WESTERN

Rugged men looking for love...

Fortune's Mystery Woman

Allison Leigh

The Cowboy's Rodeo Redemption

Susan Breeden

MILLS & BOON

Allison Leigh is acknowledged as the author of this work
FORTUNE'S MYSTERY WOMAN

First Published 2024
First Australian Paperback Edition 2024
ISBN 978 1 038 93908 1

THE COWBOY'S RODEO REDEMPTION

First Published 2024
First Australian Paperback Edition 2024
ISBN 978 1 038 93908 1

Published by
Harlequin Mills & Boon
An imprint of Harlequin Enterprises (Australia) Pty Limited
(ABN 47 001 180 918), a subsidiary of HarperCollins Publishers Australia Pty Limited
(ABN 36 009 913 517)
Level 19, 201 Elizabeth Street
SYDNEY NSW 2000 AUSTRALIA

Printed and bound in Australia by McPherson's Printing Group

Fortune's Mystery Woman

Allison Leigh

MILLS & BOON

Though her name is frequently on bestseller lists, **Allison Leigh**'s high point as a writer is hearing from readers that they laughed, cried or lost sleep while reading her books. She credits her family with great patience for the time she's parked at her computer and for blessing her with the kind of love she wants her readers to share with the characters living in the pages of her books. Contact her at allisonleigh.com.

Books by Allison Leigh

The Fortunes of Texas: Fortune's Secret Children

Fortune's Mystery Woman

Cape Cardinale

The Pilot's Secret

Return to the Double C

A Weaver Christmas Gift
One Night in Weaver...
The BFF Bride
A Child Under His Tree
Yuletide Baby Bargain
Show Me a Hero
The Rancher's Christmas Promise
A Promise to Keep
Lawfully Unwed
Something About the Season
The Horse Trainer's Secret
A Rancher's Touch
Her Wyoming Valentine Wish

Visit the Author Profile page
at millsandboon.com.au for more titles.

Dear Reader,

What a whirlwind it has been since the Fortunes of Texas hit the little town of Chatelaine, Texas, where scandals and secrets—old and new—abound!

The secrets that are locked in the mind of the young woman Ridge Fortune calls "Hope" are on the verge of breaking through the amnesia that has plagued her for months. The only thing Ridge can hope for is that those memories of her life "before him" won't take her away again when they do. Only Ridge isn't entirely innocent of keeping a secret or two himself...

I hope you'll enjoy this trip to Chatelaine and that you'll root for these two young lovers to find their way to a future together as much as I did!

All my best,

Allison

For "Fortune" lovers everywhere,
including the fine authors with whom it is
my privilege to work, plus the spectacular
team at Harlequin that supports us. In particular,
thank you to Susan Litman, who manages to keep us all
on track and never seems to lose the smile in her words.

CHAPTER ONE

THE CAR.

It was *the* car.

Late-model sedan. Four doors. Charcoal gray.

The sun reflected blindingly off the windshield, preventing her from seeing who was behind the wheel, but it didn't matter. The car was steadily approaching. Coming her way.

Nausea clawed up Hope's throat, and sweat suddenly beaded on her lip despite the sharply cool January day. She nearly slipped when the forward momentum of her fake-leather boots stalled, and she wrapped her arms tighter around the carrier strapped against her front.

Protect the baby!

The words screamed through her head as she shrank back against the solid building next to her. As soon as her shoulder felt the contact, she whirled. The back of her winter jacket crinkled and caught against the rough brick as she rolled around to escape. Heart hammering in her chest, the recessed doorway right behind her felt like a godsend, and she ducked into it, not daring even a single glance back as she yanked at the glass-fronted door.

The jingle of bells above her head were an assault on her heightened senses despite the merry little tone of them. She started forward, but something from behind tightened around her throat.

Choking.

She gasped, taking another step, frantic to escape, but it tightened even more. She squeezed her eyes shut.

Protect the baby!

"Hold on there, hon. Your scarf's caught in the door."

She hardly heard the words over the racket of her heartbeat.

"There you go." The constriction around her throat abruptly eased, and a smiling middle-aged face swam into her vision. "That wind out there is crazy today, isn't it? Just blew the door shut right on you. Saw that right away." The woman was tugging her hood off her own head as she peered at the bundle strapped against the front of Hope's coat. "What a darling girl," she cooed. "My youngest granddaughter just had her first birthday. She was a Christmas baby. Bet you're not *quite* that old yet, are you, ladybug?" She laughed delightedly at the animated leg kicks her comment seemed to earn, and wiggled Evie's fuzzy-lined boot for half a second before she turned her smile to Hope's face.

The nausea was starting to fade, but Hope felt as breathless as if she'd run a marathon.

Not that she could remember ever running a marathon. It was just one detail among hundreds of others—like her own name—that Hope hadn't been able to recall for the last six months.

She cradled Evie's comforting weight against her but couldn't keep from looking over her shoulder back through the windows of the door.

The rear end of the dark gray car was just rolling past.

Her mouth dried all over again, even though the vehicle kept traveling, innocuously moving through the intersection.

When it had gone far enough that she couldn't see it anymore, her breath silently eased out between her clenched teeth.

She turned again and realized the lady was still looking at her, the smiling question in her eyes shaded by more than a little concern at Hope's behavior.

"I, uh, I thought I saw someone I knew," she said with too much cheer that didn't seem to fool the woman at all. "Time flies really fast, doesn't it?" she added quickly. "Evie's eight months now."

At the sound of her name, her daughter garbled nonsensically and kicked the little fuzzy boots that had been under the tree on Christmas morning just two weeks ago.

Another gift from Ridge.

He'd given Evie so many things.

Hope, too.

The knowledge was like a little weight inside. Comforting yet very, very disturbing.

At least the woman stopped eyeing her as if she suspected Hope was someone who needed eyeing. "It does go fast. Enjoy every minute of it," she said. Then she caught the little starfish hand that Evie had extended and laughed lightly. "Even more so when you get to my age." She wrinkled her nose, still smiling engagingly. "You realize it's all gone by in the blink of an eye."

"Hi, Miranda." A slender brunette carrying a stack of hardback books appeared nearby, prompting Hope to take proper stock of her surroundings.

A bookstore. Cozy. Slightly crowded. Entirely charming.

Her breath evened out a little more.

"I thought I heard your voice." The brunette was speaking to Miranda. "I've got your special order in the back." Her bright smile took in Hope and Evie. "Are you here for our story hour?" She tilted her head toward the back of the shop. "They're just getting started, and we always have room, particularly for new faces. I'm Remi, by the way. Are you new in town? Visiting someone for the holidays?"

Panic had driven Hope inside the shop, not the lure of story hour. In all the months since she'd inexplicably found herself in Chatelaine, Texas, she'd only ventured into the town proper a handful of times. She started to shake her head. "I, um—"

"You should join them," the woman—Miranda—encouraged. "Nothing like forgetting yourselves in a good story hour. Remi here has amazing taste in books, whether for children or old ladies like me." She winked. "Books. Always good for what ails you."

"Truer words," Remi quipped with a smile, "but *old ladies*?"

She rolled her eyes, giving Hope a conspiratorial grin. "We should all have the energy of Miranda Tibbs." She maneuvered the stack of books in her arms and extended her hand toward Hope. "I'm Remi Fortune."

Fortune.

Undoubtedly another relation of Ridge. He was almost as new to the Chatelaine area as Hope—and in addition to his siblings who'd also recently relocated there—the whole region seemed riddled with members of the extensive Fortune family.

All of whom had been nothing but kind to her and Evie.

"Hope," she returned, quickly shaking Remi's hand before resuming her usual position of cradling Evie against her. She didn't give her last name. How could she? It wasn't the first time she'd felt a moment of awkwardness from that telltale omission. One would have thought she'd have learned how to deal with it by now. "I, um, we can't stay. I'm supposed to be meeting someone at the Daily Grind."

"Maybe next time, then," Remi said easily. "We have story hour every Wednesday at ten. Mondays, too."

"Thanks." Now that she'd mentioned the coffee shop, she felt inordinately anxious to leave, so she backed up again to the front door, pushing it open with her weight. "It was nice meeting you."

"You, too, Hope."

The two women continued smiling at her as she went through the doorway, and if there was speculation in their eyes, Hope pretended not to see it.

Once outside, she turned again into the stiff breeze, pressing her lips against her daughter's silky hair before tugging the hood of Evie's tiny jacket in place. Looking over her shoulder, she searched the street for a glimpse of the dark gray sedan.

From what she could tell, traffic in downtown Chatelaine was never all that heavy and this Wednesday was no exception. Which is probably why it had been so easy to see that car.

Why had she thought she recognized it?

There was nothing special about a dark gray car. There was one right now, in fact, parked not far ahead of her in front of the feed store, and *it* wasn't filling her with the screaming meemies.

It didn't have to mean there were people in town again asking questions about a young woman and baby…

So what was it about that *other* sedan?

She'd known it was *the* car. The one that Ridge's brother Nash had talked about seeing only a few months ago.

She pressed her fingers against the pinpoint of pain behind her right eyebrow. It was coming more frequently lately. Ever since she'd started getting flashes of memories.

If they *were* memories.

For all she knew, she was just losing her mind.

She blinked against the tears that threatened and ducked her head against the cold wind.

Focus. Just focus on one thing.

How many times had Ridge said those words to her?

Take a breath and let everything else go.

He could have been standing right there next to her, saying the words in his low, deep voice.

She took a deep breath, inhaling the presence of her daughter. "We're going to be fine, Evie," she murmured against the baby's slick hood. "Ridge—"

Her throat closed.

He was their rescuer. Their safe harbor. She'd known it from the moment her blurred vision had cleared on his face six months ago when she'd woken up in his stables one night with no memory of how she—or the baby who'd been crying in her arms—had gotten there.

Nothing in the time since had convinced her otherwise.

He was wonderful. Perfect. Handsome. Gentle. Kind. He never lost his temper. Or raised his voice. Evie loved him and so did—

She gave a sharp shake of her head, focused on the cracked cement sidewalk under her boots and started down the street again. They were already ten minutes late, but she knew that Ridge would just blame that on their appointment with the pediatrician's office.

Evie started fussing, and Hope quickened her pace, looking up and down the now-empty street before jaywalking across it, angling toward the bunch of vehicles parked diagonally in front of the Daily Grind.

She was jiggling the baby to no avail as she went inside, following in the wake of a wizened old gentleman wearing a cowboy hat big enough to house a family of squirrels. Her gaze immediately settled on the tall man leaning against the far side of the counter.

He'd been watching for her, too, and his smile was slow and slightly tilted as he straightened.

She kept herself from skipping—jogging…okay, *racing*—to him with an effort and tried not to fall into a pathetic heap when his focus went from her face to Evie.

"What's the matter, baby?" Ridge's eyes were as brown and delicious as a shiny dollop of dark, melted chocolate.

Predictably, Hope's mouth seemed to water and feel dry all at the same time, and only several months' worth of practice kept her from visibly reacting when his hands brushed against her as he deftly undid the fasteners of the carrier before lifting Evie out of it.

He swung the baby above his face and tilted her until her nose touched his. "What're you sounding so cranky about, Little Miss?"

As soon as he'd lifted her, Evie's fussing had magically stopped, and now her little hands closed in his brown hair—just as glossy as his eyes—and she yanked enthusiastically. "Ba-be-ba-ba!" Her fuzzy boots frog-kicked so hard that one of them flew off.

Hope laughed and caught it before it could land in someone's coffee.

And right then and there, the entire charcoal gray car reaction became a thing of the past.

Ridge was laughing, too, and he deftly twirled Evie in his arms until she was cradled high against his chest. "You're gonna roast in that thing," he told the baby, tugging off her little puffy purple coat to reveal the red T-shirt with Mommy's Bestie printed on the front. He tugged the hem of the shirt down over the slight pudge of her tummy and the stretchy denim leggings. Only after he'd dealt with Evie did his gaze finally focus on Hope. "How was the doc?"

"Fine." She took the coat from him before working the boot back onto Evie's stocking-clad foot. It wasn't easy with the way she curled her toes. "She's grown an entire inch since her six-month checkup." Not that this was a surprise to either one of them, given the rate Evie had been growing out of her clothes.

"And the cough?"

The cough Evie's developed in the last few days was the reason for the appointment in the first place. "Dr. Monahan said she'd prescribe something if it doesn't clear up on its own, but she doesn't have an infection or anything." Hope patted her daughter's padded rump, and when her fingertips brushed accidentally against Ridge's forearm, she curled her fingers as tightly as Evie's toes. "Have you ordered?"

He shook his head, and she made a point of looking at the laminated coffee menu lying on the counter. He stood close enough that she felt surrounded by the warm scent of him. Soap. Fresh air. *Him.* "She said to call again if it worsens or starts affecting her eating and sleeping."

"Hear that?" Ridge was addressing Evie. "No more waking up at three in the morning, or it's back to the doctor for you."

"Ba-ba-ba!" The baby's blue eyes were adoring as she hung her head back, arching herself over Ridge's arm and clasping her hands together.

The empty carrier sagged from Hope's torso, and she unconsciously rotated her shoulders. Ridge was a foot taller than she was. Evie's height was no burden at all to him. "Did you get your business finished okay?" Ridge had also had an appointment in town that morning, which is why he'd said they'd meet up in the Daily Grind after.

"For now." He didn't elaborate. Not that Hope expected him to.

Yes, they had fallen into a certain familial-like routine since he'd found her unconscious last summer. But Hope wouldn't make the mistake of forgetting that they were *not* a family.

Evie had a father. He'd been Hope's husband. She was almost certain of that now, and Ridge was perfectly aware of that fact, too, since he'd been present when she'd remembered that she used to wear a wedding ring. She'd also remembered her husband's funeral. Or at least she thought she'd remembered it.

Her memories were so disjointed, she was afraid to trust anything as real. What if she was confusing real facts of the past with the jumbled dreams…nightmares…that plagued her?

Why didn't she feel *grief*? Was there something more wrong with her? Was her mind coming up with a horribly convenient way to justify the life she was living now?

Until she could trust her own mind, there was no hope of going back.

Nor any hope of moving forward.

Certainly not with Ridge.

Because as much as he adored her daughter—and everyone, including his mother and his five brothers and sisters, freely acknowledged that this was so—he'd never once crossed the line where Hope was concerned.

He'd held her when she'd needed comfort.

Wiped her tears when they'd needed wiping.

But he'd never kissed her.

Not even close.

She wasn't sure what she would do if he ever tried.

And what sort of woman did that make her?

"Decide what you want?"

She jerked slightly, looking up from the laminated menu that was clenched between her fingers. She hadn't even realized that she'd picked it up or that she'd shoved Evie's coat into the already strained-at-the-seams diaper bag.

Her throat felt tight, and she shrugged, forcing a smile that she didn't feel. "I can't. There're too many choices." She knew the Daily Grind had the best coffee in the county, but in her heart of hearts, she was a tea girl.

He plucked the menu from her fingers. "Close your eyes."

She obediently closed her eyes.

"Now stick out your finger and point."

She pointed, feeling the slick menu against her fingertip.

"Mocha latte," he gave the order as she opened her eyes and saw that what she'd really pinned the finger on was espresso.

Only he'd known better. "Americano with two extra shots for me," he added.

The coffee shop was busy, and it was obvious it would take a few minutes for their order to be prepared, so Hope headed to one of the few empty tables while they waited. She pulled off the carrier and looped it and the fraying strap of her pink-and-white-gingham diaper bag over the back of her chair before sitting down and peeling off her own coat.

Ridge had offered more than once to get her a larger, sturdier diaper bag, but she kept refusing. If it wasn't for the name *Evie* embroidered in minty green on the flap of the bag, she wouldn't even know the name of her own daughter.

Her eyes prickled, and she turned to stare out the side window. By the time Ridge joined her at the table, managing both Evie and a paper plate nearly too small for the large chocolate croissant it held, she'd banished the tears once more.

He set the croissant in the middle of the table beyond Evie's reach and tossed down a bundle of napkins he'd pulled from the pocket of his leather jacket.

Despite herself, Hope's mouth watered, and she immediately reached out to break off a corner of the warm, flaky pastry and popped it in her mouth.

The croissant was buttery. The chocolate was rich and slightly bittersweet. The combination was addictive. She reached again and her fingers knocked into Ridge's.

"Sorry," she mumbled and snatched her hand back, twisting her fingers together in a knot atop the table. Her skin hummed, feeling warm from the steady look he gave her.

"You seem antsy."

The observation didn't help her nerves. "Not at all." The lie was obvious even to her.

He shifted Evie on his lap and reached forward, settling his palm over Hope's white knuckles and pressing slightly to keep them in place when she automatically tried to withdraw. The gleam of his gold watch peeked from beneath the edge of his leather sleeve.

He was Rolex watches and designer duds, whereas she was

homemade diaper bags and discounts. No matter what she remembered or didn't remember, she needed to keep that in mind.

Ridge Fortune was in a class all his own.

"Did you have another memory?"

Her throat felt tight, and there was no scarf caught in a closed door to blame this time. "No."

"But…?"

She shifted in her seat. "It's nothing." She didn't want to tell him about the car. About her illogical fear of it. But when he looked at her the way he was now, she knew from experience that she had no willpower whatsoever.

"Hope—"

"Order up for Ridge." The call came from the clerk at the counter.

Ridge's lips tightened slightly.

"I'll get it," she said in a rush and slid out of her seat.

Saved by the coffee.

CHAPTER TWO

THE DRIVE FROM Chatelaine to Ridge's house on the north side of Lake Chatelaine was a little more than ten scenic miles. That morning, though, Hope's usual appreciation for the beautiful Texas landscape was absent.

Evie was silent from the back seat of Ridge's luxurious SUV; she was sound asleep and not providing the least distraction from Hope's troubled thoughts.

In six months, she'd learned more about Ridge than she had about herself. He'd always been unfailingly patient with her, but she knew even the deepest well had a bottom, and judging by the lines forming alongside his lips, she couldn't help wondering if he was reaching it.

If she told him about the car, she knew his first reaction would be to go all protective.

That had been his response from the moment he'd found her unconscious on his property. Instead of immediately calling 911 or the police, he'd called a physician friend of his. To deal with her health more immediately than the authorities…because who *knew* what situation had driven her into the horse barn of a complete stranger, with an obviously young infant strapped to her chest and no identification on her at all?

"Why *didn't* you call the police?" The words came out utterly without thought, and she wanted to kick herself for not having better control.

He was slowing the vehicle as he turned up the road leading to the Fortune Family Ranch—which was a lot more than a single ranch to her mind, but his family could call the compound whatever they wanted.

"What?" His attention remained on the road that ran along the sometimes jagged perimeter of the enormous lake. "When?"

She glanced over her shoulder at Evie, but the sleeping baby still provided no distraction and Ridge was waiting expectantly. "When you found me." She faced forward again. "You, um, you called your friend Mitch, instead."

He didn't answer immediately, though she felt his gaze through the dark sunglasses he wore. He slowed slightly as they neared the ranch headquarters—a cluster of red-bricked barns and a long, low building that housed the offices—before picking up a little speed again as the road straightened out and moved toward the main lakeside house where his mother resided. "Mitch is the best doctor I know around here. Would you rather I'd have called the police?" he finally asked.

"No!" She shifted. "I wasn't thinking that at all," she said truthfully. "It's just not what most people would do. Most people would want to wash their hands of the situation as soon as they could."

The corner of his lip quirked. "I'm not most people."

How well she knew that.

She chewed the inside of her cheek and stared out the side window again. His family ranch numbered more than three thousand acres and employed more than a dozen people from outside the family. She'd met most of them at one point or another. Easy to do when nearly all of them lived on the property or nearby.

Once they passed the turnoff to his mother's house, the road meandered more, cresting a hill and then another before passing the first of the six luxuriously modern log homes occupied by him and his siblings. Hope knew they'd been built as guest cabins for the original owners of the ranch who'd retired to

Arizona. But calling them cabins was as accurate as the whole ranch/compound thing, as far as she was concerned.

The first of them was occupied by his eldest sister, Jade, who'd established a petting zoo on the property, mostly as an attraction to get kids involved in the educational workshops she taught.

The zoo was probably Evie's favorite place in the world, and a part of her couldn't help imagining her baby girl someday participating in a workshop, too.

Wishful thinking. That was years down the line, and who knew what their situation would be by then.

The thought was still plaguing her even when they reached the turnoff for Nash's place. Nash was Ridge's eldest brother and acted as the ranch foreman. He'd always been nice to her—they all had been—but Hope had also always felt a little intimidated by him.

"I wanted to help you," Ridge finally said when they'd driven past Nash's property and were about halfway to the next gate leading to Arlo's place. "That's why I didn't call the police. Would you rather I'd have handled things differently?"

She made a face. "It would be proof of being the biggest coward in the world if I'd waited six months to tell you so, wouldn't you say?" She looked down at her ringless fingers, focusing on the memory of when that hadn't been the case. When a narrow band had adorned her wedding ring finger.

She concentrated on the image. Could almost feel the faint weight of the gold.

She curled her fingers. Trying to savor it? Or rid herself of it?

"You're not a coward."

She flattened her fingers against her thigh, looking at him from the corner of her eyes. "How do you know?"

His lips quirked again. "I just do."

"Same as you just knew I needed help?"

"Maybe."

What could she say to that?

She exhaled and looked out the side window again. They passed the stone pillars and open gate marking Arlo's property, and she mentally paced off the distance to the next gate. She knew it was roughly a mile between them. She also knew that it was almost exactly five miles from Ridge's front door to Jade's petting zoo. Even though there was a perfectly good golf cart at her disposal, Hope had probably walked the distance a hundred times now, pushing Evie in the fancy all-terrain stroller that Ridge had bought for her. His gate was as big as Arlo's, but slightly edgier with its deceptively simple bronze metal lines.

Gravel spun slightly under the SUV wheels as he turned from the paved road and drove through the opening. She'd never seen his gate closed, either. "Do you ever close it?"

"The gate?" He smiled faintly and shook his head. She wasn't sure if it was in answer to her question or in judgment of its inanity.

"When Evie's older, might have to," he mused after a moment. "Just to keep her corralled."

The notion was disconcerting.

Somehow, months had passed without her making any serious effort to leave.

Why would she when Ridge had made staying with him so impossibly easy?

She chewed the inside of her cheek again. Would she be thinking the very same thing a year from now? Two? Five? Ten?

Ridge was an eligible bachelor. The youngest son of the Windham Plastics magnate, Casper Windham. But Casper had died last year, and the company had been sold. Which left Ridge and his siblings even richer.

Sooner or later, he'd want a real family of his own.

Her stomach clenched painfully at the notion, and she suddenly sneezed, burying it in her elbow.

Dust was clouding up from the gravel as Ridge drove. He'd been talking about having the long drive up to his house paved, but so far hadn't done anything about it. She felt certain it was because he, himself, wasn't certain just how long he'd be living there.

Her life was in limbo because she couldn't remember where she *really* belonged. However, his life was too, because—so far—he didn't want to disappoint his mother who'd been the one to transplant herself and her six adult children here when she'd found herself a widow *and* an heiress to a father she'd never known.

Sooner or later, all limbo had to end.

Didn't it?

She abruptly sneezed again. Dust had always bothered her. "'Scuse me."

He pulled into the circle drive that fronted the beautiful house, with its pitched roof and wings extending from the central A-frame, and parked. "I'll get Evie and you get the door."

Since he was better than Hope at extracting the sleeping baby from her car seat—again, purchased by Ridge—she didn't argue. She gathered up the carrier and diaper bag and walked up the stone steps of the house. A swipe with the fob he'd given her months ago after installing a fancy security system and the door unlocked with a soft snick. After a nudge, the big, heavy door swung inward, revealing a view straight through the center of the house to the gleaming lake on the other side.

She didn't have to possess her memories to feel certain that her life BC—before Chatelaine—had not involved luxurious "cabins" with million-dollar lakefront views.

Evie was still sound asleep as he carried her past Hope, her lips pursed into a sweet bow and her cheeks rosy in her otherwise porcelain complexion. Hope pressed her lips to the baby's forehead when Ridge paused as he stepped into the foyer. Despite the flushed cheeks, Evie didn't feel any warmer than usual, and Hope stepped away again. She looked up at Ridge as she did so and felt her breath catch slightly when she found his gaze on her.

He'd left his sunglasses in the SUV, and his pupils seemed dilated a little in the change from outdoors to in. "Want her in her crib?"

Her throat managed to allow some nonsensical sound to escape, and she nodded jerkily.

A vertical line creased between his brows. "It would be easier if you'd just say what's bothering you, Hope. The things I'm imagining are bound to be a lot worse." His thumb brushed Evie's flushed cheek. "Dr. Monahan really said she's fine?"

Remorse was swift, and she was squeezing his forearm before she even realized it. Of course, his first thoughts were always about Evie. "Really," she assured him and by some miracle disconnected her fingertips from the roping sinew barely disguised beneath soft leather. "I would tell you."

"Then it's another memory." He waited a beat. "About *him*?"

He meant her husband. Former or otherwise. The man who'd put the wedding ring on her finger who may or may not even be alive. She sighed. The twisted memories were riddled with both love and pain. She couldn't tell which one superseded the other and that alone was tormenting.

She turned away from Ridge, tossing up her arms in defeat. "I saw the car."

"What car?"

She looked over her shoulder at him, and his lips tightened. "That car," he muttered. "The one Nash—"

"Yes."

Ridge exhaled slowly, though he looked more angry than worried. "I'm going to put her down." He turned on his boot heel and silently disappeared down the wing where the nursery and Hope's bedroom were located.

His bedroom was on the opposite side of the house.

He wouldn't even let Hope clean over there, though she'd tried to offer cleaning house for him in exchange for the shelter he'd been giving them all this time. The end result was that she had never even seen past his bedroom door.

She knew it would be tidy and clean. The housekeeper he *did* allow to clean was named Terralee, and she kept the entire place spotless despite the presence of an eight-month-old baby.

Any other details, though?

They existed only in Hope's imagination.

She walked through the great room and around the enormous kitchen island. In the current home-designer world of white and more white, Ridge's kitchen was an entirely different animal, with the cupboards finished in a warmly muted and antiqued green, juxtaposed against caramel-colored wood counters that almost exactly matched the color of the narrow strip of sandy shoreline only yards away from the house. The result felt cozy, despite the oversize footprint and wall of windows that spanned the back side of the house.

The view wasn't merely of the spectacularly beautiful Lake Chatelaine, but of the multilevel deck protruding from behind the manor. It worked its way from a covered area, complete with two stone fireplaces, down to a dock that extended far out over the water.

Every inch of that deck begged a person to go out and enjoy it.

The pot of Irish breakfast tea that she'd brewed earlier that morning was cold, and she filled a mug and stuck it in the microwave situated below the countertop on the island. While it heated, she leaned her arms on the tawny counter and moved the small baby monitor closer. The image from the baby's room was full color, the sound perfectly clear.

Another Ridge purchase, and he hadn't skimped. There were four other monitors situated around the house and a fifth outside on the covered deck.

Everything inside her felt melty and soft as she watched him lean over the crib, gently depositing Evie onto the mattress. She squawked only once and immediately rolled onto her side, one hand going to her cheek and the other clutching the corner of a crinkly fabric book that Hope had given to her for Christmas. In the two weeks since, Evie had rarely let the book out of her sight.

Books just made Hope think of the bookstore, Remi's Reads, which just further made her think again about the car.

She turned down the volume on the monitor and, since she was able to see when Ridge left the nursery, perched herself down on a bar stool, more or less prepared for his return.

"Where?"

She didn't pretend to misunderstand. She set the mug on the counter and slowly turned it in a circle. "In front of the feed store. Before I got to the Daily Grind."

"Who was driving?"

She shook her head. "I don't know. I couldn't see."

His lips compressed. He yanked open the refrigerator door and pulled out a glass bottle of milk, taking a swig straight from it. He replaced the cap and stuck it back on the shelf.

She couldn't help staring. He bought the expensive milk from a small dairy farmer who actually delivered the stuff twice a week, and she'd never once seen Ridge do such a thing.

He turned back to her, and his lips were twisted again. "This whole situation is giving me an ulcer," he muttered.

Dismay sank through her. "It is?"

He made a rough sound. "No." As if to prove it, he grabbed the twin pot next to hers that held his black-as-tar coffee. He filled a mug and repeated her steps of heating it in the microwave. "What did the car look like?"

She told him.

"That describes probably half the cars around town."

She wanted to find comfort in that logic, but didn't. "I know it was them."

Them being the couple Nash had told her and Ridge about. Middle-aged. Seemingly nonthreatening. Yet when they'd described a woman who looked like Hope, Nash had instinctively denied seeing anyone in the area who fit the description.

In some of the worst half-dream-half-memories that tormented her, there was a couple. Seemingly nonthreatening.

Until they were.

Not for the first time, she wondered if she'd done something bad.

If that was why she'd taken her baby and run. Run from her life.

There simply was no other way to describe what seemed to have happened. Hiding away in a wealthy man's stable among his prized racehorses with no identification or money on her at all. She'd been running. Either from something someone else had done, or from something *she* had done.

She inhaled shakily and adjusted the baby monitor an infinitesimal centimeter. The perfect beauty of her sleeping baby was solidly real.

Then the microwave dinged, startling her.

She was turning into a basket case.

Hope watched Ridge remove his mug from the microwave and take a swig of the steaming contents. She couldn't help wincing just a little. Whether or not his stomach was lined with titanium, his mouth seemed to be.

"They're the only ones who've looked for you," he said. "If you were really on the run, there'd be police reports."

"Stop reading my mind," she murmured and picked up her own mug, burying her nose in it.

"I don't have to read your mind. Your face telegraphs every thought you have."

That remark was hardly comforting. Half her thoughts were about *him*. Her cheeks felt as flushed as Evie's had been, and she was grateful for the distraction of her tea.

"Remember anything else?" he asked.

"About the car?" She shook her head.

"Well. Whoever it is, they can't get to you here."

By *here*, he meant his house with the fancy security system. Even if he did start using the gate at the end of the long gravel drive, it wouldn't keep out someone who was determined to get past it. They could simply climb over.

It would be a hefty climb, but not an insurmountable one.

She tried imagining the middle-aged couple that Nash had described scaling Ridge's gate—which, at its highest point, was probably at least eight feet—and couldn't. The fencing beyond the gate pillars was just plain old barbwire. A good set of cutting tools could take care of that.

"What if they come with lawyers?" Equally worrisome.

"We have lawyers, too."

Her throat tightened. There were days and days that had gone by when she wasn't beset with anxiety. When she could almost forget that she hadn't sprung to existence last summer on this piece of Texas land.

And then there were days like today.

Which were coming ever more frequently.

"Maybe I should see a therapist," she murmured. It was what Mitch had suggested on his most recent visit. He, Ridge and several other guys had gotten together for poker just after New Year's Day. Testosterone town while she and Evie had hunkered down on their side of the house, even though Ridge had assured her that she didn't need to stay hidden away.

"If that's what you want."

She couldn't tell one way or another what he thought about it. Her facial expressions might be an open book for him, but she couldn't say the same about him. Sometimes she could read him perfectly well. Like when he was with Evie. And other times…

She sipped her tea again. What she *wanted* was the certainty that she belonged right where she was. And that wasn't going to happen regardless of what she did or did not remember. She knew more than a few things about Ridge Windham slash Fortune. Or Fortune slash Windham. Or just Fortune, if he kept to his mother's desire to embrace everything about her newfound family name, even if it meant wiping out her children's connection to their late father.

She knew he'd grown up with privilege and wealth in Cactus Grove, near Dallas. That he'd always had his pick of women—and there'd been plenty, if the gossip sites were even remotely accurate. She knew he could tolerate everything from the strongest coffee imaginable to even the hottest chili peppers served at Harv's New BBQ in town.

She knew he never lost at poker. That he could sit for hours doodling on a piece of paper and end up with some new contraption to sell that would save someone time and money. That he'd accepted this house that his mother wanted to provide him only because he loved her and didn't want to cause her more upheaval than she'd already endured, but that learning all the ropes around the ranch was a poor substitute for the engineering work he'd done for his father's company. A company that appeared to have been sold right out from under him and his siblings.

She knew that the diamond key pendant he'd given to her as a Christmas gift was little more than a trinket to him, even though she suspected the cost of it would buy her and Evie a very long way down the road if she sold it.

Which she would never do.

But she couldn't bring herself to wear the incredibly beautiful platinum and diamond pendant. Nor could she ever bear to part with it.

What she also knew was that, right or wrong, she was in love with him.

But he was *not* in love with her.

Evie? Most certainly.

But Evie's mom?

CHAPTER THREE

RIDGE WATCHED THE pull of Hope's soft pink lips as her frown deepened. "If it upsets you that much, *don't* see a therapist," he said. He knew he was equally as anxious for her memories to return as he was for them to be forever gone.

Hell of a note.

Her lashes swept down, hiding the periwinkle blue. "I'm just afraid of what my brain isn't willing to give up. What could be that bad?"

She wasn't quite telling the truth. He could see that, but he couldn't *really* read her mind. His mom had always told him he was too intuitive to waste himself on engineering. He'd always considered the combination of the two made him better at each.

He was good at figuring out things, but he'd definitely dragged his feet where Hope was concerned.

Sure, he'd monitored every news feed he could find for details about missing women matching her description. He'd even hired a private investigator—something that he hadn't admitted to a single one of his family members. The only one who knew was Beau Weatherly, who'd recommended Gordon Villanueva in the first place. Ridge's meeting that morning while Hope had been at the pediatrician with Evie had been with Beau.

Not at the coffee shop, though.

Just because the retired rancher and investor placed a mildly tongue-in-cheek sign out on a table in the Daily Grind most mornings offering Free Life Advice didn't mean that Ridge intended for his personal business to be discussed in public. But there was no denying that the man unfailingly had sensible advice.

Despite Ridge's efforts, though, he'd only met dead ends. Whoever *was* out there looking for Hope wasn't doing so because of a missing person's report. Not in the state of Texas, anyway, where he had limited the search at first.

As soon as Ridge had hired him four months ago, though, Villanueva had expanded that territory into the surrounding states, and more recently the entire country.

There had been three women fitting her general physical description with criminal charges of child abduction—all of which the investigator had determined were unrelated.

Until the middle-aged couple that Nash had come across, there hadn't been a single person out there seeming to make a diligent effort to find her. And so far, Gordon Villanueva hadn't been able to locate the couple, either.

Ridge never doubted that Evie was Hope's biological child. They shared the same birthmark on their necks. It was small, but distinctively star shaped. In the months since he and his sister Dahlia had found Hope in his stable, Evie's hair had come in even more, just as auburn as her mother's. And though he knew the color of babies' eyes often changed, it seemed to him that Evie's were only becoming more periwinkle blue like Hope's.

Evie was Hope's. Unquestionably.

But who else's was she?

The specter of Evie's father—Hope's husband—was always there. Had he died? Or was Hope's memory as faulty as she feared and he was still alive?

If he was and everything had been normal and fine in their marriage, why hadn't the man been turning over heaven and earth to find them? Even if their marriage hadn't been happy, what about the baby? If he wasn't alive, why had she run? What did she have to fear?

Ridge felt Hope's gaze on him, and he realized he'd been rubbing the pain in the center of his chest that was a constant companion whenever he speculated on the circumstances that had brought her and her baby into his life.

Circumstances that would take them away again.

He pushed away the annoying thought. He'd had plenty of practice at it since last summer, but since Christmas, it was getting even harder.

He never should have given her that necklace.

Because now he kept noticing how she never wore it.

She was still watching him with a slightly pinched expression, drawing the corners of her lips down.

"Don't suppose you got a license plate or anything on the car?"

She was shaking her head before he finished speaking, her frown deepening. "I hid in a bookstore," she admitted huskily. "A total coward. I should have—" She broke off, pressing her lips together.

He set down his coffee mug and went over to her, dropping his hands over her shoulders. "It's okay," he murmured. He squeezed slightly, and her head tilted, resting against him. She exhaled softly, and the pressure in his chest grew. His jaw tightened until it ached. "It's okay," he said again, more firmly, before releasing her.

Nash hadn't gotten a license plate, either. Just the description of a late-model gray sedan. Of which hundreds of thousands were purchased every year.

"I'll see if there is a therapist Mitch recommends," he said, picking up his coffee again and moving around the island, well away from the lure of touching her. "You can decide if you want to pursue it or not."

"Okay."

But still, the white edge of her teeth worried at her lower lip. Then she shifted as though she was shrugging off a weight, and her gaze skipped around the kitchen. "Aren't you supposed to be working this afternoon?"

He glanced at his watch. "Yeah." The farrier was coming that afternoon, and Ridge was supposed to meet her down at the main barn. He worked his head around, trying to loosen the tightness in his shoulders. "I'd better change. What about you?"

Hope picked up the baby monitor and showed him the screen. Evie was awake. Lying on her back and kicking her legs while she chewed on the corner of her fabric book. "I figure I have two minutes of grace before her contentment disappears," she said wryly. "Just enough time to make you a sandwich if you want one."

A part of him wanted to blow off the farrier and the ranch altogether, just to stay there with her and the baby. "We still have leftovers from that roast you made?"

"Yes, including a few slices of the sourdough loaf I squirreled away before you could eat it all."

Now the corners of her lips were tilting a direction he far preferred. The slight smile always struck him as slightly impish, whereas a full-on smile from Hope pretty much felt like a celestial event.

She set down the monitor and slid off the bar stool, and when she moved past him toward the refrigerator, he breathed in the scent of her hair. He was twenty-nine years old. He didn't know if she was eighteen or twenty-five. He seriously doubted she was older. There wasn't a single line on her youthful face.

"I'll change," he muttered, and escaped the kitchen. His bedroom was at the end of the opposite wing, and he made short work of exchanging what were dress clothes for him these days for old jeans, work boots and a flannel shirt. Gone were his days of bespoke suits, high-rise Dallas offices and manufacturing plants, though half his closet was still filled with those suits.

When he returned to the kitchen, a fat plastic-wrapped sandwich was sitting on the island next to the baby monitor, on which he could see Hope changing Evie's diaper. The sound had been turned down, and he thumbed the button until he heard the sound of her softly singing to the baby.

You are my sunshine, my only sunshine...

A fresh pang in his chest, he turned down the volume, took the sandwich and left the house. Bypassing the SUV, he ate as he walked past the pool and the small guesthouse that was on his property, and headed toward the barn and stables that were only a fraction the size of those located at the ranch headquarters.

He stopped long enough to check the water and feed the three retired racehorses he hadn't been able to give up when he'd moved from Dallas. He called 'em Larry, Moe and Curly. Their official registrations, however, were Toddy Boy, Winter Sun and Ali of My Heart. They had forty-nine starts between them and over a million in winnings. Now they were out for stud.

"Living the dream, right, guys?" He rubbed their foreheads one last time, tossed the plastic wrap in the trash barrel and climbed behind the wheel of the dusty pickup truck he used while he was working around the ranch. A wind was kicking up, and it blew through the passenger window that would no longer roll up all the way. He pulled out the puffy vest that he kept stuffed behind the seat along with an assortment of other handy items and put it on before starting up the engine.

The steering was a little loose and the shocks were almost shot, but he did find something vaguely satisfying about driving the thirty-year-old bucket of bolts. It was a helluva change from the sports car he'd driven in the city. And though money had always been easy in his life, he couldn't see plowing through creeks and muddy bogs with the Escalade that had replaced the Porsche.

He drove through the gate, smiling a little to himself despite the restlessness that had plagued him ever since his mother purchased the property last summer.

The ranch had already been a fully functioning cattle operation when they'd taken it over, lock, stock and barrel. Since then, Ridge had been learning all there was to learn by working alongside the fifteen employees who did everything from cooking to cowboying.

Not because he figured he'd ever be running the place.

Nash had already staked out his position as foreman, and once his older brother decided on something, that was all there was to say about it. Sabrina handled the books. Arlo was already a successful investor and was busy turning around ranches that were failing—which was not the case with the Fortune Family Ranch, as it was known now—and Jade and Dahlia were doing their own thing and were all about the animals. Jade with the nonprofit petting zoo she'd established, and Dahlia raising sheep of all things, right in the middle of a cattle ranch.

Ridge was the youngest of them all and the only one who didn't have a place where he actually belonged. And unlike Dahlia and Jade, he couldn't see inventing—or reinventing—himself.

He was an engineer, for God's sake. He'd figured his place was at Windham Plastics.

His father had had other ideas, and in the months since the company had been sold, Ridge had faced the fact that his father would have felt that way even if he hadn't been stricken down by the pancreatic cancer that killed him.

Casper hadn't been an easy man. He'd been cold and distant. To his wife and to his children.

The only time that Ridge had felt like he and the old man were even close to being on the same page was when Ridge worked at Windham Plastics. But where his interests fell more heavily on solutions for the healthcare industry, Casper had chased the best profits. Period.

None of Ridge's brothers or sisters had wanted to work at Windham. Only Ridge had. And despite the battles he'd had with the old man, in the end—despite being blindsided by Casper's decision to sell the company to his biggest competitor—Ridge had made his peace with him.

The company's not for you, Ridge. Those were the last words his father ever said to him. *Find out what is.*

A day later, his father was dead.

Ridge didn't think he was going to find out what "it" was by stringing fence and learning the ins and outs of cow-calf pairs.

But he also had Wendy to consider.

Ridge knew his parents' marriage had been far from perfect, but she'd still been rocked by Casper's death. And it was obviously important for her to make a connection to this Fortune side of her family that she'd never known existed, or she would never have thrown herself so precipitously into this new life. As a parent, she was the opposite of Casper, and she wanted her offspring along for this new ride.

As much as Ridge wanted to find "it" for himself, he wanted to see his mother happy. She, more than anyone, deserved it. For all the disappointments they'd suffered with Casper as a father, Wendy had been the opposite. Ridge couldn't count the number of times his mother had kissed him good-night. "Good day, bad day," she'd whisper, smoothing his covers even as she tugged away the building blocks he'd usually been clutching, "you are loved, and love is everything."

He automatically turned onto the frontage road leading to the headquarters and returned Sabrina's wave from where she was standing in front of the offices talking on her cell phone.

He could see the farrier's trailer before he reached the barn. He parked alongside Nash's truck and went inside. He figured the only reason Nash—four years older than Ridge—didn't give him a censorious look for being ten minutes late was because he was busy jiggling the crying baby he was holding.

Ridge was still trying to get used to the idea that Nash was a father, much less that he'd so readily given up his longstanding insistence that fatherhood was *not* for him. But there he was, carrying around a bundle of baby who was about the same size now as Evie had been when Ridge first discovered Hope in his stable.

Mentally tabling his intention of rehashing Nash's initial encounter with the gray car and the only people on earth who had seemed to want to find Hope, he stopped next to his brother and peered into the wailing, unhappy face of his nephew. "Colt is giving you quite a ride, I see."

His brother shifted the baby to his shoulder, patting his back through the snug swaddle of pastel blue and green stripes. "You'll never make it in comedy, dude. Stick with the day job."

Ridge grinned a little and turned to greet Lucille, the sixty-some year-old farrier. Her hair was as bright a red as Lucille Ball's had ever been, and he couldn't help speculating whether or not the deliberate color choice was because of the name. Not a person to waste time or mince words, she was already hard at work, and even though he was only a few minutes late, he could see she was already cleaning and trimming the fourth hoof of Goldie, one of the oldest horses they had. Goldie was also one of a handful of horses that were shod. She would be getting a new set of shoes today, which lengthened the period of time Lucille would have to spend on her. For those horses that went barefoot, it only took her about twenty minutes to clean and trim their hooves.

In addition to Goldie, though, there were eleven other horses that Lucille would see that afternoon, and it was Ridge's task to make sure all of them were ready. All but three of them were still out in the pasture, and he started gathering up halters.

"Imani busy this afternoon?" Nash was engaged to Colt's mama, and even though Imani Porter ran her own successful specialty baby gear company, it wasn't that often that Nash brought their son to work.

"She and her mother went to Corpus for the day." Nash repositioned his son again, trying the pacifier that was fastened to his blanket with a bright red clip, but the infant wanted nothing to do with it.

Ridge couldn't help feeling a little pleasure over his brother's awkwardness. It wasn't often Nash seemed out of his element. But Ridge also knew very well that sense of helplessness.

Just because Evie wasn't his by birth didn't mean he loved her any less, and the worst thing he'd ever felt was not being able to soothe her when she'd needed soothing and Hope wasn't there to do it.

"Try flipping him over," he advised. "Hold him like a football." He mimed what he meant before heading down the aisle between the empty horse stalls toward the opened doorway on the opposite end that led to the nearest of their pastures.

A whistle brought three quarter horses immediately toward him, and he led them into their barn stalls with ease. He might be an engineer, but he'd still been around horses for most of his life, and remembering that he liked caring for and riding them as much as he liked racing them had been welcome. Every time he could feel his stress level where Hope's situation was concerned, hands-on time with the horses had proved a good way to help dispel it.

Nowadays, instead of recreational romancing, he was practicing recreational horse maintenance.

The gossip rags back in Dallas who'd loved recounting his social life would have had a field day with it.

Eyeing his big brother, Ridge was pleased to see that Nash

was holding the swaddled bundle of his son like a pro footballer, his big palm seeming to be exactly the cradle that Colt had wanted for his head.

"It's something about the pressure on their bellies," he told Nash as he grabbed a few more halters from a peg. "Worked great with Evie, too." He raised his voice a little to be heard over the loud sound of Lucille working a red-hot horseshoe over the anvil.

The noise wasn't bothering Colt at all.

His eyes were closed, his lashes long and dark against his pudgy cheeks, his pink lips drawn up in a bow like he was nursing in his sleep. Meanwhile, Nash was staring down at him with naked adoration.

Was that what Ridge looked like, too, when he held Evie?

Probably.

He just hoped that emotion wasn't so obvious to everyone and their mother's brother when he gazed at Evie's mother.

He went back outside. Gathered up two more horses, though he had to do a little chasing this time. Despite the cold wind, the vest was no longer needed, and he pulled it off and hung it in the tack room when he got more leads.

Lucille worked thoroughly, but fast, and if he didn't want to be outpaced by a woman older than his own mother, he didn't have time to lollygag. By the time he'd gotten the rest of the horses stalled, she'd finished with Goldie and three more horses, and Nash had taken the baby inside the ranch office.

Ridge kept himself busy in the barn while Lucille worked. She couldn't abide someone hovering over her and there was plenty of grunt work for him to take care of while still making sure the next horse was ready and waiting when she was ready.

She worked steadily, breaking only when her equine pedicure client needed a break. By the time she was finished and he had turned all the horses back out to the pasture, he couldn't understand how she could even stand up straight. Farriering was backbreaking work.

But she did stand straight and give a cackling raspy laugh when he pointed it out. "Sonny, I'd rather do *my* work than yours."

That was true. At least *she* had a purpose.

He helped her load up her equipment and opened the door of her dually pickup for her. "Nice manners," she said as she heaved herself up onto the high seat. "Be back around next month," she told him and drove off just as the sky opened.

He watched her taillights wink through the drenching curtain of rain.

No purpose. But good manners.

He supposed things could be worse.

CHAPTER FOUR

IT WAS NEARLY dark when Ridge let himself into his house through the back door of the laundry room.

The rain had let up, but only slightly. He pulled off his boots and grabbed a few towels from the stack that Terralee had left folded on a shelf. Then he proceeded to mop up the puddle of rainwater he'd made on the floor with one and raked the other over his head. He could smell something good coming from the kitchen, and his stomach growled right on cue.

Ridge yanked the wet flannel over his head without even bothering to unbutton the shirt and tossed it into the deep sink next to the washer and dryer that were so modern he didn't have the first clue how to run them. The shirt landed with a wet slap. If he didn't have to walk through the kitchen and the great room, he'd have left his soaking jeans there, too. Instead, he peeled off his socks and added them to the pile, then, with the towel hanging around his neck, he walked barefoot into the kitchen.

He'd expected the usual sight of Hope and Evie—bright eyed and pink cheeked as she smashed some unidentifiable substance against the tray of her high chair—but he stopped short at the sight of his sister Jade sitting at the big island, too.

She was Nash's twin, but the resemblance stopped at their coloring. Nash liked being captain of everything. Jade, however, rivaled Ridge when it came to blending into the background among the rest of their siblings. Funny, really. The eldest and the youngest sharing the same trait. But since starting up the zoo and becoming engaged—for real—to Heath Blackwood, she'd seemed to come into her own. She'd obviously found the "it" that Casper had told Ridge to find.

The basset hound by her feet was the same as always, though, and Ridge leaned down to scrub Charlie's ears on his way to peek at whatever deliciousness was happening on the stovetop. So what if his arm happened to brush against Hope's when he lifted a lid on a big pot to look?

She avoided making eye contact with him as she waved the wooden spoon to keep him at bay. From the soup or from getting too close to her was up for debate.

"It's minestrone," she said. "And it's hot." Another wave of the long-handled spoon, this time aimed even more directly at him. Her blue eyes looked at him and skittered away as fast as a drop of water on a screaming hot pan. "You'll burn yourself."

Too late. Since he'd met her, he'd been on a long walk to incineration.

But he knew enough to focus on the here and now. And right now meant the aroma coming from the pot. "Smells great," he said truthfully. Whether or not Hope ever remembered her entire past, she was a terrific cook and seemed to relish pouring over cookbooks and trying out new recipes.

It was a good thing he was working his tail off physically around the ranch. If he hadn't been, he'd be wearing a larger size by now for sure.

He grasped the ends of the towel hanging over his chest just to make sure he didn't do something stupid, like grasp *her*, and caught Jade's measured gaze.

Probably thinking she could read his mind.

She, like the rest of his family, had embraced Hope and the baby. They all shared that same protective instinct that had kept Nash from admitting anything to those strangers. But Jade also was clearly worried what it would mean for Ridge when Hope's memory *did* return.

For once, though, his sister held her tongue about the matter, but only because both Hope and Evie were right there.

He moved over to Evie and, thanks to weeks of practice, was able to avoid her grasping, sticky hands as he leaned down to kiss the top of her head. She babbled nonsensically and slapped her hand down on the goop on her tray, obviously delighted at the way it splatted out from beneath. Then she immediately lifted her hands, her eyes sparkling up at him.

To hell with a little sticky gunk.

He lifted her out of the high chair and laughed when her hands went right to his hair. "Messy girl." He blew a raspberry against the polka-dotted shirt that had replaced the red one from that morning, and she gave a belly laugh that wrapped him right around her sticky little fingers.

He nuzzled her warm cheek and slanted his gaze toward Jade. "Where's Heath?"

"He had a business meeting at the LC Club this evening." Heath was something of a wunderkind in the agriculture and tech field. Self-made, successful and only a year older than Ridge. Which also made him three years younger than Jade. But there was no reason to suspect that Heath was after Jade for her money, because he already had plenty of his own. "And then he's hoping to meet the triplets for a drink afterward."

The triplets were Heath's half sisters. All of them had been separated as babies and reunited only recently. Proof that Casper Windham's family wasn't the only screwed up one around these parts.

"I came over to see you about this." She was fluttering a simple embossed white card between two fingers.

"If that's a new wedding invitation for you and Heath, fine. But if it's that strange one we got last month—"

"Heath and I haven't set a date yet." Her cheeks flushed a little as she spoke, like she couldn't quite believe *she*—a tomboy according to their late father, who'd never find a man—was getting married.

She squared up the rectangular wedding invitation on the counter. The invitation had been preceded each month with one oddball request or another back to July when they'd all received the initial save the date.

Unfortunately, neither the first missive nor any of them since gave them a clue to the identity of who was actually getting married. Which, as far as Ridge was concerned, was a good enough reason to ignore the whole thing despite his mother's insistence otherwise.

"There's a rumor that you're not planning to attend the mystery wedding," Jade said.

Ridge glanced down at the likely culprit to spread that news. "A rumor, huh?"

Hope didn't meet his eyes as she lifted Evie out of his arms. Her knuckles brushed against his bare chest before she turned quickly away. "She's a mess." She sounded a little breathless. "I'm going to pop her in the tub real quick. Turn off the soup so it doesn't boil over. It'll be ready soon as I add the *ditalini*." She practically jogged out of the kitchen.

Jade was still watching him.

Waiting.

"I told Hope I didn't see the point of going to a wedding where we don't even know who the bride and groom are," he admitted gruffly. "Nothing I haven't said before." He turned off the stove burners.

"Ummm." Jade pressed her lips together for a second. "Think you were supposed to leave the one under the pasta going."

He made a face and took a minute figuring out which switch controlled the right burner.

Jade was rolling her eyes when he'd completed the task. "For Pete's sake, Ridge. How'd you fend for yourself before Hope came along?"

"I was still in Dallas," he reminded her.

"Oh, yeah." She wasn't impressed. "With a new date every night of the week."

"Not *every* night." But when he wasn't going out, he'd had a housekeeper who'd kept him in meals that usually just needed a minute or two in the microwave. He wasn't sure he'd ever had cause to turn on his own stove and honestly couldn't remember if the thing had been a gas monstrosity like the one he had now, or if it had run on electricity.

He'd had meals regardless, and beyond that, he just had not cared.

He stepped over Charlie, who'd camped his sturdy self directly in front of Ridge, and ran the end of his bath towel under the sink faucet, using it to wipe the drying goop—banana, he realized—off his chest and his chin. "Why does it matter to you, anyway?"

"We've *all* been invited. It's not like it's a fluke. A mis-delivery or something." She waved the invitation between her fingertips again. "Back in July when the first save the date came, I agree that it was easy to just dismiss. I mean, who sends out a wedding notice and leaves off the identity of the people getting married? It seemed like a mistake. But since then?" She shook her head. "It's obviously intentional."

"Inexplicable, you mean."

"Inexplicably intentional," she returned, ever the more-knowing big sister. "We're supposed to provide a meaningful photograph." She ticked off one finger. "Then be prepared with a meaningful quote." She ticked off another. "And the text messages?"

At one point, everyone in the family had gotten text messages like some damn survey, asking which of the example wedding attire they preferred. A, B or C.

They weren't living in some television game show, but every time one of those mystery-wedding missives showed up, it felt like it.

The text had sparked quite a discussion among his sisters and his mother. As far as Ridge knew, his brothers had ignored responding the same way he had.

"The wedding's this month," Jade said. "Three weeks from Saturday, to be specific."

He squinted at her. "Think I've got to see a man about a horse that day."

She let out an exasperated tsk. "You know that Mom wants us all to go. Present our united support."

United *front*, maybe. But Jade, like all the rest, knew their mother was his Achilles. "Go for the jugular, why don't you?"

She lifted her shoulder. "Whatever works. *Obviously*, the bride and groom are from around here. We have Fortune relations coming out our ears. Some we haven't even met yet."

She tsked again and leaned toward him over the massive island. "It's a few hours out of your Saturday. Don't be like Dad, Ridgy Rigid. Come on."

He gave her a look.

"I call them as I see them, brother mine."

"If I was as rigid as he was, I wouldn't be living here." He raised his arms, encompassing the lavishly appointed home.

"As if you don't *like* living with Lake Chatelaine right outside your back door," Jade chided.

"You know what the problem is? All of you girls have weddings on your brains."

"That's kind of the normal thing that happens when you fall in love for keeps. And it isn't just the twins and me." The twins being the *other* set of twins—Sabrina and Dahlia. "Arlo and Nash are chomping at the nuptial bit, too."

The topic was wearing too thin for Ridge's comfort. There was only one wedding that he cared about these days. The one wedding he dreaded knowing more details about.

Hope's. To another man.

He flipped the towel back around his neck. "If I say I'll go, will you get off my back about it?"

"I haven't been *on* your back," she said sweetly. "I *could* be if—"

He staved off her words with his hand and nearly tripped over Charlie, who'd moved again to lie right under Ridge's feet. He leaned over and rubbed the dog's head. "Dude. You know how to pick the spots, don't you."

"This says to bring your plus-one." Jade propped the invitation against the mason jar that was filled with the remains from a fancy Christmas bouquet that Ridge had bought for the holiday. "I assume that plus-one won't be Terralee."

He nearly snorted. Terralee Boudreaux was a bold-as-brass transplant from New Orleans who was twenty years older than him. "She'd make mincemeat out of me."

"Whereas Hope won't?" His sister's voice was soft and abruptly serious.

"Leave it alone, Jade."

She sighed audibly but didn't press. "So, you'll go. Both of you. What about the photograph thing?"

"What about it? Think I'll be kicked out if I show up without one in hand?" He tossed up his hands. "I'm not one for taking pictures. You know that." He didn't even keep photo albums.

"You take pictures of your engineering—" she swizzled her fingers in the air between them "—thingamajigs all the time."

"Designs," he deadpanned. "They're called designs, Jade."

He was earning the eye rolls from her big time.

"Whatever." She slid off the bar stool and patted her thigh. "Come on, Charlie. Let's go home and wait for Heath."

The dog lumbered to his feet. He was so short legged, his long ears practically dragged the ground. But he gave Ridge's bare foot a drooly swipe of his tongue as he headed toward Jade.

"At least your dog loves me," Ridge told her.

Her lips stretched. "I love you, too, you big dweeb." Her gaze flicked toward Hope's wing of the house. "I also worry about you."

"You don't have to."

"Might as well ask the moon to stop rising every night."

"Speaking of the moon." He followed her to the doorway. "There isn't any moonlight out there with the rain." He flipped on the exterior light, but the circle of illumination that it cast reached only as far as the wide shallow steps that led up to the front door. They glistened wetly. "It's dark as hell. Sure hope you drove over in something better than that golf cart you use at the zoo."

"That golf cart has headlights *and* fog lights," she returned. "Which is more than I can say about my real vehicle." Jade patted his cheek before scooping Charlie up in her arms and skipping down the steps.

He watched her jog through the rain—now more a drizzle than a curtain—and disappear into the dark. A moment later, headlights beamed out from what was obviously the golf cart.

The headlights were better than nothing, but even after she'd driven out of sight, he still felt like he should have driven her home.

"Jade decided not to stay for soup?"

He nudged the door shut as he turned to see Hope coming into the room. Evie was clean again, her damp hair glossy and dark and slicked back from her forehead in a tiny little ponytail that stuck nearly straight up. "Yeah. She wanted to get home to Heath."

Hope's lips twitched. "Can't really blame her there."

She missed his grimace because she was leaning over, deftly spreading a jungle-themed baby quilt on the floor. Then she set Evie down on it with her favorite chewy book and some big plastic keys on a ring before going to the kitchen. She checked the pasta in the pot, adjusted the burner and turned to wipe down Evie's high chair with a wet cloth.

Hope had a graceful economy of movement and he could always tell when she was flustered because that's when that economy faltered.

"Are you, uh, going to clean up before we eat?"

He usually took a shower and shaved before sitting down with the ladies for dinner. But since he'd had a shower thanks to nature, he shook his head. The way her gaze slid to his bare chest prompted him to at least go and put on a clean shirt.

When he returned to the kitchen, she'd tucked the high chair away in a narrow alcove between the fancy built-in gas stove and a tall glass-front cabinet. She jumped a little when he pulled out the bar stool and turned away from the glass. Almost as if she'd been using it to check her reflection.

Despite himself, he reached for the wedding invitation sitting against the jar of still-piney scented twigs. Pressing it flat with two fingers, he slid it a few inches back and forth on the satiny wood surface while he watched Hope stretch up to pull two wide, white soup bowls from inside the cabinet. The action stingily revealed a narrow swath of creamy skin between her jeans and her dark blue sweater.

The invitation bent slightly under the pressure from his fingers, and before he did more damage to it, he stuck it against the mason jar again. Then he folded his arms, leaning on them against the island. "I think the price of you spilling the beans to Jade that I didn't plan to go to this thing is for you and Evie to come with me."

The slotted spoon she'd picked up banged against the side of the pan, spilling water down onto the hot burner. "I don't have anything suitable to wear to a wedding." She started to turn toward the sink, checked the motion and then turned back again to the stove. Dipping the spoon in the pot again, this time she successfully transferred the helping of pasta into one of the bowls. She followed it up with a ladle full of soup from the other pot.

He picked up the invitation yet again and tapped the edge on the counter. He absently adjusted a piece of greenery in the mason jar. "It's at the Town Hall," he said. "Two in the afternoon. Hardly black tie." He slid his glance her way. "The dress you wore at Christmas was—" *Captivating.* He cleared his throat a little and set aside the invitation before reaching for the bowl she set on the island for him. "It would work fine."

He reached over and pulled a soupspoon from the drawer of flatware. "For that matter, what you're wearing now would be fine."

She stopped halfway between the stove and the island and gave him a look. "I may not remember the mascot from Central High, but I *know* this—" she spread her arms and looked down at herself "—is *not* appropriate wedding guest attire." She looked up again and flushed slightly. "What?"

"Did you hear yourself?"

Her lovely lips pressed together. "Yes, I heard myself. And don't pretend that *you* were raised to think that frayed blue jeans are appropriate for a wedding." She faced the stove again with her ladle and the second bowl. "At least one that isn't being held on some mountaintop," she added in a scoffing manner.

"Central High," he repeated. "That's what you said."

It took a moment, but then her shoulders visibly stiffened.

The bowl clattered a little when she set it back down on the counter next to the stove. "Central High," she said softly.

Wonderingly.

She angled her head slightly and closed her eyes, obviously concentrating. "The home economics teacher was Mrs. Jones. No. Johnson." She shook her head again. "That's not right, either. Something like that. But it was my favorite class." She gave a faint laugh. "Because it was easy."

Ridge was already thumbing his phone, running a search for Central High School. Dozens of locations came up. Not just in Texas but in the surrounding states. He was afraid of pushing Hope for more details, though. It had never been successful in the past and usually ended up doing more harm than good, leaving her drained and disappointed.

It was hard, but he took the opposite tack. "Soup's really good. Minestrone's one of my favorites."

"Your mother told me." She sounded absent as she picked up her bowl again, added pasta and then the aromatic, vegetable-studded soup.

She carried it to the island and took the bar stool next to him. "Jenson. Jordan. What *was* her name?"

"It doesn't matter," he said. Even though it did. Any piece of the puzzle of her past was invaluable. "When were you talking soup with my mom?"

"A few days ago. She came by with another outfit for Evie. I told her she had to stop buying clothes for her, and she said she'd picked it up for nearly nothing at a thrift store." She made a sound. "As if your mama *ever* shops in a thrift store."

"She wasn't always wealthy," he replied mildly. Wendy Wilson had been raised in near poverty in Cactus Grove, believing herself to be the daughter of a single mother named Gertie Wilson. Poor or not, though, she'd been an honest-to-goodness Texas beauty queen who'd caught the eye of Casper Windham, and from then on, poverty became a thing of the past.

But his mother had never forgotten the value of a hard-earned dollar. And now, she knew the truth about Gertie. That she'd only been Wendy's babysitter when Wendy was an infant, left in her care by her real mother, who'd perished in the same terrible mining accident sixty years ago that had claimed the lives of fifty miners.

With nobody else coming forth for the baby, Gertie had taken the baby away from Chatelaine altogether and raised her as her own in Cactus Grove.

All of which had come to light bare weeks after Casper's death, when Wendy learned the truth about her real family. Both her parents had died in the mine accident. But her maternal grandfather was a millionaire named Wendell Fortune with plenty of secrets in his own life, not the least of which had been faking his own death for many, many years, riddled with guilt over the mine tragedy that had also claimed the life of his secret, illegitimate daughter. He'd left the country, only returning a few years ago, but even then, he'd used an assumed name until his failing health prompted him to begin fessing up to his remaining family.

But there'd still been a missing puzzle piece—the baby of the daughter he'd never had time to publicly acknowledge.

He finally located her—Wendy—shortly before his ill health claimed him for good. Wendell's bequest to Wendy?

A castle.

Turrets and all.

Located just outside of Chatelaine.

Now, Ridge's in-with-both-feet mother was embracing her newfound Fortune roots and remodeling the castle into a boutique hotel. She'd gotten all six of her adult children to move to town along with her, and he was still sort of shaking his head, wondering exactly how she'd accomplished it.

"You should know by now that when Wendy Fortune has her mind set on something—even if it's baby clothes—she's not going to let anyone get in her way," he told Hope.

"A trait she seems to have passed on to all of you."

And yet, she'd stayed with Casper. From the time Ridge was old enough to realize that there seemed little love between them, he'd wondered why she had never left him.

"Well." He got up to refill his soup bowl and glanced over at Evie, who was still chewing on her book, but only half-heartedly since she was nearly asleep. "I'm set on you and Evie making that infernal wedding tolerable. I couldn't care less what you decide to wear, but you've got three weeks to figure it out."

Her lips tilted, but there was an air of sad confusion in the faint smile. "Why do you do all of this, Ridge?"

He felt his chest hollow out a little. "You don't really want me to answer that, do you?"

A flush blossomed over her cheeks and her pupils seemed to flare for a moment.

Then Evie let out a loud squawk.

Hope's throat worked and her gaze dropped away from his. "I need to feed her and put her down," she murmured, as if she needed to explain, even though this was their usual routine and had been for weeks. She slid off the bar stool. "I'll clear up all of this later."

He watched her collect Evie and the blanket and head out of the great room.

And he continued watching long after he heard the soft sound of a door closing.

Central High.

It was a start.

CHAPTER FIVE

"I'VE CHECKED SEVENTEEN schools between Texas and New Mexico," Gordon Villanueva reported two days later, "with Central in the name."

Ridge could hear the squeak of a chair through the phone and easily pictured the investigator sitting in the battered chair at his Corpus Christi office.

"I know you estimated Hope to be in her early twenties," Villanueva said, "but to cover our bases, I added another seven years to the window. But none of the schools had a home economics teacher with a last name starting with *J* during that period."

"What if she was wrong about the teacher's name?" The way she'd spoken about the school had been entirely unforced, unlike the name of her home economics teacher.

"Anything's possible. Which is why I still have my assistant tracking down yearbooks. I've sent you what we have so far because it'll take a helluva lot of time going through them manually to see if she's a student in any of them. But in the meantime, while she works on the rest, I'll start on states east of Texas. The term 'Central High' covers a lot of possibilities, but we'll get there."

Ridge propped his arm on the top of the handle of the post-hole digger he'd been using and squinted against the sunlight.

The rain from two days ago was gone, but it had left unseasonable warmth and humidity in its wake.

There was nothing around him except a few head of cattle. Jaime, who'd been working with him earlier, had needed to run home to take care of his toddler son because their usual babysitter had flaked out and his wife had a meeting she couldn't miss.

Ridge hoped the ranch hand wouldn't be gone the rest of the day. The fence they'd come out to repair had turned out to be worse than expected. If he had to do it all alone, it would take him twice as long as expected. And he'd have a long walk back to his pickup truck at the ranch headquarters since Jaime had taken the work truck.

He swiped his sweaty forehead with his arm and switched his cell phone from one hand to the other. "Money's not an object. If you need to bring more people on to help—"

Villanueva's laugh was almost as raspy as Lucille's. "Already done that. I know you're champing at the bit for answers, Ridge. This is the most concrete information we've gotten. But it still takes time. Eliminating seventeen possibles narrows the remaining field. You should have the first box of yearbooks today or tomorrow. Maybe Hope looking through them will shake more memories loose. But if they don't, we'll still get there."

Ridge squinted even more. Once they did "get there," what was he going to do about it?

"And if she remembers any other details, no matter how small, let me know." The investigator rang off and Ridge pocketed his phone.

He looked at the holes he'd already dug for the new line of fence and angled his head, eyeing the invisible line where he still had to dig a half dozen more. Only a handful of days after a rain, but the ground was as unforgiving as if there'd been no rain at all.

While he didn't necessarily mind the physical work, the drawback was it left his brain plenty of time to roam. And not even imagining a half dozen ways to make the process more efficient was enough to keep his thoughts from turning back to Hope.

Eventually, Jaime returned, muttering complaints about wives and kids and the cost of everything under the sun.

He didn't seem to need any input from Ridge, which was good, since his experience with any of that was nil.

By the time they planted the remaining posts and finished stringing the wire, the sun was giving out. Jaime dropped him off at the office and drove off without delay. It was Friday, and for him, the end of a workweek.

Ridge, on the other hand, went inside long enough to grab a cold drink. Sabrina was still at her desk, her blond head bent over her work.

"Aside from it being past quitting time, shouldn't you be sitting somewhere with your feet up or something?" She still had a few months to go in her pregnancy, but she was carrying twins and was—in his inexpert brotherly opinion—sporting a whale.

She smiled at him and leaned back, showing that she did, in fact, have her feet propped on a cardboard box of files underneath her desk. "I'm just finishing up the payroll for the week," she told him. "Zane's picking me up soon. We're having dinner at the LC Club."

"Nice."

"I think so. What's this baloney about you not going to the big mystery wedding?"

He eyed her over the cold can of soda. "Where'd you hear that?"

"Jade."

Naturally. All his sisters were uniquely different. And nonetheless thick as thieves. "Is there anything the three of you *don't* share?"

She lazily smoothed her hand over her ginormous belly, and the sapphire engagement ring on her finger winked under the fluorescent lights. "Oh," she mused, her eyes looking suddenly...feline-ish. "There might be a few details."

He held up his hand. "Just stop there. I don't want to know."

Sabrina's smile widened mischievously. "You think you're the only one of us who gets to have a sex life?"

"Gack." He pulled a face.

She laughed and pulled her feet off the box, sitting up to the desk as much as her pregnancy allowed. Then she plucked a perfectly sharpened pencil from a pencil cup. It exactly matched the other dozen pencils still in the cup, not to mention the one that was already tucked behind her ear. "If you're just going to stand there drinking a root beer, find somewhere else. *I* still have work to do."

"I told Hope I'd go but only if she and Evie come, too," he admitted without having any real intention of divulging anything.

Sabrina raised her eyebrows slightly. "Was there ever any likelihood of you going *without* them?" She pulled a sheaf of papers off the printer adjacent to her desk and placed them precisely on the blotter in front of her. With one eye on him and one on the papers, she ran the tip of her pencil down the printed columns, checking for God only knew what. Her progress halted only once. She circled something, turned the page over and gave him a look, as if she was still waiting for an answer to what he'd considered a rhetorical question in the first place. "Don't pretend you're not falling for her. We've all seen it."

He ignored that. "She made some comment that she doesn't have anything suitable to wear."

His sister's eyebrows rose again. "There's nothing in my closet that would work for her," she stated the obvious. "Even from before these two soccer stars growing inside me. Hope's tiny. I'm the Jolly Green Giant standing next to her."

It was an exaggeration, but only slightly. Pre-preggers, Sabrina had been just as slender as Hope. But Sabrina was considerably taller. "I was thinking something more like a shopping trip."

She still looked uncertain. "You think she's not going to find it odd if I approach her out of the blue for a shopping trip?"

"She won't think it strange if you tell her you're shopping for something for the baby girls there." He gestured, taking in the jut of her belly. When she was still deluded enough to think that she and Zane could just share parenting duties when it came to their children without her falling head over heels for him, she'd done a stint of babysitting for Evie. "Tell her you want her advice or something and you can slide in the wedding part."

"Well." Sabrina absently tucked the pencil behind her ear,

dislodging the first one, which slid behind her to the floor, unnoticed. "It's not a bad idea. Whenever I start looking at all of Imani's stuff that she carries at Lullababies, I want everything under the sun, and I *know* we don't need that much. Zane didn't become responsible for his brothers until they were already adolescents, so he's new at this whole part of things, too."

"Just don't forget it's not all about you," Ridge reminded.

"I know. Wedding guest attire." She plucked another pencil from the cup and pointed the pink eraser tip at him. "Who do you think you're talking to here? But as it happens, what I *thought* I'd wear is already getting too tight to accommodate these two—" the eraser tip aimed toward her belly "—so I actually ought to get something as well." She flipped the pencil again, swirling it dismissively in the air at him. "Now get out. I don't want to be late meeting my fiancé."

He left and was just passing Arlo's gate when his cell phone rang again. Answering, he heard Beau Weatherly's deep voice boom through the cab. "You alone?"

It wasn't Beau's typical greeting, and Ridge felt a surge of anticipation. "Yeah." Even though he knew nobody would likely overhear, he still rolled up his truck windows and turned down the volume a little. His foot eased up on the gas pedal until he was barely rolling along. "What's up?"

"Have a friend in the probate court. Nonny Zazlo's spread's going to be approved to sell in the next week. Maybe two, depending on the judge's schedule. That's one of the ranches I was telling you about last week. The one on the other side of Chatelaine. About thirty miles out." Beau cleared his throat. "House leaves something to be desired, but the land is in good shape. Excellent carrying capacity. Reliable water source. Good forage. If you're really serious about buying your own place, you could do a lot worse. Nonny sold off all the livestock when he first got sick, but he didn't have a chance to get around to selling the equipment. So, it's all going to be available, too."

Ridge's hands tightened on the steering wheel. Adrenaline shot through him, and he started to pick up speed again. Almost from the very beginning, he had confided to Beau that he wasn't entirely set on accepting his piece of the Fortune Family Ranch.

Not when he couldn't figure out how in hell he was contributing in any meaningful way. He wanted—*needed*—something of his own. His father had recognized that, too, before his death.

If Ridge had a ranch of his own, he'd sink or swim on his own.

Problem was, land in these parts was pretty locked up. Wendy being able to buy the ranch had been divine timing, both for her and for the former owners who'd moved to Arizona. The employees who already worked there were a mix of day hands who helped keep the ranch side of things working—like Jaime—a few office workers, kitchen help and a crew of all-around handymen and women who could put their hand to nearly any task, whether it was keeping the roads graded, fixing toilets or setting out spring plants around the main house.

As far as he was concerned, the place was top-heavy with employees, but he knew Nash didn't necessarily agree. And it was a given that their mom would never think of cutting down the payroll. The only time she'd give someone the axe was if they did something outright unethical or illegal.

Ridge's needs were a lot simpler, however. He didn't need a lakeside compound complete with a half dozen guesthouses or a weighty payroll. But he also wanted more than a little spit on the ground with barely enough room for a few head of cattle and a chicken coop.

He wasn't looking for a hobby. He was looking for a *life*.

"You think it'll go quick?" he asked Beau.

"Let's just say it'll be a miracle if Zane Baston doesn't snap it up before the probate clerk types up the sale approval." Beau's tone was dry.

Sabrina's fiancé was well-known for his ability to sniff out desirable parcels of land. If he wasn't an entirely decent guy who'd adjusted his entire life when he'd become guardian of his younger siblings, he'd have probably been reviled for it as much as he was admired.

That was the nature of success, it seemed.

One person loved you for it.

Another person hated you.

Ridge turned through his gate and felt the crunch of gravel

under his tires. Through the darkening evening, he could see the welcoming glow of lights coming from the house up ahead.

If he bought a place of his own, would Hope and Evie even still be here to share it with him?

"I can finagle a look-see if you're intrigued," Beau offered. "Properties like it are getting as rare as hen's teeth around here. We've got more time with the other property I mentioned if you're concerned with the short timeline."

The other ranch on Beau's radar was located in Oklahoma. A lot farther away. It was larger, but less expensive. The house and barn had also burned down a while back, meaning a lot more work would be required.

"I don't want word getting back to my mother," Ridge cautioned. The other man knew perfectly well that Ridge didn't want to chance upsetting Wendy. "She's had enough to deal with this past year without worrying about my defection from the family compound."

"I've met your mama a time or two." Beau's tone remained dry. "Seems to me you might be underestimating her a mite. I think y'ought to just tell her what's in your mind."

"On the other hand, I've been her son my entire life," Ridge countered. "You don't know her like I do. She has a smile that's as sweet and agreeable as lily of the valley. But get past the pretty flowers, and a person's smart to exercise caution."

"Your mother's not toxic." Beau suddenly sounded a little testy. Not surprising. Most every male who ever encountered his mother tended to get protective. Even though Ridge was no different, he also recognized the fact that his mother was probably the least likely person to need protection, whether provided by her sons or the local wise man.

"Not saying she is," Ridge answered easily. "But she's got a will of iron and a way of getting what she wants without seeming to lift a single one of her elegant fingers. Probably be good to remember that when she's involved with local charities and such. She'll have you offering up your wallet *and* begging her to please take some investments off your hands, too, while she's at it."

Beau let out a bark of laughter. "Yeah. Well, mebbe I can sort of see that. She sure is wrapped in a pretty package, though. So, I can set up a time for you to see Nonny Zazlo's old place if you want. I'll just make sure they think *I'm* the one interested in it."

Ridge smiled ruefully. The retiree could talk about Zane's propensity for buying up property, but Ridge knew that Beau had a nose for wise investments, too. It had made him a very wealthy man—probably more so than ranching ever had. "Just don't make them think you're too interested, or the price'll go up even more just from the rumor of it." He had his own financial resources, but they were no match for Beau Weatherly. Or Zane, for that matter.

He parked in front of his house, his gaze following Hope, who was visible through the front window as she moved rapidly around the great room, doing something that he couldn't make out. "Go ahead and arrange it. Sooner the better as far as I'm concerned."

Beau rang off, and Ridge went inside the house.

The sound of his entry was masked by the loud song that Hope was singing, and he realized then what she'd been doing. Singing "Skip to My Lou" and skipping around with Evie in her arms like they were square dancing.

He leaned against the doorjamb, watching silently. His smile widened when she hit the words *my darlin'* with particular enthusiasm and spun on her stocking-clad heel, spotting him halfway around.

She skidded slightly, and he launched forward, prepared to catch her and the baby, but she righted herself first with a breathless *"oofph!"* and Evie chortled with delight.

"I didn't hear you come in," Hope admitted. Her cheeks were rosy, whether from her square dancing or getting caught at it.

Either way, he couldn't have gotten the smile off his face even if his life depended on it. "Square dancing, eh?"

"Teach them young, that's what I've always heard." Her chin had a little bit of a point to it, and when she angled it upward like she was doing, he imagined fairy-tale elves dancing in some woodland glen.

The fancifulness of his own thoughts was almost excruciating. But he still couldn't stop grinning at her.

It had been that way almost from the first.

He reached out, realized he'd been about to tuck her glossy auburn hair behind the pretty shell of her ear, and instead, lightly tweaked Evie's button of a nose. She beamed at him, and even through the drool he could see the edges of her two upper teeth.

"They finally cut through, eh?"

Hope nodded, huffing out a puff of air that stirred the disheveled locks straying across her forehead. "Finally. Maybe now she'll sleep more than three hours at a stretch at night."

Evie stretched her arms toward him, nearly launching herself out of her mother's arms, and Ridge quickly caught her, trying not to get distracted by the soft curves under Hope's long-sleeved T-shirt along the way.

He propped the baby high on his chest and dabbed her wet chin with the candy-cane patterned drool bib fastened around her neck. "Let's see those choppers, baby girl." He tickled her chin easily into another happy grin, and she showed off the stubs of her lower teeth as well as the new teeny, pearly edges poking through her upper pink gum. Her bluer-than-blue gaze was fastened on him as if he was the most fascinating thing she'd ever seen. "Are you going to give your mama a break now at night?"

Ridge could count on one hand the number of times he had *not* awakened to the sound of Evie stirring in the middle of the night. Twice, he had made the mistake of shuffling across the house in the dark, and both times were seared into his memory.

Hope, dressed in a thigh-length nightie that one of his sisters had provided in those early days when all Hope had besides Evie was a diaper bag and the clothes on their backs, leaning over a hastily obtained bassinette while the small lamp in the corner of the room made the nightie nearly transparent.

And the second time before Christmas, when he'd had an unreasonable panic attack at the sight of an empty crib on the baby monitor, and burst into Hope's bedroom, afraid he'd find her room empty as well.

Only the two of them had been curled together on Hope's bed, both so deeply asleep that neither one of them had awakened despite his noisy clumsiness.

That had been the night after she'd remembered wearing a wedding band on her finger.

He'd leaned against the doorjamb, one hand pressing against the train charging inside his chest until it slowed. Knowing he couldn't stop her from leaving if she decided to, whether she went because of her memories or not.

Ridge had finally gone back to his own bed, but it had been a long time before he'd slept.

He still found himself waking in a cold sweat most nights, padding out to the kitchen to check the baby monitor and assure himself that the two females who'd turned his world upright were exactly where he wanted them to belong. The only reason he didn't keep a monitor right in his bedroom anymore was because it had started to feel uncomfortably voyeuristic.

"I have fantasies about sleeping the whole night through." Hope's voice lured him outside of his head again.

Evie was blinking her ridiculously long eyelashes as she continued gifting him with her beatific smile.

Hope's expression, however, was entirely rueful. "I can't really remember what it feels like, and—" her fingers flitted with the tendrils of hair drifting over her temple "—it has nothing to do with the blank space up there."

Evie suddenly decided that twisting her fingers in Ridge's hair was a brilliant idea, and she started yanking away like a bronc rider, squealing with such fierce delight, he couldn't help laughing despite the sharp pain.

"Aww, baby." Hope quickly reached up to disentangle her grasp. "You're going to leave a bald spot," she tutted.

Ridge winced, more from the feel of her breasts pressed against his arm than the damage the baby might cause. In pure self-defense, he bent away from her, extending his arms in an abrupt game of airplane until Evie could no longer reach his head at all.

He zoomed her through the great room, not stopping until he was next to the fireplace that—for the first time since New Year's—was cold.

"I made enchiladas for supper," Hope said, seeming not to have noticed his physical reaction as she went into the kitchen and peeked quickly into the oven. "They still have about ten minutes to go if you want to clean up first." She rolled the high chair out of the alcove and over to the island, looking at him expectantly.

"Yeah." He pivoted Evie over to the high chair, tucked her in and gave her the crinkly fabric book that he found half hidden in the couch cushions before heading to his bedroom.

Sabrina had joked about having a sex life, but his had been stored in cold showers for months now.

When he returned, freshly showered and barefoot but dressed in jeans and the plaid flannel shirt that "Santa" had magically left under the Christmas tree for him, Evie was flinging puffs of cereal from the tray of her high chair, and they were landing on the large packing box that was now sitting on the floor near her.

"A courier just dropped it off," Hope answered his questioning look.

"The yearbooks," he realized aloud.

"Yearbooks?"

He hadn't told Hope about Gordon Villanueva before, but it was obvious he would need to, now.

What he didn't expect though was the way her face tightened when he admitted to hiring the investigator to help in his search for answers about her past.

She shook out a clean dish towel with a sharp snap, folded it in fourths and left it on the island before picking up a quilted pot holder shaped like a daisy and turning to the oven. "You've been working with him for four months?" She extracted the pan of enchiladas and thumped it down on the folded towel. The daisy pot holder was tossed down beside it, and it slid across the island, falling onto the floor on the far side.

He narrowed his eyes. "Why are you upset?"

She propped her hands on her hips and directed her attention at her feet. She took a few breaths, and he wondered if she was counting to ten. Or even twenty.

When she finally lifted her head, the color that had filled her cheeks had subsided, though the stretch of her lips still looked annoyed. "It would have been nice to be informed."

Hope pulled open a drawer, then grabbed flatware and two

folded cloth napkins. With deliberate care, she placed a knife, fork and spoon on each before turning back to the cabinets and pulling down two plates that she set beside the napkins. She dished up several enchiladas, steaming hot and covered in dripping, melted cheese, and transferred them to one of the plates. Then carried it to where he sat at the end of the island, set it in front of him and handed him the napkin and flatware. As soon as he took them, she turned away. "If you were anxious for me to go, you should have just said so."

He reached out and grabbed her arm, stopping her before he even thought about what he was doing. "I *never* said I was anxious for you to go."

She pulled on her arm and gave him a look over her shoulder when he didn't release her. Periwinkle blue had turned to bruised navy. She tugged again, prompting him to let her go, and circled her arm with her hand as if he'd marked her. Though he knew he had not. "Then why didn't you tell me?"

"Because I was afraid of what I'd find."

Her lashes fell, casting dark shadows against her pale skin. "Then you do have doubts about me."

He muttered an oath. "I have doubts about the reason you ran!" He shoved his damp hair back from his forehead. "Was anyone abusive?"

She shook her head. "No."

"How do you know? Have you remembered something you haven't told me? Why are you so fearful of the people in the gray car? Are they your parents?"

"I don't know!" She dropped her hand and went over to Evie, who'd started fussing.

"I *said* I would talk to a therapist." Evie started crying in earnest, and Hope lifted the baby out of the high chair. Hushing her softly, she pointedly stepped around the big box on the floor.

How had the evening devolved so rapidly?

"Where are you going?"

From behind, her shoulders looked rigid beneath the bounce of her hair as she ambled away. "To take care of my baby."

He'd have had to be deaf to miss the emphasis on *my*. Ridge grimaced and kicked the big box with his bare foot. All it earned him was a stubbed toe.

CHAPTER SIX

KNOWING SHE WAS overreacting didn't make it any easier for Hope to conquer it.

He'd hired a private investigator.

She carried the wailing Evie into the nursery and sat with her in the upholstered rocking chair in the corner of the room, next to the multipaned window that looked out over the moonlit lake.

The frantic rocking eventually soothed Evie out of her crying, but it didn't help Hope at all.

Her gaze swept around the room. The walls were painted a soft beige with a hint of pink that was repeated in the pattern of the artfully faded rug covering most of the wood floor. Wainscoting behind the beautiful blond-wood crib was painted a rich forest green that complemented the long leaves of a six-foot ponytail palm, potted in an ivory pot as wide around as a wine barrel.

Softly colored artist prints of giraffes and monkeys hung on the walls, and a stuffed gray elephant that was as tall as Evie sat in one corner of her crib. On the opposite side of the room, an oversize woven basket contained at least two dozen stuffed animals. There was everything from a cartoonish alligator to a sheep, like those that Dahlia was raising, to tigers and lions and a zebra with a bright red ribbon tied around its tail.

She pinched the bridge of her nose, willing away the sudden burning of tears.

It was a rare week when Ridge didn't come in without some new addition for the jungle collection.

It could have been a nursery in a magazine. Designed for beauty but even more so for the burgeoning imagination of a child.

Her child.

She didn't doubt for a second that the room would have remained a perfectly attractive guest room if there'd been no Evie.

The nursery had a spacious Jack and Jill bathroom that connected on the other side to Hope's bedroom, which was exactly that. An attractive guest room, with every convenience a person could want, right at their fingertips. From the luxurious bedding on the wide bed to the television that was cleverly disguised as a mountainside painting, until you turned it on and the painting disappeared as if by magic.

If she'd found herself rescued by someone in a single-wide trailer with no luxuries beyond running water, would she have been convinced so easily to remain?

She knew she needed to face Ridge and apologize for overreacting. But she put it off.

First, she bathed Evie, even though she didn't really need it that day. Then she changed her into her footie pajamas, nursed her, read two board books about a curious penguin named Monty, and finally laid her in the crib, though she'd fallen asleep long before the second penguin book.

She went into the en suite, angled the door into Evie's bedroom to prevent the light from disturbing her and tidied up the mess left over from the bath. And she spent much too long staring in the mirror at her reflection, seeing...what?

Last summer, Ridge and Dahlia had found her in his barn, unconscious and collapsed against a hay bale. Only later did they figure out that she'd hit her head on the middle wood rail of one of the horse stalls, and that was only because Ridge had gone looking, determined to figure out if the wound on her head was caused accidentally or from something more...nefarious.

He'd found a smear of blood, though, on the underside of

the wood that seemed to imply she'd been crawling between the slats.

To hide inside the stall or to get out of it was something they wouldn't know until she remembered.

Now, Ridge had a security camera installed in the barn. But back then, there'd been nothing.

When she'd regained consciousness, she'd known what month it was. What day, even.

She knew with unshakeable certainty that Evie was her baby. She just couldn't remember the actual event of giving birth any more than she could recollect how she'd come to be inside the barn in the first place.

She knew how to fry an egg and bake a loaf of bread. But when it came to any personal details, whether as momentous as giving birth or as insignificant as her favorite flower? She'd been a total blank.

She knew. She knew. She knew.

But the most important things? She didn't know at all.

Hope finally tugged down the hem of her blue sweater, turned away from her reflection and forced her feet to carry her back to the great room.

The only thing left on the kitchen island was the stalk of lavender she'd placed in the mason jar that morning after she and Evie returned from their daily walk. The casserole dish of enchiladas was cleared away. No plates in the sink. Oven turned off and the high chair tucked in its usual alcove.

Ridge was sitting in the middle of the wide leather couch that faced the fireplace. Aside from the dimmed light fixture hanging over the kitchen sink, a lamp on the end table provided the only other illumination in the room. The courier-delivered box was on the floor next to him.

Opened.

She walked up behind him and saw the stack of high school yearbooks on the coffee table. He held one in front of him, slowly turning the pages.

"I'm sorry."

He angled his head slightly in acknowledgment. His fingers turned another slick, oversize page covered with dozens of small square headshots of high school students. "I'm sorry, too. I should have told you."

She chewed the inside of her lip, studying the back of his neck. At the way his glossy brown hair whorled slightly. Not exactly a curl but not exactly a wave, either.

Pushing her fingers into the front pockets of her jeans, she slowly walked around the couch. There was plenty of room on either side of the couch to join him, but instead, she perched on the edge of one of the squarish side chairs that sat adjacent to it.

She clasped her hands in her lap. Her heart was beating so hard, she could hear it pounding inside her head. "Why didn't you?"

"Because I was afraid of how you'd react."

She chewed the inside of her lip again.

"I didn't want you to bolt."

"I wouldn't have."

His fingers pinched the corner of the page, and he slowly flipped to the next. "We'll never know, I guess."

She untwisted her fingers and rubbed her palms down her thighs.

"You should eat something," he said. "Enchiladas are in the fridge."

The thought of food made her stomach twist. "It's not the fact that you hired someone to help find out who I am that upset me," she said slowly. Feeling her way carefully as much for herself as for him. "It's that you didn't tell me before. It felt—" She searched for an adequate word. "Bossy," she finally settled on.

He stopped his thorough perusal of the oversize book he held and looked at her. The lamp was on the other side of him, which meant his face was more in shadow than not. But she could still feel his gaze like a physical thing.

She moistened her lips. Swallowed past the irritating lump in her throat. "You made a decision that affects me without—"

"Consulting?" His tone was less than encouraging.

"Giving me the courtesy of *sharing* the information," she finished.

"Potay-to, po-tahto," he muttered and flipped another page.

"It's easy for you to say. You have all the control!" She pushed restlessly to her feet.

He closed the yearbook and tossed it onto the coffee table. "What the freaking hell do you mean by that?"

She huffed and spun around, spreading her hands. "Have you ever had to accept someone's charity?" She huffed again and turned once more, pacing across the generous space between the coffee table and the fireplace wall. "Of course you haven't. You're Ridge Fortune Windham. Owner of racehorses and inventor of—" she waved her hand "—whatever that gizmo was you invented for your father's company."

Ridge felt like ants were crawling beneath his skin. He remained seated only through sheer willpower. That "gizmo" was changing a small but incredibly relevant part of the medical plastics field. And the patent for T349, which naturally had been held by Windham Plastics, had been sold off along with everything else. It didn't matter that Ridge had been paid handsomely along the way. It was the way his father had done it that still burned even after Ridge had more or less made his peace with Casper before he died.

The way.

Suddenly, the starch drained out of him, and he sank back against the couch cushions.

High-handed.

Bossy.

He scrubbed his hand wearily down his face. Jade joked about him being Ridgy Rigid. Was he really more like Casper than he thought?

"I was trying to protect you," he said again and lifted his hand, staying, when her soft lips opened again. "But I was also—" dammit, the truth tasted sour "—trying to accomplish something nobody else was." It was the reason he hadn't told his family, either. All of them worried about him, and he was determined to prove they didn't need to.

He could take care of himself *and* the females living under his roof.

Hope's lips closed again. Pressed together for a long moment. Then she sighed faintly and moved from the chair to sit on the couch.

The thing was huge. There were still two solid feet separating them, but it felt like the world shrank a little with her beside him.

"I've never looked at it as charity," he admitted thickly.

"And I've never seen it as anything but," she countered. When she turned to look at him, there was a sheen in her eyes that made him hurt inside. "You won't even let me do the housekeeping here—"

"Hold it." He cut her off. "It's not true that you don't do your share." He patted his stomach. "I've never eaten as well as I do now."

"It's not the same. I have to cook, anyway."

He shook his head. "Sweetheart, you and I are going to have to agree to disagree here, because we are not ever going to be on the same page about it. But if it makes you feel better, you can start mopping the floor to your heart's content. I don't care! What I care about is that you're safe and healthy and—"

Not going to leave.

He propped his elbows on his knees and raked his hand through his hair. "I'm not trying to be high-handed, Hope. I'm just doing the best I can here."

She inched closer, but only—he realized—so she could reach the yearbook he'd tossed aside. She sat back again and rubbed her thumb against the cover. It was embossed and designed to look like leather, he supposed.

"Central High," she said. "Bodecker, New Mexico."

"There are seventeen Central Highs just among Texas and New Mexico," he shared the detail that Villanueva had given him. "These are the yearbooks from the years when you might conceivably have attended from only eleven of the schools."

She looked at the large box. It was filled almost to the top with yearbooks. "How many—"

"More than a hundred. This is only one of many boxes the lawyer is sending."

She blew out a soundless whistle. "Good grief."

"If we knew exactly how old you are, it would help trim the number, but since we don't—"

"Maybe I'm older than you," she said.

He smiled a little at that. "I'm more on the hopeful side that you're at least legal to drink," he admitted gruffly.

Her eyes widened. "Of course I am."

He just looked at her. "And you know this because…?"

Her lips parted. Closed again. "Because I just do," she finally said. "I was married, for heaven's sake. That I'm sure of. I've been here for six months. Based on Evie's development, the pediatrician is fairly certain that she's about eight months old now and—" she broke off, eyes narrowed in thought "—and I remember when I was first able to vote in the *last* presidential election and thinking how stupid that I was finally legal to drink while kids three years younger were getting to help decide the leader of the free world and—"

He cut her off, laughing despite himself. "Would've been helpful if we'd have figured *that* out before now."

She spread her hands. "Better late than never, right?"

"And you—" he closed his hands around one of hers and squeezed "—must be at least twenty-five."

Ridge hadn't thought it was bothering him so much that it was technically possible that she could be so much younger than him, but judging by the almost comical relief he felt…

He blew out a long breath, but even as he did so, he was becoming aware of her palm pressed against his. In an instant, he was less interested in breathing easier than he was the feel of her warm skin. The curve of palm. The slide of fingers against fingers.

His gaze traveled down her arm. Her impossibly narrow wrist. The long, slender fingers.

He heard her inhale on a quick hiss, and slowly—so slowly it was almost painful—her palm slid away from his.

The loss shouldn't have left him aching, but it did.

She was inching along the leather couch again, only this time putting more distance between them as she tapped the year embossed on the cover. "This one is too old." Her voice sounded husky, and he ached a little more.

Setting the book off to one corner of the coffee table, Hope began checking the others that he'd already gone through, separating the *possibles* from the *impossibles.*

He got up and grabbed the ones that she'd eliminated.

"Where are you going?" she asked.

"Getting 'em out of the way." He didn't look at her, turning swiftly around the side of the couch opposite her and dumping the stack on the corner of the kitchen island. Then he headed into the laundry room on the pretext of getting a beer he didn't really want from the spare fridge out there, threw open the door and stepped outside into the chilly night.

It wasn't a cold shower, but beggars couldn't be choosers.

He walked around to the deck and twisted off the bottle cap, tossing it down on one of the side tables situated artfully around the spacious deck. Exhaling deeply, he went down the six steps to the lower level and leaned against the railing. The lake was large enough that it created its own breeze, and he was grateful because it increased the cooling effect.

As long as Hope didn't join him, he'd be fine.

If she did—

He clamped down on the thought. Having a closer idea of her real age would be extremely helpful in the investigation, but it didn't change anything else. Her ties to her past were still too much a mystery.

Ridge decided the beer was a good idea, after all, and tipped the bottle to his lips, taking a long, needy drink.

Far out in the lake, the water rippled black and shimmering beneath the moonlight. Fish jumping. Maybe someone out on a boat, stupid enough not to have a light going. He'd seen worse.

He stiffened when he heard footsteps and turned to see Hope, wearing her puffy coat, making her way down to the railing beside him. The same moonlight that glistened on the water shone on her head, picking out an occasional strand of auburn-hued hair and turning it almost gold. But her expression was a pool of mystery.

"You okay?" Her voice was soft.

"Peachy." He lifted the beer again and took another draught. Then he tilted it toward her, offering.

Her fingers brushed his as she took the bottle. "What is it?"

"IPA I discovered at the LC Club."

"I don't usually drink beer."

"How do you know?"

She gave a muffled laugh. "True." She lifted it and took a sip, placing her mouth right where his had been.

Desire stirred all over again.

She pressed the back of her hand to her lips and quickly held up the bottle for him to take again.

He deliberately brushed his hand over hers as he took it.

Masochistic, but did he really care?

"It's from a brewery called Fortune's Rising."

"Is the name a coincidence or yet another thing that your family is into?"

"Distant cousin, I think. The brewery is in Rambling Rose. Do you know the town?"

She shook her head, and he could hear the soft swish of her hair sliding over her coat. Then she pulled something from her pocket, and he realized she'd brought one of the baby monitors with her. She shared the screen with him, catching Evie in the act of turning around until her feet were where her head had once been. "She's a traveler," she murmured and tucked the monitor back in her pocket.

"It's a few hours from here. Rambling Rose."

"Oh?" She sounded only mildly interested, but something kept dogging him to continue.

He leaned his arms against the railing again, which brought him much closer to her level. He could angle his head and look right into the pale gleam of her elfin face.

"It's not a sprawling metropolis, but it's bigger than Chatelaine."

"Everywhere is bigger than Chatelaine," she said dryly.

For some reason, that remark managed to derail his odd discomfort. This was the woman who'd been sharing his home for six months. Sharing his life, whether they called it that or not. "But we still have a castle," he defended.

She shifted, and he could feel her against his shoulder. "That's a whole weird story, isn't it? Who builds a castle in a place like Chatelaine?"

"My great-grandfather, evidently," Ridge said. "And only my mother would decide to turn it into a spa and boutique hotel."

She laughed softly, and every nerve in his body seemed magnetized toward her.

"Now we're part of this family that has members far and wide. And in my head, I'm still—"

"A Windham."

"Yeah." He took another drink and offered her the bottle again.

She accepted it even though she made a face. "Maybe it's easier not remembering than knowing you have so many connections you don't know, anyway." She made a sound. "That sounded convoluted."

He still thought he understood.

Without drinking, Hope set the bottle on the wide wood rail and held it there. "It's amazing here, you know. You and your brothers and sisters all have houses right on the lake. But—" she shifted again, and he felt the press of her shoulder even more against his "—you can't even see their places. It's like you have this piece of the world all to yourself."

"True." The meandering, sometimes jagged shoreline meant absolute privacy, unless there was someone on the lake itself. "Can stand out here stark naked if I want."

She made a sound. Maybe a laugh. Or perhaps a groan. He wasn't sure and he didn't care.

"*Do* you?" she asked.

"Not so far." His hand covered Hope's, and he straightened, pulling her around to face him. "But privacy does have its advantages."

Her hair stirred in the breeze as she looked up at him. "It does?"

"Definitely," he rasped. With his free hand, he slid her hair out of her face. Tucked it slowly behind her ear.

She swayed a little. "I think…" She trailed off when he brushed his lips over her temple.

"You think…?" He kissed her smooth cheek. Slowly slid his lips toward her ear. Her hair smelled like spring. "What?"

But she didn't answer with anything except a quick inhalation as she angled her head, but not toward escape at all. He felt the press of their clasped hands against his chest. The beer bottle was hard and intrusive but everything else about her was soft and inviting.

"Ridge," she whispered.

"Yeah?" He slowly meandered from her ear along her jawline. His fingers explored the shape of her neck where her pulse beat almost frantically.

"Nothing." Her other hand closed over his shoulder, her fingertips flexing against him. She tilted her head, allowing him better access to taste that throbbing pulse that so intrigued him. "I just like your name."

Draping his arm against the small of her back, he pulled her closer. Whatever common sense he once possessed was gone. "Then say it all you want." His mouth found hers, lifted right to his as if she'd only been waiting.

He was vaguely aware of the bottle sliding from between them and excruciatingly aware of every other thing about her. From the way she tasted to the way her fingers traveled just as greedily as his. It was only when he pulled her down with him onto one of the deck chairs that he realized the fumbling motion she was suddenly making wasn't directed at him, but at pulling the baby monitor out of her pocket again.

Then he heard it. Evie crying. Not just a little cry that would quickly abate as she settled herself again. Nah. This was the kind of cry that meant "I'm awake *now*." And it brought him back to his senses with the gentleness of a sledgehammer.

He started to set her from him. "I'm sorry," he said gruffly. "I shouldn't have—"

But Hope was already levering off the chair even without his help and taking the steps to the upper level of the deck two at a time. "I'm coming, baby," he heard her say to the monitor.

A moment later, all he heard was the slam of the side door as she went inside.

He exhaled noisily and stared up at the man in the moon. "You look like you're laughing," he accused.

The moon just continued to look back at him.

The laughter didn't stop one little bit.

CHAPTER SEVEN

"REALLY?" SABRINA STOOD in the aisle of a Corpus Christi GreatStore and eyed the small box that Hope was holding up. "A manual breast pump? Everyone I know says to get one of those electric ones." She pointed at the display of breast milk pumps.

"I had an electric one," Hope said. She waggled the small box she was holding. "*This* one never lets you down. Doesn't take up half the space in your diaper bag. Doesn't wait until you have a convenient electrical outlet nearby." She shrugged. "But you know. Get both. You'll decide for yourself what works best." And goodness knew that Ridge's sister could afford to buy whatever she wanted. Her budget was undoubtedly unlimited.

As it was, she was still surprised that Sabrina had asked for Hope's help to start outfitting the nursery for her and Zane's twins. She could have just as easily asked Imani Porter, who was Nash's fiancée after all and the owner of Lullababies, which *catered* to people in their economic stratosphere.

The closest Hope could get to anything the high-end specialty baby store carried was a cutout from one of their chic catalogs.

Not that Imani herself was as snooty as some of the clientele that Hope felt certain shopped at the exclusive boutique. She was incredibly warm, and Hope knew that Ridge's family were all happy that Nash and Imani were together again after a six-month-long breakup. But Hope was *also* certain that Ridge's mother didn't drop by Nash and Imani's home with thrift-store finds for baby Colt, no matter how perfect their condition. Hope doubted a single thing touched Colt's beautiful skin that wasn't curated from the Lullababies collection.

Sabrina, on the other hand, was all about the numbers. Regardless of her own wealth, or that of her fiancé, she must like a bargain.

It was the only explanation that Hope could think of that made sense of this little excursion that Ridge's sister had talked her into. She'd even roped in her mother to babysit Evie for the afternoon.

"It'll be our girls' afternoon out," Sabrina had said when she'd picked up Hope in her fancy SUV.

"You know they pretty much carry this same stuff at the GreatStore in Chatelaine," Hope pointed out as she followed Sabrina, who was pushing the cart up one aisle and down the other as they picked out baby bottles and burp cloths and breast cream. "We could have saved ourselves the hour drive here."

"I know, but I fancied a trip where everyone I run into isn't someone who wants to ask me about Mom or the castle or how does it feel to learn I'm a Fortune." Her smile was more rueful than anything. "Don't tell me Ridge doesn't feel the same way sometimes. I think he, more than any of us, has found it hard to embrace the whole Fortune existence."

"I don't think it's *embracing* the Fortunes as much as it is turning his back on being a Windham," she said, then wondered if she was telling Sabrina something she shouldn't.

"Yeah." Her expression pinched. "Our father's cancer progressed so fast. We barely knew about it before he was summarily selling the company and we were trying to find something suitable to wear for the funeral."

"I'm sorry. It must have been very painful."

"We all deal with loss in our own way." Sabrina looked almost as if she wanted to say more, but she suddenly pointed. "Office supplies!" she said with deliberate brightness, aiming the cart out of the baby section and making a beeline for the school and home office displays. She snatched up a package of bright yellow pencils. "I go through these faster than you can imagine."

Hope smiled, content enough to follow Sabrina's lead away from the depressing subject as well as her surprisingly aimless progress around the giant discount department store. Even though it was Saturday, Ridge was working, so it wasn't as if Hope had needed to be home for him.

Her cheeks warmed, thinking about the night before. The kisses on the deck.

She feared he regretted kissing her altogether. *I'm sorry*, he'd said. *I shouldn't have.* He'd been pushing her away even before she'd realized Evie had awakened.

What else was that to mean? She wasn't entirely oblivious. She *knew* he'd wanted her as much as she wanted him. She'd felt the proof.

But even if she'd had the nerve, it wasn't as if she could've asked him. He'd been closed up on his side of the house when she'd finally ventured out again once Evie was asleep—something that had taken almost two unbearably long hours. After hovering in the great room, feeling torn between the desire to boldly cross to his side of the house and confront the matter head-on, and the cowardice of leaving sleeping dogs alone, cowardice had won out.

She'd spent a nearly sleepless night tormenting herself over every word spoken and every breath shared, only to sleep long past his departure from the house that morning, aided considerably by the fact that Evie had also awoken later than usual.

Ridge's only communication had been the note he'd left in his slashing handwriting that he'd be working all day.

So when Sabrina unexpectedly called her for advice, Hope had pounced on the opportunity like a gift from above. She would have agreed to nearly anything just to avoid the way he was obviously avoiding *her.*

"Let's go to lunch," Sabrina said once she aimed her cart through the checkout. "Or are you in a hurry to get back to that precious Evie of yours?"

Wendy had been periodically sending Hope snapshots of herself and the baby. To be honest, Hope wasn't sure which one of them looked like they were having more fun.

"I'm not usually away from her for more than an hour or two at a time...but we could have lunch," she agreed faintly. Sabrina was something of a force and it was hard not to get swept along. Particularly when the woman tucked her arm through Hope's as if they were the best of girlfriends.

"Excellent! I know the cutest place at the shopping center next to the FortuneMetals complex." Sabrina laughed as they started across the busy parking lot. "Wonder if Cousin Reeve is there?" She wrinkled her nose, looking surprisingly mischievous. "Have you heard of him? Reeve Fortune?"

Hope lifted her shoulders. "Erm—"

Sabrina laughed again. "The surname notwithstanding," she said drolly, "he's a big-time overachiever. Runs FortuneMetals *and* FortuneMedia."

Hope's eyebrows rose. "I've heard of FortuneMedia at least." One of the business offices in Chatelaine near the Daily Grind, in fact, had a big FortuneMedia sign on it. Considering the building used to be an old house, the sign had always struck her as too modern. "Isn't that the company that keeps buying up smaller media outlets?"

"So I've heard. Bought up the company that produces *The Chatelaine Report*. Have you seen it?"

Hope shook her head.

"It's a community event blog. We've been promoting the petting zoo on it for the last month. Anyway, Reeve ended up marrying the woman who used to write it, Isabel Banninger. Was apparently all the scandal around here a year or two ago. She was engaged to Trey Fitzgerald and made it all the way to the church but ran out on him 'cause his cheating was caught all over the internet. You've *surely* heard of the Fitzgeralds? Daddy is big-time into politics?"

Hope tapped her forehead. "Sorry. If I have, I've forgotten."

Sabrina gasped and pressed her hand to her mouth. "God! How insensitive I am." She looked so genuinely distressed that Hope would have done a backflip to ease the moment.

"It's fine," she insisted. "Some things I *do* remember. And some things I don't. That's just the way it is." It sounded so much easier to deal with than it really was, but she loathed the idea that people who knew felt sorry for her because of it.

"Well, I just can't imagine it." Sabrina beeped the doors of her vehicle as they approached it, and the liftgate automatically opened. "But I think you're handling it amazingly well."

"I'm only handling it because Ridge insists on taking care of everything." The words came out before she could stop them, and she felt her face flush. "I'll get all this." She quickly reached for one of the overloaded bags. "You already look like you're ready to pop."

For a second, she thought Sabrina was going to argue. But Ridge's sister's smile widened ruefully. "Yeah, I feel like I'm about ready to sometimes, too." She blew out her breath, rubbing her back as she moved to the driver's side and hauled herself up behind the steering wheel.

Hope quickly transferred the purchases into the back of the SUV. She looked up at the opened liftgate above her head. Even if she jumped, she didn't think she'd reach the button to close it. "Can you close it from up there?"

"Sure thing."

Hope ducked out of the way when the wide door began descending again, and waited until she heard the secure sound of it locking into place before she climbed up into the passenger seat. "Does your OB think you'll make it to your due date?"

"Hopefully, but we're keeping close track. One scare to the hospital was enough for Zane and me." Rather than backing out of the parking spot, though, Sabrina sat there for a moment, tapping the steering wheel with her thumb. "He's like that, you know," she said quietly.

Hope's mouth dried a little. Sabrina wasn't referring to either her obstetrician or fiancé, but to Ridge. "Generous to a fault?"

"That. But also, he's a fixer by nature."

Hope looked down at her clenched hands in her lap. "I don't like knowing I need fixing."

Sabrina's hand immediately reached over and covered Hope's. "Not *you*," she said firmly. She squeezed her hand in emphasis. "Fixing your situation."

"But I should be doing more for myself," she said huskily. She looked up at the other woman. "Shouldn't I?"

Sabrina's brows twitched together for a moment as she placed her hands on the steering wheel again. She was obviously taking Hope's words to heart. "Like what? You mean like getting a job?"

She lifted her shoulders. "Maybe? I can't imagine who'd hire me, though. I can't even say whether I have a college education. What kind of experience I have." She made a face. "If any."

"Well, I'd hire you in a second," Sabrina said so matter-of-factly that Hope believed her. She started backing out of the parking spot. "Regardless of what you remember about yourself, you're honest, conscientious and motivated. I can't tell you how many people I've met who have a basketful of degrees yet possess none of those attributes. I'll take one employee who is interested in learning and showing up over five who aren't. If we had a spot at all in the ranch office, I'd tell you it's yours."

"I wasn't asking—"

"I know you weren't," Sabrina assured just as swiftly. "If you could choose to be anything at all—without regard to education or experience or any of that—what would it be?"

"A good mom," Hope said immediately.

Sabrina pressed her hand to her swollen belly. "Amen to that." Then she gave Hope a quick wink. "I know it's probably annoying to hear but have patience. Things will unfold in time. I'm certain of it."

How many times had Ridge told her something similar?

"Patience is overrated," she muttered and then huffed out a deep sigh.

Sabrina smiled at her. And Hope smiled back.

As they continued driving through the streets of Corpus Christi, Hope peered through the windows, wondering if she'd spot anything that might be familiar.

As far as she knew, none of the yearbooks came from a Central High School located there.

"Talking about patience, though, I have to admit I wouldn't mind being a few weeks early," Sabrina said suddenly. "Nothing crazy of course, but how *huge* am I going to get?"

Hope laughed. "I was enormous." She pressed her hands against her belly, looking down at herself, and so easily picturing her abdomen. "It was like having an alien living inside me, watching Evie moving around inside that huge belly!"

"Try having two of 'em," Sabrina said feelingly.

Hope's mind immediately took a detour into the land of make-believe. Twins obviously ran in Ridge's family. When he had a baby—

Her phone pinged with another picture from Wendy, and Hope managed to get her mind off of Ridge making babies.

She flashed the picture of Evie and Wendy grinning into the camera at Sabrina when she stopped at a light.

"I think they're having more fun without us," Sabrina chuckled.

Hope smiled, too, and saved the picture to that great, mysterious thing called the cloud. She already had hundreds of pictures filling up her cloud. The cell phone was yet one more thing that Ridge had provided for her as well as an email account and that metaphorical puffy white storage space.

Whatever the future held, at least she'd have the photos she'd taken. The phone might need to be left behind, but that email account and all of its trappings were forever hers.

When she and Sabrina were seated in the cute little café, which overlooked the park next to the FortuneMetals skyscraper, and had ordered, Sabrina pulled a notepad out of her purse and spread it on the table. She flipped a few pages, all of which were covered with lists of one sort or another.

"What *is* all that?"

"Lists," Sabrina stated the obvious. "In the last month I can't seem to stop making them. I'm afraid I'm becoming obsessed, actually. This one—" she flipped to one page that was covered with neat handwriting and wildly colorful checkmarks "—is an inventory of all the bed linens we have!" She shook her head at herself and turned to another page. "Honestly, I don't know how Zane stands it."

Hope grinned. "Because he adores you," she said. "Lists and all."

Sabrina was flipping more pages, murmuring slightly to herself. "Thank God," she replied. She pulled out a pencil and busily marked off items under a large heading of NURSERY, then she turned another page and sat back slightly. "The wedding."

Hope was doctoring the iced tea the waitress delivered. She knew Sabrina and Zane were thinking sometime after the babies were born, and a part of her couldn't help wondering if she and Evie would still be there to see it.

The knot twisting in her stomach was becoming much too familiar.

"Have you set a date, then?" she asked a little desperately.

"Not yet." Fortunately, Sabrina noticed nothing amiss as she tapped her page with the eraser end of the pencil. "This is about the mystery wedding." She sat forward, lowering her voice confidingly. "I think I've figured out who is getting married."

Hope raised her eyebrows, surprised. "Really! How? And who?"

"Process of elimination."

Hope waited. "And?"

Sabrina sat back to let the waitress place their orders on the table. As soon as she was gone again, Sabrina leaned forward again. "Belinda and Javier."

Hope blinked, taking a fraction of a second to place the names. "Belinda Mendes?"

Sabrina was nodding. "And Javier Mendes."

"Aren't they already married?" The middle-aged couple were longstanding employees at the ranch. They even lived in one of the bungalows near the ranch headquarters. Hope walked past it every time she and Evie went to the petting zoo. Belinda's flower garden was a treat almost as sweet as the zoo.

"Married *and* divorced. Three times. And from what I hear, they're overdue to remarry." Sabrina picked up one of the wedges of her sliced club sandwich. "And it would make sense why we've all been invited."

"But why not just let everyone know it's them?"

"Who knows?" Sabrina waved her hand, and a little slice of tomato slid out of her sandwich and landed on the plate. "Hedging their bets? Less embarrassment if they cancel out altogether before the big day?" She took a quick bite before her gesturing lost even more bits of sandwich ingredients. "And I bet you that my *mother* knows the truth. Which is why she is making sure that we all attend."

Hope thought it was a bit of a stretch, but who was she to judge? "I guess it makes about as much sense as anything else."

"Well, I'm pretty sure I'm right," Sabrina said, looking satisfied with her conclusion. "Wish they would've just done it a month ago, though. I've grown out of the dress I was planning to wear." She shook her head. "Won't fasten over the boobal region anymore." She patted her cleavage.

Hope couldn't help but laugh. Yes, Sabrina was *very* pregnant with an impressive watermelon-sized baby bump and a bosom to match. "I'm sure you'll find something that works."

"Easy for you to say, Miss Size Two."

Hope gave a snort of laughter. "Not even in my dreams anymore. When I was in high school, I was a zero." She didn't really know where the knowledge came from. Like the other memories, it just seemed to be *there*. As if it had never been missing in the first place.

"You're killing me." Sabrina pulled a comical face. "A zero. Good grief. Now, the least you can do is help me find a dress, too."

Hope started to shake her head again. She knew how close Sabrina was to her sisters. Surely, they'd be better at the dress matter. "I—"

"There's a boutique right here in the complex," Sabrina interjected. "DD's Designs. We could pop in after we finish here. The owner's a friend of mine from a women-in-business association." She seemed to realize she was still holding a pencil in one hand and her sandwich in the other and stuck the pencil behind her ear.

"A maternity boutique?" Hope immediately envisioned something as chic as Lullababies.

"Not exactly maternity clothes. But if I could find something flowy enough maybe I could get by without having to visit Ollie the Tent Maker."

"You hardly need a *tent*."

"Perhaps not. But we're here." Sabrina gestured toward the

windows that lined one wall of the fancy little café. "And I hate wasting a good opportunity."

Hope wavered. She glanced at her phone again.

Her companion noticed. "My mother and Evie will be fine for an extra few minutes," she promised.

"I know, but I don't want to take advantage of—"

Sabrina let out a laugh. "Seriously? Nobody takes advantage of my mother. She'd make mincemeat out of them without turning a single blond hair and smile graciously right through the bloodletting."

"Now I *know* you're exaggerating." Wendy Fortune was the epitome of classy elegance, even when she was mugging for a selfie in the company of an eight-month-old. "Bloodletting?"

"Might be a slight exaggeration," Sabrina allowed. She reached over and squeezed Hope's hand. "Come on. How often do we get a chance to indulge ourselves with just some girl time?"

She made it sound so appealing that Hope found herself capitulating even before she'd made the conscious decision to do so. "But just the one shop, right? I really *don't* want to be away from Evie too much longer."

"Well, when you put it like that..." Sabrina winked. "One shop." She gestured at their plates. Her sandwich was half-eaten already whereas Hope had barely taken a single bite of hers. "So get cracking there, girlfriend. Eating is fine. But it has got nothing on shopping for clothes, and you have a baby to get back to."

Two hours later and driving up the ranch road once more, Hope knew she'd never doubt Ridge's sister when her mind was set on something.

Not only had Sabrina found herself a lovely dress to wear to the "sshh, Mendes wedding," but she'd gotten two other casual outfits for herself, one for her twin, Dahlia, and when that hadn't proved fulfilling enough, she'd insisted on turning her focus on Hope.

Which is why Hope had stored three shopping bags in the back seat of the SUV and not two.

"I'll pay you back," Hope said for about the fifth time since

Sabrina had insisted that the watercolor silk dress was positively made for Hope.

"Whenever," she said with the careless ease that only someone who has never worried about money could carry off. "You heard Deedee yourself when she rang it up. Friends and family discount she said."

In the great blankness of her past, Hope was certain that she would never have paid such an extravagant amount for a dress, no matter how beautiful. If it weren't for that discount—nearly 75 percent off the full price—she would have certainly been able to resist Sabrina's well-intentioned coaxing to buy the thing. "Well, as a friend of her friend, thank you."

"Wait until Ridge sees you in it. You'll knock him speechless."

Hope pressed her tongue against the back of her teeth, trying and failing to suppress a little shiver. Regardless of his reaction, though, she no longer had an excuse to avoid attending the Mendeses' mystery wedding. Because whether or not he regretted kissing her, she didn't doubt for one second that he wouldn't hesitate to use her as an excuse not to go himself if she refused.

She didn't want that on her conscience, too.

Her gaze lingered on the headquarter buildings as Sabrina drove past them. "You really think it's Belinda and Javier, huh?"

"Pretty positive. Dahlia, Jade and I started a pool to see who's right. Not that I should admit to having insider knowledge, but Belinda and Javier both requested vacation beginning the day before the wedding. Perfect timing for a honeymoon. That's what clinched it for me, anyway. It's just too coincidental to ignore, don't you think?"

It did seem like a reasonable conclusion to Hope. She cordoned off the part of her mind that was intent on conjuring details of a ceremony that had culminated in a wedding ring on *her* finger and prayed that her fractured mind wasn't visible on the outside. "Who do Dahlia and Jade think the couple is?"

"Dahlia's betting on Dr. Mitch and his office manager, Alondra. Jade's undecided."

"*My* Dr. Mitch?"

"If Dahlia's right, he's Alondra's Dr. Mitch," Sabrina said

humorously. "Pump my brother on it. If I'm backing the wrong horse, I want to know. It'll keep me from losing any money on Belinda and Javier!"

Hope tried not to choke. The idea of "pumping" Ridge for anything was too disturbing. But somehow, she managed to produce a chuckle in response.

Sabrina's steady stream of chatter fortunately didn't require a lot of input, and it wasn't long before she dropped Hope off at Wendy's house.

Ridge's SUV, which she had used that morning when she'd met up with his sister, was still parked where she'd left it.

Sabrina hung her head out the window after Hope had her shopping bag in hand. "Tell Mom I'd have stopped in, but I'm dying to get out of these pants, and I'll see her tomorrow for brunch!" Then she waved and drove off.

Hope headed toward the beautiful house, the shopping bag from DD's Designs swinging from her hand. Before she could even ring the doorbell, though, the door swung open to reveal Wendy's smiling face. She was a tall, slender woman with enviably sleek blond hair cut in a flattering bob and striking green eyes.

"Come in, darling. I didn't even hear you drive up. I was just showing these gentlemen out." Wendy wrapped her arm through Hope's and pulled her right into the house, stepping aside while several of the ranch hands trooped out—Javier Mendes among them. They all tipped their hats politely as they departed. "Just had to discuss a little ranch business." She shut the door after them. "Now, tell me all about your day. Did Sabrina wear you out?"

"No…not entirely." She felt a quick jab of self-consciousness when she heard more male voices from inside the house and recognized Ridge's right away. Sighing, she pushed her fingers self-consciously through her hair. She'd had the window partially down for part of the drive, and her hair was probably a mess. "She said she'd see you tomorrow for brunch."

"I've talked all of my children into brunch at The Chef's Table," she said. "You and Evie included, of course."

Hope knew the fancy restaurant was located at the LC Club

and opened her mouth to demur, but they'd just entered the great room and she spotted Ridge standing next to the enormous stone fireplace.

He was holding Evie, who was, not surprisingly, giving him the usual looks of adoration. Ridge, however, was looking at Hope, and she felt a kaleidoscope of butterflies suddenly take flight inside her. It was a wonder she didn't sprout wings herself and flutter her way right on over to him. Her lips even tingled, as if it was only moments ago that his lips had been pressed against them rather than the better part of an entire day.

Mercifully, Wendy's arm around Hope's kept her grounded while she doggedly recalled Ridge's *I'm sorry, I shouldn't have* and peripherally noticed Arlo and Nash were also present. Whatever ranch business it was had been important enough to call them all together on a Saturday afternoon.

"I was just telling everyone how much I enjoyed watching Evie today," Wendy was saying. "She's an absolute joy. Brings me right back to when my little ones were little."

"Mom's in the mood for reminiscing," Arlo deadpanned. Like all of Wendy's offspring, Arlo was tall. But where Ridge and Nash both were dark-haired and dark-eyed, Arlo was blond like Sabrina and Dahlia. "Next thing she'll be telling us who had diaper rash and who didn't."

Wendy reached out and cradled Arlo's cheek in her palm. "I could recall who was the one most likely to run out of the house stark naked," she said with a fond tap as his cheek turned a little ruddy.

"Busted," Nash drawled. He was leaning on the enormous kitchen island, a squat glass of something amber held in his long fingers. "I dearly hope it's a habit you've finally outgrown."

Arlo raised his eyebrows. "At least I never got poison oak on the parts the sun's not supposed to see like *someone* I know."

"Oh, my. Nash really was truly miserable," Wendy said. "Easy to laugh about now."

"Easy for you to say," Nash grumbled. "I was eight and the memory still pains me."

"And this one—" Wendy let go of Hope and poked Ridge

in the center of his chest "—had to be watched every minute of the day, too."

Ridge shook his head, but his mother just laughed and moved across the room to where an array of cut crystal bottles were arranged on a tray. She eschewed the liquor, though, for a bottle of water. "He was forever trying to fix things."

Hope set her shopping bag on a side table. Some things didn't change, she thought.

Wendy threw herself down in the corner of the oversize leather couch, leisurely crossing her long legs. "I had an antique table in my dressing room," she said. "And my youngest there—" she tilted the bottom of her bottle in Ridge's direction "—decided the legs were an inch too long. So, with his toy toolbox full of *supposedly* toy tools, he cut exactly an inch off each leg." Her sparkling gaze focused on Hope. "He was five," she added. "My advice to you is to never allow Evie to own a toy toolbox no matter how harmless the tools appear to be."

"Five!" Hope didn't have to work hard to imagine a little boy with waving brown hair, inquisitive brown eyes and an unexpectedly mischievous grin. "And you had an actual saw?"

"Didn't need a saw." Ridge shrugged. "I used the hammer and the screwdriver like a wedge."

"And sanded it all when he was done with my set of vintage steel nail files," Wendy finished.

"The table legs were about two inches in diameter," Ridge retorted. "It wasn't as though I was cutting chunks of wood like the legs on that." He moved Evie to his other arm and gestured carelessly at the solidly framed coffee table in front of the couch.

"By the time he was eight, he'd moved on from redesigning furniture to blowing up stuff," Nash said.

Hope raised her eyebrows. *"Stuff?"*

"I liked experimenting," Ridge said dismissively. "And not all mints dropped into a bottle of soda react like the old Mentos in soda trick."

"There were times I think you liked the *mess*," Wendy said wryly. "Particularly when it ended up dripping down from the ceiling."

"Well. Speaking of messes…" Hope bent and gathered up

Evie's scattered toys. "I hope Evie didn't make too much of one." She straightened and stuffed them in the diaper bag that sat on the other end of the couch.

"I look forward to many messes with that little one," Wendy assured.

As if cleaning up the toys were a signal, both Arlo and Nash began making their exits. They kissed Wendy's cheek, bumped Ridge's fist, tousled Evie's hair and tipped nonexistent Stetsons toward Hope as they left.

All perfectly normal behavior.

But Hope still felt a faint frisson of unease that had nothing to do with Ridge and a moonlit lake and whether or not he regretted kissing her.

It wasn't unusual for his siblings to gather together for no reason at all. They were a close family.

And her being a worrywart was starting to spill over onto too many unrelated matters.

Focus. Just focus on one thing. Take a breath and let everything else go.

She exhaled slowly as she shouldered the diaper bag and held out her arms for the one thing that never failed. Evie. The pale skin around her daughter's eyes was looking pink—a sure sign that she was getting sleepy. "I should get her down for a nap. Any later and it'll be impossible to get her to sleep tonight at a reasonable hour."

"I'll come with you." Ridge transferred the baby to her. "I rode with Arlo earlier."

Hope nodded and snuggled Evie's neck, inhaling the sweet baby scent for a long, needy moment before she looked at Wendy once more. "Thank you ag—"

The older woman cut her off with a languid wave. "Enough thanks, my dear. She's a delight, and I'll be begging you soon enough for a repeat." She stood and picked up Hope's shopping bag, peeking through the tissue paper that poked artfully out the top of it. "What lovely colors," she murmured.

"I needed a dress for the M—" She almost said Mendes but corrected hurriedly with, "mystery wedding."

If anything, Wendy looked even more pleased. She tilted her

cheek to accept Ridge's light kiss before they all headed into the foyer. Then his mom pulled open the door and handed Ridge the shopping bag. "Don't forget brunch tomorrow."

"How can we? You've put reminders on all of our calendars," he told her.

"A mother learns these things," she said blithely, and watched them until they reached Ridge's SUV before she went inside and closed the door again.

Hope fastened Evie into her car seat and hoped she wouldn't fall asleep on the short drive to his place. If she did, she'd probably figure the five minutes would be enough of a nap to last her, and Hope knew from experience that would mean a very cranky Evie come nighttime.

She climbed into the passenger seat and took the shopping bag that Ridge handed over to her. The tissue paper crinkled softly as she set it near her feet and fastened her seat belt.

"So." She folded her hands in her lap and looked at him. "Is it my imagination or—" she swirled her index finger in the air "—have you all been circling the wagons?"

CHAPTER EIGHT

TIMING, RIDGE THOUGHT, was everything.

It was impossible to ignore the inquisitive, vaguely imperious expression on Hope's face. It reminded him, strangely enough, of the way his mom could look sometimes when she knew something was off.

If she'd have arrived just five minutes later, everyone would have already been gone from Wendy's house and Hope would have never known a thing about the impromptu meeting Nash had called after one of the hands reported seeing that suspicious car again.

"It's—" fully prepared to lie, it aggravated the life out of him that he couldn't "—not your imagination." The gravel spun a little under his tires as he accelerated down his mother's drive toward the gate.

He could sense Hope's muscles tensing, though her expression didn't change.

"A gray sedan was seen on the access road that runs back behind Dahlia's place," he admitted. "One of the hands reported it to Nash. Everyone on the ranch has been told to keep an eye out for it."

Her lips compressed slightly. She nodded and turned forward. Her profile was sharply outlined by the deepening afternoon sun. "When?"

"When were they told or when did they see it?"

Her eyebrow lifted slightly. "Is this why Sabrina took me out of town today?"

"What?" He felt his neck get hot. "No. The car wasn't spotted until you'd already left. It was around noon today." While he'd been on the other side of Chatelaine, traipsing around the Zazlo place with Beau Weatherly.

She sucked in a breath. Exhaled even more slowly.

Then she shifted and crossed her arms over her chest.

The bag near her feet crinkled.

What would Hope think of the property? The house was half the size of the one they occupied now.

He cleared his throat. It was always too easy for his thoughts to get ahead of himself where she was concerned. "Since Nash saw the car the first time, he spread the word to keep watch. After you saw it in town, we've emphasized it to everyone. The good news, though, is this time we got a partial license plate."

Surprise softened her stiff posture, and she looked at him again. "How partial?"

"First three numbers. But it's a Nebraska license plate. I got the information to Villanueva. Nash also has someone with the sheriff's department working on the number. The focus is narrowing."

"Nebraska..." she murmured.

His hands felt sweaty around the steering wheel, and he lowered his window all the way down. "Does it feel familiar?"

She was looking out the side window. The wind from his window stirred her hair. She made a soft sound as she shook her head.

Ridge glanced in the rearview mirror. Thanks to the mirror that hung on the back seat to reflect the baby's rear-facing car seat, he could see Evie's head bobbing. Nearly asleep but determined to stave it off.

How could he bear to lose either one of them?

He cleared his throat yet again. "Meanwhile, I think it's time we started using the gate at the end of the drive."

She gave him a look. "You're *that* worried?"

"Cautious," he corrected. "Everyone is going to be using

their gates. It's already been agreed upon. We'll stop again when…" He shrugged. "When we have all this figured out," he finally concluded.

"Great. I'm inconveniencing everyone now."

"You're not inconveniencing anyone. I told you…we're all on the same page." He drummed the steering wheel with his thumb a few times. "How, uh, how was Corpus? Sabrina leave anything on the shelves for someone else to buy? Figure she's going to have a baby shower at some point. Is there anything left to get her?"

"She didn't buy a lot of diapers," Hope said. "Diapers are always a good shower gift." She was quiet for a moment. Then tucked her drifting hair behind her ear.

He'd spent an inordinate amount of time studying her ears. Along with every other little detail about her.

She had pierced ears. But had never worn any earrings. Did she dislike them? Was she allergic?

The key pendant he'd gotten her was platinum and diamond.

Sabrina told him that lots of people had sensitivities to jewelry but not usually platinum.

"Diapers." His thumb drummed the steering wheel. Why wouldn't Hope wear the damn necklace? "I'll have to remember that."

Her hand fluttered to the paper twine handles of the shopping bag. "I bought a dress," she said.

His neck got a few degrees hotter. Short of turning on the air conditioning in fifty-degree weather or sticking his head outside the open window like a dog, he had to live with it. "Yeah?"

"For the, um, the wedding."

As if he didn't know that.

"Sabrina loaned me the money," she added a little pedantically. "I intend to pay her back."

He was pretty certain that Sabrina didn't worry about getting repaid. He also thought he showed good sense not mentioning that, however. "Great. That's great."

"It's not from GreatStore."

"I don't care where it's from. As long as you feel good about it and don't leave me to fend for myself at the thing."

She faced him once more, arms crossed again. "Aren't you the least bit curious who is getting married? Your sisters have started a pool on it, you know."

He didn't, but even if he did, he just did not care. He spread his fingers away from the steering wheel. "I have the feeling that an honest answer is going to get me into hot water."

She made a sound and shook her head. "Men," she murmured.

He managed not to smile, but it was an effort. "I have it on good authority from my mother that we're an impossible lot." He glanced in the rearview mirror again. "We're not going to make it before she's asleep."

She craned her head around to look back at her daughter's reflection in the specialized mirror. "Thirty minutes," she said. "If she just could sleep for thirty minutes, then we'll all sleep better tonight."

They'd reached the closed gate for his turnoff. He drove right past it.

"Where are we going?"

"Anywhere. So long as it takes at least thirty minutes."

"I *knew* she kept you awake at night, too."

Yeah. It was *Evie* who kept him awake at all hours.

He just smiled wryly and kept driving.

They made it all the way around the entire lake. They drove by the Fortune Castle, where only one tradesman truck was still parked outside. His mother's renovations of the place to turn it into a boutique hotel were nearly complete.

He'd seen it only a few times before she'd started the mammoth undertaking. From what he could see, the outside had changed little, except the moat of unruly bushes that had surrounded the property had been eradicated and new landscaping installed in its place.

He knew better than to stop entirely, though. It was the constant motion that kept Evie sleeping soundly. Instead, he trolled past the unlikely structure, while Hope made admiring sounds about the blooming sunset behind the turrets.

When they hit the thirty-minute mark, he looked at Hope. Her head was resting against the seatback, her eyes at half-mast as she watched the sky. She was almost as relaxed as Evie. One hand resting on the console between them. The other hand occasionally pulling her hair away from her face.

It was all he could do not to pull over and reach for her. Kiss her all over again, even if it did mean waking up the most effective eight-month-old chaperone who'd ever existed. "Keep going or head home?"

"Keep going." Her gaze slanted toward him. Periwinkle blue at dusk. "Only if you don't mind…"

If it meant a few more minutes between now and the reality of returned memories, he'd drive forever.

Instead of turning back toward the lake, he drove instead toward the town of Chatelaine.

The air blowing through the window was getting chillier, but she wasn't complaining, so he left it alone. "Haven't taken you to Harv's New BBQ yet, have I?"

She shook her head. Brushed her hair back from her face again and gave him a sideways look. "What happened to Harv's Old BBQ?"

"Who knows? Guess you'd have to ask Harv."

She smiled slightly, then turned her palm upward against the console between them. "Maybe I will."

He'd been kicking himself for kissing her the other night. Not because he regretted it. Kissing her had been a long time in coming. But he felt like a man dying of thirst who'd been given the faintest taste of water. It only worsened the wanting.

None of which stopped him from settling his hand lightly atop her palm. And why something so simple could feel so freaking erotic, he had no idea. But he was glad the wind blowing through his window was on the verge of cold.

He was pretty sure she'd wonder why he'd suddenly stick his head out the window otherwise.

"Ridge?"

Heat was streaking down his spine. "Yeah."

She hesitated, and he moved his hand away, so he wouldn't have to endure her doing it first.

"Last night. I'm sorry about—" her fingers curled into a

small fist, though her hand remained on the console "—about throwing myself at, uh, at you—"

His head whipped around. There was still plenty of light to see her cheeks had turned red. "What are you talking about?"

"On the deck. I kissed—"

"*I* kissed you," he said over her. He closed his hand over her fist. "And the only thing *I'm sorry* about is moving too fast for you."

"*That's* what you regret?"

"Who said anything about regret?" He realized he'd tightened his hand around her fist and deliberately lightened his grip.

"You. You said you were sorry, you shouldn't have—"

He checked the road and pulled abruptly off onto the shoulder, kicking up a cloud of dust. He shoved the gear to Park and turned to look at her. "I *shouldn't* have rushed you," he said flatly. "I'm not sure what would have happened if Evie hadn't started crying when she did."

Hope's face looked even rosier. "Would that have been so terrible?"

The desire that was a constant simmer inside him went straight to boil. "You're the one who is doubting your own memories about your husband's funeral. Are you married? Not married?"

She sucked in an audible breath. "I don't feel married."

"Right now? Or period?"

She didn't answer and his head felt too heavy. He closed his eyes and ground his teeth for a short millennium. He felt her shifting and looked at her again. She was staring at her palms in her lap.

Imagining a band on her wedding finger, no doubt.

He reached over and deliberately covered her left hand again with his. "I don't want to be something *you* regret, Hope. Not now. Not later." His voice sounded as raw as the words felt.

"Why did you call me that?"

The question threw him. "Call you what? Hope?"

"You're the one who gave me the name in the first place. Why Hope?"

"Should I have stuck with *Hey You*?" He immediately regretted the sarcasm. "Because it was the first thing that came to me," he said. "I looked at you and I thought—" his jaw felt tight "—I *felt* Hope."

His admission seemed to echo around them.

Then her palm shifted, pressing up against his, molding them together. Her fingers slid slightly, gliding through his fingers.

If the way her palm curled against his was any indication of how other elements would fit, he could die a happy man.

But only if he could be certain she didn't belong to someone else.

"I don't want to be something you regret, either," she said softly.

Honk!

They both startled, sitting back in their seats when the semi-trailer blew past their SUV, leaving it rocking in its wake.

"Jerk," Hope muttered.

Ridge had a stronger word for the honking driver, who had also woken Evie.

Hope unfastened her seat belt and leaned over into the back seat, getting the baby situated again with the pacifier. Then she slid back into her own seat beside him. She fastened her seat belt. "We agree, then." Her voice was soft but steadfastly calm. "We don't want to do something we'll regret."

That hadn't strictly been what either one of them had said, but just as he was set to gnaw on it, she shook back her hair and lifted her chin slightly. "Doesn't stop us from being friends. And friends—" she moistened her lips "—can hold hands." She set her hand on the console again in an unmistakable invitation. "Right?"

His blood pounded in his ears. Nothing about Hope would ever be *just friends*.

He shifted into Drive, threaded his fingers through hers and steered back onto the road with his other hand. "Right." Some lies were meant to be forgiven.

For a small-town Saturday night, Harv's New BBQ was hopping.

He dropped Hope and Evie off in front of the restaurant since the crammed parking lot meant he had to park down the block.

When he joined them, they were in line with another dozen people after them.

No table service was available at Harv's. You waited your turn to order at the counter, carried your own food to one of the many picnic tables lined up outside the place and cleared your own mess away when you were done.

Big propane heaters were scattered among the tables, casting enough heat that you didn't really feel the cold. String lights bobbed lightly overhead, suspended in a long crisscross pattern between the Harv's rooftop to the tall poles that separated the perimeter from the used tire place next door.

They sat across from each other, shoulder and hip against complete strangers who were just as neck-deep as they were in some of the best BBQ that Ridge had ever tasted. A three-piece band was wedged into the only speck of covered patio that existed. The enthusiasm in their music definitely superseded their talent, but nobody seemed to mind. There were as many people two-stepping between the tables as were eating.

A young couple one table over had a little boy. Definitely older than Evie, but between the food that Hope cut up for her and the entertaining faces the child was making at her, she was as happy as a piglet in clover.

Ridge went back to stand in that godforsaken long line, after they'd stuffed themselves to the gills with brisket and pulled pork and hot sausages, just to buy a wedge of chocolate cream pie topped with half a foot of whipped cream. And knew he'd do it twenty times over, just to see Hope's face wreathed in laughter at the way Evie wanted to dive into the stuff.

Then the three of them did their own share of two-stepping, only to lose their seats at the picnic table to usurpers who were just as neck-deep in their own food.

Hope took Evie into the restroom and returned with a considerably less sticky baby. He scooped her daughter into his arms, and they walked, hand in hand, the two blocks back to the Escalade while she raved about Harv's food, and he wondered what she'd think of Nonny Zazlo's spread only another ten minutes or so straight up the road.

Then she spotted his SUV. "For heaven's sake," she exclaimed. "What's wrong with people?"

"Hunger for Harv's, I guess." Two ancient pickups had parked so close he was nearly blocked in. He almost wished they had because it would have delayed the end of their evening. But thanks to the technology on his SUV, he could have maneuvered his way out of nearly anything, and while she and Evie waited off to one side, now was no exception.

He pulled abreast of the first pickup. It had a cracked windshield, a bench seat patterned in fraying plaid and a flag hanging from a pole mounted in the truck bed.

Hope fastened Evie into her seat and climbed into her own. "There is no way that guy could have parked any closer to you."

"Not without making baby trucks."

She fastened her seat belt and jabbed the button for her heated seat. "I hadn't realized how cold it was getting."

He'd take credit for that fact if it wasn't for all those propane heaters.

Unlike the crowded Harv's, the main drag of Chatelaine was quiet, and moments later, he pulled out in a U-turn and aimed toward the lake.

"It's been a good day." Hope broke the silence when they were halfway home.

"Yeah." And he would have traded his fancy-ass SUV for a pickup truck with a cracked windshield in a hot second, just to have that bench seat, so—*friends* be damned—he could put his arm around her and pull her close to his side. He'd keep her there for as long as he could.

Timing. It was everything.

And Nebraska—and whatever was lurking there—was getting closer by the minute.

THE NEXT MORNING, Hope was getting Evie buckled into her car seat when Gordon Villanueva called Ridge.

They were already running late to meet his family at The Chef's Table for brunch, but Ridge stepped away from the SUV to take the call. "What've you got," he greeted.

Some people would be offended by the lack of niceties. Villanueva wasn't one of them. "We've narrowed down the vehicles to six. Two are rental cars. Four privately owned. I'm emailing you the list of full plates. Meanwhile, I'm headed to Nebraska in a few hours. Want to see the registered owners in person."

"You're not telling them what you're—"

"Cool your jets, son," Villanueva said mildly. "I'm seeking information. Not planning to dole it out."

Ridge's shoulders came down again. He smoothed the tails of his necktie. He'd worn one only a handful of times since moving to Chatelaine Hills, but The Chef's Table called for a certain amount of formality. "Sorry," he muttered.

"No need to apologize. It's a stressful situation for y'all. Anyways, I should have more news for you by the end of the day, even if it is just to say there's no connection at all."

"Thanks," Ridge said, but Villanueva had already ended the call.

He pocketed his cell phone and walked back to the vehicle.

Hope was already sitting in the passenger seat. She was wearing skinny black jeans tucked into knee-high boots and a bright blue turtleneck that she'd gotten from one of his sisters for Christmas. The color made her eyes look even bluer.

"That was Gordon Villanueva." He climbed in beside her and conveyed the latest. He turned the engine over and put the SUV in gear. It wouldn't take long to get to the LC Club, but they were still going to be nearly a half hour late. His fault for losing track of time that morning when he'd gone down to the barn early to work with Larry, Moe and Curly.

"So, we might know who I am by tonight." Her voice was as tight as the pinched line that had formed between her eyebrows.

"We might know who *the driver* of that car is," he corrected. "It's a piece of the puzzle, but it doesn't necessarily mean we'll have a direct line pointing to your real identity."

"I wish Hope *was* my real identity," she muttered.

"Once you know the truth, you'll feel differently."

"Will I?"

It was a question that he was wholly unequipped to answer, and they both knew it.

He slowed as he neared the gate, waiting for it to slowly

swing open when he hit the switch. But it only swung a few feet before it ground to a halt.

"Sit tight." He got out and checked the mechanism that powered the heavy steel. After making a few adjustments, he got the gate going again, and soon they were speeding along the ranch road. It was nearly eleven thirty in the morning. The sun was shining, and there was a faint breeze causing ripples on the lake. As they drove around the lake, he saw at least a half dozen small sailboats out to take advantage of the day.

He envied them a little. Most of his experience with boats was of the luxury yacht variety.

"I left a phone message at Mitch's office this morning," she said when they'd finally reached the farthest point of the lake and turned onto the main drag, which wound between the cluster of businesses and the shoreline walk that was busy with joggers and skateboarders. "Asking for a recommendation for a therapist."

He stopped at a crosswalk, and while they waited for a woman pushing a stroller to cross, he looked from Hope to the sandy beach that stretched from the walk to the glittering water. A kid ran in the sand while trying to get his red kite aloft.

Had Ridge ever looked that carefree?

Felt that carefree?

The roadway cleared, and he hit the gas again and glanced at Hope. "I could have just called Mitch directly."

"I know you could have." She crossed one slender leg over the other. The toe of her boot bobbed up and down. "But I need to start doing more for myself." She shoveled her lustrous hair away from her face. "Can't expect you to take care of everything forever."

Why not?

He didn't voice the words, knowing how antiquated he'd sound if he did, but he meant them all the same.

What was wrong with a man who wanted to take care of those he lo—

A low-slung sports car suddenly shot out of a side road right in front of them, and Ridge jammed the brakes, automatically throwing his arm out in front of Hope, who'd pitched forward despite her seat belt. He glared at the departing license plate—TFIII. "You okay?"

"Fine." She sounded breathless. "Um—"

He belatedly realized the arm he'd thrown in front of her had landed squarely over her breasts. One of which fit oh-so-neatly in the cup of his palm.

He rapidly moved his hand away. "Sorry."

But he wasn't.

Not even a little.

CHAPTER NINE

THE LC CLUB was a sprawling multistory building of cascading terraces and balconies topped with red slate tiles that sat right on the shore of Lake Chatelaine, and on that day, one entire terrace level of The Chef's Table—just one of the designated restaurants at the LC Club—was occupied by Ridge's family.

The wall of windows that were opened when the weather was warm were currently closed, but that didn't hinder the spectacular view of the seemingly endless lake.

The brunch that Wendy had arranged might have sounded simple when his mother talked about it, but the lavish buffet that had been set up for them was anything but. She could take the Windham out of her name, but some things where Wendy Fortune was concerned didn't change. Entertaining in style—even if the guests were just her family—was one of them.

"She's very good with children," his mother said.

She was sitting beside Ridge in the easy chairs situated closest to the windows. On the enclosed terrace several feet below their window, Hope had command of both Evie and Colt, as well as little two-year-old Aviva, who was being raised by Arlo's fiancée, Carrie. Their terrace fed right out onto the beach, though the windows were also currently closed, and they had it all to themselves. Which meant the colorful beach ball that Aviva was chasing endlessly didn't bother a single other soul.

For most of the time since they'd arrived at the restaurant, Hope had seemed to deliberately occupy herself with someone *other* than Ridge. The fact that those others happened to all be miniature people was moot.

"She is." He watched Hope lightly bop the beach ball so it landed perfectly enough that Aviva could catch it. The toddler's squealing laughter penetrated the windows separating them. "Hope's good with people, period."

His mom made a soft little *mmm* sound.

"So, what really spurred this brunch thing?" He swept his arm behind him. Sabrina and Dahlia were heads together at one table, leaving their fiancés to the football game playing out on an oversize television. Nash and Imani were ensconced together on a love seat as if they'd gotten stuck together by glue, and Arlo and Carrie were still picking at the array of bite-size desserts set on a multitiered glass display.

"Not a single thing," she said so airily he didn't believe her for a second.

He scooped a tiny spoonful of caviar from the tin and dabbed it on a crème-fraîche-topped blin. Nobody else had been eating the blini so he'd commandeered the whole dang tray of them, as well as the crystal bowl of ice holding the caviar tin. "Are you sick?"

She frowned at him. "Whatever makes you ask a question like that?"

Gauche or not, he folded the small blin in half and ate the entire thing in one bite. When he'd swallowed, he wiped his mouth with a napkin that he tossed atop the remaining morsels. He'd already eaten so many of them he was stuffed. "That time that Dad scheduled a family dinner." Tried to, anyway, since nobody had agreed to go.

Only after the fact did Ridge realize that was probably about the time that Casper knew he was dying.

His mother's complexion lost a little color. "Oh, honey," she sighed. Then shook her head slightly and tucked her hair behind one ear. She reached over, squeezing his hand. "I've never been healthier." Her cheeks regained their usual color. "Or, for that matter, happier. But time does move swiftly. All of you—" her nod took in the others behind them "—are on the cusp of the most wonderful life changes, and I want to savor it all."

"Mom," he chided in a low tone. "You begged, cajoled and pretty much bribed us with *cabins*—" he accompanied the mocking term for their lavish lakeside homes with air quotes "—to move to Chatelaine Hills. We see each other nearly every day."

"You don't have to analyze everything in life, Ridge. Sometimes you can just enjoy for the sake of enjoying."

His gaze drifted out the window again. Below, Hope was holding Colt on her lap while Aviva, apparently disinterested now in the beach ball, played with Hope's long hair and Evie crawled over her legs. "Enjoying with no concern for consequences is a little dangerous, don't you think?"

"Honey, my entire life has been about the consequences. Consequences for my own choices when I was younger than you are now. Consequences of the choices made by parents I never even knew. Choices by your father, by Wendell Fortune. The list goes on and on…"

"You're making my point."

"Ridge." Her tone held a gentle reprimand. "My point is you can't *always* worry about consequences. Things happen in our lives over which we have absolutely no control. If you're not careful, happiness can slip through your fingers like sand in the wind. You couldn't have changed your father's choice to sell Windham Plastics even if he'd given us all some notice about it."

"Why'd you stay with him?" Ridge suddenly pinned his gaze on her. "Seriously. Why?"

She blinked slowly. "When I married Casper—said those vows—I was head over heels in love with him. All of you were conceived in love, Ridge. I know you don't believe it but it's true. I thought I'd married my knight in shining armor. He'd wed the poor little Texas beauty pageant trophy winner and turned her into his queen. And our fantasies lasted, until they didn't. But we'd still said those vows."

"But you weren't happy."

"Neither was he," Wendy said gently.

"I don't see how he suddenly has your understanding."

She smiled faintly. "It's not all that sudden. I'm sad for the handsome knight who became too blind and callous to appreciate the family he'd had right under his nose."

"But not sad enough to keep his name."

Her gaze softened even more. Typically, she was reading his thoughts before he could even articulate them. "If I'd divorced him, do you think I would have kept my married name?" Her gaze went to the rafters.

He hadn't inherited her ability to read minds and he wondered what thoughts were in hers.

"You'd have gone back to being Wendy Wilson," he concluded.

"Ah." She lifted her index finger. "But even that wasn't accurate, was it? My real mother's surname was McQueen. If she hadn't been illegitimate, it would have been Fortune." She spread both palms, and the collection of diamond bracelets on her slender wrist sent prisms dancing. "And here we are."

"Embracing all things Fortune," he muttered.

"You know that I appreciate the…loyalty…you all showed by taking the name. But if you're happier still being Windham, I would understand."

"Maybe you take understanding too far, Mom. Instead of brunches with *us*, you should be looking for something for yourself. You've still got a few good years left—"

She snorted inelegantly. "Oh, Ridge. Thank you *so* much for *that*."

"You know what I mean."

She just laughed good-naturedly and pushed herself out of the deeply cushioned chair. The lines of her narrow fitting ivory suit fell perfectly into place. "I've said it before, and I'll say it again. When I'm interested in changing the current state of my love life, I'll be sure to let you know. Until then, save all the suggestions and leave me in peace. Trust me." Her smile took on a mocking tilt. "I am doing perfectly *fine*." She picked up the napkin-covered plate of blini and carried it over to the buffet table, where Carrie was laughingly trying to finger-feed a bite of something to Arlo, who was steadfastly shaking his head.

However, Ridge's attention wasn't on his siblings or their partners.

It was on Hope.

And a partial Nebraska license plate number.

"Hey." Jade nudged the elbow he'd propped on the arm of his chair and snickered when he jerked. "Heath and I are going to do one of the Chatelaine mine tours and take a little hike. He picked up a map from the Chatelaine museum last week, and it has all the old, abandoned mines marked on it. You and Hope want to come along? Everyone else has already bowed out. Don't you do it, too."

"I wouldn't suggest holding your breath. I doubt Hope'll want to leave Evie for two afternoons running."

His sister raised her eyebrows. "Maybe *ask* her what she wants to do rather than assume?"

Ridge grumbled under his breath. Save him from women who always thought they knew better than him.

"Fine." He pushed to his feet. "I'll ask her. But I'm telling you…" He went out the swinging glass door that was barely distinguishable from the windows that surrounded it.

His assessment had been spot on.

Hope did *not* want to leave Evie for another afternoon. "Can't we take her with us?" she asked instead. "She loves being outside and never minds the carrier."

He wanted to traipse around the countryside looking at boarded-up mines about as much as he wanted a hole drilled in his head. But he also wasn't inclined to disappoint Hope. So, he nodded, and they all agreed to meet up again a little later after they'd had a chance to change into more suitable clothes.

When they did reconvene on the other side of Chatelaine, it was at a dusty spot marked with a big sign that proclaimed Joyride Silver Mine Tour!

While Jade and Heath purchased tickets for the four of them, Hope slathered baby-safe sunblock all over Evie, tied a flowery-patterned bonnet on her silky auburn head and deftly maneuvered her into the baby carrier. Now that her daughter was getting so much bigger, she could position the carrier either in front of her or in back.

That afternoon, she chose the back. "She's gaining weight," Hope said. "It's getting easier to carry her this way."

"I could carry her," Ridge offered. He wasn't sure why he hadn't thought of it before.

But she was shaking her head. "I don't think the carrier would fit you."

Considering Hope was no bigger than a minute and he topped her by a foot, he didn't bother arguing.

Jade was holding up the colorful brochure that contained the map of the other mines nearby. She'd marked a route on it in yellow highlighter. "Here's your copy," she told him. "Just in case we get separated after we're done with the tour here."

Ridge glanced at the map and was more than a little disconcerted to realize one of the stops colored in yellow was squarely within the Zazlo property. He also noticed there was no mention in the brochure or on the map of the silver mine Wendell Fortune and his brother had owned. Before its deadly collapse, it had been the most profitable mine around. "Surprised the Fortune Mine isn't listed despite the way it ended."

Heath reached out and tapped a spot on the map some distance farther out from town. "It was around there. The museum where I picked up the brochures has a whole display."

"Have you always had an interest in abandoned mines?" Ridge asked as he tucked a bottle of water in the mesh side pocket of Evie's carrier for Hope.

"Only since I'm marrying the great-granddaughter of a mine owner," Heath replied humorously. He leaned over and kissed Jade's nose. She positively glowed as she beamed back at him.

Ridge sincerely hoped they didn't plan to be all lovey-dovey the entire afternoon. It was his sister, after all.

And judging by the vaguely goading glint in her eyes as she slid a look his way, Jade knew exactly how he felt.

"Tour in two minutes!" An ancient-looking old man with a beard that could have housed a flock of birds stood in the doorway of a modest-looking rustic building. "Don't matter if you got tickets or not. You're late, you're out of the tour. No refunds." He stomped back inside.

"Friendly guy," Hope said under her breath.

Stuffing an extra bottle of water inside one of the cargo pockets of his pants, Ridge silently agreed.

They all filed through the narrow doorway into the building, which turned out to be a gift shop selling a myriad variety of snacks and cold drinks, jewelry, and simple toys like jacks and bouncing balls and not-so-simple things like hand-carved slingshots.

While they waited for the second hand to tick down the last minute, Ridge glanced in one of the glass jewelry displays. It held dozens of silver rings. Some with stones. Others without.

"Afternoon." He smiled at the old woman guarding the case, and she preened a little, plumping up her gray hair that was so wild it needed no plumping whatsoever.

"Afternoon," she returned and tapped the glass case with a gnarled finger. "Silver in these rings comes from this very mine," she said. "Artisan crafted and all." She smiled broadly, showing off a missing molar and creating dozens more wrinkly intersections on an already lined face. "They make a fine wedding band." Her gaze went tellingly toward Hope, who blushed and hurried over to the elderly man who had pulled a hardhat fitted with a light on the front down from a peg.

He plunked the hat on his head. "I'm Harv," he yelled so abruptly that Hope nearly jumped back a foot. "I'm your tour guide here at the Joyride. And don't be asking for discount coupons for my goodfernuthin' grandson's bar-bee-cue down the road." If the derision in his voice weren't apparent enough, the sneer curling one corner of his lip put a magnifying glass on it. "Boy's got no family loyalty." He turned and pushed at a rough-hewn section of wall behind him, and it slid back to reveal a yawning cavern with a set of steps going down into the darkness. "Don't see *him* sending folks my way, do you?"

Hope's round gaze sought Ridge's as if to ask *are we sure we want to do this?*

Suddenly, he forgot about wondering what sort of wedding ring Hope had remembered wearing and found himself stepping closer to her. He gently nudged Evie's hat in place where it had slid to one side. Her eyes were nearly closed, but she still held fast to her crinkly fabric book.

Jade and Heath followed Harv down the steps, quickly disappearing into the gloom. The old man's voice echoed back up to them.

"Mind your heads," he warned. "Them wood beams go back more 'n a hunnert 'n thirty years when the Joyride was first established in 1894."

The gray-haired woman handed Ridge a sturdy flashlight before he passed through the opening after Hope and Evie.

He flipped it on and directed the strong beam down the steps. While he'd never considered himself claustrophobic, those steps seemed to go down forever.

Hope had hesitated a few steps down from him, and she looked back up at him. Anticipation lit her features as brightly as his flashlight did the steps under their feet. "Come on," she said, beckoning with her hand. "They're going to get too far ahead of us."

"Wouldn't matter," he said wryly and ducked his head to avoid hitting the first of the series of beams that held the earth at bay as they descended. "Could hear old Harv from a mile away."

The old codger's voice was booming back to them, recounting the trials and triumphs of mining through the ages, and by the time Ridge and Hope reached the bottom of the stairs and the tunnel widened out, he'd gotten sucked into the tales just like the others. He brought up the rear, the beam of his flashlight bouncing around the pathway and walls despite the ancient lanterns that were spaced out along the way. Whether intentional or not, the bulbs flickered intermittently.

The lure of silver, copper, gold and whatever else they were finding down in these depths that had ensnared his great-grandfather, Wendell Fortune, and his brothers hadn't transmitted down through the genes to Ridge, that was for sure.

Only by looking at his cell phone was he able to tell how long they'd been walking when they finally stopped in a large, mostly square room crammed with ancient wooden crates, coiled ropes, bed rolls and tools gone red with rust. Ridge could feel a draft of cool, fresh air, and imagined what it would have felt like when there'd been no ventilation pipes hiding in the dusty corners.

He pulled the water bottle from his pocket and took a long drink. He, for one, was grateful for modern conveniences. He was also glad that Evie was sound asleep.

No future bad dreams for her, at least.

Heath and Jade were roving around the room, peering at this, asking questions about that. Telling ol' Harv that their great-granddaddy had been none other than Wendell Fortune.

Hope, however, edged closer to Ridge. "You alright?" she whispered.

"Swell." He guzzled another quarter of his water bottle.

The flickering lantern lights sent shadows dancing over their faces, but Ridge could still see the curve of her soft lips.

She leaned even closer. "We're almost through," she whispered.

"How do you know?" Harv's tales were interesting, but the man sounded as though he could go on forever.

"Tour lasts an hour," she said. "It's more than half over now."

If his cell phone was to be trusted, more like 70 percent over now.

Thirty percent to go. He could stand that.

Particularly when Hope slid her hand through his arm and stood so close to him. Probably just because of that cold air coming through the pipes, but he wasn't going to look a gift horse in the mouth.

"O' course, you don't need me to tell you about the Fortune Mine collapse." Harv's booming voice was only slightly toned down in the room. He hitched one skinny hip up on the corner of a slatted crate, which held a facsimile of bags of flour alongside at least a dozen sticks of dynamite.

Ridge hoped they were fakes, at least.

"Mining's always been a dangerous pursuit," Harv said. "But all them folks dyin'..." He tsked and shook his head dolefully. "Tragic is what it was."

A tragedy that had lived on even longer thanks to the years of deceits and secrets maintained not just by Wendell and his brothers but by their future generations.

Seemed like Casper Windham had been truer to that nature than Wendy. He'd only seemed to find more caring for his fellow humanity when he'd learned he'd been dying. Only last month had Arlo shared his discovery that Casper had paid for the cancer treatments of everyone else who'd been in the hospital at the same time he'd been there. That he'd made sure that all of the patients' kids had toys at Christmastime.

"Did you lose family or friends in the mine collapse?" Jade asked Harv.

The old man shook his head. "No family. A couple of friends, though. The Joy here—" he hopped back to his feet, surprisingly spry, and clapped his hand around a support beam "—was competing against the Fortune Mining Company. Much as she could, anyway. The Fortunes were always a lucky bunch of cusses." His face screwed up for a minute. "Beggin' pardon, to ya'll. Don't mean to offend."

In his odd, rolling gait, he started out of the room again, switching on the headlamp on his helmet as he went.

As far as safety gear went, if it was actually necessary, he ought to have handed out hard hats to all of them.

Once again, Ridge looked beyond the obvious trappings and started to see the nearly invisible signs of modern day. He was an engineer, after all. He could appreciate ingenuity.

The Joyride Silver Mine tour might look like it was still living in the early 1900s. But it was all for show.

And he'd gotten sucked into it as much as anyone else.

Even having figured that out, though, he still breathed more easily after they reached the top of the earthen steps and Harv pushed the mock wall back in place.

"Hope you enjoyed the tour," he said. "Appreciate you tellin' your friends about us if you did." Harv offered a squinty smile at them. "And if you didn't, appreciate you keepin' that all to yourself."

Heath pushed a wadded bill into the jar sitting next to the whisky barrel that apparently doubled as a seat for Harv when he wasn't conducting business. A hand-printed sign above the jar said TIPS. "We did enjoy it," he assured the old man, reaching out to shake his hand. "Very informative. Thank you."

"Glad to share." Harv tapped his temple with his index finger. "Worst thing a man can do is go to his grave hoarding stuff up here."

Hope turned away from Harv before he could see her expression tighten, but Ridge saw it and knew she was thinking about the memories that *her* mind was currently hoarding.

He added his own tip to the jar and followed her out into the sunshine, where she was loosening the straps of her carrier and deftly maneuvering Evie around so that she was facing Hope.

"Want to call it a day?" he asked her. There was still the hike that Jade had mapped out that included the abandoned mine on the Zazlo spread.

"Not at all," Hope said quickly. She cradled Evie's padded rear through the carrier, huffing a little as she tried to re-configure the straps for the new position.

"Here." Ridge wrapped his hands around the upper straps, taking Evie's weight off of Hope long enough that she could complete the task. And somehow, by the time she was successful, they were standing as close together as two people could stand, considering the eight-month Evie right between them. "Better?"

Hope's throat worked. She moistened her lips, her gaze landing on his and flitting away again. Pink color rode her cheekbones. "You, um, you can let go of the straps now," she whispered.

His knuckles were pressed against her flesh. If he stretched out his fingers, they'd brush her breasts. He cleared his throat and let go of the straps. Jade and Heath had exited the gift shop and were coming their way. "Gonna refill my water bottle," Ridge said and turned in the other direction.

The last thing he needed just then was Jade and her hawk-like attention noticing he was more in need of a dunk under cold water than he was a paltry drink of it.

CHAPTER TEN

"LOOK." MORE THAN an hour later, two pit stops to change and feed Evie, who'd woken up, and a lazy debate with Jade, who'd decided to go one way when they reached a fork in the trail while Ridge wanted to go the other, Hope stopped in the middle of the shrubby field they were walking. "That's a farmhouse. We *are* on private property." She shaded her eyes with one hand and propped the other on her hip, slowly turning in a circle. "Did we lose the trail you think?"

Ridge shook his head. He'd shed his sweatshirt before they'd left the Joyride and wished that he could shed his shirt, too. He contented himself with adding another roll to his rolled-up sleeves. As far as he was concerned, it wasn't supposed to be this warm in January. "We didn't lose the trail," he assured.

Her brilliant blue gaze turned his way. "How do you know?"

"This is the Zazlo ranch," he said. "We crossed onto it when we passed the water tower a while back. Nonny Zazlo died last year. Has no relatives to inherit it."

"Surprised Zane Baston hasn't bought it up." She said the same thing that Ridge had. She turned in a circle again and automatically caught the crinkle book when Evie tossed it at her head. "I guess that means nobody's living in that cute farmhouse." She sent a grin toward Ridge. "At least I don't feel so bad trespassing now."

He suddenly felt as inept as a teenager with a crush on the untouchable homecoming queen. "You think it's cute?"

"Big old covered porch and all those shutters? It's like something Joanna Gaines would design. Who *wouldn't* love it?"

He didn't know who Joanna Gaines was, but he didn't care. "I'm thinking about buying it," he admitted even though he hadn't intended on admitting any such thing.

Her jaw dropped slightly, and her cheeks paled. "You want to move?" Her lashes swept down suddenly. "C-congratulations." She looked down at Evie, crinkling the book even more as she lightly tapped her daughter on the head with it, and the baby babbled nonsensically as she took the book from her mother and then shoved one corner in her mouth.

Full of crinkly fabric book or not didn't stop Evie from chattering away.

Hope retied the baby's hat under her chin and pulled out the water bottle from the mesh side pocket. She flipped the pull top, squirted water into her mouth, then Evie's, then sent a small stream of it down the back of her shirt before she tucked it back in the pocket. "Awfully warm for January." She briskly set off in the direction they'd been walking. "How much further to the mine?"

She'd already pushed up the long sleeves of her T-shirt. Now the wet fabric clung to her spine before disappearing under the waist of her faded blue jeans. As she quickly picked her way over and around sage-green clumps of scrubby grass, Ridge couldn't keep his attention off the sway of her hips.

"Not far," he answered belatedly. He didn't have to pull the map out of his pocket to know that. The mine was near the northern border, which he knew was marked by a shelterbelt of trees that ran perpendicular to the creek that marked the eastern border. "And I haven't decided for sure about moving."

She lifted one hand, obviously using it to keep her balance as she stepped over a decaying log. He caught up to her, prepared to help.

"I've got it," she said a little testily.

He turned up his palm.

"And of course you want to move," she added, still cranky.

"Everyone wants something they can call their own. Dahlia has her sheep. Jade the petting zoo. Nash runs the show. Sabrina writes the checks. Arlo already had his own business, and you—"

"Fill in the gaps," he said shortly.

"I was going to say that you had Windham Plastics until it was taken away."

"Good to know I'm an open book," he muttered.

"Don't expect me to feel sorry for you," she said tartly. "You can buy anything you want." She waved her hand in the general direction of the farmhouse that had already fallen far behind them thanks to the new clip in her step. "Including Zaney Nazlo's place."

"Nonny Zazlo," he murmured.

She flapped her hand. "Whatever. Ranch. Don't ranch. Invent another gizmo. Your choices are endless." She snatched her water bottle again and took a drink, her pace never slowing. "How soon?"

"Before I decide?"

"Before you move."

He was starting to feel testy himself. "Hard to say when I'm not sure if I want it bad enough to break my mom's heart."

"Your mother practically worships the ground you walk on. She's like that with all of you. She's not going to stop just because you decide to leave the nest."

He grimaced. "I left the *nest* when I was twenty."

"Bully for you. At least you had a nest. I didn't even have—" She stopped abruptly, and this time when Evie tossed her crinkle book, it sailed right beyond her mama's shoulder.

Ridge scooped it up and caught up to Hope. "What?"

She just shook her head a little, pinching her eyes closed. "I didn't have parents," she said thickly. "I grew up in foster homes. Group homes."

He stifled an oath and started to reach for her, but she shook her head. "Don't."

He curled his fingers into fists. "Hope."

"If you touch me right now, I'm going to start crying, which will only upset Evie." She didn't look at him. "All I remember were group homes. No specific foster parents."

"Anything before the group homes?" If she'd lost her parents as a young child or a baby even, surely she would have had an actual foster family. He didn't know a lot about it, but group homes were designed for older kids. Weren't they?

"No." Her voice was so brittle, it hurt to hear it. "So just, just tell me where the stupid *mine* is so at least I can say it's something I've achieved."

He swallowed a dozen questions that didn't want to be swallowed.

"We keep walking until we reach those trees." He pointed toward the horizon where the tops of the trees were just becoming visible. The land sloped downward toward them, so the distance was deceiving.

She nodded silently and set off once more.

Where were the foster homes?

Did she remember any other names?

"I think the last group home was called something like Goldstone." Her voice floated back at him, uncannily responding to the questions pounding inside his head. "I remember going on a ski trip to Gatlinburg. On a bus. I think it took an entire day getting there."

He just managed not to pull out his cell phone to start calculating how many places were a day's bus ride away from Gatlinburg, Tennessee. "Do you remember how old you were?"

"No. Yes." Her footsteps paused. "Thirteen." She waited a beat. Then repeated it with more certainty. "Thirteen. I had a friend. She was sixteen. Amy Smith. She wanted her driver's license *bad.* That ski trip was the most fun we'd ever had," she said finally, and started walking again.

It was a treasure trove of information.

He quickly thumbed the details into a text and sent it off to Villanueva, fortunately managing not to trip over his feet from not watching where he was going as he followed her.

They crested the gentle hill and descended into the valley on the other side. The mine was marked only by a boarded entrance bearing a heavy latch that was chained and locked.

Hope walked over and crouched down on one knee in front of it. A faded placard was nailed into the wood. "Fester Mine," she read. "The images *that* evokes are lovely. I thought it was just called Mine 32."

"Mine 32 is what the map says. Maybe Fester was someone's name."

"Rough name. Fester like an untreated wound. Of course, my real name could be equally as awful."

He didn't know why, when it was so important to find out her real name, it was a relief that she hadn't remembered it along with the details about living in foster care. "It won't be awful."

"When it turns out to be Gangreenia Crudbucket I'll remind you of that." She pushed to her feet and rattled the chain and lock.

He was glad to see that both were in good shape. They'd obviously been replaced fairly recently. Beau Weatherly hadn't mentioned the mine, which made him wonder if the other man even knew of its location on the property. It was only a minor curiosity. Weatherly couldn't *really* know everything, though there were times that it felt like it. "Gangreenia?"

She lifted her shoulder. "Live without knowing your own name a while," she said. "You'd come up with dozens of possibilities, too. I must admit I prefer the name Hope."

He wrapped his arms around her and Evie. Felt Hope's stiff resistance for only a few seconds before it drained away and she gave an exhausted sounding sigh.

"Did Amy get her driver's license?"

She shook her head. "Nobody willing to sign the paperwork for her." Her forehead fell to his chest. "She ran away a few months after that ski trip. Never saw her again. I don't think I made a lot of friends after her," she added quietly.

He pressed his cheek to hers, holding her even closer until Evie squawked a protest over being squashed between them.

Hope's eyes looked drier than his felt. "Ready to go home?" he asked.

"Ready to go back." She gave a twisted smile that held no humor. "But it seems like it's not really home. Not for either one of us."

She jiggled Evie and shook her head a few times. "Enough depressing myself," she said determinedly and once again set off in the direction they'd come.

When they passed the empty farmhouse again, she waved her arm, encompassing. "Totally Joanna," she pronounced. But after that, it was only Evie who kept up a running litany of ga-ga-gas and ba-ba-bas.

Jade and Heath were already waiting when they reached the spot off the highway where they'd left their vehicles. The two of them were sitting next to each other on the opened tailgate of Heath's truck.

"Find Number 32?" Jade hopped off the tailgate when Hope blew out a long breath and began detaching Evie and the carrier.

"Yeah." Ridge thought it was pretty noble of him not to point out that the buttons on Jade's shirt were buttoned all wrong. "Aka the Fester Mine. You find yours?"

"Um, no." His sister shook her head. "It was so hot, and we found this sweet little lake that was all shady, so we hung out there for a while instead."

"Mmm." Explained the misaligned buttons.

He lifted the back hatch of the SUV, and Hope set Evie in the cargo area while she dug in the diaper bag for a change of clothes. Evie's clothes were as damp from sweat as Hope's were.

"Thought we'd stop at the Saddle and Spur," Heath said. "Grab an early dinner."

"Steak with a side of steak," Jade quipped.

Ridge knew without having to ask that more socializing was the last thing Hope wanted to do. "It's been a busy day for Evie," he said.

Jade nodded. Her gaze was busy moving between him and Hope. At least *they* didn't have mismatched buttons.

At the rate they were going, would they ever?

Jade and Heath departed, and Ridge got behind the wheel and started up the engine and the air-conditioning while Hope finished up with Evie.

Not for the first time, he checked his cell phone for some response from Villanueva, but there was none.

He knew the investigator would check in at some point. He

always did, even if the report was only that there was nothing new *to* report.

"Know what it's like to be waiting for answers," he'd said when Ridge had first hired him. Now, while trying to distract himself from everything in his life that felt undone and unfinished, Ridge wondered what unanswered questions had tormented Villanueva.

He also wondered what the odds were that one of the registered owners the investigator was planning to meet had been involved in foster care.

Then Hope opened the passenger door and climbed up beside him and sent his thoughts scattering. He realized she'd fastened Evie—now dressed in a plain white T-shirt and a diaper—into her car seat already.

They drove back through Chatelaine. The town seemed even sleepier than usual on a Sunday evening. Only a few other vehicles besides Heath's were parked next to the Saddle and Spur. They left the town behind, and with no traffic to speak of, soon reached the lake.

He stopped long enough to pick up pizza from Shoreline Pizza, and then turned toward Chatelaine Hills. The aroma of the pizza had his stomach growling by the time they finally turned through the gate, which this time opened and closed right on command.

After parking along the side of the house, they went in through the back door.

Hope settled Evie in her high chair with a squeezable food pouch and a handful of cereal puffs. "Can you watch her for a few minutes while I change?"

In answer, he pulled out the bar stool next to Evie, and Hope practically jogged out of the room.

He stole one of Evie's tasteless cereal puffs. "Do you know who Joanna Gaines is?"

She smiled toothily at him and pitched her food pouch over the side of her high chair. He picked it off the floor, wiped the squeeze top and gave it back to her. But when she went to throw it again, he pulled it out of her reach. "Ah, no. I'm on to your games, princess."

Evie swept her hand across the tray, scattering as many puffs as she caught, which she lifted to her mouth and shoved inside with all the busy diligence of a squirrel readying for winter.

He got up and retrieved her sippy cup, filling it with water, and set it nearby. Then he sat back down and flipped back the pizza box lid.

The pie inside was still hot, the melting cheese bearing just the right amount of overdone brownness and the pepperonis curling crisply around the edges. He started to lift out a piece when his phone chirped.

He dropped the piece back onto the cardboard box and picked up his cell phone.

Villanueva.

His hand felt strangely unsteady. He ran his other hand over the baby's head. "What're we hoping for here, Evie?"

She opened her smiling mouth to show him the puffs she was still munching.

He leaned over and kissed her forehead. "You keep me sane, baby girl."

He straightened again and thumbed open the message.

No luck in Nebraska. None of the auto owners have an apparent connection to Hope. Will verify but don't expect to find they weren't all on the up and up. Good details about foster care. Tennessee is a long way from Nebraska. Will dig further.

Ridge closed the message and turned his phone face down on the counter.

He picked up the pizza again.

He'd eaten two pieces and successfully fed Evie half the food pouch when Hope returned, freshly showered and dressed in a loose-fitting gray T-shirt dress that reached all the way down to her bare toes.

She took the bar stool across from him and folded her hands together atop the counter. "I think it's time for Evie and me to move out."

"No." He pushed the box of pizza toward her. He'd saved his crusts for her.

Her lips compressed for a moment. But he could see her eyeing the crusts.

They were her favorite part.

Not the cheese. Not the toppings.

Just the crusty edge.

It could be doughy. It could be browned and nearly burnt to a crisp. Didn't matter. She ate them regardless, as if they were a delicacy.

He took a third slice for himself, starting at the pointed end like any sane person did.

She shifted on the bar stool, as if she was trying to make herself physically taller. "I really think it'd be best if—"

"No," he mumbled around the pizza in his mouth. He swallowed. Got up to retrieve an IPA from the fridge for himself and a bottle of cola for her. He sat again and picked up the slice once more.

"I'd rather have a beer," she said and returned the cola to the fridge. She set the IPA deliberately in front of him and twisted off the cap.

He watched her over the pizza, wondering how long it'd be before she caved. She liked beer even less than she liked strong coffee.

She took a swift sip, tried and failed to hide the resulting grimace, then chased it down with a huge bite of pizza crust.

She lifted her chin a little. "Just because you say *no*—" she growled out the word in a deep tone that he assumed was meant to mimic him "—doesn't mean I have to listen."

"Where would you go?"

Her brilliant eyes darkened almost to navy. "There's a shelter in—"

"Definitely no. I don't care *where* it is." He pushed aside the box and clasped her hands, beer bottle and all, between his. "Why the sudden urge to abandon me?" He tried, yet failed, to keep his voice light. Easy.

"Well, *you're* going to move."

Realization dawned. His sisters had accused him more than once of being obtuse. Now he had to wonder if they'd had a point. "*If* I move, and that—" her mouth opened, and he spoke over her "—is a big if, of course you and Evie would come with me."

Her eyebrows pulled together. "You need to stop feeling responsible for us, Ridge. Just because you found us in your barn—"

"I don't feel responsible for you." A bigger lie didn't exist. "I want you both with me." The raw truth of that part balanced things out. "I've gotten used to you."

"Like what? A pair of slippers?" She rolled her eyes.

"Don't knock a good pair of slippers." He released her hands and picked up his pizza again. "If it's so important to you, though, you could use the guesthouse."

She stared. "What?"

He'd considered the idea before—inspired by Nash, who'd done that very thing with Imani only a few months ago. But Hope had seemed content to be right where she was. With him. And he had no interest at all in changing that.

But he had enough smarts to know that standing in her way wasn't the right thing to do, either. And if she was in his guesthouse, she'd be closer than some *shelter* in Godknowswhere, where he'd have no chance of protecting her at all from whatever—or whomever—lurked in her past.

"It's not much more than a studio setup," he warned. "No real proper bedroom and just a kitchenette." But there was a full bathroom and some ancient furniture the previous owners had left. "The kitchen in the house is always open for you to use, of course."

He'd have had to be sightless to miss the sudden light in Hope's eyes. The way her entire body seemed to lean forward with interest. "But what about you and the Nazlo farmhouse?"

"Zazlo."

"Whatever."

"Even if it works out, if I decide I *want* it to work out, it'll take time. It's not the only place to consider."

Her eyes widened. "Y-you're looking at more than one place?"

"Well, so far I've only seen—" He shook his head. They were getting off track. "The point is nothing is imminent."

"Where else, though?"

He was starting to feel a little harried. "Oklahoma."

Her mouth rounded. "That's…a bit further."

Understatement of the year. "It's just a thought. The place doesn't even have a ranch house because it burned down."

"Oh, well, then you have to go with Fester Mine's house."

"Nonny Zazlo," he said crisply. "That house needs some renovations—"

"Not too many, I hope." Her cheeks flushed. "I mean, it looked charming from the outside at least."

Exasperation was building. The topic wasn't about his problems. It was about hers. "Do you want to use the guesthouse or don't you?"

She pressed her lips together for a moment. Then nodded, which was at least one thing he'd fully expected.

"Yes, please," she said fervently.

"It's still full of crap from my place in Dallas." A small mountain of stuff that he hadn't decided to part with but also hadn't had room for in the fully furnished house from his mother. "It'll take a day or two to clean it out."

"I don't care." She hopped off her bar stool and darted around the island, throwing her arms around his neck. "Thank you." She pressed her lips against his cheek.

His hand automatically went to the small of her back. She smelled like morning rain and midnight desire.

"Didn't know you were that anxious to leave."

She pulled back only slightly. "I'm *not* anxious to leave." She barely waited a breath. "When can we start cleaning it out?"

Given that he was voluntarily putting space between them, it was odd that he couldn't suppress a sudden laugh. Even if it did feel as rusty as the tools down in the Joyride Silver Mine. "Next week?"

"Perfect." She kissed his cheek again and then practically danced over to Evie, who had sucked down most of the contents of the pouch and was only half-covered in the rest, and lifted her free of the high chair. Hope held her high above her head and laughed up into her baby's face. "Guess what you and Mommy are going to do?"

He pushed aside the pizza and reached for his beer.

Ridge knew exactly what Evie and her mommy were going to do.

Break his heart.

CHAPTER ELEVEN

"AND WHAT ABOUT THIS?"

Dahlia's tone was waspish, and Ridge looked over at his sister. It was Monday morning, and she was the only one who'd volunteered some time to help him deal with the mess of items he'd more or less dumped into the guesthouse last summer. "It's my polo gear," he told her.

"You haven't played polo in years."

"So?"

She rolled her eyes and tossed the bulging sport bag out of the closet that she'd been mining. The bag landed atop the pile of similar bags, teetered a little and started to slide down the side. "So why did you bother bringing it here?" She pushed her hair back from her face and stretched her back. "Along with the boxing gloves and the tennis rackets and the fencing gear?"

He turned back to the stack of packing boxes that he hadn't had the sense to label and now, all these months later, didn't have a clue what they contained. "Because I didn't take the time in Dallas to clean out. Obviously." He sliced through the packing tape and flipped open the cardboard flaps.

Ski boots.

A wad of T-shirts that he'd had since college.

A wooden crate from Mendoza Winery.

No wonder the box was so heavy. It was full of booze and boots.

Last time he'd used the boots was in Gstaad. He'd gone there after earning his most recent master's degree. For a while, he'd been an avid skier. But he'd never gone to Gatlinburg, Tennessee.

The boots didn't interest him, but the wine was another story, and he lifted the crate out of the box. The dozen bottles of wine it contained had been packed by the winery in millions of pieces of crinkled cardboard that scattered over the floor as soon as he extracted one of the bottles. Merlot. "I forgot all about the wine."

"Think you forgot all about a lot of stuff," Dahlia muttered. "I had no idea you were such a pack rat, Ridge."

"Not even close to a pack rat," he said absently. The bottle was slightly dusty from the packing material. He rubbed his thumb over the foiled label, polishing. "Dad sent me the case when we got the patent approved on T349."

His sister stopped next to him. Dahlia's relationship with their father, on the surface at least, hadn't been as fractious as some of theirs. "The case is still full. You never drank any of it?"

He shook his head. He remembered how surprised he'd been reading the card that came with the wine. Written by Casper himself, rather than by his secretary.

Ridge hefted the crate out of the way of the mess of packing materials and packing boxes. He made room for it on the crowded granite breakfast bar and then turned back to survey the progress they'd made.

He'd begun clearing things out after Hope and Evie had left for their daily trek down to Jade's petting zoo. Ridge had finally learned to keep his trap closed when it came to Hope's insistence on walking, even though there were perfectly good golf carts around that would have made short work of the distance. And that morning, he'd been glad of her choices, because it meant he could estimate pretty well the amount of time he had before she'd return.

While he'd hoped to surprise her by having the place cleared out by then, he hadn't counted on the breadth of the task until he'd actually gone inside the guesthouse for the first time since moving there.

"I'm gonna pull the truck around," he told Dahlia. "Toss everything in the back that'll fit and drop it at the donation center in Chatelaine." He blew out his breath. "It should only take me about five trips," he muttered.

"I realize it sounds odd when I've been complaining for the last hour, but are you sure you want to give it *all* away?"

"I'm sure. Get rid of everything. Except this." He thumped his hand on the wooden wine crate. "So, if you want something we've already unpacked, now's your chance."

She immediately reached for one of the sport bags.

"You and Rawlston taking up disc golf?"

"The sheep like to play chase," she said and flapped the Frisbee she'd taken out of the bag.

The idea of his sister casting Frisbees around to entertain one of her designer-wool sheep ought to have seemed laughable. Yet it fit her entirely.

"You still have that stack over there you haven't opened."

"I think it's clothes." He hadn't missed them up until now, which seemed like a good reason to avoid even going through them. "Only thing I care about keeping is the wine."

Her expression softened, but he pointedly ignored it. Instead, he hastily stepped over a small mountain of crumpled newsprint that had been wrapped around a set of dishes he hadn't known he possessed, which Dahlia had loaded into the dishwasher, and then he escaped out the door before she could make more of the wine situation than he wanted.

His dad gave him some of his favorite wine.

Nothing to get all worked up about.

The sun was straight up, and he blamed it for the burn in his eyes.

Squinting at the ground, he trekked around to the front of the main house to retrieve the rusty old pickup, only to stop in surprise at the sight of his mother's car just parking in the drive.

He waited while she turned off the engine and climbed out. She was dressed in black yoga pants and a snug zippered top that he supposed was meant to be a jacket. With her blond hair pulled back in a slightly messy ponytail, she could have passed for one of his sisters, versus his mother.

"What're you doing here?"

She smiled and pushed her dark glasses up onto her head. "Good morning to you, too." She stretched up and kissed his cheek. "A little birdie told me you were getting your guesthouse ready for Hope. Thought I'd come and see how it was going."

"Dahlia texted you and told you we could barely get through the door," he deciphered.

Wendy didn't deny it. "I was surprised, though. Hope's been living with you for months."

"She's been living in *my house* for months," he corrected. "Two different things."

She gave him a look. "Keep telling yourself that, honey. So, what prompted the change? Is everything okay between the two of you?"

"What do you mean *between*? We're not—"

She raised her hand. "Enough. If you want to keep your head in the sand, you're the one who gets to pick the grains out of your teeth." She tugged at the hem of her short jacket. "You know that I believe it's healthy for a woman to have a sense of independence. Just as I believe it's healthy for an individual to be honest with themselves." She shot her cuff and glanced at her diamond wristwatch. "And honesty makes me admit that I don't have time to stand here yammering. I have marketing meetings soon at the castle about the launch." She patted his cheek in obvious dismissal and strode off in the direction of the guesthouse.

He squinted into the sky. How much would his mother appreciate his honesty when he told her about the Zazlo place? He rubbed his hand down his face and yanked open the squeaking pickup truck door and coaxed the engine into starting.

Wendy was showing something on her phone to Dahlia when he pulled up at the guesthouse a few minutes later. He ignored them both in favor of loading up the truck bed and driving off with the first load. Far as he could tell, neither one of them gave him any notice.

He drove into Chatelaine and dropped the load at the thrift store, waiving off the donation receipt that one of the volunteers there wanted to give him, and made the return drive back out to the lake. The biggest nuisance was dealing with manually opening and closing the gate, which had stopped working again. Still, all told, the round trip took less than an hour, and when he got there, Dahlia and his mother had been joined by Sabrina, who was looking particularly round sitting on a stool with her arms propped over her immense belly.

At least Jade was busy with the petting zoo, he thought as he made quick work of taking off with a second load.

He loved his sisters, but when they all got together, they always fell way too easily into the "tell baby brother what to do" mode.

This time, when he returned, his sisters and mother were gone. But the furniture that had been pushed to one side of the place had been rearranged, and Hope was sitting on the short, overstuffed couch, fiddling with a bunch of orange and red wildflowers that she'd placed inside a clear mason jar. She looked across at him when he entered and pressed her fingertip to her lips.

He spotted Evie sound asleep on a blanket on the floor next to the couch, her rump stuck in the air and her little crinkly book clutched in her fist.

He ignored the hollow pang inside his chest and quietly sat down opposite them both in the side chair that was just as dated as the puffed-up couch and—he figured—just as uncomfortable.

"You'll need new furniture," he said in a low voice. "This stuff is older than I am."

"It's perfectly fine," she said, equally soft. "You just don't like the pattern of gigantic mauve and teal palm fronds."

That was true enough. "The furniture came with the place."

"Your mom mentioned that."

He lifted a brow. "You saw her, then?"

"She and Dahlia were just leaving when Evie and I got back." She fluffed the clutch of wildflowers once more and set it in the middle of the square coffee table. The flowers clashed with the overwhelming amount of teal and pink. "When you said next week, I thought you meant next weekend."

"I wanted to surprise you."

"You did." She leaned forward again to slide the mason jar to the corner of the coffee table and sat back yet again. "There're even dishes and pots and pans in the kitchen cupboard."

"And wine." The crate was still sitting where he'd left it on the breakfast bar. It seemed to be the only thing that hadn't been moved during his last trip to Chatelaine. "Did you arrange everything?"

She shook her head. "This is how the furniture was when I came in here."

Evidently, his mother's meetings at the castle hadn't been quite as imminent as she'd implied if she'd taken the time to rearrange furniture with Dahlia. It was a sure bet that Sabrina hadn't been up to moving the stuff. She'd looked like she was lucky to be able to just move herself around.

"How was the petting zoo?"

"Fine. A new potbellied pig arrived just before we left. Evie was so enthralled, it was hard to tear her away."

He glanced around the corners of the guesthouse, wondering why he'd thought this was a good idea at all.

There was no good place for Evie's crib, much less the menagerie of stuffed animals he had been giving her almost since day one.

"I didn't think of saving some of the boxes," he said. His whisper sounded more ragged than he liked. "Could have reused them to move your stuff over here."

"I don't have a lot of stuff, remember?"

As if he could forget. "More than a few laundry basketsful," he countered.

Her lips stretched slightly. "Evie has more things than I do." She moved the jar of wildflowers a third time.

Was the reality of having her own space less appealing than she'd thought?

"There's still no news about the car?"

How could he have forgotten? She, more than anyone, wanted those answers. He shook his head. "Sorry. Villanueva is still drawing a blank on it. I should have told you." The investigator had sent a text late the night before that he was done in Nebraska, having confirmed his belief that the "possibles" living there were unrelated to Hope's case. "He's gone back to Corpus already."

"I'm not any worse off with no answer now than I was before," she murmured, and brushed her hands over her jean-clad thighs as if brushing off the topic altogether. Then she stood and moved around him, coming to a stop in front of the wall adjacent to the breakfast counter. She propped her hands on her narrow hips and just stood there. Her hair was getting so long now that it reached halfway down to her waist.

He curled his fingers into a ball, trying to rid the itchy need to run them through those shining waves.

"Evie's crib could go here," she finally said, sweeping her hand in the air. "Maybe a shelf there for some of her stuffed animals and toys. Sort of like she has now?"

He got that familiar pang in his chest again.

He'd be afraid he was afflicted with some disease that caused heartburn if he didn't know that both the cause and the cure resided with her.

"Sure," he replied a little belatedly. The wall she was looking at was pale white with a distinct yellow cast. "If you want new paint, it'd be better to do it before you move in." He waited a beat, studying the ugly couch. "What about your bed?" The place didn't allow for much more furniture, and the crib would take up most of the space against the wall she was considering.

"I'll sleep on the couch for now, I guess." She walked back around him and flipped up one of the cushions to look beneath it. "Too bad it's not a hide-a-bed."

"Hide-a-beds are never comfortable."

She looked over her shoulder at him, her eyebrows lifted with skepticism. "*You* have slept in a hide-a-bed before?"

"Not specifically slept," he allowed. "But back in college there was a girl—"

"Say no more." Her cheeks pinked and she rolled her eyes. "Please."

He could feel his grin sneaking out despite his effort otherwise. "Maybe a Murphy bed would work. At least you'd have a real mattress—" He broke off when his cell phone buzzed. Pulling it from his pocket, he showed her the name on the screen.

Villanueva.

Speak of the devil.

Her eyebrows immediately pulled together, and her gaze cut to Evie still sleeping blissfully with her little book.

Ridge stood and went outside onto the porch before swiping the screen and holding the phone to his ear. "What's up?" He felt Hope come up behind him, standing close enough to feel the warmth of her.

"Finally got some useful info from one of my cop friends," Villanueva said.

He turned slightly and put his arm around Hope's shoulders, holding the phone between them so she could hear as well. "That's good." His pulse shifted into higher gear, but he kept his tone even.

"The car was rented in St. Louis at the airport," the other man continued. "Same car. Six different times over the last seven months. Driver's name was Howard Marks of Nashville, Tennessee."

Hope sank down until she was sitting on the porch step. But she shook her head slightly in response to Ridge when he immediately sat beside her. Her cool hand slid into his, and he curled his fingers around hers.

"Wife's name is Petunia." Villanueva was still speaking. "They're the only ones who match the general description your brother provided. I'm texting their DMV photos. They're nearly eight years old but I'm working on getting more recent ones."

"What's the guy's story? Who is he?"

"Don't have all of that yet," the investigator said. "Expect to by the end of the day. We're looking at the foster care angle in particular. The only thing I know so far is he's a stockbroker. But I wanted to let you know so you could run the photos by your family. I'm texting them to you now."

Right on cue, Ridge's phone pinged softly.

Hope's fingers tightened on his. Her cheeks were pale.

"Let me know if your brother recognizes them," Villanueva added.

"I will. Either way," he added, but the investigator had already ended the call.

Ridge's thumb hovered over his cell phone screen. With a simple brush, he'd be able to reveal the texted photos.

"You ready for this?" he asked Hope.

She shook her head. "But that's not a good reason to wait."

He wasn't so sure about that, but he swiped the screen and the text message opened.

The two photos were small, but remained clear enough even after he'd expanded them to fill the screen.

Howard had a head of fading brown hair and nondescript features. Petunia had darker brown hair with bangs that were cut too short over a narrow face. She was equally average looking.

He studied Hope's auburn head. "Anything?"

She took the phone from him and made the photos even larger. Swiping between Howard, then Petunia, then back again. "Nothing," she said finally and handed him back the phone. "No reaction even."

"Reaction?"

She took his free hand and pressed it to the center of her chest. "No racing heart."

Ridge couldn't say the same.

He slid his splayed fingers away from the gentle swell of her breasts and stood.

"If even my subconscious knew them, I'd have a reaction," Hope said with enviable certainty. She stood as well and swiped her hands over the seat of her jeans as she went back inside. Only then did Ridge realize that Evie was making noises.

He paced around in a circle in front of the guesthouse, squeezing the back of his neck with one hand and strangling his phone with his other hand.

Then Hope reappeared with a sleepy looking Evie in her arms. "I'm going to fix her lunch," she said and started off toward the house.

He watched her for a long moment, before forwarding the photos to Nash.

Recognize them? Old DMV photos.

Nash replied immediately.

It's them. He's nearly bald now and she had short gray hair, but I'm dead sure. Who are they?

Ridge blew out a long breath. He sent the information along to Villanueva and wished to hell he'd never offered up the guest-house for Hope to use. She and Evie were a lot safer under his roof than they would be two hundred and fifty yards away.

He sent another text to Nash.

I'll fill you in later. But keep watch.

Then he followed behind Hope, deliberately not catching up to her before she reached the house.

She'd have been eight years younger when those photos were taken. Maybe it was the reason why she hadn't recognized either one of them. An explanation for her "no reaction."

Yet, eight years really wasn't such a long time. The annoyingly logical voice inside his head seemed determined to debate the matter.

A middle-aged person's looks didn't change *that* much in less than ten years.

How could Hope panic so much over the sight of a car, but not the images of the people who'd occupied it?

Once again, he was left with more questions than when they'd started.

And one of them now was whether or not he should tell Hope about Nash's confirmation.

Instead of going inside, he diverted around to the deck and walked all the way down to the cantilevered rail.

The lake—his portion of it, anyway—was quiet. He called Mitch's office. Not surprisingly, he wasn't available on a Monday afternoon.

Ridge left a message to call him and finally went inside.

Evie was in her high chair, shoveling her fingers through her cooked green beans in favor of the spoon that Hope was trying to use. "Come on, baby," he heard her coax, but Evie wasn't having any of it. She wanted both the spoon and to squish and squeeze her beans, and that was that.

"It'll take her two hours to eat at this rate," Hope said ruefully as she surrendered the spoon again.

"What about one of those squeeze pouches?"

"I need to pick up more from GreatStore. And it's important that she figure out the utensils, too."

He leaned down to Evie's level. "Hard being eight months old, isn't it, Little Miss?"

She grinned and tossed a handful of green beans into his face.

Hope muffled her laugh, but her eyes sparkled as she yanked a paper towel off the roll and handed it to him.

He didn't have the heart to kill that sparkle just yet. He'd wait until Villanueva found the link between Howard and Petunia Marks and Hope. Until then, he'd just have to make sure that everyone on the ranch remained vigilant.

Six times, Villanueva had said. Ridge, though, only knew of three times. Did that mean Howard and Petunia Marks had been sniffing around three other times that they hadn't known about? Or were those incidences unrelated to Hope altogether?

The likelihood of that seemed small. They'd traveled each time to St. Louis before beginning the hunt.

The location had to be significant.

Had Hope lived there? If so, how...why...had she ended up in Texas? Last month, she'd had a memory flash of riding a bus and running, somehow landing in his barn, no less, but even she had admitted the memory felt typically garbled and confusing. Like some sort of bad dream that felt real but wasn't quite.

"If you have work to do, you don't have to hang around here," Hope said. "Not on our account."

He looked at her.

"You're frowning." She waved her hand as if to encompass his entirety. "I thought it was maybe because you were thinking about everything else you have to do."

The "everything else" was already being capably taken care of by ranch employees who'd been there well before his family had come along.

But now that Hope had pointed out his frown, he realized

that his jaw was so tight it ached, and no amount of willpower let it ease up. But it was easier letting her believe he was thinking about work than worrying about her. "How about a trip to the hardware store?" he suggested abruptly.

Her eyebrows lifted.

"You can choose paint colors for the guesthouse." And he could get the parts to fix the gate opener for once and for all.

She angled her head, and her hair slid over her shoulder. "I suppose you think it'll be necessary to hire a painter again like you did with the nursery."

It was exactly what he'd been thinking. "That *is* how the paint gets on the walls."

"You are such a Richie Rich." Her smile widened. "You're a *Ridgy Rich*." She actually giggled. "We could paint it ourselves you know. It's not that much work. And I already know what colors I want for Evie's wall. The same colors she has now."

"Hiring professional painters helps keep the economy turning," he defended.

She laughed outright, and Evie joined in, adding the accompaniment of drumming her spoon against her high chair tray.

The ache in his jaw suddenly eased.

Amazing what a little laughter from his ladies could do.

CHAPTER TWELVE

THEY SPENT THE rest of the day painting the guesthouse walls.

To be strictly accurate, Hope spent the day painting while Ridge—after banishment from ever touching a paintbrush or roller again—spent it keeping Evie occupied.

"You should have said the real reason you wanted to hire painters was because you'd never done it before," Hope told him when she finally climbed down from the ladder after repainting over his apparently subpar attempts.

"I've painted before," he defended.

She pressed her lips together. "Okay," she said after a moment. "It's just not everyone's forte."

He might have felt more crestfallen if he'd cared a jot about his skill as a housepainter. "You're not perfect, either."

Her lips parted, and she whirled around to face the wall that was an almost exact replica of the nursery in the house. There was no wainscoting, but she'd done some magic with painter's tape and the two colors of paint—blush above and rosemary below—looked just as good. "Did I really miss a spot?" She started up the ladder again. "I'm certain I didn't get any paint on the ceiling like you did."

He chuckled and caught her around the waist, lifting her off the ladder. "The walls are perfect," he assured. "It's *you* who's got the spots." He slowly let her slide through his arms until her feet touched the ground. Then he lifted her chin and took the damp rag out of her fist to wipe her chin.

"Oh, well. Getting paint on myself is okay," she said, though she sounded decidedly breathless.

He rubbed another spatter from her temple. "You have some in your hair, too," he murmured, *finally* threading his fingers through her hair that she'd smoothed back into a long ponytail.

Her lashes fluttered closed, and her hands clasped his shoulders. "It'll wash out in the shower," she breathed.

He was an idiot, was what he was. Lighting matches even though he knew better than to start this particular fire. "You might need help."

Brilliant blue peeked at him from beneath her long lashes, and she leaned into him. Her lips parted softly, and she rocked her hips ever so slightly against him. "I might," she agreed.

He almost groaned aloud and clamped his hands on her hips to stop the maddening motion. At least that was his intention. But good intentions were futile when she was stretching up against him, her hands sliding from his shoulders to his neck, and her fingers roved through his hair as if they'd felt just as greedy for the sensation as he had. Her breasts were flattened against him. He could feel the point of her tight nipples and the unevenness of her breath.

Evie was fed and safely confined in her play yard with her stack of toys, and all it would take would be a second to rid himself and Hope of a few pieces of clothing to feel every inch of her against him.

He kissed her temple. His fingers drifted to the hem of her T-shirt. Slid beneath. Her skin was like velvet. Warm. Smooth. Enticing.

She made a soft *mmm* sound that went straight to his head, and he dragged aside the stretchy fabric cup of her bra to palm her breast. She moaned a little more, and he lowered his mouth to take that tight nipple between his lips, T-shirt and all.

Her moan turned to a throaty groan, and when she dragged his free hand to her other breast, he was nearly undone.

"Don't stop," she begged.

He wasn't sure he could even if he wanted.

And he seriously didn't want to.

He yanked her shirt upward, and she accommodated by lifting her arms. As soon as the fabric cleared her head, he sent it sailing while he lowered his head to her neck. The warm curve of her shoulder. Down to the valley between her breasts, still plumped up from the bra cups he'd pulled aside. Her skin was creamy…her nipples rosy and rigid. He circled one with his thumb while he tasted the other, and she cried out.

He paused instantly, not sure he hadn't hurt her.

"Don't stop," she gasped again. Her lips were parted. Her cheeks flushed. He dragged his thumbs slowly over her nipples again, and the flush deepened.

She writhed against him.

He'd never seen anything more arousing.

Ridge turned and lifted her to the back of the ugly sofa that they'd pushed away from the wall and to the center of the room, and she dragged at his shirt. He yanked it off and sent it the way of hers. She immediately pressed her mouth against his chest and linked her ankles behind him, tightening him into the V of her thighs. He ran his hands down her back. Up her sides. Felt her shiver. But he knew now that her nipples were the fuse to fireworks.

He was more than ready to set that flame…but in time.

For now, he drew the cups of her bra down a little more and her breathing quickened. He tasted the creamy flesh. Kissed his way from one mound to the other, and her inhalation was a hiss when his lips barely whispered over the tight peaks.

Her head fell back, and she rocked against him.

"You're going to come, aren't you," he whispered against the pulse throbbing madly in her throat. "If I do this." Light as air, he drifted his fingers over her nipples.

She groaned. "Ridge, please."

It was the only kind of begging he ever wanted to hear come from her lips. "I don't have to touch you anywhere else," he rasped. "Just—" he drifted again, barely a whisper of a touch "—there."

Her mouth was open. Her body quivered. "Don't tease."

"Not a tease," he assured. "A promise."

Blue fire looked up at him through her lashes. "Prove it," she said throatily.

The need inside him was feral. He lowered his mouth to her breast, watching her all the while. He didn't touch her, though. Just breathed on that sweet, tight, ruby peak.

"You're going to pay for this," she promised huskily.

He smiled slowly. "Now who's the tease?"

"Oh, it's a promise," she said.

He touched the tip of his tongue to her nipple.

She jerked, and he felt the ripple that worked through her abdomen.

"More?"

She nodded restlessly. "A lot more."

He laughed soundlessly and circled all the way around. Drew it lightly between his lips while his fingertip flirted with the other.

Hope's breathing was almost a sob. Her legs were a vise around his hips.

"More?" he asked again.

She didn't answer. Just lifted her hand to his and boldly pressed his thumb and index finger around her nipple.

Fire licked down his spine. If he wasn't careful, he would beat her to the fireworks.

He caught her nipple between his teeth and bathed her with his tongue while he gently compressed the other, until he finally cupped both her breasts, squeezing her nipples tightly between his fingers, and he found her mouth with his.

She convulsed, her pleasure seeming to go on and on before she collapsed bonelessly in his arms.

His own breath was raging from his chest, and he lifted her onto the couch, nearly falling over her. Their hands collided as they worked at their jeans, and then she was guiding him into her and they both groaned. Everything about her was exactly perfect for him. She wound around him, her mouth on his. "Faster," she begged.

What else could he do but comply? Particularly when her hands were racing over him, threading through his hair, and she was murmuring his name as though it was the only name in the world for her.

And then she was quaking around him all over again, and if he'd ever had any fantasies about making this last, they went right out the window as he succumbed to the mindless perfection of his Hope.

He was still panting like he'd climbed Everest when she shoved at his shoulders a short time later. "Did you hear that?"

All he could hear was his heart still clanging inside his head. He kissed the tiny birthmark on her neck. "No."

"Anyone home?"

He jerked his head up, too.

Met Hope's wide blue gaze.

Her cheeks were red from razor burn. Her lips almost swollen from his kisses. He pressed her head down to the cushion and out of sight and looked almost fatalistically at the door. Just waiting for the knob to turn.

Which it did.

Then the door opened, and Jade stood there in the wash of the porch light. "I knew you had to be somewhere around here," she said, as if there was nothing at all unusual over finding her brother sitting on an ugly mauve and teal couch partially shrouded in plastic drop cloths without a shirt.

Their only saving grace was the fact that the couch was facing away from the front door.

Jade had no way of seeing that he didn't have anything else on, either, and that Hope was still mostly underneath him.

"Oh," his sister said, as if she'd just realized something.

Ridge's neck burned, but then he noticed her attention on Evie's play yard near the door and the fact that she'd fallen asleep amongst her toys.

Jade pressed her finger to her lips. "Sorry," she whispered. "I'll wait over at the house." She slowly pulled the door closed again, and the breath that he hadn't realized he was holding escaped.

He sat back against one arm of the couch and raked his hand through his hair while Hope untangled her legs from his. She set her bra to rights and slid down to her hands and knees on the floor to crawl after her clothes.

"I don't think Jade's going to look through the windows," he said.

Hope just gave him a harried grimace before she yanked her T-shirt on and tugged her ponytail free of the neckline. Flinging his shirt in his direction, she slid on her jeans and then pulled up her knees, wrapping her arms around her legs. She lowered her head. "This is mortifying." Her voice was muffled.

"Why?"

She lifted her head just long enough to give him a scandalized glare before dropping her forehead back to her knees again.

He stiffly got to his feet and yanked his jeans back on. Shaking out his shirt, he saw the splotches of dried paint on the front.

He figured not even Terralee's talents would be enough to save the thing. "At least Evie fell asleep," he said as he pulled the shirt over his head.

Hope groaned, and this time there was nothing erotic about it at all.

He went to the door. "I'll go deal with my sister."

"Good luck."

The house was only a few minutes away. He wished it was farther.

He went in through the back kitchen door. Jade was sitting at the island.

"This is becoming a habit." He closed the door behind him.

"Yeah, and I had to drive around the back sides of our property to get here. Did you know your gate opener isn't working?"

"I'll get it fixed," he told her.

"Soon, I hope," she groused, pushing a shoebox-sized plastic container toward him.

He reached instead for the refrigerator door and pulled out a beer. "What's that?" He gestured with the bottom of the bottle toward the box before taking a quick drink, then following it with a near guzzle.

Jade noticed and raised her eyebrows. "Hard day?"

"Implying that my work isn't taxing enough these days to qualify as hard?"

"Good grief." Her eyebrows went even higher. "I wasn't even remotely thinking that." She shook her head slightly. "When did you get so touchy?"

"I'm not touchy," he denied and lifted the bottle again. "What's in the box?"

"Family photos." Jade was still giving him a strange look, but apparently her agenda was already full enough without adding the task of figuring out what was stuck under Ridge's saddle. "Therefore—" she jabbed a finger in the air between them "—I don't want to hear any more excuses about not having a photo to give as a wedding present to our mystery couple."

That stupid wedding had been about the furthest thing from Ridge's mind.

His sister dropped her finger to the box and pushed it toward him. "Pick one. Any one. I don't care which." She looked beyond him, and he realized that Hope—mortification be damned—had followed him through the back door. She was carrying a still-sleeping Evie and walked past them both, disappearing down the hall.

She returned a few minutes later. "A successful transfer to the crib," she said. "Amazingly enough." Her eyes bounced between Jade and Ridge before she turned away and yanked open the refrigerator door with only a small clatter of bottles inside. "Can I get you something to drink, Jade?"

"I'm fine."

Hope extracted a bottle of water and pushed the door closed with her hip. She maintained a healthy distance between herself and Ridge as she moved to the other side of the island. Aside from a few wrinkles on her T-shirt, there was no evidence that, not too long ago, Ridge had kissed his way through the cloth long enough to leave a wet mark on it.

"I just brought these by for Ridge." Jade tapped the plastic container. "Will you make sure he chooses a photo before the mystery wedding?" She didn't wait for an answer and looked back at Ridge. "You can return the box to me later."

"Fine. Whatever," he said.

"Happy day. Aren't you all agreeable now?" She took the beer bottle from him only long enough to look at the label. "Fortune's Rising IPA." Her lips twitched. "Figures." She handed it back to him. "I'm introducing the new potbellied pig in the morning at the petting zoo. We're definitely going with your idea of holding a contest to name him. Will you be coming by?"

Ridge didn't make the mistake of thinking she was addressing him. Hope was the one who took Evie down to his sister's passion project every day.

She was nodding as she pulled an apron over her head and tied the strings around her waist. "We should be there right after opening time. If I have some ideas for names, can I participate, or am I disqualified because I know you?"

Jade laughed as she headed for the door. "Hardly. I just want a fun event that garners interest in the petting zoo. The more proceeds we make, the more kids we can accommodate in our free workshops," she said on her way out.

Ridge pulled out a bar stool and sat. The ever-present mason jar sat on the island, filled with several gray-green stalks. He absently pulled the jar closer and sniffed the tight buds.

Lavender.

He didn't even know where lavender was growing around here any more than he knew where the orange and red flowers she'd placed in the guesthouse came from, but he knew Hope was forever finding one sort or another. He moved the jar aside and reached for the photos, flipping off the lid. With little interest, he pulled out a stack of color snapshots and started flipping through them. "Potbellied pig names, huh?"

"You bet." Hope sounded determinedly breezy. She set an oversize bowl on the counter and opened another cupboard, pulling out a hand mixer. "Torvis." She opened a drawer. Dropped the metal beaters she extracted on the butcher-block top. "George the Great. Donald."

Ridge smiled. "Do you always have a stockpile of names at your fingertips?"

She opened the pantry and hefted out an enormous canister. "Just for pigs, I think." She set the canister next to the bowl and rummaged in another drawer until she came up with a metal measuring cup. "Choosing Evie's name was a much lengthier pro—"

The measuring cup clattered to the floor.

Her eyes were saucers when they turned his way. "Rebecca," she whispered. "Amelia. Danny wanted—" Her face paled even more, and she swayed a little. "Petal." The word came out through clenched teeth as she pressed her hands to both sides of her head as if pained.

He dropped the handful of photographs and caught her just in time to save her from crumbling when her knees went out from beneath her. Sweeping her up in his arms, he carried her to the couch, kneeling down to deposit her.

Her eyes were closed.

His phone.

Where the hell was his phone?

He swore and pressed his knuckles lightly against her pallid cheek. It was cool. Vaguely clammy.

Or maybe that was just him.

He'd forgotten all about the landline. That's how dependent he was on his cell phone. But there was the cordless phone sitting in its cradle practically in front of his nose on a side table. He snatched it up and returned to the couch, kneeling on the floor next to her while he made sure there was a dial tone before he started to punch out 911 with his thumb.

With his other hand, he yanked at the strings of the chef's apron she had tied around her waist in accordance with some deeply buried factoid to remove constrictions when a person fainted.

Hope's hand drifted over his arm. "Stop," she whispered.

Her eyes were slits of bruised periwinkle looking up at him.

He didn't punch out the last number, but he held on to the phone, anyway. His fingers were clamped around the hard, oddly substantial handset so tightly they wouldn't have obeyed any sort of command to loosen.

"I'm okay," she continued, still in a whisper that seemed like she was anything *but* okay. "Danny wanted to name the baby Petal, after his mother. It was better than Petunia."

Puzzle pieces fell into place.

If his head wasn't pounding with his own pulse, he would

have probably heard the sound of them all clicking together. Completing the picture of Hope's real story.

Real family.

"Danny's mother." He managed to get the words out through a throat that felt as locked up as his fingers.

"Danny Marks." Her face crumpled, and she began crying softly. "My husband."

CHAPTER THIRTEEN

HOPE FELT RIDGE'S arms come around her and even though she knew she ought to be stronger, she clung to him as the tears racked through her. Tears for the past. For the present. For the future that would never be.

She cried until there was nothing left inside her but a hiccup and a stitch in her side and the front of Ridge's shirt was damp and wrinkled.

His gaze was dark and searching when she finally made herself push away from him. She only got as far as the corner of the couch, though. She didn't seem to have the strength to go any further.

She didn't know if she appreciated the fact that he didn't say a word or if it would have been easier if he'd started peppering her with questions.

That's what Danny would have done.

She closed her eyes again and rubbed her cheeks. "I'm sorry," she said thickly.

"Don't be sorry."

"I remember everything."

Ridge's expression didn't change, but he seemed to tense.

Or maybe that was just her.

She ducked her head, using the hem of her shirt to wipe at

her cheeks even though his shirt had already absorbed the brunt of her tears.

He got up and went to the kitchen, returning a moment later with a damp towel. He rolled it into a compress then tucked his hand beneath her chin and gently swiped her face with it.

She nearly started crying all over again and to stop it, simply pressed the whole damp bundle against her eyes. "My head is pounding." It wasn't untrue, but it was still just an excuse to put off the inevitable.

"I'm calling Mitch."

She lifted the compress to look at him. "I don't need a doctor."

But he'd already reached for the phone again and began dialing. "Mitch or 911. Humor me."

She chewed the inside of her cheek and applied the damp compress to her closed eyes again while he spoke briefly into the phone.

"He's on his way," he said.

Then silence stretched between them and it felt like a living thing, pulsing right along with the rhythmic pounding inside her head.

She lifted the compress once more and waved it in the air. "Who knew the key to my memory would be a pig-naming contest?" Her desperate attempt at flippancy fell miserably flat.

The corners of Ridge's mouth lifted slightly, but not even he could keep up the pretense. "Want to tell me about… Danny?"

Was it her imagination that he'd hesitated before speaking her husband's name?

Hearing him say it made her wince slightly.

And no, she didn't want to tell him about Danny. She didn't even want to think about Danny. But of course, that seemed almost all she could do.

Every single detail had come pouring back. Just as Mitch had suggested it would. The whole lot swung from one side of her mind to another with the delicacy of a wrecking ball.

The good.

The bad.

The tragic.

She unfolded the towel. Refolded it. Then just twisted it together between her hands. “My name is Holly,” she said instead.

Holly.

Marks.

Her name joined the pounding inside her head.

“My mother was fifteen when she had me and sixteen when she dumped me off at a fire station.” She grimaced. “Not that I remember it.”

Ridge’s features tightened. “You were an infant. But you ended up in group homes?”

There were more important things to tell him. Life-changing things to tell him. “I guess I was sort of sickly. That’s the reason I was never adopted. At least that’s the story I got.” She realized she was picking at her thumb, creating a hangnail where there’d been none and made herself stop. “I was with a bunch of different foster families. Nobody lasted more than a few years.”

He muttered something under his breath. Shook his head. “I’m sorry,” he said.

“For all I know, it might have been worse if she’d tried to keep me,” she said. She’d never really hated her mother for abandoning her when she’d been just a child, herself. Holly had learned quickly enough that her situation was better than some.

But that didn’t mean she hadn’t longed for a family of her own.

A real family.

The image of Danny’s face swam inside her head and her stomach churned.

She pressed the compress against her face again, swallowing down the wave of nausea.

Then the doorbell chimed and Ridge bolted off the couch again. “Finally.”

He sounded as anxious to escape as she felt.

Yet, after escorting Mitch inside, he didn’t leave them alone. Choosing instead to pace around the couch while his friend sat down beside her and gave her a calm smile. “How’re you doing?”

She gave him a shrug. She was busy watching Ridge from the corner of her eyes.

What was he thinking?

She realized Mitch had opened his medical bag and was pulling out his stethoscope and blood pressure cuff. She chewed the inside of her cheek, enduring his attention and counting her way through the blood pressure check, as if she could control the results with a slow, measured one-to-ten. He pulled out a light and shined it in her eyes, asked her if she had any pain—she did, but not the kind that he could help with—and then returned everything to his bag again and just sat there for a moment, watching her.

"Are you okay staying here now?"

The question surprised her as much as it did Ridge.

"Why the hell wouldn't she be," he demanded.

Mitch just raised his eyebrows slightly at his friend, who seemed to take whatever message that was meant to convey, and started pacing again, with a fresh rhythmic flexing of his jaw.

"I'm fine," she answered belatedly, realizing that Mitch was still waiting for her answer. Aside from a massive headache, the emotional pain that surpassed it wasn't something that a pill was going to help.

Another wave of tears was building behind her eyes and she pinched her eyes shut. She couldn't do a thing to stop the hitch in her breath, though.

She'd tried so hard to make everything better, to disastrous effect.

"I can give you a sedative—"

She shook her head hard. So many times she'd heard that offer back then. After the accident. Didn't matter that she'd been pregnant—

A piercing cry erupted from the baby monitor, seeming to make them all jump.

She snatched up the monitor and muted the volume.

Ridge took a step away from the fireplace. "I'll get—"

"No!" She shoved the monitor into his hands, pretending not to see the frown on his face. "She needs feeding." She practically ran from the room, but not fast enough to miss the cautioning grip that Mitch took on Ridge's arm when he would have followed her.

Tears leaked down her face as she closed herself in the nursery with Evie, who wailed even louder and stretched out her arms.

"I know, baby." She lifted her daughter out of the crib and pressed her face to her sweet cheek, hauling in a shuddering breath. "Everything's going to be okay."

Considering the tumult of memories accosting her, the assurance was hollow, but Evie didn't know that.

Or maybe she did, because it took her daughter longer than usual to settle down back to sleep after feeding and it took three tries before she settled back down to sleep after an exhausted sigh.

Hope wished she could remain in the nursery forever, but of course, she couldn't. She went into the en suite bathroom and snatched a tissue from the box. She blew her nose for what felt like the hundredth time. She splashed cool water over her face in hopes of alleviating the red circles around her eyes.

But when she straightened and looked in the mirror, she still looked a wreck.

As if there'd been no passage of time at all since that last, dreadful argument with Danny.

Fourteen months ago.

How much had occurred in that span of time?

It was no time at all, and yet an entire lifetime.

Evie's, at any rate.

She slid open a drawer and stared hollowly at the contents.

Hairbrush. Ponytail holders. Tweezers and face cream and a small quilted cosmetic case that Wendy Fortune herself had given Hope.

"Just a few things," she'd said only a few days after they'd met and she'd come to visit Ridge, bearing a bag of things for the baby and the little quilted case for Hope. "Essentials that every girl needs." Wendy's smile had been almost unbearably kind. Lip gloss. A tube of mascara. Blush. And a wad of twenty-dollar bills that Hope hadn't touched until Christmas arrived and she'd still had no memory of who she was, and a stronger desire to purchase a few gifts than to keep from touching that money because of pride.

She pulled out the brush and drew it almost manically through her hair until her scalp tingled and the strands were crackling with static electricity. Then she raked it all back again in a tight ponytail.

But it only accentuated the pinched lines around her eyes and mouth, and she let it down again.

She knew she was wasting time, hiding in the bathroom. Knew that Ridge was out there, waiting. Questions still dammed up in his beautiful brown eyes.

She opened the cosmetic case from Wendy. The distinctive blue box inside contained the diamond key necklace that Ridge had given her, tucked in the very same spot that had once held the wad of twenties.

With trembling fingers, she thumbed open the jewelry box and traced the outline of the key with the tip of her fingernail. The diamonds winked softly.

She closed the box. Pulled out the blush and smoothed some on her pale cheeks. It wasn't much in the way of armor, but it helped just a little.

Selfishly she wished that her daughter would start fussing again. Offer up a reasonable reason for Hope to stay in the nursery.

Not Hope.

Holly.

Another numbingly loud metronome took up residence inside her head, and she pressed her fingers against her aching temples.

Only a few hours ago, Ridge had given her the most intense orgasms she'd ever had in her life.

She was every bit the horrible person that Petunia and Howard believed her to be.

Just go out there, Hope. Tell Ridge the truth.

That you're the reason your husband is dead.

She let out a deep, shuddering breath.

Avoiding her reflection in the mirror, she returned everything inside the quilted case, zipped it shut and closed the drawer. Then she turned off the light and left the bathroom.

Mitch was gone. No surprise. And Ridge was sitting on the

couch but there was nothing relaxed in his demeanor. As soon as he heard her, he rose. His gaze searching.

So close, she thought with a deepening ache inside. She'd been so close to real happiness with him. And now—

"Evie okay?"

She nodded.

His jaw shifted. "And you?"

This time, her nod was jerky. She sat on the arm of a side chair and tucked her hands beneath her thighs to hide the way they'd started trembling again.

Just tell him.

"I thought I could take Evie to Mexico," she blurted baldly. "I had my passport and a little cash with me." What she'd managed to hide away without Danny's knowledge before she'd even become pregnant. "I took a half dozen different buses from St. Louis to hide our trail. By the time I reached Texas, I thought we were nearly home free." She pressed her lips together against an ugly wave of nausea. "Obviously I was wrong."

"Why were you heading to Mexico?"

"Because Howard and Petunia were going to take Evie from me."

She realized she was too restless to sit.

Instead, she stood and paced across the room, tucking her shaking hands in her back pockets. She stared blindly at the artful arrangement of books and candles on one end of the mantel. Terralee's doing.

Hope's—*Holly's*—contribution to the household had mostly been limited to jars of wildflowers that she stole from the roadside.

"Why do you think they were going to take Evie from you?"

"I *know* they were going to," she corrected. "I had pounds of paperwork from the attorneys who told me so."

"But why?"

"Because I'm not a suitable mother."

"Bullshit."

She winced a little. Not so much at the word but at the passion in the delivery.

Her eyes burned. She was still facing the mantel. Easier that way. She couldn't look at him and tell him the truth. To see the warmth in his expression wither and die.

Get it over with.

Rip off the bandage and be done with it.

"They knew I caused Danny's death," she said thinly.

"He's dead then. You weren't mistaken after all." Ridge moved around to stand in front of the fireplace where she couldn't avoid seeing him. "You're *not* married." His tone was neutral, but she could see the effort it cost in the white line of his rigid jaw. "You're a widow?"

She nodded, pinching her eyes closed. Ridge's image was seared in her mind anyway. "A car accident."

"An accident is an accident. How'd you cause it?"

"A car wreck," she said. "I should have been more specific."

"It still doesn't mean it was your fault."

She opened her eyes again, throwing out an arm. "Tell your investigator my real name. That I used to live in St. Louis. Tell him about Howard and Petunia. He'll confirm it all."

"He already knows about Howard and Petunia Marks. At least he knows they were the ones driving the rental car."

Right. The investigator had told them about the car earlier that day. He'd sent the old DMV photos of Danny's parents. She ought to have recognized them, even though they'd both aged a lot by the time she'd met them.

Villanueva's text message seemed so long ago, though.

Before the hardware store.

Before the painting.

Before.

She wrapped her arms around her waist, trying to staunch the ache she felt inside. She was trembling so badly her teeth were chattering. "We were at one of Danny's endless work parties. He'd been drinking. I hadn't."

"Because you were pregnant."

She nodded. "It was t-time to leave, and I wanted to drive, but to Danny that was tantamount to saying he couldn't. Not just a basic fact that he *shouldn't*. He'd already been complaining all night about the amount of starch I'd let the dry cleaners use on his dress shirt." Recounting the utter ridiculousness of it stirred up the resentment and powerlessness she'd felt then. "As if a random wrinkle was the reason one of his c-clients hadn't shown up to the party. And I lost it." She shuddered, and Ridge flipped a switch near the mantel almost roughly.

A small flame immediately licked its way around the gas logs in the fireplace.

She moved jerkily closer to the heat. "I s-stood there on the sidewalk outside the f-fanciest hotel in the c-city and screamed at him like a lunatic until a security guard had to separate us.

"Like all things Danny, though—" she lifted her shaking hands slightly "—he talked his way out of it. The s-security guard gave Danny his keys and then he put me in a taxi. I got home. Danny didn't. He ran off an overpass."

"I'm sorry." Ridge turned up the gas flame even more. It burned hotter. Brighter. Then he braced his hand on the mantel. "That must have been awful."

Her nose felt like fire ants were crawling inside it. She focused on Ridge's hand. The long fingers. Square palm. The ridge of calluses that belied the fancy gold watch on his perfectly shaped wrist.

"I was relieved," she whispered. *That* was what was awful.

Ridge's fingers curled until his knuckles whitened. "Then he *was* mistreating you."

Her knees felt like jelly. The warmth from the fireplace had been immediate, but it didn't help her vibrating bones.

She angled sideways and slid down onto one of the armchairs that flanked the hearth. "Danny was a stockbroker. Like his father. Only we lived in St. Louis because Danny didn't like Tennessee. It was far enough away—"

She cleared the growing knot from her throat. Far enough away to keep his parents from getting too close a look at their son. She realized it now. But hindsight was always clearer, wasn't it?

"He said he wanted to move far enough away to be outside the range of his father's influence," she managed evenly. "So that he could be sure his success would be *his*."

"Was he? Successful?"

She chewed the inside of her lip. "From the outside, I'm

sure we looked like the perfect couple. Handsome stockbroker and the little wife. Living in their brand-new, perfectly lovely house. Large enough to be impressive, but not so large that it was ostentatious." She looked down at her hand. Remembering the enormous diamond ring that had turned out to be fake when she'd tried to pawn it.

As if he'd known she would try to do so at some point.

"Having a lovely house doesn't guarantee everything going on inside of it is lovely, too." Ridge blew out a rough breath. "My family is proof of that."

"Did your family control every minute of your day? Twenty-four seven?"

"I think you already know they didn't." He was silent for a moment. "How long ago was the accident?"

She leaned her elbows on her knees and pressed her face to her hands. "Fourteen months."

"You must have barely been pregnant."

"I wasn't even three months along." Danny had been crowing about her pregnancy to everyone they knew from the moment the test stick had turned positive. A month later at his funeral, they'd all been whispering how tragic it all was.

It *had* been tragic.

And avoidable if she'd have just faced the truth and escaped before it had been too late.

She'd been the proverbial frog in the kettle—not smart enough to recognize the water surrounding her was getting hotter by the day.

She thrust her fingertips through her hair, digging her fingertips into her scalp. "I was stupid enough to think being pregnant might change things. But I should have known better. I'd already quit my job at the day care center because he didn't want me to work. Not even the fact that they wanted me to take over for the director who was retiring made any difference to him." She deepened her voice. "Any wife of Danny Marks will never need to work."

She yanked on her hair as she raked it back from her face. Pulling tightly because the pain of it was more welcome than the memories. "When you're young, it might sound romantic.

But in reality?" She sniffed. "The one thing in my life that I'd accomplished on my own, and I gave it up without so much as a whimper. People like Danny don't change," she said huskily. "They just get more so." And she'd been no better. Just taking the blows that life kept giving her.

"You didn't answer if he was successful."

She grimaced and looked at Ridge. Her eyes felt gritty, but she could still see that he'd already come to his own—correct—conclusion.

"Everything was appearances for Danny. Including his career." She moistened her lips. "The house was mortgaged beyond its worth. The fancy car was a lease. He was a stockbroker, alright, but not a very good one. His parents never saw that, though. He was their only child. They believed he hung the moon and the stars."

"How did the two of you meet?"

"A coffee shop of all places." She shook her head. "I had just turned twenty-two. He was thirty. It was like something out of a romantic movie, and I fell, hook, line and sinker. We were married in less than six months." She made a face. "I'd say let that be a cautionary tale to all young women, except I'm the perfect example of how pointless cautionary tales are."

She leaned forward and dropped her voice to a facetious whisper. "The big secret is that we ignore them. Every. Single. Time."

He didn't smile. Proof that he couldn't relate to a twenty-two-year-old girl who watched too many romantic comedies. "Back to the parents," he prompted instead.

"They swooped in after the funeral. At first it was a relief. They took care of everything. Arranged the funeral. I didn't know how to do any of that. And then they insisted that I go back to Nashville with them. Saying I was family. Carrying their only grandchild. They wanted to take care of me, too. So. I went."

She pinched back the tears collecting in her eyes. "I never had a family. Then there was Danny. And after him, there were his parents. But I hadn't learned my lesson enough. I had to wait until Evie was born to realize how insidious their helpfulness really was. And then they talked about how much more they could do for Evie than I could, especially knowing how my background hadn't taught me anything about being a proper mother, and suddenly there were legal papers getting drawn up. And Petunia reminding me that if I'd have been a better wife, Danny wouldn't have died, and—"

"Enough." Ridge crouched in front of her. "Look at me."

She shook her head.

But he gently clasped her face between his palms. Those large square palms with calluses that ought to have felt rough but didn't. "Look at me, Hope."

"Holly," she said thickly, but she focused on his face. Felt herself start to slide down into his warm brown eyes.

He brushed his thumb against her cheek, wiping away a tear. "You'll always be Hope to me. I'm in love with you, you know."

She drew in a jagged, stuttering breath. "No. I c-can't do this now."

"I'm not asking you to do anything," he said. "I'm just telling you the truth."

She couldn't form a single, coherent thought.

And maybe he realized it. Because he just lifted her hands and kissed her knuckles lightly before dragging the chair on the other side of the hearth closer.

He sat on the edge of the cushion, not even ten inches away from her. She could feel the warmth of him. But he didn't touch her.

For once, she was grateful for that.

"Tell me how you ended up in my barn."

It was a logical question.

But still she hadn't expected it. A few weeks ago, she'd already had a flashback about buses and panic and running. "You already know—"

"Go through it again," he said. "Step by step. Break it down."

"Break down more stupidity on my part?"

"Hope," he chided softly.

Holly.

She didn't voice the correction.

"The bus I was on made a stop near the LC Club. A bunch

of us who'd been on the ride the longest got off to stretch our legs. We'd done it dozens of times before. I had Evie in the carrier. It was hotter than blazes. We all left our backpacks behind on the bus. The driver would lock the door. And that's what I did. Left my backpack. Which had my passport. My money."

"Someone stole it?"

"That would be pathetic, right?"

He sighed. "I once had my wallet stolen out of a gym locker I forgot to lock. It happens."

She wasn't sure she believed him. But she didn't mind so much if he was making it up to make her feel better.

Proof that she was still a sucker for self-delusion.

"I'm twenty-six, by the way," she said abruptly. "Old enough to know better."

He slid a lock of her hair away from her cheek and tucked it behind her ear. Then his hand fell away again. He waited.

Quiet.

Patient.

The Ridge who didn't seem rigid at all.

"Anyway, it wasn't stolen," she said. "Not in the true sense of the word. But while we were stretching our legs, I saw Howard and Petunia. They were in a gray rental car, pulling up almost right next to the bus. And I panicked. You know that ice cream place on the shoreline walk? Just down a ways from the LC Club."

He nodded.

"I ducked in there with Evie. I could see them from the window. They finally pulled into the parking lot at the LC Club, but by then my bus—along with every measly dollar I possessed—left without me."

He made a soft groan. "Seriously."

"I know. It's one disaster after another."

"Those disasters brought you and Evie into my life," he said gruffly. "You'll have to pardon me for having a different take on it."

Despite everything, something dangerously sweet squiggled around inside her chest, and it alarmed the daylights out of her.

It was all she could do not to snatch Evie from her crib and bolt all over again.

"So." Ridge's steady, calm voice lured her thoughts back down from the panic level. "You saw Howard and Petunia. And their rental car. Always gray. Sounds a little OCD to me. What's the deal with that?"

"It's not OCD. It's the contract Howard's company has with the rental car company. All they have are gray sedans. Part of the *brand*." She put air quotes around the word.

"Keep it simple, stupid," Ridge murmured. "It wouldn't have mattered what the license plates on the car was, so long as it was the right color."

"I knew I needed to catch up to the bus. I realize now that the nightmares I have sometimes of running are running after that big, lumbering bus." She blew out a sigh. "Someone in the ice cream shop said the bus route always took it to Chatelaine Hills for a stop before it headed to San Antonio. I bummed a ride with some kid who looked barely legal to drive, and he let me off near the stop. It's right at the turnoff to your family's ranch."

"There's a bus stop there?"

"Quite a popular one." Some vestiges of humor twisted dryly inside of her. "For those of the non-Ridgy-Rich variety."

"Just finish the story."

"It had been a longshot in the first place. I missed the bus by nearly a half hour. By then it was starting to get late. Evie was fussing. I walked until I found a private enough spot to stop and nurse her. And then—" she shook her head again "—that bloody gray car came trolling down the road. I knew it wasn't safe to stay near the road like I had been, so I started cutting across the fields."

She tried to remember her path all those months ago and thought she must have somehow skirted to the farthest boundary of Jade's property, then angled across the somewhat wedged-shaped back sides of Nash's and Arlo's places, before finding a shelter that hadn't been lit by fancy security lights.

The clearest memory of all was the panic that had been driving her.

"When it was too dark to go any further, I ducked into what

I *thought* was an empty barn. And then I heard some voices and—" she spread her palms "—the next thing I remember, I was waking up with you and Dahlia hovering over me, and everything else was just…gone."

A muscle ticked in his jaw. "You know how lucky you were to end up somewhere safe?"

"Yes. If Howard and Petunia had found me, I'd have been the living proof of their claim that I wasn't fit to raise my own child. I had no money. No roof, no food—" She broke off when he took her hands in his and squeezed slightly.

"That's not the case anymore," he reminded her. "Not only do you have food and shelter, but you've got a support system. People—not just me—who care about you. Our lawyers can—"

"No."

He gave her a look. "They're the ones who brought lawyers into it, sweetheart. The best way to deal with them is with better lawyers. And we've got plenty of them."

Her nerves felt suddenly pinched. "I don't need you fighting my battles, Ridge!"

"Well, *somebody* better," he countered, sounding suddenly a lot less calm and reasonable. "Villanueva found them already. It's only a matter of time before the reverse is true and Howie and Pet talk to the right person who remembers seeing you or Evie. And then what are you going to do? Mexico's out, babe. No passport."

She yanked her hands from his and shoved to her feet. "Don't call me babe. My name is Hope! Ach! Holly." She waved him off. "And don't touch me right now, either. You're the reason why I can't think straight."

He lifted his hands away from her.

Once again, Evie started wailing. She hadn't remained settled after all, and the sound was magnified several times over by the assortment of baby monitors lying around.

She spun on her heel and started to head down the hallway.

"This will seem easier tomorrow." His deep, husky voice followed her.

"Easy for you to say. You don't have a child of your own that someone's threatening to take." She pushed open Evie's nursery door and went inside.

She never heard Ridge's response.

"Sure feels like I do."

CHAPTER FOURTEEN

"MORNING." BEAU WEATHERLY lifted his mug of coffee in greeting when Ridge slumped down at his table in the Daily Grind.

Ridge buried his nose in his own coffee and grunted.

"Is it Zane Baston putting in an offer on Nonny's place yesterday that's got you so chipper or the new living situation I hear you've got going for yourself?"

It had been two days since Hope moved over to the guesthouse. She'd only waited until the next morning after her memory had returned because Evie had already been asleep for the night. If not for the baby, Ridge was certain she would have moved over there that very night.

Now here it was halfway through the week. Villanueva's involvement was no longer necessary. He'd sent Ridge some links about the accident that claimed Danny Marks's life, along with his final bill. He'd done everything he could. The protection that Hope needed now would come from having better lawyers than Howard and Petunia had.

Lawyers that Ridge could provide, but only if Hope agreed.

Which she was refusing to do.

"I'm not taking more charity than I already have," she'd told him the evening before. "Soon as I can find a paycheck that doesn't get swallowed up by day care for Evie, I'll start paying you back for everything you've done for me."

No mention whatsoever about the fact that he'd told her he loved her.

And damn sure no response in kind.

When he'd made the suggestion that she didn't *need* to work, he'd immediately recognized his monumental error.

But no amount of apologizing seemed to help.

Now, he wasn't just afraid of not being able to protect her and Evie from her former in-laws, he was half afraid she'd decide she didn't want the use of the guesthouse at all. It wasn't as if it was perfect. Didn't even have an actual stove in it. Just a microwave and a dorm-sized refrigerator.

"What do you do with a stubborn woman, Beau?"

The older man chuckled. "Love 'em anyway."

"Nobody said anything about love."

"Son, you've been in love with that young lady and her baby girl for months."

Ridge squared himself to the table and circled his coffee mug with his hands. He'd never once subscribed to Beau's "free life advice." Aside from consulting him about real estate, which was just good business sense as far as Ridge was concerned. "Was your wife a stubborn woman?" He knew Beau's wife had died quite some time ago. And they'd been married a long, long time.

"She was." Beau's eyes were reflective. "When she needed to be."

Ridge grimaced. "That's real helpful, Beau. Thanks."

"Every relationship is a give-and-take. Problems can get real interesting when you both are taking opposing stands over something at the same time. Otherwise…" He shrugged and glanced at the door when it opened.

The faint smile around his lips returned as they both watched Ridge's mother sail through the doorway.

They weren't alone. Every other person in the place also took note when Wendy entered.

"You have a fine-lookin' mama," Beau murmured under his breath. His gaze followed her to the counter, where she propped an indolent elbow and bestowed her brilliant smile on the barista before tossing back her hair and laughing at something the teenage boy said. She was dressed in winter white, from the skinny turtleneck down to the tall leather boots she had tucked her jeans into.

"Yeah," Ridge said tartly, "and she's not looking for romance. She told me so herself just a few days ago. So, cool your jets, old man."

Beau grinned. He shifted and hooked one arm over the back of his chair as he maintained his attention on Wendy. "I'd be careful about who you're calling old," he warned. "I can still wrestle a steer when the need arises."

"Is that the sum of your life advice today?"

Beau picked up his coffee mug and nodded. "Seems so. Although, I'll add free of charge—" a big offer since the placard on the corner of Beau's regular table at the Daily Grind announced *Free* Life Advice "—that Zane's offer on Nonny's place was with the intent of subdividing it for a housing development."

"Chatelaine needs a housing development?"

"Not now," Beau said. "Down the line? Who knows?"

"You're the local wise man. Aren't you the one who's supposed to know?"

"Chatelaine's not a burgeoning market. It's small, but it's held its own for a lot of years. Not shrinking. Just plodding along. Might be time for some growth to hit. 'Specially with that castle of your mother's bringing in new sets of eyes."

"Where you going with this, Beau?"

The other man squinted slightly as he sipped his coffee. Ridge wasn't sure if it was from the hot drink, from contemplation, or because he was getting a better bead on Ridge's mother's figure.

"Just that the probate judge was an old friend of Nonny Zazlo. He'll know the notion of the family ranch getting chopped into rows for ticky-tacky houses would make him turn over in his grave. If there were a competing offer from someone who intended to continue using the land for ranching..." He squinted and sipped again.

"The last thing I'm thinking about right now is that property," Ridge said under his breath because his mom had straightened from the counter and turned their direction, carrying her tall coffee cup in one hand.

"Sometimes fixing one thing can lead to another thing getting fixed almost all on its own," Beau told him cryptically.

Then he pushed to his feet and swept his Stetson off the table in invitation in the same motion that he practically yanked Ridge's chair out from under him. "Morning, Miz Fortune. You're looking mighty cheerful."

"Beau Weatherly," Wendy greeted. "Just the man I'd hoped to see." She presented her cheek for Ridge's kiss and gracefully sank onto his abruptly vacated chair. Then, setting her boxy leather purse on one corner of the table, she smiled brilliantly at both men. "Ridge." She tsked. "You look like you've been pulled backward through a knothole. When's the last time you shaved?"

He didn't feel self-conscious all that often, but if someone could inspire it, it would be his mother. He rubbed his palm down his scratchy jaw.

"Hope's living in the guesthouse," Beau said, as if it would be news to Wendy.

"I know. And we had a wonderful chat just this morning." Her gaze drifted over Ridge again. "Don't you have somewhere else to be, honey? I thought Arlo and Nash were meeting this morning."

"They are. And there's nothing particularly important that I can contribute," Ridge answered flatly. "Unless we buy more land, we don't have room for more stock. We're running as many cow-calf pairs as we can. Dahlia needs her parcels for her sheep. Jade needs hers for the petting zoo. Status quo is maintained whether I show up to look at Arlo and Nash's weekly charts or not."

Wendy's eyebrows had risen slightly. "Well, I suppose you could take a look at the castle—"

He swore. Then grimaced. "Sorry," he muttered. He usually tried not to swear around his mother. "That's the problem in the first place, Mom. I don't need you to make up another job for me." He exhaled loudly. He was more annoyed with himself than he was with her. "Ignore me. I'll figure it out."

"I've never doubted it," Wendy assured blithely. "Perhaps you could check in on Sabrina. She has a new project on her hands."

Ridge jerked. "That's not some clever way of saying she's having the babies, is it?"

"Good Lord, Ridge. Of course it isn't. Do you think I'd be sitting around here—albeit enjoying some very fine company—if I had two more grandchildren making their entrance to the world?" She looked across at Beau, who had seated himself again across from Wendy.

"Stress," Beau mused. "Does things to a person's reasoning unless they find some outlet."

Ridge shook his head, stomped over to the counter to get a lid for his coffee and left.

He drove back to the ranch and stopped at the petting zoo. But Jade just shook her head when he appeared outside, where she was refilling one of the enormous buckets of feed that dozens of little hands would spread around for the goats and the pigs. "Hope didn't bring Evie this morning," she told him. "She did send me a text message, though, to let me know not to worry."

The only other time that Hope hadn't taken Evie to the zoo had been when her baby was sick.

He turned to go, making his way through the gift shop back to the entrance. The sight of a tall giraffe caught his attention, though. He went back out to catch Jade's eye. "When did the giraffe come in?"

"Yesterday morning. I can't keep too many of them in stock. They take up too much room."

"Not this one," he told her and went back inside the shop again. He purchased the giraffe from the volunteer operating the cash register—he could never keep up with the names of the people who cycled through Jade's place on a regular basis—and maneuvered the stuffed animal into the back of his SUV. He had to let the giraffe's head stick out the window because it was so tall, which earned a few amused looks when he drove out of the parking lot and turned toward his place.

He doubted that he'd find Hope and Evie inside the house. Even though he'd told her she could use the kitchen in the main house, she hadn't done so yet. He wandered down through "her" wing.

The nursery looked painfully empty without Evie's crib. The rocking chair sat forlornly in the corner. The other toys and stuffed animals were gone, as were the lithographs from the wall.

He walked through the bathroom to Hope's bedroom on the other side.

There wasn't a single thing left to say she'd ever occupied the place. Not even a strand of auburn hair.

Terralee was nothing if not efficient.

He went back outside and wrestled the giraffe out of the back. It wasn't that the animal was particularly heavy, but it was as tall as Ridge. He grabbed it around its brown and yellow torso and lifted it off the ground to carry around to the guesthouse.

The door of which was locked.

He set the giraffe on the porch and looked through the windows, but the wood blinds were angled so that all he could see inside was a few inches of sun-dappled floor.

He tried the doorknob again. Just to be doubly certain it was locked.

Hope didn't have any money. The golf cart was parked in its usual spot off to the side of his house. He texted his mom.

Where was it that you talked to Hope this morning?

But his mother didn't reply. No dancing dots even to indicate that she was in the process of it.

The weather was calling for rain again, so he took the giraffe back over to his house and left it inside the foyer. Then he got in his SUV and headed back down the drive.

Stopping to open and close the gate again was a pain, but until he fixed the opener, there wasn't anything he could do about it.

He aimed the SUV toward the ranch headquarters and called Evie's pediatrician office along the way. No, they hadn't made an appointment that morning to see the baby.

It was something at least.

Gravel spun under his tires when he turned off to the headquarters. His mood was even darker as he spotted Zane standing in front of the massive photocopier. Ridge stopped next to him. "Tract housing, Zane? That's what you have in mind for the Zazlo spread?"

Zane raised his eyebrows, his expression mild. "It's one possibility," he said. He took a sheaf of papers from the copier bin and dumped them in Ridge's surprised hands. "Take those for Hope."

Frowning, he looked down at the stack of colorful sheets in his hands. Boot Camp for Dads!

"What the hell are these?"

Zane shrugged. "What it says. Boot camp for dads. Sabrina asked me to copy 'em so I copied. I was going to drop them off at your place, but now I don't have to and—" he looked at his watch "—I'm late for a meeting." He lifted his hand and strode away.

Ridge turned to head toward Sabrina's office. He got halfway there when Nash stuck his head out of his office. "I thought I heard your voice," he greeted. "You missed our meeting this morning."

"I missed your and Arlo's meeting," Ridge corrected, but he stopped in front of Nash, who'd retreated back into his office. "Here." He slapped down a half dozen of the flyers on his brother's desk. Nash was a new dad. He could use pointers just as much as anyone.

"What're those?"

He regurgitated the brief exchange he'd just had with Zane. "Talk to Sabrina if you have questions."

Nash showed about as much interest as Ridge felt and pushed the flyers to one side. He took a folder from his desk and extended it. "Take a look. It's the budget for the next fiscal year. Want your take on it before we finalize it."

"I've already told you what I thought. We can't expand without acquiring more land."

Nash flicked his fingers. "And we listened. Stop thinking we never do, Ridge." His phone pinged, and after a glance, he immediately answered. "Imani."

Ridge could see the change in his brother's expression just

from saying the woman's name, and he wondered if he looked as besotted where Hope was concerned.

Probably.

Did it bother him?

Not in the least.

He just wished he could *find* her. He left Nash's office and went down to Arlo's. His brother didn't work there all the time since he had his own business to take care of, but he used his office more often than Ridge did. He glanced in. Arlo was leaning back in his chair, his ankles crossed atop his desk. He was talking on the phone. Obviously a business call.

Ridge left him a few flyers, too. Aviva was a toddler already, but the flyer didn't specify any particular age of kids as a focus for the boot camp.

Finally, he went down to Sabrina's office.

And sitting right there, her head bent over a bunch of forms on the desk, was Hope.

His heartbeat jerked around a little as he stood there watching her unawares. Evie was sitting in her stroller next to Hope's chair, and she spotted him, though, and squealed, stretching out her hands, her fingers opening and closing.

Hope looked up then, and her periwinkle gaze crashed into his.

"Where's Sabrina?" he asked thickly.

"Ladies' room."

He dropped the flyers on the desk next to the papers that Hope had been poring over and plucked Evie out of the stroller. "I went looking for you," he said. "I was a little worried when I didn't find you." He buzzed Evie's neck, and she gave a satisfyingly joyful belly laugh. At least one of his ladies was still happy with him.

"I left a note on the counter in the kitchen where I'd be."

He hadn't gone *into* the kitchen.

"Your mom offered me a job," she said. She lifted the paper, and he realized it was an employment application.

"Doing what?"

She frowned slightly at his tone. "Does it matter?"

He exhaled. Nuzzled the other side of Evie's neck until he

earned another belly laugh. Listening to her laugh was the best de-stressor that he could think of.

While she was still chortling, he propped his hip on the corner of Sabrina's desk. "It doesn't matter," he said more reasonably. "Whatever it is, I know you'll be great at it."

Her lashes swept down but not quickly enough to hide the gleam of pleasure. "She wants me to open a day care center to serve the children of all the ranch workers," she told him.

"Are there that many?"

"Ten so far on the waiting list. I happen to know that Chatelaine Hills doesn't have a single day care center."

"Probably a lot of private nannies," he said.

"Yes, but—" she lifted her index finger "—sometimes that is by necessity because there aren't any other options. And particularly affordable options. But, anyway, I wasn't thinking so much about the people who can afford to live in the fancy houses out here as the workers, who more likely live in Chatelaine where it's more affordable and have to drive out here to the lake to make a living. With a good childcare center in the area where they work—"

"You don't have to sell me on this, Hope. I think it's a great idea. But starting small with just the ranch kids isn't a bad thing."

"I know. And that's what I'll do. I have to hire enough staff to meet the local regulations and find a facility that—"

She broke off when Sabrina waddled back into the office, her hands pressed against her back as if she needed a counterweight for her belly.

Ridge swung her chair around for her to sit. He'd sort of been joking earlier about her having the babies, but now he wasn't so sure. "You okay there, sis?"

"Just experiencing the joy of gestating," Sabrina assured breathlessly. She rolled her chair closer to the desk, which wasn't very close at all, and reached for one of her trusty perfectly pointed pencils. "If you haven't seen Nash, he has a copy of the proposed budget for you."

"I've got it." He'd flattened it into a cylinder and stuck it in his back pocket. He actually had some interest in reading it now that he knew about the day care thing. "Did you know your fiancé's planning to build tract houses in Chatelaine? Out near the water tower?"

"If you have a problem with Zane's business, talk to Zane."

"I don't have a problem with it—"

"Zane is buying the Zazlo property?"

He looked at Hope. "That's what I hear."

She frowned slightly. "I'm sorry."

Sabrina's gaze was bouncing between them. "What's going on here?" she said slowly. Suspiciously.

Ridge grimaced. He set Evie back into the stroller and waggled a squishy pink octopus in front of her. She grabbed at it and greedily shoved one of the legs into her mouth. "I was considering buying it," he admitted.

"Kind of far for an expansion of the ranch, isn't it?"

"I wasn't thinking of it as an expansion. I was thinking of it as something *I* would run. Me."

Comprehension dawned on his sister's face. "Oh." She winced slightly and rubbed a soothing hand over one side of her belly. "Foot, I think. Under the ribs." She leaned back in her chair. "You need to tell Mom," she said bluntly.

"How do you know I haven't?"

Sabrina gave him a look.

"I know I need to," he muttered. "I came close this morning, too." Even though Beau knew more about Ridge's plans than anyone—save Hope—he hadn't felt like having that discussion with his mother in front of the other man.

"Excuse me," a timid voice from the doorway interrupted them, and they all looked around to see the mousy receptionist who sometimes filled in when the regular woman was off. Miriam. Marjorie. Something like that. "There's someone here to see Miss—er—Mrs. Marks."

Hope's gaze flew to Ridge's. Her alarm was plain.

"Who?" Ridge's question was sharp.

"Uh. I—" The girl looked uncertain. "I didn't ask his name. He's older, though. Almost bald. Should I go—"

"It's fine, Mariah," Sabrina said. "Thank you."

At least he'd been close on the woman's name. He didn't take his attention from Hope. "I'll go see—"

Despite her obvious alarm, annoyance flickered in the blue depths. "No." She placed her pen carefully on top of the employment form she'd been completing.

There was only one nearly bald older man who'd be seeking Hope out from anywhere, and they all knew it.

"Would you keep Evie back here for me?"

Every instinct he possessed wanted to argue. Only the sudden warning tug on the back of his shirt by his sister reminded him to tread cautiously. Acquiescing, he picked Evie back up from the stroller. She batted him on the head with her octopus. "I'm two seconds away," he told Hope, following her out of the office.

She nodded. She was wearing another bright sweater—this one red—over leggings, and she smoothed the hem as she walked away from him.

Ridge pressed his forehead against Evie's. There was no way in hell he was going to let anyone take her away from Hope.

Sabrina tugged his shirt again. "Look."

He turned to see her holding a monitor almost like the ones that he'd gotten around the house for Evie. It showed a color image of the reception area. "I got this because it was simpler than having to haul myself to my feet and see who was here every time I'm working alone," she explained. "Zane's idea."

The camera showed the top of Mariah's head as she returned to her desk, but it was mostly focused on the entry. His chest ached as he watched Hope cross in and out of the camera's view. Sabrina nudged the control on the camera and followed after Hope.

The guy sitting in one of the chairs was lanky. Definitely balding.

And definitely *not* Howard Marks.

"Holly Marks?" His voice was loud through the monitor.

Hope nodded.

Ridge saw it coming then. And there wasn't a thing he could do about it.

The man extended an envelope, and Hope automatically reached out and took it.

"Consider yourself served," he said with a smirk of satisfaction. Then he walked briskly out of the door.

Ridge met Sabrina's eyes. "Damn," she murmured.

And then some.

"SHE HAS A POINT. Meeting her husband's parents face-to-face for a discussion might defuse the situation. Keep the lawyers out of it. Maybe they can come to a resolution without Hope ever needing to return to Nashville next month for that subpoena."

Ridge glared at Beau, not really sure why the man was there for what Ridge considered a private family matter, but he'd arrived along with Wendy when Sabrina had sent out her bat-signal text to the family and that was that.

"Meeting with Howard and Petunia isn't what I have a problem with," he said now, pacing across the empty break room. Nash had sent everyone home so they could have the building to themselves. He glanced at Hope, who sat at one of the tables scattered around the utilitarian room. "It's meeting with them *alone*," he clarified pointedly.

Her lips tightened and her chin lifted slightly. His mother was seated next to her. She was bouncing Evie slightly on her lap. "This is Hope's decision," she said.

Ridge's nerves tightened. "You agree with her, Mom? Really? You think this is the way to fix—"

Hope suddenly stood. "I'm sorry. Would you all excuse us for a sec?" She wrapped her hand around Ridge's forearm, her fingertips digging.

He followed her out of the room and closed the door to the break room. But that wasn't far enough evidently, because she kept walking, dragging him after her.

All the way outside the building.

Fitting that the clouds were dark as tar and a wind had kicked up.

She let go and turned on him. Her hair lifted around her shoulders. "I don't need you to *fix* me." Her voice shook. "I thought you understood that!"

What he understood was that—once again—what he wanted most in this world was just out of his grasp. "I didn't say fix *you*. I meant this fu—" He ground his teeth together. "This situation," he said finally. "This is how we work, Hope. This family. We do it together."

"Oh, like you're doing Mr. Rancherman together with them," she scoffed. "You won't even tell your mother that you want a ranch of your own. How is that *together*?"

Sometimes he was slow to the party. "Picking a fight with me isn't going to change my mind. Meet Howard and Petunia if you think it's what you need to do. But for God's sake, don't do it all on your own, Hope. You don't need—"

"My name is Holly," she yelled. *"Holly!"*

It felt like a punch to his kidneys.

It hadn't been so long ago that she'd told him she'd wished her name was Hope for real.

"Right," he said. "I'm sorry."

Her shoulders sagged. "I'm sorry! Try to understand, Ridge. Getting my memory back is...hard."

"I know."

"No! You don't know. You can't possibly. You can sympathize, but you can't know." Her hair whipped across her face, and she pushed at it, futilely. "I need to figure out who I am. Who I...who I *want* to be. And I... I can't do that." Her voice thickened. Sounded choked. "I can't do that with you always right there. Ready to save the day when I screw it up."

"You're not screwing up anything."

"I'm screwing up *us*!" She pulled her hair back from her face again, and he could see the tears in her eyes. "You love *Hope*," she said thickly. "The person you found unconscious in your barn. The person you've been playing house with. Evie's mom, who takes her to the petting zoo and steals flowers from people's gardens to put in jars."

His mother was right, he thought.

Happiness slipped through a person's fingers like sand.

"That's *you*," he ground out. But until she could merge her past with her present, he could finally see that no amount of trying on his part would convince her of anything.

He'd known it all along. That she'd break his heart.

Strange that he hadn't been more prepared.

"Stay in the guesthouse as long as you need," he said. "I'll stay out of your way. I'd just like to—" he stared into the wind "—to see Evie now and then."

She sniffled. Wiped the tears with the backs of her hands. "Of course. Evie loves you."

But her mother didn't.

He wiped a raindrop from his cheek.

Maybe it was a raindrop.

Maybe not.

"I appreciate that—" he steeled himself "—Holly."

Then he did the only thing left to do.

He turned and walked away.

CHAPTER FIFTEEN

"BUT YOU *HAVE* to come," Sabrina said. She waved her hand at the lovely watercolor dress that was hanging on the closet door of the guesthouse. "That dress deserves to see a wedding. And Javier and Belinda's grandson is the first one on the list for Fortunate Futures. You can't *not* go!"

Despite the misery that she'd felt ever since Ridge had called her Holly the week before, she couldn't help smiling a little. "We haven't decided on Fortunate Futures as the name for the day care," she reminded Sabrina.

"It's better than Little Darlings or Precious Footsteps." At the first planning meeting for Wendy Fortune's latest business brainchild, both names had been tossed into the hat along with Fortunate Futures and a half dozen more. "It's too bad that we couldn't make use of the space at the castle." Sabrina twitched the fabric of the watercolor dress, and it seemed to shimmer slightly in the sunlight angling through the window.

It was the window that faced directly at Ridge's house, and Holly had taken to keeping the blinds closed. Sabrina had opened them, though.

Holly would have to close them again later.

It was just easier. Stave off temptation and not find herself wallowing at the window, hoping for some fleeting glance of him coming or going.

The only times she had seen him since that awful day the week before were when she took Evie to the petting zoo.

He'd give her a polite nod, take over the stroller and go off with her daughter for a brief period. Proof that he'd meant what he said about keeping his distance, it was always Jade who brought Evie and the stroller back to Hope.

She shook her head. She was worse than all of them.

Holly.

Her gaze landed on the giraffe that had appeared on their doorstep a few days ago, and she looked away again.

She knew things were over for her and Ridge. Had known it when she'd screamed at him like a banshee and he'd used her name. Her *real* name.

For him, Hope was no more. She'd seen it in his eyes.

But things weren't over for Evie and Ridge.

Hope—*dammit*—Holly wasn't sure how she'd be able to stand it.

"The castle is a little far from the ranch," she reminded his sister a little belatedly. "We need a location that is readily accessible for the parents who'll be using the center."

"I know." Sabrina rubbed her back and paced across the small room. "This place isn't even half the size of the guesthouse at Nash's," she said. "What gives with that?"

Holly lifted her shoulder. "Complain to the builder I guess." She knew what Sabrina was really doing there. Trying to keep her mind off the looming meeting that she was having with Howard and Petunia that afternoon. In an effort to find a neutral location, they'd settled on one of the private meeting rooms at the LC Club.

She'd given in on having legal assistance from the Fortunes. Wendy had talked her around on that. So it had been a kindly bespectacled man named Luther Cook who'd reached out to the Markses' lawyer to arrange the meeting, during which both lawyers would remain outside the room. If one was needed to intervene, both would.

Her phone pinged softly, and she picked it up to see the image of Aviva and Evie playing together with a stack of blocks and dolls. Arlo's fiancée, Carrie, had offered to keep Evie, and she'd been providing reassuring messages and pics throughout the day.

"I suppose we should go," Sabrina finally said. She was in charge of delivering Holly to the LC Club.

Holly chewed the inside of her lip and nodded. She brushed her hands down the front of the black slacks she was wearing with a white blouse and black jacket.

"Sometimes a suit is called for, honey," Wendy had said when she'd delivered it the day before. "Whenever I'm feeling nervous, a little Prada or Chanel always helps."

Thankfully, the label inside the garments had been much more mainstream or she would have been too intimidated to wear them.

Holly went into the bathroom long enough to make sure her hair was still smoothed back in a neat ponytail and that her mascara hadn't smeared. She looked like she was on her way to a job interview, quite frankly.

But the suit did make her feel like she walked a little taller. She picked up the leather purse that Wendy had loaned her and opened the door.

Despite herself, she couldn't help looking over at Ridge's house when she opened her umbrella and followed Sabrina to her SUV. Neither his Escalade nor the rusty old pickup were there. Whatever that was supposed to mean.

The umbrella collapsed, she bit back a sigh and fastened her seat belt, closing her eyes. Tried a few of the breathing and visualization tips she'd gotten from the therapist she'd seen at the beginning of the week. She'd already made the appointment before her memory had returned. When she'd gotten the text message reminder about the appointment, she'd decided to go.

Couldn't do any more harm than she'd already done all on her own.

Syrie Landers had proved to be surprisingly down to earth and practical. None of the woo-woo stuff Holly remembered from some of the social workers who'd passed through her youth. "Small steps," she'd told Holly. "Every journey starts with one step. Remember that."

When she opened her eyes again, Sabrina was pulling into

a parking spot at the LC Club. The lot wasn't even half-full. Rainy Thursday afternoons evidently weren't prime time. Sabrina handed her the compact umbrella. "I'll be waiting right here. Luther should have already arrived."

She nodded. "If I forget to tell you later—"

Sabrina squeezed her hand. "I know." Her eyes looked a little damp. "Now, go get 'em."

Holly opened the umbrella and quickly crossed to the entrance. A slender girl in a knee-length sheath dress pointed out the way, and a few minutes later, she was greeting Luther, who was sitting in a chair outside a closed door. He introduced her to the stoic-faced woman who occupied the chair on the other side of the door. "Wanda Ledbetter," he said.

Holly shook her hand. She'd be damned if she'd say "pleased to meet you," since she was anything but. "I appreciate you taking the time today," she settled on.

Then she steeled herself, pushed open the door and went inside. "Hello, Howard." She looked at Petunia sitting next to him at the end of a long table that could have sat sixteen. "Petunia."

She could see Danny's mother looking behind her, as if she expected the door to open again.

"I didn't bring Evie, if that's what you were hoping for. I'm certain your attorney informed you that I would be alone."

Petunia's lips tightened. She whispered something to Howard.

Holly deliberately uncurled her fingers from fisting. She walked over to the table. Pulled out the chair at the end and sat with her hands folded on top of the table in front of her. The power position. She'd seen Wendy Fortune do it many times now. "Thank you for coming."

Petunia's eyes flashed. "As if you gave us a choice?"

"You still have a choice," Holly said. "No one is forcing you to be here. You could have chosen to wait until next month at the courthouse in Nashville. You're the ones bringing a suit against me to take custody of my child."

"*Danny's* child," Petunia said harshly.

"Yes," Holly agreed evenly. "And Danny is gone. Sadly, he's never going to know what a beautiful girl we created."

"He's *gone* because of you."

Howard put a calming hand on Petunia's. "You agreed," he said under his breath, but not so much so that Holly couldn't hear.

Petunia looked angry, but she clamped her lips together.

Funny. But Holly had never realized how much more Danny had resembled her than he had Howard. She'd always thought he'd looked more like his dad.

"How *is* Evie?" Howard asked gruffly.

"She's fine. She's starting to talk some. Crawls like a fiend." She leaned down and pulled the manila envelope from the purse. Then stood and carried the envelope down to him. "She loves her bath time and being outdoors." She set the envelope on the table near Howard and returned to her seat. "She's a good eater and a good sleeper and she's the light of my life. And—" she folded her hands again and hoped that her white knuckles weren't visible from their end of the table "—she deserves to have a relationship with her grandparents."

"*We* should be raising her," Petunia said, obviously striving to keep herself in check.

"Why? Because you think I don't know the way families should behave? That somehow, because I was pretty much raised in the foster care system my whole life, I lack something that *you* possess?"

"Danny told us about your past."

"My past that could be a lot worse than it was? I never did drugs. I could have. The opportunity was there almost every day of my life. I graduated from high school. Earned a scholarship to get a child development degree. How about you, Petunia? What's your *past* like?" She squeezed her hands tighter, counting in her head until her racing heart slowed back down again.

"If that's some sort of threat—"

"You beat Danny once with a pair of scissors," she said quietly. "He had a scar on his shoulder from it."

"Enough," Howard said heavily. "Nobody's life looks perfect when you shine a magnifying glass over it. Including Danny's." He'd slid the photographs out from the envelope, and they were spread across the table in front of him. She saw the way his fingers trembled a little as he touched the most recent one of Evie, with her hair tied up in a tiny ponytail on the top of her head while she reached out to pet one of Jade's bearded goats. "She looks like you," he said.

"I think she's beautiful, so I'll take that as a compliment."

"Howard, this is a waste of time," his wife snapped.

"If you don't behave yourself, Pet, you can sit outside with that termagant of a lawyer you hired."

Holly sank her teeth into her tongue to keep from reacting.

Howard looked at Holly. "I'm sixty-five years old," he said. "By the time Evie's school-age, I—*we*—" he gave his wife a pointed look "—will be seventy. When you say you want Evie to have a relationship with us, what does that mean?"

"Not having *had* grandparents," Holly said carefully, "I can only say that I think it means extra hugs. Extra love. Phone calls just to chatter together. Trips to a zoo. Maybe an overnight now and then." She lifted her palms. "It means what it needs to mean. But it doesn't mean usurping my role as her *mother*."

"I'm telling you, Howard—"

"I warned you, Pet." He gave his wife a look. "I let you spoil Danny his entire life, and he became an unhappy, discontented adult who'd sooner lie to us about the color of the sky than tell the truth. And I bear just as much blame as you for not stopping it when I had the chance.

"Now." Howard turned back to Holly. "Let's cut to the chase, shall we?"

She realized her mouth had dropped open and quickly shut it. She nodded once. "Let's."

"STILL IN THERE, I take it." Ridge stood outside of his sister's SUV, his shoulders hunched against the damp.

"Yeah." Sabrina eyed him. "You could sit inside you know. The LC Club. My car. Either would be better than standing out in the rain."

"I don't want to chance her knowing I'm here."

She quirked a brow. "Taking the distance thing a little far, don't you think?"

"I'm giving her what she wants."

"Right now, Hope doesn't know *what* she wants. Zane called it, you know. Said she's in survival mode. Just trying to get through. He'd felt that way when he'd ended up being responsible for raising his siblings. It won't last forever."

"It's been almost two hours. Let me know what happens." He flipped his collar up and angled across the large parking lot. He'd parked around the block in the lot for a small strip of medical offices.

Ridge was soaked through by the time he reached the Escalade. The only thing he had to dry himself with was a forgotten blanket of Evie's. He ran it over his face and head and sat there for another hour with the pink fabric twisting in his hands before he got a text from Sabrina.

No words. Just a thumbs-up.

He lowered his head and breathed fully for the first time in days.

CHAPTER SIXTEEN

HOLLY STOOD OUTSIDE of the town hall building and wondered what she was doing there.

Javier and Belinda Mendes would have plenty of people present to celebrate their latest nuptials without Holly being there.

A thin man wearing a cowboy hat and dress boots brushed past her and pulled open the heavy door. "Going inside?"

She brushed her hands down the sides of the watercolor dress. Her cell phone was tucked in one of the hidden side pockets. A small jeweler's box was in the other.

Holly knew what she was doing there.

She'd left Evie in Howard's care back at the guesthouse. Her former father-in-law had told her he'd sent Petunia back home to Nashville the morning after they'd met.

She wasn't sure she would have left her baby with him if Petunia had still been there.

Yes, they'd all agreed to some general terms.

But Holly would believe Petunia could refrain from trying to take over again when she saw it.

Howard, though? He'd been a lot more convincing.

She only needed to stay long enough to get through the wedding ceremony. Maintain her self-control long enough to give Ridge back the pendant. She could wait until she got back to the guesthouse before falling apart and then somehow summoning the willpower to do everything else that needed doing.

Finding a more permanent place to live was at the head of the list.

She obviously couldn't remain in Ridge's guesthouse.

Another person brushed past her, heels clicking loudly on the floor tile and clearly following one of the signs with the word *wedding* flowing in elegant script across the board.

She followed, too, and caught her breath a little in pure feminine appreciation when she slipped into the back of the event room. Clearly, practice made perfect where the Mendeses' wedding decor was concerned. Her intention of remaining in the back of the room went by the wayside when Jade and Heath came in right after her. Jade wrapped her hands around Holly's wrist and pulled her down the aisle between the seats to the bunch of chairs surprisingly near the front that were still vacant.

If she'd had more of her wits about her, she would have realized she'd let Jade shuffle her into the seat right behind Ridge.

He looked over his shoulder at her. Then his sister.

Jade immediately shuffled one seat over, making room for Ridge, who made Holly gape when he stepped right over the back of the pretty white folding chair to take the seat next to her.

His hand closed around hers almost the way that Jade's had, except *his* touch made her tremble, and when he pressed his thumb against her pulse, she was left wondering if it was hers that thumped so hard, or his.

"Stay," he said. "The music's already starting."

And it was. Amid the lovely swags of white fabric and the clusters of palest pink roses, the string trio seated in the corner of the room had begun the traditional wedding march.

A smiling man wearing a black suit moved to the center at the head of the aisle and opened a Bible. He was obviously the officiant.

Sabrina, who was sitting in the row behind Holly, leaned forward as they stood in preparation for the "mystery" bride to enter. "Pool's up to two hundred bucks," she whispered.

Despite everything, Holly had to bite back a smile. Far as

she was concerned, Sabrina still had the inside track, knowing about the Mendeses' vacation requests.

The music reached a crescendo, and the doors at the back of the room opened again. She craned her neck to see, but all she got was a glimpse of a flowing champagne-hued gown.

All around her, though, she heard gasps.

"I'll be—"

"*No* way!"

"Ssh!" Jade was trying to hush her siblings without success.

"Holy sh—" Ridge cut off his stunned reaction when Holly hastily poked him in the side before snatching back her hand and clasping it at her waist.

And then she, too, could just stare as the bridal couple came level with their row.

Wendy Fortune, radiant in silk and lace and carrying an elegantly simple bouquet of long-stem roses, smiled at them and gave a little wink before she continued forward on the arm of a very handsome-looking Beau Weatherly.

Holly looked at the faces around her.

To say they all looked shocked was putting it mildly.

"Please be seated," the officiant invited, and there was a general shuffling in the room as the music trailed away and the guests sat.

And watched in dumbfounded consensus as Wendy Windham Fortune became Mrs. Beau Weatherly.

Later, of course, it all made sense.

The mysterious requests for a favorite photograph as a gift. For a meaningful quotation.

After the ceremony, Holly, still unable to extricate herself from the throng of Ridge and his siblings, found herself sitting in the adjacent room that had been decorated just as beautifully for the reception. The string trio had been replaced by a small live band, and servers were moving in and around the tables offering food and drink while the bride and groom took command of the dance floor in a wholly *un*traditional tango that left Wendy's sons looking up at the ceiling and down at the floor and Wendy's daughters muffling their delight behind their hands.

The rest of the guests all stood up with a whooping holler

when the dance concluded with Beau leaning Wendy over in a swoon-worthy dip.

Then the radiant bride rose and kissed her new husband and spontaneously tossed the long-stem rose bouquet she'd been holding all the while.

It sailed through the air and landed squarely in Ridge's lap.

He looked chagrined and after a moment handed the bouquet to Holly.

Her face felt on fire. She wanted to push it away but she also didn't want to make a scene. She ended up setting the beautiful stems in the center of the table. "We'll all enjoy them," she said.

Fortunately, Wendy and Beau were beckoning others to join them on the dance floor, and amid the commotion, Holly was able to finally escape.

She made it as far as the bathroom down the hall before the tears came. She closed herself in a stall and cried until she couldn't cry any more.

She cried for the naive girl who'd married for all the right reasons but still hadn't found happiness. Mostly, she cried for the Hope she'd never really been. She cried until someone tapped on the door. "Y'alright in there, hon?"

"Fine," she said thickly. And waited until the woman had flushed and washed and left again.

She left the stall and shook her head at her reflection. Eyes swollen. Nose red.

"Lovely," she muttered.

"You are." Ridge stepped into the room and closed the door.

Her heart climbed into her throat. "You can't be in here."

"And yet—" he spread his arms, looking ridiculously handsome in his perfectly tailored black suit and caramel-colored silk T-shirt "—I *am* in here." As if to drive the point, he flipped the lock on the door.

She pressed her hands behind her against the marble counter. The wedding decor had continued even into the bathroom, she realized. A vase of glorious roses sat next to the sink, and in the little sitting area, the bench was draped with oyster-colored satin.

"Sabrina told me you left Evie with Howard?"

She lifted her chin slightly. "Yes. I'm sure you think that was a bad idea."

"I think it was the *only* idea." He stepped closer. "He's Evie's grandfather. Villanueva did a check on him. Seems to be a stand-up guy except for his taste in a wife."

"He sent her back to Nashville."

"I heard." He took another step toward her.

She sidled around him, almost surprised that he let her reverse their positions. Only, once she'd succeeded, she didn't really know what to do next. The music from the reception was still perfectly audible—a painfully romantic "Someone Like You."

She nervously shoved her hands into her pockets. She could unlock the door. Leave.

Why didn't she?

"The giraffe is huge," she said abruptly.

His hooded gaze was serious. But his beautiful mouth smiled slightly. "It was huge. Head stuck out the window like a happy dog when I drove it home."

She pressed her lips together. The image in her head was priceless. "Evie loves it," she managed after a moment.

Her fingers toyed with the jeweler's box.

The reason she'd come to what she'd thought would be a mildly interesting wedding. "Quite the surprise from your mom and Beau."

"Quite. Apparently, they've been involved all along. Kept it quiet at first because it was so soon after my father died. Then kept it quiet longer because..." He shrugged. "Who knows? My mother is nothing if not surprising."

"You *never* suspected?"

He shook his head. "Probably should have. But I've had a pretty big distraction of my own."

She felt her skin flush and realized she'd retreated again only because the back of her knees bumped the satin-covered bench, and she sat with an inelegant plop. "You don't have to worry about distractions anymore," she said. "So you can move on to Oklahoma or...or wherever and—"

"I'm not going to Oklahoma or any other wherever."

"I thought Zane was buying the Zazlo property."

"Got it right that time," he murmured. "He is. At least that was the plan last I heard." He stepped closer.

She was having the hardest time breathing normally. Maybe she was allergic to roses and had never known it before. She fastened her hands around the jewelry box and yanked it from her pocket. She stuck out her hand, the box between them. As if it would ward him off or something. "You need to take this back."

He didn't reach for it.

She thumbed the box lid. Pushed it open. The beautiful key pendant nestled among the velvet exactly where it had been the day he'd given it to her. "It was your Christmas gift to me."

"I know what it is." His deep brown gaze had hers ensnared, and she couldn't seem to look away to save her life. "It was a gift, Holly."

The name was like a nail in a coffin. How could she not have known that?

"It's too much."

"If you don't want it, sell it. Start Evie's college fund or put a down payment on a car."

"I could never—"

"What? Sell something that has value but is otherwise meaningless?"

"It's *not* meaningless!"

His eyebrow peaked. "You've never worn it. I assumed you didn't care for it."

"It's from you. Of course I cared for it." The words felt wrenched out of her. "I loved it just like I lo—"

His eyebrow went up another millimeter.

She swiped her face, looking away from him. There was a window above the locked door. A little cascade of ivory and a rosebud was fastened in the corner.

Wendy didn't miss a detail.

Her hand was shaking. She finally lowered it to her lap. "Why did you change your mind about leaving?" She thumbed the lid down on the blue box. "Realize you don't have to go anywhere to invent your next gizmo?"

"I don't want to go any place where *you* are not," he said evenly.

She trembled. "You don't mean that."

"One of these days—" he went down on one knee next to the bench "—you're going to get tired of telling me I don't mean what I very sincerely do." He opened the box and extracted the pendant.

It swung from the fine chain, glittering gently.

"The key is to my heart." His voice was suddenly gruff. "I thought it was a pretty obvious symbol. And you didn't want it." His fingers looked too big to work the tiny, delicate clasp, but he succeeded anyway. He leaned closer to her, bringing with him the scent that had always been faintly heady. Reaching behind her neck, he fastened the necklace, then trailed his fingers down the length of the chain to the pendant that nestled right above her heart.

"But like it or not, it's yours." His fingers went from the pendant to tuck beneath her chin. "I told you before, Holly. You are my *hope*."

Tears sprang to her eyes.

"You are everything I want in this life. You and Evie. And I am not going to go *anywhere* unless you're by my side. Since you're here, that means I'll be here, too." His gaze roved restlessly over her face. He lightly brushed his thumb over her lip.

She could hardly breathe, waiting almost desperately for his head to lower. To feel his kiss again.

His hand fell away.

He pushed to his feet.

"I know you're not ready. But that doesn't change the way I feel. I want to marry you. I want to give Evie my name and a passel of little brothers and sisters to boss around. And if you're never ready?" His lips twisted ruefully. Sadly. "Holly." He flipped the lock and pulled the door open. "Gangreenia Crudbucket," he added. "I'll still love you until there's no more me left."

Then he excused himself and sidled past the line of women that had formed outside of the door.

"So romantic," the first to rush inside gushed. She slammed herself inside a stall.

Another woman followed. “Honey, if you don’t want him, I do.”

Holly pushed to her feet. “Sorry,” she said thickly. “He’s taken.”

She looked up and down the hall for him but didn’t see him. There were so many wedding guests milling about and the music was loud enough that when she called his name, her voice was just swallowed in the noise.

She hurried to the main staircase and looked down. Just in case.

The only person at the base of the stairs was the security guard, leaning against his post and tapping his highly polished boot in time to the music.

She whirled on her heel and hurried back to the reception hall, working her way through the tables and the servers still bearing more food. More wine. Champagne. Cocktails.

She grabbed a sparkling flute as one passed by her and gulped down half.

And then she spotted him.

On the dance floor, doing a very sedate waltz with a woman who looked old enough to be his grandmother.

She left the unfinished champagne on a table and crossed the dance floor. She tapped the woman’s brocade-covered shoulder. “May I cut in?”

The woman had snapping black eyes. “If I were a few years younger,” she quipped, “I’d tell you no way. But I’ve got a mile-high slice of wedding cake waiting at my table along with a double bourbon, so.” She grinned and surrendered her spot.

And suddenly, Holly’s confidence wavered.

She stared up into Ridge’s beautiful eyes. The eyes that had never once wavered in kindness. In caring.

In love.

He stood there, hands waiting for her while the dancers moved around them.

Take a breath, she thought. Every worthwhile journey started with just one step.

“Hi,” she said, feeling giddy happiness start to swell inside her. This time, she knew whatever was to come, she wouldn't be alone.

Ridge loved her.

And she loved him.

She stuck out her hand as if they were meeting for the first time. "Call me Hope."

He closed his hand around hers. "For the rest of our lives," he said.

Her eyes filled again. But there was no grief. No pain. Only joy. "I love you." She cleared her throat. "For the rest of our lives."

His smile was slow. He drew her against him so closely she couldn't tell his heartbeat from hers.

And they danced.

Across the room, Beau pressed his lips against his bride's temple while they watched her youngest son circle the dance floor with his beloved. "I told you it would work out," he said.

Wendy leaned against him. How quickly and how easily he'd become her strength. Her roots. "You did," she said a little tearfully. "I was so afraid he would want to go."

"He still might."

"But they'll go with him. He'll have that."

"Yes. And he'll always come back home."

She sighed and turned into his arms, looping her hands around his neck. "Have I told you how handsome you look today? The suit is *very* sexy." She tucked her tongue lightly between her teeth for a moment. "But I happen to know what's underneath is even better."

"Are you propositioning me, Mrs. Weatherly?"

"Every chance I get, Mr. Weatherly."

He looked over her shoulder at the satin-draped table of cards and gifts that people had brought, even though their deliberately cryptic invitation to all their guests had plainly stated that the only gift desired was the invitee's presence. "Maybe we should glance through some of that stuff," he said. "Because darlin', once we start our consummating it's going to be a long while before you're interested in doing anything else."

Wendy's laugh came from her very soul. It was the first thing that had attracted her to Beau. His ability to make her genuinely, truly laugh. Life had given them a second chance together, and they were both grabbing on with ten fingers and ten toes each. "Consummating," she mimicked his drawl. "As if you're some backwoods moonshiner hitchin' his wife."

"Don't knock a good moonshine."

She laughed again and swept up a handful of the cards. Around his shoulder she could see that all of her children were on the dance floor. Even Sabrina. "I hope she doesn't overdo it," she murmured. Much as she loved them, she didn't want to cut short the *consummating* for an emergency trip to the delivery room. "Here." She handed Beau a few cards. "We'll open these and then—" She batted her eyes at him.

He tore open the first of the cards with almost indecent haste. "Congratulations to the happy couple," he read. "From the mayor." He tossed it aside and tore open the next. It contained a similar sentiment. "Pretty hard for people to be personal when they don't know who they're sending the card to in the first place."

"Very true. Look at this one." Wendy was wagging a gold rimmed card that she'd pulled from its heavy, unmarked envelope. "A weekend awaits you as our guest at the Fortune's Gold Guest Ranch," she read. She turned the fancy white card over. The printing on the other side was in gold. "Gift of Fortune," she said. She tapped the card against her chin. "Interesting."

"Fortune's Gold is hours away," Beau remarked. "The guest ranch there's pretty famous." He tugged everything out of her hand and tossed it all aside before drawing her to his feet. "Wouldn't be the worst place to spend a weekend." He kissed her lips. "Probably find some random connection to more of your wild and crazy family."

"We're not wild and crazy," she defended. "We're—"

"Perfectly unique," he assured. Then he wrapped his arm

around her waist. The band had struck up a rousing "Celebration" that had nearly every person in the place crowding onto the dance floor.

He caught his bride around the waist. And giggling like young new lovers, they snuck out.

Because.

Consummating awaited.

* * * * *

The Cowboy's Rodeo Redemption

Susan Breeden

MILLS & BOON

Susan Breeden is a native Texan who currently lives in Houston, where she works as a technical writer/editor for the aerospace industry. In the wee hours of morning and again at night, you will find her playing matchmaker for the heroes and heroines in her novels. She also enjoys walks with her bossy German shepherd, decluttering and organizing her closet, and trying out new chili con queso recipes. For information on Susan's upcoming books, visit susanbreeden.com.

Books by Susan Breeden

Harlequin Heartwarming

Destiny Springs, Wyoming

The Bull Rider's Secret Son
Her Kind of Cowboy

Visit the Author Profile page at
millsandboon.com.au
for more titles.

Dear Reader,

I suspect many of us have a special someone who "got away" but maintains permanent residence in our heart. In *The Cowboy's Rodeo Redemption*, the heroine does more than live in the hero's heart. She reappears on his doorstep after ten years.

For Nash, Jess didn't "get away." She abandoned their friendship before he could summon the courage to express his true feelings. Now, giving his twins a stable home is his top priority. By contrast, Jess wants her daughter to achieve the height of barrel-racing success—a dream that Jess herself gave up in favor of settling down. Only, she needs her former crush's help. When old and reignited feelings are revealed, they must decide whether to repeat history by hiding and running away...or embrace this opportunity.

In this third book in my Destiny Springs, Wyoming series, Nash and Jess receive a rare second chance to get it right.

I hope you enjoy their story, and that you have all the second chances in life that you want...and deserve!

Warmest wishes,

Susan Breeden

For the Joneses.

CHAPTER ONE

NASH BUCHANAN SHOULD have been stressing out. But all those daisies made it impossible.

He stared at the whiteboard that was leaning against a wall in the breakfast nook. Its designated place. A few hours ago, he'd used the board to write out his daily to-do list—a ritual that was as much a part of his mornings as the two cups of black coffee from his favorite mug. But all that productive thinking had been literally erased. Now, the board was covered in hand-drawn flowers of various colors and sizes instead.

All was not lost. He was reasonably sure that he and his ranch hand, Parker Donnelly, had completed most of the tasks already. The rest, he'd figure out. He didn't even have to ask which of his twins had cultivated this garden.

"Elizabeth Anne? Can you come here for a minute, sweetheart?"

Never one to take a proper nap, Lizzy had been playing in the den while her sister slept in their bedroom. Nash took advantage of the time to catch up on paperwork in the adjacent study, within earshot, which had given his daughter ample opportunity to do her brand of damage.

Then again, both girls had been in and out of the kitchen throughout the morning, pretending to make breakfast on the toy kitchen set that he'd assembled and placed in a corner. He would reserve final judgment until he could ask the necessary questions.

The pattering of little feet paused at the entrance to the kitchen. The fact that Nash used Lizzy's full name rather than her nickname must have tipped her off that she'd crossed a line.

He lifted the board, swiveled and held it up for her to see.

The precious giggle that followed confirmed what he already knew. There was no better sound to Nash's ears, except it tended to let her get away with just about anything. But with school starting in less than a month, he needed to make sure any boundary issues were addressed. The first-grade teachers might not be so understanding about having their lessons erased from the chalkboard and flowers drawn in their place.

"Do you like it, Daddy? I drew it for you 'cause you're sad a lot."

Sad? Preoccupied, perhaps, but he understood why he'd come across that way. Trying to take care of his sprawling Wyoming Buck Stops Ranch with little to no help, and making it a home his children could grow up in and he could grow old in, did that to a person. Now that Parker had three solid months of experience on the ranch, Nash was beginning to feel much better. Although, in all fairness, Lizzy's random crops of hand-drawn daisies deserved some of the credit.

Finally, he had time to focus on being a daddy to his six-year-old twins, even if he couldn't fulfill the role of mommy, as well. The ladies in Destiny Springs were wonderful role models, if not steady or permanent ones. He'd given up on *steady* and *permanent* long ago.

Nash returned the board to its place, pulled out a chair for Lizzy and pointed for her to sit. After she settled in, he took a seat across from her.

"The flowers are beautiful, but do you remember what we talked about? How this is my chore board and it's important? That's why I bought you and Katherine Claire your own to draw on." Nash made it a point to use Kat's formal name, as well, if only to keep things as balanced and equal as possible. Whether that was a rule for raising twins, he wasn't sure, but it felt right in most cases.

Lizzy looked to her bare feet, which were swinging anxiously while dangling from the too-tall chair. "Kat drew on half of it."

Nash studied the board again. The girls were physically identical. Wispy blondish hair, jet-black lashes, soft brown eyes. But they differed in almost every other way, including artistically. Lizzy was creative, whereas Kat was analytical.

"Is that so? Which flowers are hers?" he asked, giving Lizzy a chance to either take back the accusation or prove it.

She pointed to a couple of stick pony figures in the lower corner. He hadn't even noticed them. Definitely Kat's handiwork, but still…

"Half, huh?"

Lizzy neither denied nor confirmed. Although the little girl struggled with basic mathematical concepts, he was pretty sure she knew better in this instance.

"Stay right there." He stood, walked to the refrigerator and poured two glasses of milk, adding chocolate syrup to hers. After placing both on the table, he retrieved the last giant chocolate chip cookie, compliments of Becca Sayers at the Hideaway—Destiny Spring's local B and B. She'd brought over three yesterday as a bribe. Said she needed a favor. But two of the treats mysteriously disappeared within hours.

He sat back down. As predicted, Lizzy eyed the dessert.

"Want half?" he asked.

She nodded and sat up straighter.

He broke off a tiny piece, placed it on a napkin and slid it in front of her.

She looked crestfallen. And more than a little perturbed. Exactly the response he was going for.

"That's not half!" she said.

He took a big bite out of the cookie and pointed to the board again, hoping she'd get the point he was trying to make.

"But I like to draw more than Kat does."

Nash took an even bigger bite, taking extra time to chew and swallow. "And I like this cookie more than you do. Is there anything you want to clarify?"

Lizzy huffed and looked down. "Okay. She didn't draw *half*."

"And whose idea was it to erase the board and draw in the first place?" he asked.

"Mine. I s'pose."

Nash smiled, then broke off a bigger section from the part he had yet to bite into. He paused before relinquishing it and waited until she looked him in the eye.

"I appreciate you wanting to cheer me up," he said. "But next time, let's find a better place to plant your garden. Agreed?"

At that, Lizzy smiled and accepted the cookie. Hopefully, she accepted the lesson, as well. Time would tell.

While Lizzy proceeded to dip her cookie into her glass of chocolate milk and make an appropriate mess, he tiptoed down the hall. Kat's slow, deep breathing was noticeable beneath the thick pink blanket. That half of the twin equation had no problem with naps. Maybe because her Breyer horses were all lined up on her dresser as if protecting her in ways that her own daddy couldn't.

Which brought him back around to her horse stick figures on the whiteboard and reminded him of the most important bullet point of all. Not that he'd forgotten.

That favor Becca wanted? In Nash's opinion, it was worth more than three cookies. Although, in all honestly, he wouldn't have said no under any circumstances. Folks helped other folks in this close-knit community. One of Becca's guests was transporting a horse and needed a place to board it for two weeks. In fact, the woman should have already arrived, if his estimation was correct. Becca had texted about twenty minutes ago, indicating that the guest was on her way. What she hadn't told him was the woman's name.

At least he'd insisted on one condition: the guest had to take care of the feeding and exercising and grooming herself.

"Daddy! Somebody's here," Lizzy called out. Kat barely stirred.

Nash closed the door behind him and went into the den, where he and Lizzy watched the truck and trailer head down the drive. After parking, a woman stepped out, glanced toward the house and ran both hands through her hair in a way that was all too familiar.

He closed his eyes as if it would block out the memories. Instead, it trapped them inside, where they fully awakened.

How could something that happened ten years ago get to him now? Jessica McCoy had been one of his students. And students left sometimes, although they usually gave at least a day's notice and a reason why. Especially the ones who were responsible adults within a few years of his age. Even more so, those he also considered good friends. In every case, they'd at least say goodbye.

Make that, in every case except Jess's.

Then again, the most important women in his past had never bothered with such formalities. Why should she have been any different?

Nash opened his eyes and considered that perhaps he was wrong. Maybe this woman only resembled Jess from a distance, although eerily so. Same slender frame. Same porcelain skin. Same silky black hair, although it was cut closer to her shoulders instead of grazing her waist.

No. That was Jess, all right. Either that, or she had a twin he never knew about. And, at one time, he knew so much about her. Or so he thought.

At least he could take comfort in the fact that she was more than capable of caring for her horse, and he could stay out of it. When he'd first agreed to this, it crossed his mind that he may have to step in anyway, for the horse's sake.

He was tempted to go outside and help, but his feet felt as though they were nailed to the hardwood floor. Instead, he watched as she walked around to the horse trailer and conversed with its occupant.

"Is that my mommy?" Lizzy asked.

"No. I'm afraid not."

He should have been used to that question, but it tugged at his heart every time. His ex-wife abandoned them all when the twins were born. She'd come back around when they were toddlers, only to leave again. Without saying goodbye either time. If she ever did return one day, to stay, he wouldn't let her back in.

"She's pretty," Lizzy said.

She sure is. Even more so than he remembered.

He placed a hand over his chest to calm what felt like a palpitation. It was just stress. Yet, it hadn't happened in years.

"Do me a favor, sweetheart. Go to your room and draw me some daisies. Lots of them," he managed to say, even though a quicksand feeling in his stomach tried to tug the words back inside.

"Are you gonna give 'em to the lady?"

It was a logical assumption, but not a chance. They were for him.

"Maybe if you draw enough to share half, I will. Now scoot!" He pivoted her toward the hallway, then gave her a kiss on the back of the head and a loving shove.

Just in time. Jess was making her way up the steps but paused at the door. He was pretty sure she couldn't have seen them watching from the window, so he wasn't in a rush to answer it.

She lingered for quite a while, as well. He could safely assume why. As with Lizzy pausing at the kitchen door, Jess had to have known what she'd done. She could have returned his call with some sort of explanation. At least he'd been able to get ahold of her folks to confirm that she was all right.

Once she knocked, he paused for a few moments before answering, still unsure of what to say. One thing was for certain: maybe Buck Stops was open to board a visitor's horse for a couple of weeks.

But his heart was closed for business.

WHEN THE DOOR eased open and Nash leaned against the door frame, Jess's breath caught in her throat.

At least he didn't slam the door shut. Not that he would do something like that. Odd, but he didn't seem shocked to see her. Maybe Becca had told him her name, even though Jess had indicated she wanted to surprise Nash.

He didn't say a word, and he'd never been shy about speaking his mind. Yet, he didn't really have to. The way he cocked his head and blinked suggested he was waiting for a long-overdue explanation.

She couldn't explain it back then. How could she articulate it now? She never thought she'd land on his doorstep again. Otherwise, she would have made a more graceful exit. But how do you say goodbye to a man you're in love with but who's clearly in love with someone else? A smarter, prettier, more talented someone at that?

Easy. When you're Jessica McCoy, you don't say goodbye. You simply leave.

They stood in silence until she couldn't take it any longer. She stepped forward and embraced him. Even though they'd been in a student-teacher situation, they'd also become friends. Hugs had come naturally. This one, however, was anything but.

He tensed at first, then softened a little.

"It's good to see you again," Jess whispered, before taking a step back.

He didn't return the sentiment, and he'd barely returned the hug, yet his soft brown eyes suggested that perhaps he felt the same. Then, just as swiftly, he straightened his posture and looked past her.

"Becca tells me you need to board your horse for a couple of weeks."

Jess scraped her splattered ego off the ground after that obviously unwelcome display of affection, pulled her shoulders back and looked out to the trailer. "Two weeks. Then we'll head to Montana for the rodeo there in three. And it's Taylor's horse."

"Your husband?"

"Daughter. She's back at the Hideaway. Becca graciously agreed to babysit for me while I came over here."

"Your daughter is in good hands," Nash said without so much as looking at her.

"That's what I hear." His words further confirmed what Jess had already concluded. Even though she'd talked to Becca only a few times over the phone, they shared a mutual acquaintance who couldn't speak highly enough of the B and B and its sweet owner.

After several moments, they settled back into that place of silence. The whole thing was awkward, to say the least, which was the reason she hadn't wanted to bring Taylor with her. That would have really put Nash on the spot with what she was about to ask.

Her talented eight-year-old daughter had hit a plateau and needed help from the best barrel racing teacher Jess could think of. She wasn't going to let a little thing like her pride get in the way of giving Taylor the type of career Jess herself could have had.

Not that she'd trade having Taylor for anything, even with everything else it had entailed. Specifically, giving up that career to be a full-time stay-at-home mom and wife after taking what was supposed to be a brief sabbatical. Being anchored to one place, rather than traveling the country. Then giving *that* up to be a widow who was left without a financial safety net.

Maybe she would've seen it coming if she hadn't trusted a man who was less than transparent. Lesson learned…and ultimately rewarded, with Taylor picking up where her abandoned stirrups left off. And making a lasting impression in the rodeo world. *Their* world.

She couldn't undo her mistakes, but hopefully she could correct the one that was right in front of her. But that would have to wait anyway, because a sweet little voice called out from behind Nash.

"Daddy! Here's your flowers!" The beautiful little girl handed him a board with a colorful drawing, which made Nash himself blossom.

There's that smile I loved.

"So, you have a little one, too," Jess said.

Nash looked up as if he'd momentarily forgotten she was there. "Where are my manners? This is Elizabeth, but she goes by Lizzy these days."

Jess didn't even have to ask. Although Lizzy favored Nash, she was definitely Roxanne's little girl. Which meant that Nash had ended up marrying Jess's main competition after all.

Even though she shouldn't have been surprised, the gut punch caught her off guard. At the same time, she knew Roxanne was now married to someone else and continued to compete.

Speaking of manners, Nash had yet to ask her inside. But with Mischief waiting in the trailer, she didn't want to linger.

"Go wake up Kat, please. Then you two can come join us on the porch."

"Okay, Daddy," Lizzy said, disappearing down the hall.

Nash stepped outside and left the door cracked open behind him.

"Is Kat your wife?" she asked.

"Daughter. Lizzy's twin. Double trouble, but the good kind."

Raising even one child alone was a challenge—albeit also the good kind. But two? Then again, she simply assumed he was raising them by himself. She could be very wrong. Part of her was aching to ask. He wasn't wearing a ring, and she always figured him for the ring-wearing kind of man. Traditional and loyal.

"And double fun, too, I imagine," she said.

That didn't earn her the warm smile she'd hoped for. More of a slow nod.

"Tell me about the horse," he said, switching the topic again as if Jess was getting too personal. That was fine, because she needed to keep her focus on the reason why she was there in the first place.

"Mischief is a quarter horse. Eight years old, like Taylor, and he's her secret weapon in barrel racing. She's been called The One to Watch. Maybe you've heard of her? Taylor Simms?"

"Simms, did you say?"

"Taylor wanted to keep her daddy's last name after he died. I get it. I changed mine back to McCoy."

Jess wanted to add that she felt it impossible to move forward with the life she and Taylor envisioned without changing hers back. But it didn't feel like the appropriate time for that kind of disclosure.

Nash's eyes softened. "I had no idea. I'm sorry for your loss."

She simply nodded. She hadn't meant to even say that much. Time to get the conversation back on track.

"We're doing good, though. Especially Taylor with her barrel racing. She could be even better. You know how stiff the competition is."

Nash blew out a long breath, then straightened his shoulders and looked straight ahead again. "I exited those circles several years ago, and I don't keep up. No desire to get back into it, either. Don't have the time."

Jess gulped. Had this trip been for nothing? "You don't teach anymore?"

"No, ma'am."

There was a resoluteness to his answer. A "this topic is closed" quality about it. Furthermore, their lives had drifted further apart than she'd ever imagined they'd be. That's what ten years could do. Prior to that, they'd had a strong connection. The rodeo was his world.

And he'd been more open back then. No emotional walls like the one she was slamming into today.

The door opened, and the twins joined them outside. Both wearing matching rubber boots but otherwise dressed quite differently. Lizzy was in the same flowered long-sleeved dress as she'd been a few moments ago. Her twin sported tan breeches and a pink puffer jacket. At least their daddy would be able to tell them apart.

"Lizzy and Kat, this is Jess. She'll be keeping her horse on our property for a couple of weeks," Nash said.

Kat looked up at her. "I like the horses more than I like the cows."

"That's an understatement," Nash said. "Let's get Mischief situated, shall we, ladies? Jess, follow that dirt road. We'll meet you there." He pointed to a path that led to the stables in the distance, even though he hadn't needed to. She remembered.

Jess drove solo while the Buchanan clan walked, with Nash anchored by a twin on each side. All holding hands.

Once they got Mischief situated in his temporary digs, Nash insisted on giving Jess a tour of the property, even though once again, she didn't need one. Not much about it had changed except the arena was so stark. No barrels. Not even any circular scars in the dirt to indicate they'd ever been there.

His horses were out in the field, lingering by a fence. Probably curious about their new stablemate. The girls ran over to pet them while Nash watched the goings-on with that warm, familiar smile again. All of a sudden, it seemed as though no time had passed.

"What did the bartender say to the horse when he sat down at the bar?" Jess asked.

Nash cast her a questioning look. "I have no idea."

"Why the long face?" she answered.

Nash shook his head and laughed under his breath. She waited for him to tell the next joke, like they used to do during their weekly training sessions. Rule was, the one who dropped the thread had to make Juicy Lucy burgers after practice.

He seemed to think about it as he watched his daughters in the distance, but no joke was forthcoming. Perhaps he'd forgotten about the ritual altogether.

"I have a favor to ask, Nash." Might as well come right out and say it before they got bogged down in an awkward silence again.

At that, he looked at her. "I thought boarding Mischief was the favor."

Nash's response was so swift and pragmatic, it took her breath away.

"One of them, yes. But I also wanted to ask if you could help Taylor. She's hitting a wall, and I suspect she can do more. I'll pay you for however many sessions it takes."

Once again, he looked away. "Sorry, Jess. I don't teach anymore."

"I know. You did say that. I guess I was hoping you would consider making an exception. For an old friend."

She inwardly winced at the last half because it wouldn't add any points in her favor. In fact, a joke even formulated in her mind. *You may be old, but you're no friend...*

But their friendship had meant something to him at one time, hadn't it?

He put his hands on his hips and surveyed his property while seeming to contemplate it. In the distance, a man was exiting the greenhouse. Nash waved, and the man waved back.

"Friends don't usually up and leave without saying a word, do they?" Nash looked straight into her eyes this time, then added a half smile to apparently soften the accusation. Then again, someone had to say it. In that moment, she realized that maybe he hadn't simply been disappointed professionally and as a friend. She'd hurt him on a deeper level.

But that couldn't be. He'd never so much as hinted at such feelings, and she'd been on the lookout for them.

"I halfway agree," she said. "A good friend wouldn't do such a thing. But a bad friend obviously did. And that friend is truly sorry."

That earned her an accepting nod. She'd take anything she could get.

"Truth is, I'll do anything for my daughter. That includes admitting I was wrong and begging for help from the best barrel racing teacher I've ever known. You'd do the same for Lizzy and Kat if you were in my shoes. I'm quite sure of it."

"Best, huh? What's the punch line?" he asked, pulling his hands from his pockets and folding his arms instead.

"It isn't a joke. But the punch line *could* be that you owe this bad friend a Juicy Lucy. Since I'm trying to be a better friend, I'll let it slide this time."

Attempting to joke around at such a serious, soul-bearing moment was a bold and presumptuous approach, but she wasn't getting through otherwise. Desperation was setting in.

"You've made a good argument, Ms. McCoy. But I don't want your money."

"Because a bad friend's cash is no good?"

Nash softly laughed. "Actually, you prepaid for a couple of lessons that you never got around to taking. But I'm afraid the statute of limitations for using those credits or collecting a refund has expired. I'm not saying that to be cruel. It was in the training contract."

She had to think about it, but he was right. She had bailed before taking the last three lessons. "You remember that?"

"I remember a lot of things."

Whatever that meant. There was lots to remember. Clearly, he wasn't going to elaborate. The old Nash would have.

Once again, that strange silence fell between them. In the background, the girls were arguing about something.

In that moment, she began remembering a lot of things, too.

Clear signs. Like the admiring looks he'd give his now ex-wife. Or the way he'd allowed Roxanne to interrupt Jess's lesson time with a question or two. Not that Jess could blame any man for being distracted. In fashion terms, the future Mrs. Buchanan had been a ball gown, whereas Jess had been a gingham day dress.

Furthermore, she still was.

Now that she'd experienced a mental refresh and fast-forwarded to the present, it was her turn to look away.

"So you'll consider it?" she asked.

If he did, it certainly wasn't going to be as a favor. She'd been saving up for this. Sewing until her hands were chafed. Not only for Taylor, but for other mommies on the rodeo circuit.

"I insist on paying you," she said, hoping to prompt a commitment.

Nash pivoted and faced her.

"Okay. You can babysit the twins while I'm with Taylor. That's the only form of payment I'll accept. That said, I'll do an evaluation first. In a couple of hours, if that works for you. If I think I can help, we'll decide whether to proceed."

Not the answer she was expecting. She was counting on the extra hours she'd have with Taylor being gone to catch up on outfits that the ladies were expecting in Montana. Word of mouth had elevated her business. It could also bury it if she didn't deliver the goods. If she accepted Nash's offer, not only would she *not* get that work done, she'd need an extra pair of hands and eyes to watch two little girls instead of only one.

It was the worst form of payment he could ask for. Thoroughly inconvenient and stressful. Furthermore, she didn't have to think twice.

"You've got a deal, Mr. Buchanan."

CHAPTER TWO

TURNED OUT, erasing daisies was no easy task.

Not when his rambunctious little Lizzy had put so much love and effort into her bad decision to draw on his board instead of her own. But as difficult as it was for him to wipe the artwork clean, it was nothing compared to what he'd gotten himself into with Jess.

So much for extricating the rodeo from his life completely. After Jess had stopped taking lessons, she disappeared from the circuit. He never imagined she'd be back, full force, as a rodeo mom. She'd caught him totally off guard.

Offering to evaluate and possibly coach Taylor in exchange for Jess babysitting the twins seemed like a reasonable solution in the weakness of the moment. It wouldn't otherwise be possible for him to keep an eye on the girls. And taking Parker off ranch duties to babysit instead would be a business setback he couldn't afford.

Besides, he suspected this whole issue could be put to rest in one session, especially since Taylor was The One to Watch. If that was true, her skill set should be pure enough that any issue would be obvious. With awareness came correction, and she could practice on her own time, with Jess's help. Jess would have been The One to Watch herself, had she not quit. Problem solved.

Yet, even going through with one session would be enough to pique the twins' interest. They'd want to learn barrel racing, as well. Kat especially. They were like little sponges. And when that happened, he'd be forced to use the word that kept eluding him: *no*

Like he'd said to Jess, rodeo events weren't feasible. Too much travel. What he didn't mention was money was painfully tight, and his only ranch hand was still as green as a head of lettuce. Then there was the bigger issue that was nobody's business: running into Roxanne and all the complications that would involve. His chest tightened at the thought of it.

Why get the twins started only to let them down? Not that he intended to lie about Taylor if they asked. He simply wasn't going to offer up any information.

Nash grabbed his cell phone and took a picture of Lizzy's handiwork so it wouldn't be entirely erased from his life. With a couple of long swipes using a hand towel, the landscape was wiped clean.

On a whim, he grabbed a black marker and belatedly wrote *NO* in the white space. Big letters in all caps. Couldn't hurt to practice for the next time someone wanted a favor he had no business granting.

"I haven't even asked yet," a man said, startling Nash. He looked behind him.

Parker.

"You scared me." The girls often snuck up on him, but their voices were sweet and soothing—even when they were arguing about something, as they were doing in the adjacent den. Nash would eventually acclimate to Parker's deep tone.

"Sorry about that. I finished weeding, but I might have accidentally destroyed a little of whatever it is you're growing," Parker said.

His ranch hand had come a long way, considering he brought zero hands-on experience with him. But he still had miles to go. Thankfully, Nash had narrowed the weed infestation down to one variety for Parker to tackle. Even gave him pictures to refer to.

"No worries. Today is the day for altered landscapes. What is it you wanted to ask?"

"Thought I'd check the board first, then find out which task you wanted to hand off. However…" Parker pointed to the unmistakable word.

Nash picked up the hand towel again and wiped the *NO* away. That said, there was something Parker could do that he wouldn't mess up. The man was a natural with kids, and the girls adored him.

"Do you mind watching the little angels for a short while? I need to take care of something in the arena."

"You know the answer to that. But I'll be happy to take care of the other issue for you instead. Real cowboys, like me, can handle anything you throw our way."

Nash knew the guy was only half joking. A few months ago, the cowboy in front of him sported button-downs and ties and didn't even know the purpose of a hoof pick. Made sense, though. What business consultant in a fancy high-rise office building in Chicago needed such a thing? The transformation had been fun to watch, but his skills had yet to catch up with his confidence. Furthermore, Parker knew it, which made it all the more fun to play along.

"Terrific. I need a cloverleaf in the arena," Nash said, adding a grin. It wasn't nearly enough direction.

Parker rested his hands on his hips. Nash waited for it.

"Why only one? Four leaves are considered good luck."

Once again, Parker didn't disappoint. Such banter had become their shtick. But the laughter was short-lived as he thought of the joke that Jess had told earlier. For a fleeting moment, it had felt as though she'd never left. Joke swaps had been *their* shtick, back in the day. But he wasn't about to let that start up again.

Nash straightened his shoulders and willed himself to return to the issue at hand.

"That's an excellent suggestion. I need all the luck I can get. The girls are in the den. Don't mention the cloverleaf. I'll explain later." Nash grabbed his Stetson and headed out the back door.

The cool midmorning air felt refreshing. He took deep, cleansing breaths on the way to the shed that he used to store banished items.

Too bad he hadn't given the barrels away years ago when he'd first considered it. That would've provided a built-in excuse to not work with Taylor. Too late now.

Nash fished out his key ring from his jeans pocket and worked the key into the rusty lock until it gave way. With a determined yank, he opened the door. His breath caught in his throat when he spotted the fifty-five-gallon drums sitting in the far corner. They looked so…sad.

"You're back in business, girls, but don't get used to it," he said, remembering he used to think of the barrels as his children.

He cleared the path and retrieved them, one at a time. They each weighed about forty pounds—slightly less than one twin.

The rest was coming back to him, as well. The location of the score line to the first or second barrel, the ninety feet between them and the one hundred and five feet from those barrels to the third. He mentally calculated the stopping room needed and got to work.

Once done, he backed up to the fence and surveyed his work. A crisp breeze rushed over him, and it felt as though a new life had been breathed into this tired arena.

More like, the best—and worst—part of his old life.

Nash tried to shake off the feeling as he headed back to the house. The girls were snacking on peanut butter and banana slices and crackers that Parker must have fixed for them. He was busy filling in the board with a list of remaining chores and doing an admirable job of it.

"I have a nice surprise for you, girls," Nash said.

They looked up but kept eating.

"You're gonna be spending a few hours with Jess today at the Hideaway," he continued. "How does that sound?"

"The pretty lady?" Lizzy asked.

"That's the one."

Parker looked up. "Pretty, huh?"

Nash knew what his ranch hand was implying. The guy recently got hitched to the woman of his dreams and had even given up a six-figure career to muck stalls for Nash and make a life with her here. That was true love. Now, Parker and the rest of the town were itching to matchmake someone else.

Nash was tempted to tell them all to move along. Nothing to see here except a grizzled rancher who wanted nothing more than to take care of his little girls.

"Pretty is as pretty does," Nash said.

The twins nodded. He wasn't sure if that was still a saying, but it resonated. He'd fallen for another pretty face. The person behind it, however, turned out to be anything but.

He wasn't putting Jess in that category. Yet.

Truth was, he admired the lengths she was willing to go to for her daughter, and even her confidence for showing up after all these years. Furthermore, she was still a good, down-to-earth person overall. Otherwise, he wouldn't have agreed to this.

Didn't mean he was about to forget how it had ended before, or let it get to him when she left again. And she was going to leave. At that point, he'd give the barrels away completely.

He stepped over to the kitchen window and discreetly pulled the curtains closed. In retrospect, he should've waited to set them up. Reduce the possibility of the girls noticing and asking to try barrel racing, too. Then again, honesty was always the best policy. Maybe it would be the practice he needed in flexing his "no" muscle.

There was much comfort in that thought. Yet, it did nothing to persuade his heart, which was throwing a tantrum inside his rib cage. It didn't take long for Nash to admit to himself that it had nothing to do with the barrels.

And everything to do with Jess.

WAS IT TOO late to pack up and leave Destiny Springs?

That was Jess's first impulse after she got back to the Hideaway. Although even she—a card-holding confrontation avoider—wasn't going to act on it this time. She'd just taken a successful baby step in approaching Nash, which could have turned confrontational. She'd find some other way to resolve those restless, unresolved feelings she still had for him. The other challenge: taking care of his two precious little girls without getting equally attached.

Best thing to do in both cases, she swiftly decided, was to treat this situation for what it was: a business arrangement. A place where such emotions didn't belong, especially since Nash otherwise wanted no part of her and Taylor's world.

Jess got out of the truck, opened the cab and grabbed the handle of her so-called portable sewing machine case. It was an industrial model but worth its weight. She needed all the bells and whistles it offered.

Before she could so much as lift it off the truck floor, she heard the distinctive sound of boots drawing near.

"Let me help you with that, ma'am," the cowboy said, swooping in and taking over before she could answer.

Jess was starstruck. Never in a million years did she think that Cody Sayers, of all people, would be helping her with such a thing. As husband of the B and B's owner, he'd retired from professional bull riding not so long ago. But he would always be a legend in rodeo circles. She and Taylor had both been big fans. Now, Jess was an even bigger one.

"That's a kind offer. I'm in the Spandex Room," she said.

"I know. Your daughter has been making the rounds with Becca. Taylor's bragging about how her mom makes all her cool clothes."

Jess bit her lip to suppress a gigantic grin.

"Do you happen to make little boys' clothes, as well?" Cody asked. "My six-year-old son, Max, outgrows his as soon as his mom cuts off the tags. We have to drive about twenty miles to buy more."

Jess had never made little boys' clothes, although she was itching to try. But this was impossible timing for a new project, if he was even serious.

"I'd love to meet him," she said in lieu of committing.

"Oh, you will. Can't miss him. He's the little redheaded bundle of energy."

Said like a proud father. Even though his subsequent smile was infectious, Jess had to force one in return. When Taylor lost her daddy two years ago, something about her changed.

How could it not? The typical growing pains for a young girl that age further compounded it. As a single mom, Jess did her best to fill the void left behind.

Once Cody had successfully lifted the sewing machine, she grabbed the bag of groceries she'd bought on her way back from Nash's. They needed to have something in the room to snack on. Not only for her and Taylor, but now for the twins.

Cody took the lead up the porch steps, nodding politely at the endless stream of guests exiting. Mostly women, but a couple of men sprinkled in. It felt as though Jess and Cody were swimming against the tide.

"Is something going on that I should know about?" Jess asked.

Cody led them up the staircase to the second floor, taking the steps as if he were carrying a down-feather pillow rather than a thirty-pound contraption. "A group called the DEBBs are what's going on. They picked Destiny Springs this year for their annual retreat. You and your daughter got the Spandex Room. It was the only one available, and I apologize for it in advance. Becca thought an eighties-themed room was a good idea at the time. We're planning on redecorating it at some point."

Jess had to admit, the concept did seem odd. The bigger question was…

"Who are the DEBBs?"

Cody reached their room and knocked first. When no one answered, he unlocked it.

"To be honest, I can't remember what it stands for exactly. Engineering something or other. How about we set you up over there?" Cody pointed toward an empty desk.

"Perfect." She'd be able to spread out a little, with room left over for her notions.

He positioned the machine squarely in the center. "The plug is on the left. Can I do anything else for you?"

She thought about it. "As a matter of fact, I need some ideas for activities in the area that would interest a couple of six-year-old girls."

Jess never actually lived in Destiny Springs. She'd driven an hour each way from her parents' house in Sweetwater County to take lessons from Nash. But she'd worn blinders the whole time. So focused on barrel racing, and on Nash, that she never got fully acquainted with this town.

Cody's eyes widened. "Not to alarm you, but I've only seen Taylor around. Do you have another daughter or two I should be looking out for?"

Of course, he shouldn't have to look out for her daughter at all, but his concern was comforting. She was still processing the fact that she'd be wrangling twins for a few hours this afternoon. And if everything went as planned, she'd be doing it a few more times over the next two weeks.

"Not mine. Nash Buchanan's. We're doing a kid swap today for a few hours. Long story," she said.

Cody offered up a knowing smile. "Now, *that* sounds interesting. Nash, huh? Nice guy, by the way. Spoils those girls rotten. Pretty much spoils everyone he loves, come to think of it."

"I'll tell you all about it as soon as I find out how it ends," she said, doing her best to discourage any further conversation.

"I'll hold you to that promise. As far as activities, there's Sunrise Stables right down the road. Hailey Goodwin-Donnelly, the owner, offers pony rides and a goat petting zoo. The kids around here can't get enough of it. Not to mention, she's the best babysitter in town. Just ask the twins."

That was good to know, in case Jess got in a serious pinch. She could use some of the cash stash she'd saved up to pay Nash for lessons, now that she was babysitting instead.

"There's also Kavanaugh's Clothing and Whatnot and other shops in the square," Cody continued. "And a drugstore with a vintage soda fountain bar a few miles farther down. Georgina Goodwin, our part-time employee, can give you the specifics."

"Thank you. Terrific suggestions. I'll find out what the girls would prefer."

Taylor finally returned to the room, escorted by Becca, who collected a hug from the girl as if they'd known each other for years.

Becca turned to Jess. "If you ever need a second set of eyes, promise that you'll let me know. I'm always around."

"I promise," Jess said.

Becca turned to her husband and nodded toward the hallway before disappearing again.

"That's my cue to leave, ladies. Good luck in Montana, Taylor." Cody gave the girl a fist bump before making his exit.

Jess had been gone less than an hour, and Taylor had already made friends and told them all about her upcoming competition. Not that she minded sharing her daughter with others, but she could sure use a hug or fist bump, too. She took comfort in the fact that Taylor had bragged about her mom's sewing, assurance that she was still loved and appreciated, if not embraceable.

What Jess had in her favor was barrel racing. Their mutual passion for the sport was like superglue, even though it sometimes seemed as though Taylor didn't really want to travel around the country to rodeos. Yet, when Jess had suggested that they take a year off from competing, Taylor was inconsolable. It was as if Jess couldn't say or do anything right at times.

Before she could initiate a conversation about their favorite subject and find out if it was one of those times, Cody reappeared in the doorway.

"Sorry to bother you. Nash is here with the girls," he said.

Jess thanked him and turned to Taylor. "Okay, my dear. Nash is going take you back to his ranch. You can call me at any point, but I will otherwise pick you up at five. I'm babysitting his girls while y'all are working."

Together, they headed downstairs. She spotted Nash and the twins in the parlor. Not hard to do since the downstairs was otherwise empty. Lizzy was running all over the place while her daddy admonished her to stay in the vicinity. By contrast, Kat sat quietly on the sofa, clinging to a Breyer horse.

Nash stood and removed his Stetson as Jess and Taylor approached. He still had that thick, slightly wavy brown hair that had always remained on the verge of needing a trim.

"Taylor, this is your coach. Nash," Jess said.

Nash extended his hand, and Taylor reciprocated. "Nice to meet you, young lady. I've heard some wonderful things about you."

At that, Taylor beamed.

"What are you gonna coach her, Daddy?" Lizzy asked. The twins had both joined them at some point.

Instead of answering, Nash introduced their respective girls to each other, then shifted from one foot to the other as if uncomfortable about something. She could relate. This whole arrangement had caught her off guard, as well, even though they'd been the ones to negotiate it.

"Your daddy is gonna work with Taylor and her horse. You met Mischief, remember?" Jess directed the questions to the twins.

Lizzy nodded, but Kat kept staring at Taylor as if she wasn't sure what to make of this person who was temporarily replacing her in her daddy's life. How much had Nash told them, if anything? And how much should she say?

"Speaking of mischief, what kind of trouble do you and my girls plan on getting into this afternoon? Not that you've had a lot of time to think about it," Nash said.

"Cody had a few suggestions." *Or, I could let them watch television in the room while I sew.*

Nash leaned in. "Just don't let 'em out of your sight. One, in particular, goes looking for trouble."

No problem with that. She already felt a protective vibe when it came to these little girls. Besides, her sewing commitments felt like the least of her worries, as was the little troublemaker Nash was clearly referring to.

She didn't know Kat that well—more like, not at all—yet she seemed so serious. The familiarity tugged at Jess's heart. Taylor had turned serious at that age, but with an understandable reason.

Then again, maybe that was Kat's personality, but Jess was determined to get at least one smile out of her this afternoon.

"Ready to get started?" Nash asked Taylor, who nodded, turned and was halfway out the door before he finished the sentence.

"I'll take that as a yes," he said to Jess, sealing it with a wink.

Was that an accident? Didn't feel like one.

She gulped. His winks had always tended to do that to her, yet she knew not to read too much into them.

He put on his Stetson and tipped the brim. "Girls, give me a quick hug before I leave. And mind Jess while I'm gone."

The twins descended on him, with Lizzy hogging most of her daddy. He hugged them back with a vengeance, which only reminded her of the lukewarm embrace he'd shared with Jess earlier.

Kat reached up and slipped her little hand into Jess's, which made her totally melt. So much for thinking of this as a business arrangement.

As Nash stepped out the front door to catch up with Taylor, the DEBBs started pouring in. Jess nodded and smiled at a few.

One of the ladies paused, looked at Jess then down to Kat. "You and your daughter should join us in the barn. We're learning how to antique furniture!"

Jess didn't bother to correct her.

Another woman slowed down long enough to concur, then added, "We have lots of workshops lined up. Please, feel free to join us." With that, the ladies rejoined the flow until the area was once again empty and quiet.

"I don't know about you, Kat, but a goat petting zoo sounds like more fun. What do you think?"

The little girl nodded and offered up a modest closed-mouth smile, which suggested Jess was on the right track with the activity suggestion. That made two votes. Yet, she needed a consensus. That was when something beyond awful occurred to her.

She was missing a twin.

CHAPTER THREE

"IS THIS WHAT you're looking for?" Becca asked.

All the pent-up air exited Jess's lungs, and her stiff shoulders surrendered in glorious relief at the sight of Lizzy balanced on the woman's hip.

Her hand remained glued to Kat's. The little girl had been such a good sport. Poor thing, being dragged outside and even upstairs as Jess scoured the B and B for her sister. Jess released her death grip but kept Kat in her periphery.

"Where did you find her?" she asked.

"I didn't. She found Cody and me in the kitchen."

"I'm so sorry." Becca had already offered to be a second set of eyes for Taylor. How many eyes could one person spare?

"Don't blame yourself. Lizzy does this to everyone, don't you?" Becca said, directing the question to the little girl, who simply giggled as if it were all fun and games. "She never goes very far."

Easy for Becca to say.

Unifying their little tribe was now at the top of Jess's priority list, because her heart couldn't take another round. Neither could her agreement with Nash. Misplacing one of his precious girls was likely a deal breaker. She was more determined than ever to find some activities that they would all enjoy. But first, she needed to lay down the law.

"Lizzy, do you remember what your dad asked of you before he left?"

The little girl stared instead of answering. Jess could practically read her mind. *You're not my mommy. You can't tell me what to do.* Or maybe that was just the way Jess felt about it. But there were certain lines that shouldn't be crossed when it came to reprimanding other people's children. At the same time, she needed to say something.

"Please ask before you go anywhere without me. Okay?" Jess continued.

When Lizzy still didn't answer, Becca set her down but kept hold of her hand. "Jess has a point. Next time, ask her before you go running off. Understood?"

The little girl seemed to give it some thought. "Okay." She wrapped her arms around Becca's legs. The woman gave her a big hug in return.

Seriously? Jess tried to figure out the magic word because Becca had pretty much echoed her plea. She had thought Kat would be the one who would require the most effort to communicate with. Clearly, she'd need to try harder with Lizzy.

"Okay, this is getting ridiculous. You and Cody keep bailing me out. I insist on doing you at least one favor."

As soon as she said it, the regret set in. Favors were what got her into this predicament in the first place.

"The only favor we require is that you enjoy your stay. In fact, Cody has an idea for an activity you three ladies can do together. He and Georgina are putting on a fun cooking workshop tomorrow for the DEBBs. You and the girls could join in. There's room, and I'm sure the DEBBs wouldn't mind."

She didn't say it, but a couple of the women had already encouraged her to participate in their workshops. And she'd silently declined. If she could find any spare moments over the next two weeks, she'd need to sew, sew, sew. She wouldn't have the luxury of making new friends. Only new clothes.

Yet, the suggestion was not only brilliant, it felt right. Jess and her mom had so much fun together in the kitchen when she was growing up. The twins would hopefully be fully engaged. No temptation to run away. Of course, she'd have to be extra vigilant about keeping their little hands away from sharp knives and hot water and such. But with Cody and Georgina there, along with a room full of other adults, that should be easy enough.

"I wanna cook cupcakes!" Lizzy practically shrieked.

"Sugar pies," Kat countered.

That seemed to ignite a feud that threatened to escalate into a shouting match.

"Cupcakes," Lizzy insisted.

"Sugar pies."

"Ladies, let's try to—" Jess interjected.

"Cuuuupcaaaakes!"

How could a woman who had already survived the sixes with one daughter feel so helpless and ineffective?

"I'm so sorry. I'll sort this out," Jess said. "What does DEBBs stands for, by the way?"

"No apology necessary. DEBBs stands for Domestic Engineering Belles and Beaus, which is a fancy way of saying stay-at-home mommies and daddies."

That was *not* the kind of engineering Jess was expecting. All of a sudden, even one workshop felt like a bad idea. She'd gone to great lengths to avoid reminders of her previous lifestyle. Specifically, the warmth and security she'd felt when she'd been in that role, only to have it all ripped out from underneath her with the unexpected, sudden death of her husband.

Not that she dwelled on the past. If anything, she was always trying to outrun it. The thought of planting roots now felt like ropes around her ankles.

Perhaps those feelings would be manageable if her emotions hadn't been heightened after seeing Nash again. Followed by the drama of misplacing Lizzy.

After all this, Nash could still decide not to help Taylor after his evaluation today. Based on his initial reaction, it seemed highly unlikely that he'd go through with more sessions. For the first time since she'd concocted this whole plan to approach him, she was relieved that it might not go any further.

Ugh. Now she could add guilt to the thick batter of emotions.

Shame on her for even thinking such a thing. Yet, she'd gotten herself in over her head, hadn't she? Double trouble.

And not the good kind.

NASH HAD BARELY blinked when Taylor went from being a restless eight-year-old girl who was toying with her colorful friendship bracelets on the way to his ranch, to a self-assured young woman who'd strapped on her helmet and started warming up.

Then it struck him: was this how fast it would happen with the twins? That they all of a sudden would no longer be his little girls?

All the more reason to wrap up this evaluation today. Get back to spending time with his own children, like he'd worked so hard to do.

From what he'd seen so far, Mischief was sound. As was Taylor's form. During her warm-up drills, she worked both sides of the horse without needing instruction. First, with a walk, then a long trot. Once into a slow lope, she set up the horse for his turns and to stretch his muscles. Perfect.

Nash walked around the outskirts of the arena, surveying her moves from several angles. Without thinking, he settled onto his old favorite teaching spot on the fence to observe. He'd tended to avoid that perch in favor of another stretch of fence after walking away from everything rodeo.

Taylor trotted over to him after finishing her warm-up drills, obviously looking for feedback or direction. He'd reserve that for after the important part.

"Whenever you're ready, go have some fun," he said, offering up a smile, because he seemed to be fresh out of them since they'd gotten back to his place.

It had the opposite effect. She dropped her chin. What was that all about? He could venture a guess. She wasn't a grown-up young lady after all, despite the obvious maturity for her age. She was still a child.

"Hey, Taylor. Before you strut your stuff, I have one question," he called out.

"Okay."

"What did the bartender say to the horse when it sat down in the bar?" As soon as he said it, he realized that perhaps a joke set in such an establishment wasn't the best choice for a young girl. Too late now.

"Why the long face?" Taylor forced a smile, then proceeded to her starting point.

Her mama had likely told her that joke already, which would get him off the hook should she repeat it. Her expression tickled his belly and made him laugh. Nothing forced about it.

But that feeling was short-lived when he realized that the joke was on him. As soon as she rounded the first barrel, he knew Jess hadn't been exaggerating. He believed that Taylor was very well The One to Watch, because Nash sure couldn't look away.

Not that he'd ever underestimate an eight-year-old, but this gal had a level of talent and potential he hadn't seen in a long time. If ever. Except perhaps... *Jess.*

The little cowgirl executed the cloverleaf a few more times with near perfection from what he could tell. Either that, or his coaching skills were as rusty as that old lock on the shed. Her turns were solid. Her seat was secure. And the pocket was appropriate on her turns.

Then, something about the way she raced toward the finish caused the muscles in his stomach to seize. Sure, that always happened during those last few seconds that could mean the difference between first place or no place. Just never to this degree.

In this case, Nash could chalk it up to the fact that those muscles hadn't been used in a while, because nothing Taylor was doing stood out as being wrong or problematic.

This would definitely be their only session, because he had nothing to offer as far as advice, aside from a few small adjustments that wouldn't add up to anything consequential. One in particular.

"Start with the left barrel this time. For grins," he said.

He halfway expected her to defend starting with the right one, but she followed his directive. She and Mischief were equally good on both sides, which wasn't unheard of.

"I'm afraid I can't help you," he said out loud, even though Taylor was too far away to hear.

"That's disappointing, because I came all this way," someone said from behind him.

Nash tensed, then turned around. That was the second time today someone had snuck up on him. This time, it was Parker's wife.

"Hope I didn't scare you. I've looked all around for my hubby but can't find him. Is that Kat?" Hailey asked as she hoisted herself up and settled in next to him on the fence railing.

Strange assumption. Kat was quite skilled for her age, but she'd never rounded barrels, thankfully.

"Nope. That's Taylor. My former student's daughter. They're staying at the Hideaway. I'm boarding her quarter horse for a couple of weeks."

"Huh. How old?" Hailey asked.

"The horse or the girl?"

"You're funny. The girl."

"Eight."

"No way. She's phenomenal," Hailey said as she toyed with her long ponytail.

Hailey would know. She had more experience with horses than Nash, and that was saying something. She'd been part of rodeo circles when she was younger. Everything from mutton busting to barrel racing to calf roping. Now, she literally forged new trails, and a few old ones, with her trail riding business at Sunrise Stables.

"Maybe a little too phenomenal. I'm at a loss on how I could coach her."

At that, Hailey looked squarely at him. "Did you say what I thought you said? And is that a perk when someone boards their horse with you?"

"It's a long story," he said.

"The short version will do. Otherwise, I'll die of curiosity. I thought you were done with all that, even though you've never told me why, and I won't push."

Nash looked out at Taylor again, who was doing some looking out of her own. Specifically, at the Wyoming landscape. He wasn't sure where she and Jess were living at the moment, but it probably didn't have a view like his.

"I'm doing this as a favor. Jess is babysitting the twins in exchange." He looked to Hailey and waited for the inevitable comeback. That was as certain as death and taxes.

She simply raised a brow. "Uh-huh."

"What does that mean?"

"It means I bet that little girl's mom is really pretty."

"So?"

Hailey grinned and looked away. As if he wouldn't help anyone else in the same situation. Yet, would he? He'd been fiercely protective of his time—especially now that he had more of it to spend with Lizzy and Kat before they started school. That was, until Jess walked back into his life.

Speaking of which, she'd probably be heading back over with the twins soon.

Nash jumped down from his perch and made his way over to Taylor, still unsure of how he intended to handle this.

"Good job. Let's untack Mischief and get him comfortable, then we'll go inside and I'll make some hot chocolate while we wait for your mom. How does that sound?"

"Do you have marshmallows?" she asked.

"Umm…is there such a thing as hot chocolate without 'em?" he asked.

She grinned enthusiastically. So all it took was marshmallows to turn this serious barrel racer into a happy little girl again.

By the time he turned back around, Hailey was nowhere to be seen. Now both Donnellys were roaming free on his property. But he did find one of them inside. Raiding his fridge.

"Did you ever find Parker?" he asked.

Hailey nearly dropped the cheese plate. "Don't sneak up on me like that!"

"You did it first. Taylor, this is Hailey."

Hailey extended her hand. "You were amazing out there."

"Thank you, ma'am." Taylor accepted Hailey's hand and shook it.

Nash laughed under his breath. He'd always thought of Hailey as a little sister. Not a *ma'am.*

Hailey jabbed him softly in the side with her elbow, then stuffed a large square of cheddar cheese into her mouth.

"Feel free to take some to go," he said. Not that he didn't enjoy having her there. He just didn't want her around when Jess returned with the twins. Hailey had already figured out too much regarding his feelings. Or thought she had. He was still figuring that out himself, because this anxiety coursing through his body was the double-strength variety. More than one energy source was fueling it.

"All right, I can take a hint. I'll leave the cheese for you and take a hug instead." She wrapped her arms around him, squeezed tight and whispered, "I'll be back to hear that long story of yours. I'll even bring the popcorn."

Nash would have ordinarily laughed, but the seriousness of what was about to happen was settling in.

Once Hailey left, he whipped up some hot chocolate as Taylor got comfy on the sofa. Before he had a chance to do the same, there was a knock on the door.

On the other side stood Jess, Lizzy and Kat. The twins nearly knocked him down to collect a hug, which caused his hot chocolate to splash. The marshmallows on top formed a shield that helped curb some of the damage.

"Go show Taylor your Breyer horse collection, Kat. And Lizzy, maybe you could draw some flowers for her. On *your* board."

"Okay, Daddy!" the twins said in unison.

With all three girls in the twins' bedroom and out of earshot, it was down to Nash and Jess. And the decision that had to be made.

"I had a wonderful time with the girls," Jess said. "We took a drive around the square, then we watched a movie in my room. Tomorrow, we're going to help with a cooking workshop."

Tomorrow. A bold assumption.

"I have to be honest, Jess. I'm not sure I can help Taylor improve. She's everything you said she was. And more."

She looked at him but remained quiet, as if he hadn't tried hard enough. Or maybe that was his own conscience prodding him.

In that silence, he did one more run-through of Taylor's performance in his mind. Once again, his stomach seized toward the end. Although, this time, he knew why. It definitely had something to do with the way she was finishing.

Bottom line: Taylor had too much promise to ignore. Furthermore, he was itching to help. That favorite teaching spot on the fence that he'd avoided for so long was tempting him back over, although he had no intention of getting too comfortable there.

"I understand," she finally said, without any discernable emotion.

"I don't think you do," he countered, although he wasn't going to reveal the depth of that statement. Only the layer she needed to hear. He was willing to let his guard down only so far…

"I'll drop off the twins tomorrow and pick Taylor up. Midmorning. After breakfast. She and I have a lot of work to do."

CHAPTER FOUR

JESS WAS LIVING proof that one could survive without coffee for the first few hours of the morning.

Survive being the operative word.

Good thing she could practically pattern little girls' Western barrel racing shirts in her sleep. Of course, she'd preplanned the special embellishments needed to make each top unique. Just like the little equestrians themselves. So far, her vision had set her apart from other seamstresses who did similar designs for the rodeo circuit. The cloned crop topT-shirt she promised to one of the rodeo moms would be even easier to execute than the shirts.

Then there was the Dudley project. *Definitely* a job for caffeine.

Jess tiptoed past Taylor, who remained curled up beneath a pile of blankets less than ten feet away. The little girl's long, dark brown hair draped across the purple spandex pillowcase and down the side. The sunlight seeping through a crack in the spandex curtains revealed the beautiful chocolate tones within the strands. At least she'd removed the ponytail holder, along with her headphones.

Thankfully, Jess had already let Taylor know that if Mommy wasn't in the room when she woke up, she wouldn't have gone far. No farther than downstairs.

And never for too long without checking in. The trip this morning needed to be a record-breaking one.

Otherwise, she wouldn't have even considered the green spandex guest bathrobe, complete with an embroidered patch that spelled out *Hideaway* stitched in cursive and an attached tag that invited guests to take the robe home as a souvenir.

It would be good enough for a quick trip downstairs, but she wasn't going to use up suitcase space to haul it from city to city. Plus, it wasn't like she was going to run into anyone except perhaps Becca and a DEBB or two. Even if that happened, the day could only get better from there.

She slipped on the fuzzy pink house slippers that she'd brought and followed the aroma of fresh coffee to the kitchen. Hopefully, Becca would let her buy a cup.

Except the woman loading dishes onto a cart wasn't Becca, unless she'd traded her red beachy waves for a blond updo. Whoever the woman was, she must have gotten up even earlier than Jess, considering how polished she looked, from the tidy French twist to the fitted powder blue sweatshirt dress, all the way down to her impossibly white tennis shoes.

Jess was suddenly self-conscious about her own appearance. She didn't have on so much as a flick of mascara. At least her long bob didn't require much fuss. In fact, it always fell into place whenever she rolled out of bed in the mornings. She'd never been into those fancy hairstyles anyway, although they sure did look nice on others.

"Sorry to bother you." Jess tapped on the door frame softly enough as to not startle the woman. "May I buy a cup of coffee?"

The lady turned around, wiped her hands on an apron and offered a warm smile.

"Nonsense! Coffee is on the house." She retrieved a mug from the cabinet, filled it almost to the top and handed it to Jess. "I left a little room for cream and sugar."

Jess took a sip and shook her head. "It's perfect the way it is."

"Why, thank you. Made it myself. I'm Georgina, by the way. Are you one of the DEBBs?" She grabbed a fruit plate from the counter, balanced it on top of the already overburdened cart and slowly released her grip.

Jess held her breath, but the platter didn't so much as teeter.

"I'm about the only one who isn't, it seems. I'm Jess. My daughter, Taylor, and I are passing through on the way to a rodeo in Montana. We're boarding her horse at Buck Stops Ranch."

Georgina tilted her head and put her hands on her hips.

"So *you're* Nash's gal," she said.

Jess's breath hitched, and she nearly choked on the sip of coffee she'd taken. Not because it sounded so wrong, but because it sounded so...*right.* Probably because she'd wanted to wear that label so badly ten years ago.

Her shock must have been obvious to Georgina, who clapped her hands over her mouth.

"Oh, gosh! I didn't mean it *that* way. I'd heard that one of our guests was boarding her horse at his place, and that y'all went way back."

Okay. Much better. Still, her heart got a little jolt that the caffeine couldn't have achieved.

"I used to be one of his barrel racing students."

"My sister Hailey told me he used to teach," Georgina said, adding the final straw—make that strawberries—to the cart.

Jess set her cup down on the nearest counter, lunged forward and stopped the bowl from crashing to the ground. She took the initiative to rearrange a few of the items into a more stable configuration.

"Thanks. You're a lifesaver. Becca usually helps me, but eggs make her nauseous. Cody was in here earlier making his dish, so the kitchen kind of smells eggy if you didn't notice."

"Allergies?" Jess asked.

"Pregnancy. She should be over the morning sickness by now, but hopefully she'll get some relief one of these days. Until then, she can't even think about them without dry heaving. She even foregoes helping with breakfast in the barn."

"That's unfortunate. Eggs would probably help settle her stomach."

"Spoken like someone who's been there," Georgina said.

Becca appeared in the doorway, "I heard that, and I'm not going near any eggs! I'll live with the nausea. Good morning, Jess. You're welcome to my portion of breakfast."

"That's a good idea," Georgina said. "Why don't you go on down and claim a place at the community table before the other group takes over. I'll be down in a jiffy."

"I would—everything looks delicious. But I left Taylor upstairs. She's still asleep."

"I'm done here and can check on her, if you'd like," Becca said.

"That's a sweet offer, but look at me."

They both gave her the onceover.

"That's so funny. I hadn't even noticed what you were wearing. Looks good on you! But I bet you'd look good in a potato sack," Georgina said.

"I concur. Please take your time at breakfast. I'm not going anywhere except to the other room right now before I…" Becca covered her mouth and made a quick retreat toward the parlor.

The women both sounded serious about her looking fine, but Jess knew otherwise.

"I'll fix a couple of plates and take them back to the room. But first, I insist on helping you with this," she said, gesturing to the cart. Her pride could take a minor hit for a good cause.

"You're as sweet as I heard you were," Georgina said.

Jess was tempted to ask who gave her that description. The only person who knew her that well around here was Nash, and she doubted he'd describe her as *sweet*, judging by his reaction to her reappearance in his life.

"Tell you what, Jess. Come down for coffee whenever you want. If there isn't a fresh pot on, feel free to make one. You'll find everything you need in there." Georgina pointed to the cabinet directly above the coffee maker.

That was music to Jess's ears. She'd need the caffeine to get through the early morning sewing hours she had planned.

The two managed to get the overloaded cart out the door, down the trail and over the threshold of the barn without any casualties. The DEBBs were already there and milling about. A little redheaded boy was walking around to each person and offering orange juice. No one was giving Jess a second look. So far, so good.

"Help yourself to the buffet. If you need any assistance carrying breakfast back to your room, just holler at one of us. Or you're welcome to borrow a tray." With that, Georgina shifted into overdrive, placing all the food in its respective warmer or designated spot. They certainly had breakfast running like clockwork, with everyone pitching in.

Cody was stationed at the end, serving up something from one of the warmers along with that mischievous smile he'd been so famous for. Like every other woman Jess had ever known, she'd had a slight celebrity crush on the Rodeo Rascal when he first rose to fame.

But now I'm Nash's gal.

She bit her lip to suppress a giggle, then got in line.

Once it was her turn, Cody gifted her with a warm smile, although she had braced herself for a smirk. He either didn't notice her attire or was too much of a gentleman to show any reaction.

"Is that Max pouring the orange juice?" she asked as he added a dollop of *migas* to her plate.

Cody beamed. "Yes, ma'am."

Jess could understand why the man was so proud. Max obviously already had a strong work ethic. Very much like Taylor when it came to barrel racing.

"Hey, Max," Cody called out.

The little boy froze in his tracks and looked their way.

"Pour a glass for Jess, if you don't mind, sir," Cody continued.

Max practically ran to a table where the glasses were stacked. The orange juice sloshed around inside the giant pitcher.

"Slow down, cowboy!" Cody called out, then turned to Jess. "He gets a little too excited about helping with breakfast. Hope that never changes."

Jess wanted to tell him to give it a couple of years. Max would be wearing headphones all day. Then again, every child-parent relationship was different.

Jess hoped for a closer relationship with her own daughter and wasn't about to give up just because their little family suffered an unexpected loss.

"Any chance I could have an extra serving of those for Taylor? She's still asleep upstairs. That is, if it won't make you run out of eggs."

"No chance of that. Vern Fraser makes special trips over here in the mornings. You just missed him," Cody explained as he added another generous dollop.

"You have an open-door policy for breakfast?"

"Fraser Ranch provides the eggs for our morning feasts. It's the least we can do for the special folks in our lives. Just ask Nash." Cody added another lopsided smile.

"That'll have to wait until I'm appropriately dressed. I wouldn't want him to see me like this. Considering we have a business arrangement and all," she said. But in trying to clarify, she felt herself digging an even deeper hole.

Besides, she was stating the obvious. The way Cody looked past her confirmed it. She was difficult to look at.

A man cleared his throat behind her, then said, "Save some for the rest of us."

All of a sudden, Jess couldn't breathe. She looked at Cody and mouthed, "Nash?"

Cody leaned in and whispered, "I didn't see him until he was right behind you."

Jess corralled a pathetic amount of confidence, pivoted on the heels of her fluffy house slippers and put on a huge smile.

Nash smiled back, after a quick onceover that lingered on the slippers. At least he wasn't laughing.

"You're early to pick up Taylor," she said. As in *way* too early. "She's still asleep."

"Actually, I'm here to rob the buffet of some scrambled eggs for the girls. Realized I didn't have any at the house."

Jess tugged at the front closure of the robe, wishing she could somehow make it swallow her whole.

"Eggs. Nature's perfect vitamin," she said for lack of a better response.

Nash simply smiled. And stared.

Jess looked for the nearest exit but figured she'd only look sillier if she made a run for it. As if looking any worse was even possible.

"Thank you, again, for agreeing to see Taylor today, Mr. Buchanan," she said in her most professional tone.

"You're welcome, Ms. McCoy. I'll see you again in a few hours."

She was tempted to say, "Not if I see you first," but refrained. Best thing to do was to cut her losses. Although she hadn't dared to dream that this trip might result in some sort of deeper relationship, like the one she'd yearned for ten years ago, this encounter had just ensured that such a thing would never happen.

Jess pulled her shoulders back, nodded and walked around him and out the barn door without looking back.

Her pride now depleted—but with a full plate of food and a glass of orange juice in hand—Jess somehow made it back to the room without spilling anything. She temporarily set the juice on the ground and opened the door as slowly and softly as possible. Taylor was already awake.

"I brought us some breakfast," she announced.

Jess could practically read her mind. *Did you bring pancakes with fresh strawberries and blueberries and raspberries and chocolate-maple syrup and whipped cream?*

Someday, Jess would make Taylor's special dish again. But with their rodeo schedule and lifestyle, there was no telling when that would be. She didn't want to make any promises she couldn't keep.

Taylor lifted the foil on the plate and stabbed one of the strawberries with a fork, then sampled a small bite of the *migas.*

"What do you think?" Jess asked.

Taylor shrugged. "It's okay." Judging from the next huge bite, she must have decided that it was pretty good.

Jess smiled, shook her head and breathed a sigh of relief. With Taylor temporarily occupied, Jess could make progress on one of the Western shirts while the coffee kicked in.

From there, she needed to organize her thoughts for the two-piece suit that Carol Anne Dudley had requested for her daughter, Meghan. Even a mention on *Dudley's Delightful Duds* could help Jess branch out. Western tops and random clone requests were her bread and butter, but it would be tough getting Taylor all the way to nationals on that.

Mrs. Dudley's opinion was the type of advertising that couldn't be bought. Best of all, she'd given Jess creative license for the design. Hence, the black pleated chiffon bell cuffs Jess planned to add to the yellow-and-black tweed jacket sleeves. They had to be executed flawlessly. She had barely enough fabric remaining.

Same went for the tweed itself. Before she did any patterning or cutting, she'd given Mrs. Dudley a sketch for approval to proceed. Jess wasn't sure if it was good or bad news that the woman hadn't texted her back.

Not that she didn't have plenty to do right in front of her. She double-checked the direction of the grain and pinned the Western shirt pattern into place, then cut and trimmed out the individual pieces. She took one of the sleeves to the sewing machine, positioned it, then released the pressure foot. When she pushed the power pedal, the machine growled back a bit.

"Someone's grumpy this morning," she whispered softly enough so that Taylor didn't hear.

She pressed for longer this time, getting one seam done without a hiccup. Full steam ahead.

Nash's gal is on a roll. She grinned and bit her lip again. No, Georgina hadn't meant it *that* way.

Jess took a break to help Taylor finish off the *migas*. Couldn't let it go to waste. Now wide awake and focused, she positioned the second sleeve and put the proverbial pedal to the metal.

Except, this time, she got nothing but quiet in return. Not even a lazy *hmmm.* She tried again to no avail and checked the outlet and all the connections. Everything looked normal.

She pressed down a third time. Nothing. All of a sudden, those eggs weren't going down so easily. Just when she thought having Nash see her in the robe and slippers was the worst thing that could happen.

Something was broken…and her reputation would be, too, if she couldn't get the machine fixed soon.

NASH COULDN'T STOP GRINNING. Those fuzzy house slippers of Jess's had to be the cutest thing ever, next to that awful robe that she somehow managed to rock. Oh, and the way she'd said that they had a business arrangement, then proceeded to address him as Mr. Buchanan. Not that he needed reminding that it was business, but it made him see her in a whole new light.

A flattering one.

With his own smile firmly in place, his number one priority for the day was to put a smile on the faces of three little girls, as well.

Unfortunately, the odds were against him from the get-go, judging by the way the twins kept herding the *migas* around their plates with their forks.

"Miss Hailey lets us have Pop-Tarts," Lizzy said.

It was a valid point, as it had been the dozen or so times she'd mentioned it. But the answer was still no.

He allowed such sweets while Hailey babysat only because he felt guilty about abandoning them in the first place. But guilt was not going to guide such important decisions anymore.

Nash flipped the hash brown patties to the other side. A pair of crispy black circles stared back at him.

He'd like to blame the unappetizing breakfast on the fact that he barely got a wink of sleep last night. But the feel of his favorite teaching spot, Hailey's thinking it was Kat in the arena, and those old feelings for Jess that he'd thought he'd put to bed for good were now tossing and turning in his mind.

Then there was something about Taylor's sad expression when he told her to go have some fun that niggled at his conscience the entire night.

Maybe whatever she's carrying on her shoulders is weighing her down, lowering her score.

Nash laughed under his breath at the unexpected thought. If only the explanation could be that simple. Any child as young and accomplished as Taylor had to either be an old soul or have a freakishly mature side. He'd never expected his older students to be happy all the time. It wouldn't be fair to expect it of Taylor either.

With the cast-iron skillet in one hand and the spatula in the other, he walked to the breakfast table and slid a hash brown onto each girl's plate.

"How about some ketchup with those?" he asked.

Lizzy poked the patty with her finger but recoiled at the heat. Neither twin looked up.

"What is it?" Kat asked.

Nash knew what she meant, but he couldn't resist.

"Ketchup's that stuff in the fridge, in the red squeeze bottle. It's made out of tomatoes, and we dip our fries in it."

"The bottle is made out of tomatoes?" Lizzy said, then giggled.

Nash shook his head. "No, silly. The ketchup."

Kat furrowed her brow.

He tried to contain himself, but a giggle slipped out anyway. The image of Jess's infectious laugh tickled his stomach. If she were here, she'd appreciate his bad joke, and Lizzy's clever question.

Soon enough, Kat joined Lizzy with her own half-hearted giggle.

Nash waited for them to stop long enough to see his wounded-puppy-dog expression. Instead of earning some sympathy, it made them laugh until they were both practically bubbling out of their chairs.

Mission accomplished. Almost. At least he got a smile out of these two. The day wouldn't be complete until he got at least one out of Taylor, as well.

His smile was so huge right now he no longer tried to contain it. This was the best time of each day, in his opinion. Just him and his top two reasons for living. A warm, comfortable home that they'd made their own, and the Wyoming sunrise in the distance. Even Parker coming through the back door and adding more tasks to their chore board couldn't spoil the moment.

"Daddy, can I ask you something, if it's okay?" Kat asked.

That half of the twin equation was always so quiet, so this was a very good sign.

"You can ask me anything, darlin'," he said. If his heart had been any fuller, it would have burst right out of his chest.

"What do barrel racers do?"

At that, he felt his smile deflate. He'd dodged the topic before, but this thing with Taylor had brought it as out in the open as the barrels themselves. Kat had seen the beginning of a race at one of the rodeos. Roxanne was first up and started at an impressive speed. Nash didn't act quickly enough to get them all far enough away from the arena. He'd hoped the memory wouldn't stick. But it had, and now the situation promised to get a lot stickier.

"They compete in rodeos, mostly," he said. "It's like a job. Hard work. Not fun, like you and Sugar Pie have here."

Nash barely had time to blink before Kat turned back into his quiet little twin. Probably because he'd already explained that participating in rodeo events wasn't possible because traveling wasn't possible. Even though it hurt him more to say it than for them to hear it, he'd stand by that explanation.

He wouldn't think of burdening them with the fact that there wasn't enough money left at the end of the week for such things. Between the feed and the hay and the veterinary costs, that left him barely able to afford to pay Parker. Much less, their own bills.

And bringing up the topic of their mother was completely off-limits.

It had probably been a mistake to let the twins do mutton busting for a local event once. Neither had shown a serious interest. With the age limit capped at seven for most of the area events, he had a built-in excuse to say no to that without being the bad guy.

But barrel racing? That could go on for decades.

Lizzy seemed neutral when it came to the topic. Although she was crazy about her horse and was a good rider, she wasn't a rodeo gal. By contrast, Kat loved everything about the lifestyle, even though she wasn't old enough to understand the half of it.

At least he'd managed to thwart the topic, for now. Back to having fun.

Nash retrieved the ketchup out of the refrigerator and placed it in the middle of the table, hoping to invoke the giggling once again.

No such luck.

"You don't have to eat 'em if you don't want to, even though it's not good to waste food. But please eat your eggs," he said.

"If we had a dog, the dog could eat the food and it wouldn't be wasted. I'll take care of feeding him and washing his plate and giving him water," Lizzy said.

"Oh, boy," he said under his breath.

That topic again. Talk about "out of the frying pan and into the fire." Lizzy had been asking for a dog, but there was no way he could add another mouth to feed. Plus, he already knew who would end up with doggy duty, and it wasn't the twins.

Parker snorted in the background. Nash had forgotten he was even there, even though he'd babysat while Nash had made a run to the B and B.

Nash was out of fresh ideas as to how he could change the subject and get them laughing again. Something else had been invoked: the guilt. There was only one way to fix it, even though he'd vowed not to resort to it.

He walked over to the cabinet and grabbed a box of Pop-Tarts. Thankfully two remained. One for each of the twins.

"You girls get changed while I fix these for you." Nash waved the box in front of them, which put a smile on Lizzy's face and seemed to wipe away a little sadness from Kat's. They must have inhaled the sugar, because they were out of their chairs and down the hall before he slipped the treats into the toaster.

Parker had apparently sensed the seriousness of certain topics. He didn't even bother to tease. He simply wrote something else on the board, offered up a sympathetic smile and exited out the back door.

Nash looked at what his ranch hand had written.

Hang in there, Dad.

"I'm tryin'." Nash cleared the barely touched plates of food from the table. He was messing up as badly with the dog topic as he had with the hash browns. Furthermore, he didn't have a clue how to fix either except to remind himself that he was doing the best he could under the circumstances. Then there was the other no-win situation he was navigating.

Those reawakened feelings for Jess.

CHAPTER FIVE

JESS STARED AT the apron that Georgina had handed to each person in the cooking workshop. Staring back: a comical-looking purple bull, nostrils flaring, and one eye noticeably larger than the other.

"These are yours to keep as a souvenir of your stay at the Hideaway and this workshop in particular," Georgina said.

"Aww," one of the ladies said as she held up the apron for everyone to see. As if they hadn't gotten one, as well.

Aprons. Jess used to have a million of them in her past life. In this life, such a thing would stay folded up in her suitcase, which would be a waste. The thought made her feel surprisingly…*sad.*

"The artist is none other than Max Sayers, Cody and Becca's son," Georgina continued. "In case you couldn't guess, his favorite color is purple, and he adores bulls."

Jess was intrigued. "You had the fabric made from a drawing?"

"Sure did. We don't have a fabric store within a hundred miles of Destiny Springs, much less a place that could do something like this. But I'll be happy to jot down my online resource for anyone who is interested."

"Is the little artist helping us cook today?" one of the beaus asked.

"He's resting up for a trail ride this afternoon at Sunrise Stables. If you have some free time, I highly recommend going on one," Cody said.

That earned a few nods of interest and discussion among the DEBBs. But even with the chatter around her, all Jess could hear was the silent treatment that her sewing machine had given her.

What came through loud and clear, however, was a hard tug on her right arm and Lizzy practically shouting, "I wanna crack the eggs!" Those soft brown eyes pleaded with Jess as if she had a say in how the workshop would be conducted.

Thankfully, Cody stepped in.

"That's one of the most important jobs," he said. "In fact, it's a two-person task. If the others don't mind, maybe you and Kat could tackle that together."

Kat shook her head and looked to the floor. Perhaps this cooking workshop wasn't such a good idea after all. Time for some gentle persuasion because it was too late to back out now.

"It sounds like fun. Let's give it a chance," Jess suggested as she pulled Kat in for a side hug, which the little girl reluctantly accepted.

Cody fetched a couple of step stools—probably kept on hand for his own little one.

He demonstrated by tapping an egg gently on the edge of the bowl before handing the task over to the twins. After supervising their first attempt, which Lizzy hijacked and Kat was clearly okay with, Cody wiped his hands on his apron, stepped around the island and filled the void that the girls had left behind.

"Looks like the girls are having fun," he said.

Jess nodded at his generous assessment. She'd missed the target of finding something the twins would equally enjoy.

"You know them better than I do. Kat doesn't seem too interested in cooking. Maybe the next workshop will be more her thing. Any idea what the topic will be?"

"Work-life balance," he said.

They looked at each other, scrunched their noses and shook their heads at the same time.

She looked back in time to see Lizzy dip her hand into the bowl to fish out a piece of eggshell that had escaped her grip. Georgina swooped in with a fork to assist.

"I made them soap up before we got here," Jess said, loudly enough to be overheard. A few DEBBs glanced over and smiled as if to say, *No worries at all.*

Cody whispered, "When Max first started helping with the orange juice, he tried to stir it with his fingers, but I stopped him in the nick of time. You'll be relieved to know that he's a spoon expert now."

Having met Max, she could totally picture it.

"Too bad. That would have made it taste even sweeter." Jess offered up a silly grin.

Cody took a step back. "Well, there it is! I thought you forgot to bring it downstairs."

Jess cocked her head. "Bring what?"

"That smile."

Jess felt it turning back into a frown, against her will.

"Oh, yeah. That. My sewing machine decided to stop working this morning. From what I could tell after doing an internet search, there's only one place around here that might do those kinds of repairs. Hoping to get over there before they close today."

Cody pursed his lips and nodded. "I know the place. Miller Electronics. They're good, but notoriously slow and always backlogged. I have a better source."

And just like that, Cody lifted the weight of the world off her shoulders as easily as he'd carried her sewing machine up those stairs.

"Give me a few minutes." He sprinted out of the kitchen and down the hallway.

A woman tapped Jess on the shoulder. It was the same DEBB who had been the first to approach her.

"I couldn't help but overhear. Do you sew?" she asked.

"I did until this morning." At least there was a possible upside to the machine not working. She now had a built-in excuse, should anyone else want clothing made for their young sons, in case that was why this lady was asking.

"I love to sew and am pretty good at it. Haven't had time lately. Not in years, in fact. I'm hoping I can get some ideas on how to find time for it from the workshop on work-life balance. You should join us."

Rather than risk sounding ungrateful for the invitation, Jess simply nodded.

"I'm Dorothy, by the way. If you get the notion to talk about notions, I'm in the Velvet Room."

"I'm Jess, in Spandex."

"Now *that's* a tricky fabric," Dorothy said. "With spandex, you gotta stretch and hold. If your arms get tired in the middle, you could be in trouble."

"Wow. I didn't know that." Yet, it made complete sense. That was probably the only fabric she'd never handled.

The woman seemed to know her stuff. Couldn't hurt to have a sewing soulmate in the house. Not many people wanted to talk notions or listen to her ramble on about the periodic frustrations. Needles breaking. Thread bunching. Machines up and dying. Taylor would put on her headphones whenever Jess started grumbling to herself while working on a garment that wasn't cooperating.

"Ms. Lawrence, would you mind slicing some avocado?" Georgina asked.

"Not at all." Dorothy turned back to Jess. "I hope we'll have an opportunity to chat more while you're here."

Nice offer, if not doable.

Cody returned with a self-satisfied grin. "You're in luck. The best repairman in Destiny Springs can look at your machine this afternoon. He'll meet you at your room around five thirty, toolbox in hand."

That wouldn't leave much time for her to drop off the twins and pick up Taylor. But as long as she didn't linger at Nash's, they could make it back. In fact, this was a blessing in disguise, because he'd been standing on the edge of her thoughts ever since she laid eyes on him again.

"Does the repairman have a name?" Jess asked.

Cody's eyes were now trained on the DEBBs who had been corralled into volunteering, and on the girls, who literally had their hands in every task. "He sure does. He's also one of the most respected cowboys in this town."

Jess waited for a name, but nothing was forthcoming except for a mischievous smile.

So that's why they called him the Rodeo Rascal. Did she detect some sort of matchmaking going on? Otherwise, why the mystery?

Whatever the case, Jess wasn't a candidate for a relationship right now. Didn't stay in one place long enough and preferred it that way. She was tempted to tell him not to bother if that's what he was up to, but he was having too much fun teasing her. She wasn't going to spoil it for him. Not after everything he'd done.

"I've lost count of how many times you and Becca have helped me. I might as well stop trying and just take full, unapologetic advantage of your generosity," she said.

"*Now* you're catching on." He added a lopsided grin, then walked back around the island to take over the cooking once again. Lizzy insisted on continuing to help, while Kat returned to Jess's side, still stuck in a puddle of gloom.

"What would you like to do after this? We'll still have some time before I take you two back to your daddy," Jess said.

The little girl shrugged.

"Or we could talk. Woman-to-woman." Even to Jess, that sounded silly, but she was running out of ideas. At the same time, Kat looked up and stared, as if making sure the offer was a serious one.

"Can I ask a question, if it's okay?"

"Of course!" Jess said.

"What does Taylor do at the rodeo with the barrels?"

"You've never been to the rodeo?"

"Yes. But not since I was little," Kat said.

That was adorable, but strange on so many levels. Sure, he'd stopped teaching at some point. But how could a little girl whose daddy used to be one of the best teachers in the greater Wyoming area—in the world, as far as Jess was concerned—not even know the basics about barrel racing?

"The rider and her horse race around the barrels as fast and calculated as they can. The one with the best time and form wins a trophy or belt or ribbon. And usually some cash," Jess said.

"Daddy lets me ride Sugar Pie at home. She's mine, and she's a quarter horse like Taylor's. Lizzy's horse is Cupcake, but she isn't as fast as mine."

"Maybe your daddy can teach you some moves."

Kat simply shrugged and looked down at her feet.

As soon as she said it, she remembered how adamant Nash had been about not having time, or interest, in the rodeo anymore. But he didn't seem like the type of father who would deny his daughters anything if they asked.

Maybe Roxanne had hurt him so badly that he'd abandoned that part of his life. Any discussion was a reminder. That might explain his icy reaction to training Taylor. He'd definitely changed.

She wanted to bring up the topic of barrel racing to Nash for Kat's sake but didn't want him to add any more bricks to that emotional wall she'd detected. Not when she and Taylor had come this far and he was willing to help her, albeit reluctantly. Still, she ached to reach the Nash she once knew.

Then again, she wanted a lot of things.

EITHER JESS WAS twenty minutes early bringing back the girls, or Nash's usually impeccable internal clock was off.

Time otherwise felt as though it was standing still when she paused after getting out of the truck and stood there as if contemplating whether to come over at all.

Nash didn't bother dismounting from his perch on the fence. Lizzy ran over and hugged the bottom half of his legs, nearly pulling him off anyway. Kat, on the other hand, bypassed him altogether to get a closer look at Taylor, who was rounding the third barrel, then heading toward Kat instead of coming back over to him or taking it home.

He managed to tear his eyes away from that unfortunate situation once Jess approached.

"Back so soon?" He tried to hide his frustration behind a cordial smile.

Kat had already been asking about when they could all go to the rodeo again to watch the horses. Having her see Taylor in action wasn't going to help.

The fact that he'd managed to avoid barrel racing events each time, with one sliver of an exception, was partially selfish. He couldn't watch if Roxanne was competing. Not because he had any feelings left for her. He simply didn't want to risk running into her with the twins.

Of course, Jess wouldn't know that crucial fact. It was awful enough to feel like he was a "bad daddy" because of his unwillingness to even consider it, even though deep in his heart he wished he could. He didn't want Jess to reach that conclusion, as well.

"Sorry about that. My sewing machine broke. Cody lined up a gentleman to come over and look at it in an hour, and I need to be there."

Something about the way she said *gentleman* jolted his ego on an unexpected level, which was silly. It wasn't like she was going out on a date. Even if she was, it was none of his business.

Naw. Couldn't be jealousy he was feeling. Well, maybe a little, if he were being honest with himself. Helplessness, definitely. He was handy around the ranch in many ways—repairing or replacing a broken gate hinge, fixing the timing on a baler, replacing a spark plug on the four-wheeler. But he didn't have the first clue about delicate machinery.

Jess joined him on the fence. "The girls are partially to blame. They couldn't wait to get back home and see you. I put them off as long as possible."

She'd told a half-truth, at best. At least one of his girls wanted to see him. The other was more interested in the arena. Kat was practically wiggling out of her skin as Taylor showed off by finishing a figure eight on the first two barrels and was racing toward the third.

Not that he blamed his daughter for being mesmerized. He'd all but forgotten what an edge-of-your-seat sport it was. But to bypass her daddy altogether? That was a first. And hopefully the last.

He wasn't going to address the issue in front of company, however. Breakfast was always the best time with the girls as far as bringing up thoughts and feelings, so he'd let it slide for now and tackle it in the morning. He'd be smart to pick up more Pop-Tarts at the store in case he needed reinforcements.

No luck pinpointing anything today as far as Taylor was concerned. Only a rehash of his suggestions from yesterday. But he wasn't giving up yet. His intuition wouldn't allow it.

"How did you ladies spend your day?" he asked Jess.

"We attended a cooking workshop at the B and B. Lizzy had the best time. You may have an aspiring chef on your hands."

"I can definitely use one of those." Nash looked out to the girls in the distance, because looking into Jess's light hazel eyes was getting to him again.

"Did you know the first french fry wasn't even cooked in France?" she asked.

Nash's thoughts went immediately to images of his new budding chef attempting to make fries at the house. With this new knowledge that cooking was an attraction, he made a mental note to keep extra-close tabs on her. As if he needed one more thing to worry about.

"Really? I didn't know that," he said.

Jess bit her lip and nodded.

"It's true. The first fry was actually cooked in grease."

Nash thought about it for a second, then laughed under his breath.

He wanted to launch into a joke of his own. In fact, one immediately came to mind: *Is it proper to eat a Juicy Lucy with your fingers? No, you should eat your fingers separately.* But he refrained. Those old feelings were bubbling to the surface, more dangerous than hot grease in a cast-iron skillet set on high. Furthermore, it wasn't a joking matter.

"So…any comeback?"

He looked at her now, unsure of what she was getting at.

"Pardon?"

She was the one to look away now. "Seems like you've forgotten about our joke swap. I bet you still have some zingers in you."

"Not at all. It's just that…"

"Our lives have gotten more serious," she said.

She wasn't wrong. But swapping jokes would only lead to someone owing the other a Juicy Lucy. The fewer trips they made down memory lane, the better.

"And sometimes we put up a wall to protect ourselves," she continued.

Now *that* was the Jess he remembered. The woman who wouldn't let him get away with anything. Even though she used *we*, it was clear she was talking about him. She wasn't wrong about that, either.

"I suppose we sometimes do," he said, stopping short of a full admission.

Jess jumped down from the fence. "Well, then, I guess I'd better take care of Mischief and head out. Find out what's wrong with my sewing machine and if it can be fixed. Kat tells me her horse is Sugar Pie and Lizzy's is Cupcake."

"The girls picked out the names."

"I figured that much. Not that you don't have that in you, too," Jess said.

Nash tried to make sense of the statement, although he had little doubt as to what she meant.

"I'll take care of Mischief this time. You get back to the B and B," he said.

"You don't have to do that."

No, he didn't. In fact, the sooner he got Kat back inside the house and away from the arena, the less opportunity she'd have to get even more attached to barrel racing. And the greater the chance of him giving in to those sweet brown eyes of hers. But Jess needed a favor. And he needed for her to leave before he cracked a bad joke.

"Hey, ladies, Jess and Taylor need to skedaddle. Say your goodbyes," Nash called out.

Lizzy ran over first and gave Jess a big hug. "I'm gonna make some *mee-cuz* for breakfast for *all* of us tomorrow. Will you help me?"

"We made Cody's Rascal's Rodeo Scramble in the workshop," Jess explained.

"He's almost as famous for that now as he was for bull riding." Admittedly, this would throw a huge rusty wrench in his plan to spend some one-on-two time with the twins in the morning and talk about...*feelings*.

In all honesty, he used to dream of starting each day in such a way. Except with a wife. Roxanne had her good points, but she didn't have a domestic bone in her body. At least, the best he could tell. She was at out-of-town rodeos more than she was in the kitchen.

"Can we *pleeease*?" Lizzy begged.

"Jess may have plans. We should be asking her," Nash said.

Jess visibly sighed. "If the gentleman can repair my machine, I'll need to catch up on some sewing in the morning instead. I'm sorry."

"And if he can't, you and Taylor will come over?" Lizzy looked at Jess, who obviously wasn't immune to the little girl's charms.

"Sure," she said after an extended pause. Clearly, that wasn't the preferred scenario, judging by her forced smile.

"Promise?" Lizzy asked.

Jess smiled. "Okay. I promise."

It took everything Nash had not to envision Jess and Lizzy cooking breakfast for them all. Especially after seeing how comfortable the twins seemed to be around her. Ever since Jess had appeared on his doorstep for help with Taylor, he'd deferred to the professional side of his intuition, which had been waving a red flag. The personal side, however, was waving a familiar white one.

Not that it had ever fully stopped.

JESS COULDN'T HAVE timed it better. She and Taylor had no sooner settled back into the Spandex Room when there was a knock on the door.

Maybe a good-looking cowboy could provide exactly what she needed: a distraction from her thoughts about Nash. Especially since she'd had the courage to confront the issue of the jokes, and he'd acknowledged remembering. Awful jokes were the hardest to forget and often the funniest. They'd both doled out some doozies.

One thing was for certain: breakfast at his place in the morning wasn't the best idea. The gentleman on the other side of that door was the only one who could save her from having to fulfill her promise to Lizzy, because going back on promises was at the top of her no-no list.

"Coming!" she called out, pausing at a mirror for a quick hair and makeup check. Taylor had put on her headphones and was sitting on the bed, bobbing her head to whatever tunes were filling her ears.

Jess opened the door. The man who stood on the other side was most definitely a cowboy, in a loose-fitting flannel shirt and heavy denim jeans.

He removed his cowboy hat and covered his heart. His hair was as white as his whiskers. Shoulders slumped ever so slightly at the weight of the toolbox he was carrying.

"Vern Fraser, at your service. Cody tells me you're in need of a knight in shining armor. Since a real one wasn't available, he called yours truly." He added the most charming grin she'd ever seen.

"You sure look like one to me. Please come in."

It was true. Perhaps Cody had acted a little coy when she'd asked for the name. But he wouldn't have recommended Vern if the man wasn't able to help.

Vern made a beeline to the machine. "There's the little troublemaker. A Janome, huh? She's a beauty."

His knowledge put her somewhat at ease. Even more so once he began disassembling the thing and talking through the process.

Jess stepped in closer.

"There's the motor. Let's see if we can get that heart of hers beating again." He unscrewed some bolts that held the piece in place, then eased it out. Wires and all.

"Hmm. None of these are frayed. And the sensor and shield plate look clean and are on tight," he continued.

Jess looked at where he was pointing and nodded, as if she'd understood a word he'd said.

Vern started to put everything back in its rightful place but paused as if a problem was on the tip of his tongue.

"Cody tells me that Nash is training your daughter. Is that true?" he asked.

"He's going to try," Jess said.

Vern rethreaded the wires through the machine and screwed the motor back inside. Then he positioned some sort of black belt.

"That's Nash for ya. Always helping people out."

"Seems like everyone in Destiny Springs is that way. Like you, for instance."

After putting the faceplate back on and double-checking all the connections, Vern tried the pedal. No luck. He stood and rested his hands on his hips.

"I have some good news and some bad news, young lady."

"I'll take the bad news first."

"The motor needs to be replaced. Must be an internal wiring failure, is all I can figure."

"And the good news?"

"No chance Miller Electronics carries it. Not for this model."

Jess tried to wrap her mind around how that was good while Vern crossed his arms and tapped his index finger against his lips while staring at the machine.

"Do you happen to have any *great* news?" she asked.

Vern looked at her and shook his head as if he'd been lost in a trance.

"Didn't mean to scare ya. I forgot to finish my thought. I know who likely carries that motor, but they're in Casper. I can pull some strings and get it here pretty fast."

"I don't suppose you could define *fast*." She already felt as though she was being a bad customer. Which begged the question, how much was he going to charge for all this?

Vern let out a cackle that morphed into a dry cough.

"I'm pretty sure we have different definitions for what *fast* looks like. I'm eighty-four, so a turtle could outrun me. Might be able to get it shipped overnight. At this hour, it likely wouldn't go out until tomorrow morning. So a couple of days, soonest."

That was the great-news scenario? She couldn't afford to lose that much time.

"May I ask what this is going to cost?" Besides her reputation and business, which she could barely stand to think about.

Vern put the screwdriver back into his toolbox. "I can use my senior discount for the motor. The labor is on the house."

"Oh, no. Not a chance. I'm paying you for your work."

Vern patted her on the arm. "I think it was Arnold Toynbee who said, 'The supreme accomplishment is to blur the line between work and play.' If that saying holds water, it means I'm either the most accomplished person in Destiny Springs. Or the blurriest."

It was Jess's turn to cackle. That was usually the attitude she had about sewing. It also seemed to be the way Nash once felt about teaching, which made her heart literally ache now that she thought about what he'd given up. Or walked away from.

She, for one, knew how it felt to walk away from something you love. And someone.

"Do you remember when Nash used to teach?" she asked, daring to open the subject again and secretly hoping Vern would have some answers.

"Sure do. Folks around here thought he shouldn't have quit. But we all make choices that people don't understand because they don't walk in our boots."

"I know what you mean. Do you have any theories?"

"Nothing I'd bet money on. He's never talked about it. 'Course, folks around town think that some gal broke his heart."

Jess nodded. "Roxanne."

"The ex-wife? That's the reasonable conclusion. But supposedly there was another gal involved, which is why it's such a good rumor. Lots of those circulate around here, and a couple have even turned out to be true. Guess we'll never know for sure. Unless Nash ever decides to confess."

Jess was reasonably sure that wasn't going to happen. She knew he didn't quit teaching immediately after she left, so it obviously had nothing to do with her.

Whoever the other woman was, assuming the story was true, provided slight vindication that her main competition both in and out of the arena hadn't been "the one" for Nash after all. Maybe that's why Roxanne left. Maybe she didn't feel truly loved.

Hmm. Whatever the case, it seemed that neither woman was currently in his life.

Vern jotted something down on a notepad that was sitting

next to a landline phone. "Here's my number. If you come across anything else that needs fixin', you call me first." He tapped at the piece of paper as if driving the point home.

"That's too kind, really."

At that, he simply waved his hand as if swatting the compliment away. She would figure out a way to repay him, whether he welcomed it or not.

Jess opened the door for him and watched to make sure he got down the stairs safely, then returned to the room. There sure were some men of integrity here in Destiny Springs. She suspected that Nash was still one of them.

She wished she would have asked Vern if he had any advice for how to fix the other situation she was facing. But this one wasn't as simple as ordering a new part.

Her excuse for skipping making breakfast with the girls at Nash's had officially fallen through. And she'd made a promise to Lizzy, which she'd hate to break.

Maybe a good night's sleep would provide an answer. Not only to how she might bow out of the breakfast, but also why she kind of didn't want to.

CHAPTER SIX

"NOTHING LIKE A good night's sleep to help a gal see things more clearly," Jess murmured under her breath so that she wouldn't wake up Taylor.

Or so the saying goes. She personally couldn't prove or disprove it. Hadn't slept through the night in ages. Last night was no exception.

Her daughter, on the other hand, slept like a true champ.

It was one thing to get up early on purpose to work on her garments. It was another to lie awake, ruminating about the past and worrying about the future.

Ultimately, she concluded that this breakfast was a good thing for everyone involved. Then, she and her daughter could return to the B and B. Taylor could retreat back into her headphones, and Jess could continue patterning. Didn't need a sewing machine for that.

Nor did she need any fancy plans to keep the twins entertained after the kid swap later on. Jess could livestream horse shows on her laptop to keep Kat's interest, and tune into one of the food networks on television for Lizzy. Later, she'd take them out for a root beer float at the drugstore.

With the day neatly patterned out in her mind, and with Taylor still fast asleep, Jess headed downstairs. The kitchen was empty, but the coffee maker was already burping. Serving dishes were neatly stacked and ready to be filled with the morning's breakfast options.

Jess poured a cup and was right in the middle of a big, ugly yawn when someone tapped on a glass panel of the door. Her "knight in shining armor" was peering in from the other side. She set the cup down and rushed to open it for him.

The man was nothing short of amazing. How he managed to knock with his hands full was beyond her. The crate he was holding looked quite heavy and bulky. She held her breath and remained on standby as he eased it onto the counter, in case he needed help.

"I s'pose I'm a little early this morning. I was expecting to see Becca, but you're even better. Don't tell her I said so."

"I heard that, Vern," a woman called from the other room.

"Did I say Becca? I meant Georgina." Vern looked at Jess and put his index finger to his lips.

Jess returned the *shhhh* gesture. Without asking, she grabbed a clean mug from the cabinet, filled it with coffee and handed it to him.

"Well, aren't you a mind reader," he said, adding an appreciative smile.

She managed a closed-lip grin in return.

He took a long swig of the piping hot coffee as if it were room-temperature water. "It's a good thing this coffee isn't as weak as that smile of yours."

She tried to force a bigger one for his benefit, but he simply laughed and shook his head.

"I take it back about you being a mind reader. If you knew what I was thinkin', you wouldn't have to try so hard."

Jess perked up. That could only mean one thing. "You got the motor already?"

"No, ma'am, but it might be something just as good." Vern grinned as if savoring a juicy secret.

The suspense was killing her. Jess gripped her coffee mug so tightly she could have cracked the ceramic.

Vern turned and called out, "Becca, if you're still eavesdropping, please meet Jess and me in the parlor."

"Be there in a sec," she answered.

Vern set his cup down and nodded for Jess to follow. Once there, he pointed to a wooden desk. A huge arrangement of fresh daffodils sat smack-dab in the center.

"For me?" she asked, half-teasingly because what else could he be talking about? She didn't want to tell him that even flowers couldn't make her smile right now. And they couldn't begin to compete with a new motor.

"Set down your coffee. You're gonna need both hands," Vern said.

Jess did as instructed. He lifted the arrangement, handed it to her and began fiddling with some sort of latch. The top of the cabinet opened out to the side. He tugged on another flap, which opened to the front.

Becca joined them. "Are you trying to charm one of our guests by giving away our flowers, Mr. Fraser?"

Vern glanced up from his task. "Are you implying I have to try?"

"Excellent point," Becca said. "Then may I ask what you're doing?"

With some effort, he hefted something that was nested inside, and out popped a sewing machine as if rising out of bed. Vern locked it in place and gave it a couple of jiggles to make sure it was secure, then brushed off his hands.

If her jaw could have reached the floor, it would have shattered as surely as the etched Waterford vase she was holding.

"Wow. I totally forgot that converted to a sewing machine. How did you know?" Becca asked.

Vern patted its metal spine. "I've got one just like it at the ranch, but the Singer inside hasn't 'sung' in decades. Tried everything to fix her. Hopefully, this one is in working order. Miss Jess is in dire need of a sewing machine. Hers is on the blink. I hope you don't mind."

Becca stepped over and ran her hand along the machine, as well. "Of course not. You can use this anytime, Jess."

Meanwhile, Jess couldn't find the words to express her gratitude. When she could finally speak, she had to state the obvious. "I do a lot of work before dawn. I wouldn't want to wake up the others."

Vern looked around the back, found the cord and plugged it into the wall. With Becca's help, they got the pedal positioned on the floor and flipped the "on" switch. He pulled out a stool that had been tucked beneath the desk the whole time.

"Have a seat here and rev the motor while I take a listen," Vern said to Jess.

Becca eased the vase from her hands as Vern headed up the stairs.

Jess pressed the pedal, and the thing purred like a kitten. After studying the interface, she realized it wasn't an industrial workhorse like she was used to, but it would help her get some basics done for now.

A few minutes later, Vern came back down. "I doubt you're gonna disturb anyone. Can't hear a thing up there, and my hearing aids are cranked to the max."

Jess stood and gave him a hug without asking permission. She wanted to cry but managed to blink back the tears. This old cowboy really was a knight, albeit one in faded denim overalls.

After releasing her death grip on the poor man, she turned to find Becca handing her the vase. "Would you mind keeping these in your room? I don't know where else I would put them down here."

And there it was. The first time in a very long time that someone gave her flowers, even though they were technically on loan. That gift was second only to the magical machine in front of her. Plus, she now could bow out from cooking breakfast at Nash's without going back on her word to Lizzy. If she wanted. Yet, her "wants" seemed to be changing by the day.

Either way, she and Taylor still needed to run over and take care of Mischief. But now she could get some real work done before the official kid swap.

Jess returned to the room and gently squeezed Taylor's arm to awaken her.

"Looks like I have access to a sewing machine here, so we

don't have to do the whole breakfast thing at Nash's. We'll still need to feed and check on Mischief."

Mentioning Mischief always woke up her daughter better than any alarm.

Taylor sat up in bed and rubbed her eyes.

Jess glanced at the clock. Perfect timing. Nash had always been an early riser. She could deliver the news about the machine in person when they got to his ranch.

"Get dressed, please, and we'll head over there," Jess said.

While Taylor was getting ready, Jess collected the pattern pieces, along with a few notions to take downstairs so that she could get started as soon as they returned.

"Your phone rang while you were gone," Taylor called out from the bathroom.

A quick glance confirmed it was Nash. He'd left a voicemail. Hopefully, he was canceling their breakfast, which would be ideal. She wouldn't have to be the one to do it.

Instead, the message was from Lizzy, saying how excited she was about the whole breakfast thing. Thankfully, Nash hijacked the call, assuring her that there was no pressure to hang around after they dropped by to feed Mischief, and that Lizzy understood that possibility. But then he had to go and add, "Lookin' forward to seeing you."

Her heart felt as though it were about to blossom bigger than the vase stuffed full of daffodils on the bedside table. She and Taylor had to eat breakfast at some point anyway, right? And they didn't have to linger after the meal was over with. As long as the most important person in her life was on board.

"Taylor, I didn't even ask if *you* wanted to have breakfast over there."

The little girl emerged from the bathroom, all dressed except for her boots, and she was nodding.

The decision was made. Jess texted back.

I'll bring the ingredients since I know what we'll need.

After this, however, it was time to stop playing around and socializing, and instead get to work on another kind of interfacing.

The sewing kind.

IF NASH'S BOOTS could reach his backside, he'd give himself a good, swift kick in the pants. What was he thinking, leaving such a message? Especially the last part.

With phone in hand, he walked back into the kitchen, shaking his head.

"Lookin' forward to seeing you?" he muttered more loudly than he intended. Yet, it was true.

Parker glanced up from the board.

"Don't ask," Nash admonished before his ranch hand could think of a wisecrack response. Thankfully, Parker resumed his task instead. But the smirk told Nash that the subject wasn't closed.

He should have let Lizzy ramble on and on. She could have carried the message all by herself and spared him the Freudian slip. Yet, he didn't want Jess to feel obligated. No matter how hard his emotions were trying to scramble his professional common sense, he had to rein them in. No more talk about feelings. Period.

The exception would be the precious little girls who'd stayed on his heels all the way to the kitchen, arguing between themselves about who got to do what for breakfast. He hoped that didn't mean he had two budding chefs on his hands.

"I get to the break the eggs," Lizzy asserted.

"I get to make the chips, and I'm gonna use sugar and not salt," Kat said.

"You *have* to use salt," Lizzy said.

"No, I don't."

"How about we make some with each? Start getting dressed, ladies. Our guests will be arriving soon. I'll feed the horses. They're probably getting hungry by now."

"Can we feed the dogs, too, and bring one home?" Lizzy asked.

The knot that seemed to be a permanent part of Nash's stomach tightened.

"What dogs?" He was pretty sure he hadn't seen any strays near his property, much less a pack.

"The ones on TV. They live in cages, and they look so cold and sad," Lizzy said.

He knew the ones. The background music was equally heartbreaking. Those animal charity commercials sure knew how to tug on the heartstrings. If he had a million bucks, he'd help as many as possible find a home.

"No," Nash said, surprisingly swiftly and easily. He'd be proud of himself except the harshness wiped any hope right off the twins' adorable faces.

"Not today, ladies," he backpedaled. "We're expecting company, remember? Now, go change into something cute but comfortable."

At least he'd succeeded in kicking the topic down the road a little.

Once the girls were out of sight, Nash turned his focus to the task list that his ranch hand had composed. Pretty impressive. At a glance, everything looked good. Feed cows, replenish food supply, check heifers, fill water… But then Parker smirked and jotted down one last item.

Pick out a dog.

Nash grabbed the nearest rag and wiped away the words.

"Very funny. We can't let the girls see this. They already know a few words, and *dog* is one of 'em," he said.

"We can't let them know anything about the barrels, either. Anything you want to talk through? I'm a good listener."

Nash rubbed the sides of his neck and released a long breath.

"Kat's curious about barrel racing."

"Is that a bad thing?" Parker asked.

Nash's first thought was a defensive one. In his mind, there was no better sport. Kat was a natural on a horse, and she would excel. With the right teacher. She could easily become The One to Watch. But rodeo events were pricey, with the possible emotional price for running into Roxanne being more than any of them would ever be able to afford.

Just as he didn't want Kat to ask about the barrels, he didn't want anyone asking about his own feelings. Specifically, about his inadequacy as a father. But keeping a large part of the reason inside was eating away at his soul. Might help to talk it through with someone, and Parker wasn't the worst choice.

"It wouldn't be a bad thing if their daddy could afford it. Time's an issue, too. I can't be away from the ranch for as long as it would take to do it right."

"What? You don't trust me to hold down the fort? And feed the dog?"

"Oh, you'd do fine with the fort. It's a specific number I'd worry about. I'd want the same head of cattle when I returned." It was a not-so-subtle commentary on Parker's herding skills, which were admittedly improving but had miles to go.

"You'd come back to more. Aren't a few of your girl cows about to welcome little ones into the world?" Parker asked.

Heifers. But close enough. Yet another reason he needed to stay right here in Destiny Springs. Calving season, although his had been delayed this year. Even if Parker had been anywhere near ready, Nash would want to see it through.

"Speaking of little ones, Hailey tells me y'all are thinking about adopting sooner rather than later." It was a brilliant change of subject, if Nash did say so himself.

Parker simply stared and nodded.

Maybe he shouldn't have said anything, but Hailey didn't tell him not to. In fact, she could barely contain herself. Nash was getting a very different vibe from Parker.

"Sensitive topic?" he asked.

Parker raised his brows and shook his head. "Not at all. I'm happy to share."

"Then why so serious?"

His ranch hand looked back to the board. "Sorry, I thought of something..." He grabbed the marker as if he were going to jot down another point but paused instead.

That was weird. Then again, the whole day promised to be that way. Nash waited for Parker to elaborate, but no such insight was forthcoming. Maybe his ranch hand didn't want to talk about it after all.

"Since you're not gonna reveal your innermost thoughts and feelings, I'm heading to the stables." Nash couldn't help but snort, if only to add some levity to a potentially heavier conversation than either of them had bargained for.

Parker looked up. "I'll share my feelings if you go first."

With his Freudian slip, Nash thought he'd already gone first. In any case, he'd shared more than enough for one day. He wasn't about to add that sharing his feelings was at the bottom of his mental chore board this morning, because wouldn't that, in fact, constitute even more sharing?

"If you don't mind, please keep the twins occupied while I'm gone." He grabbed his jacket, Stetson and six carrots from the fridge, and headed out the door.

The cool breeze chafed, whipping across his skin like sandpaper against exposed nerves. The whole morning left him feeling vulnerable, and not in a good way. But this? The smell of the stables? The sound of wind through the aspens? The warmth of the sunlight stretching across the horizon and draping over snowcaps in the far distance? He could discuss his feelings about those things all day long.

"Here you go," Nash said as he presented a carrot to an appreciative Daisy, his oldest horse, who was afraid of children. She gave him a loving good-morning whinny in return. His two herding horses, Sassy and Tiger, both greeted him with nickers and accepted his prebreakfast treat without any drama or fuss.

By then, Cupcake had figured out carrots were involved and stretched her neck toward him as he approached, refusing to be passed over. Next door was Sugar Pie, who was waiting patiently for her treat. It was almost as though the latter two horses had picked up the personalities of their respective owners. Sugar Pie, being serious and methodical like Kat. Cupcake, their only Morgan horse, being unapologetically assertive like Lizzy.

Then there was Mischief. Nash had saved the biggest carrot for his guest, partially out of guilt for what he was about to do: feed the others. But that was his and Jess's agreement, and he'd already violated it once.

"So, Mischief, what do you think is holding Taylor back?" Nash asked.

The horse simply stared. Much like Parker had done. A giggle tickled his throat at the comparison.

"We can't help her unless we talk about our innermost thoughts and feelings," he continued.

Again, nothing but big brown eyes stared back. At least the horse seemed to be listening to him.

Instead of a full-on laugh, a chill coursed through his veins that had nothing to do with the cool breeze that had kicked up since he'd stepped outside.

That's it. Had to be. And to think he laughed off the possibility when it first crossed his mind about Taylor carrying some sort of burden on her shoulders. Maybe his intuition had been screaming at him, and he'd been too stubborn to take it seriously.

Now it was his turn to stare at the prize-winning horse in front of him. If he could help Taylor break through whatever was holding her back, it would be worth all the feelings he could stomach sharing.

The tires of Jess's truck coming down the drive interrupted the moment, but not the feeling of it. If he were to express his innermost thoughts and feelings right now, he'd have to admit that the excitement of possibly not having lost his touch was invigorating.

Most of all, it was terrifying, because his return to teaching and Jess's return to him were guaranteed to be fleeting.

Nash finished feeding Daisy, Cupcake, Sugar Pie, Sassy and Tiger, then straightened his Stetson and headed back to the house. The sooner they got breakfast over with, the sooner he could test this epiphany he had about Taylor.

And the sooner he could put all this *feelings* nonsense behind him.

CHAPTER SEVEN

BEING BACK IN Nash's kitchen again was like going back in time. Same plaid wallpaper and matching dining chair cushions. Same beige curtains. Same wall clock, with the hour and minute hands doubling as the cowboy in the bucking bronc illustration, although the hands had been frozen in time. As if no feminine force had ever been there and left her mark.

The place was so quiet. Taylor abandoned her the moment they got there and ran to the twins' room. Nash must have gone outside, because the back door was left cracked open.

One thing had been updated, however. Nash used to use a blackboard and chalk to list his daily tasks. Now, a whiteboard and dry-erase marker had assumed its corner in the breakfast nook.

Jess set the bags of groceries on the counter. While she began unloading them, her mind composed another list: additional embellishments for the Dudley project. Perhaps a yellow satin lining for both the jacket and the skirt, and a black velvet border around the collar and pockets. She had just enough scrap fabric to accomplish that.

Perfect!

Nash came in, took off his hat and jacket and hung them on the freestanding coatrack. It swayed a bit against the weight, as if its bones were getting tired.

"Taylor's down the hall with the girls. If I can pry her away, we'll feed Mischief. If not, I'll do it myself. In the meantime, Lizzy can get to crackin'."

Nash squinted. "Pardon?"

"Cracking the eggs. That's her favorite part. Make her wash her hands first. Kat can measure the cheese. I'll fry the tortilla chips, but someone will need to cut up the sausage. It's up to you, but I personally wouldn't let any of the girls do that because andouille isn't the softest and requires a sharp knife. We want them to keep all their fingers. And keep them away from the stovetop so they don't get burned."

This time, he raised his brows. "I didn't realize it would be so dangerous. And complicated."

"Oh, sorry! It isn't. I'm being overprotective."

"I appreciate it. But I have a better idea. I'll take care of Mischief while you and the girls get…crackin'. I'll cut up the sausage when I get back," he said.

Before she could answer, he called out down the hall, "Ladies? Is anyone getting hungry?"

That was enough to extract them from the bedroom.

Nash put on his jacket and hat once again and headed out the door.

She watched out the window as he walked to the stables, and the longing that it stirred in her to have someone to help with the day-to-day duties of life both surprised and overwhelmed her. She didn't get that on the road. Or living in the intentionally bland apartment in Rock Springs that she'd moved her and Taylor into after selling the ranch for barely any profit.

The new place was more a home base than an actual home, but it was a way to keep Taylor in the same school district. The teachers there had been overwhelmingly supportive in letting the little barrel-racing phenom do some remote schoolwork.

Nash's place, however… *This* was a home.

By the time she turned back around, the girls had invaded the kitchen. Lizzy had retrieved a large cast-iron skillet, which she gripped with both hands but still couldn't lift to the counter. The bowl that Kat had pulled from a bottom cabinet sported a slight chip on the rim.

We can do better than that.

After a perusal of his cabinets, Jess concluded that the girls had indeed pulled out the fancy stuff. Make that the only stuff, as far as cookware and bowls were concerned.

"Let's all wash our hands before we get started," Jess said, taking the lead and hoping to set an example. The girls followed, although she had to make Lizzy wash twice. The little girl was much too eager to get to the fun part.

Before Jess could process what was happening, Lizzy had tied an apron around Jess's waist. She had to loosen the ties a little but adored the thought.

Jess cleared a spot on the counter and retrieved a couple of painted crates for them to stand on. Lizzy didn't even wait for an invite.

While the budding chef selected an egg, tapped it on the edge of the bowl and carefully parted the halves, Jess retrieved the last items from the shopping bags and stealthily glanced over her shoulder to supervise. So far, so good. No fingers dipping into the bowl.

She collected the bag of pre-shredded cheese, fished around for a measuring cup in a lower cabinet and handed the items to Kat.

"Will you fill this halfway with Monterey Jack, pretty please? That would be a big help." She added a huge smile because it was obvious that twin wasn't thrilled with the assignment.

"I want to put sugar on the chips," she said.

"Let's make those together. I'll fry, you sprinkle," Jess said.

"Daddy says we have to make some with salt, too," Lizzy added.

"That's an excellent idea," Jess said.

At least Kat was grudgingly participating, which was more than could be said of Taylor. Her own daughter had taken a seat at the breakfast table and was toying with her friendship bracelets.

Jess understood. Taylor missed her friends back home. Although they were able to Zoom, those bracelets were the only physical connection.

Unfortunately—or perhaps fortunately—Jess didn't leave

any friends behind. She knew better than to make any new ones here, because she'd have to leave them, too. Although it felt as though she'd already made a few at the B and B.

Kat finished filling the measuring cup and did a good job of hitting the halfway mark. Lizzy was busy fishing an eggshell from her prized mix. Those washed hands came in handy after all.

With the twins' duties reasonably under control, Jess settled into a chair across from Taylor. Only a few years ago, she couldn't tear the little girl away from the kitchen. Taylor had wanted to stir the eggs or flip the bacon or do whatever task she could that involved the stovetop. Jess wouldn't let her, but her daddy would. It was their secret. Until Mommy dearest found out and put an end to it. But this wasn't their family.

And Nash wasn't her daddy.

How could I have been so blind?

Jess took a deep breath, then reached over and stilled Taylor's hands until she looked up.

"Know what all this reminds me of?" Jess asked.

Taylor blinked and stared.

"It reminds me of that time I caught your daddy letting you flip the bacon, then lifting you up and leaning over the pan so you could watch it sizzle."

A hint of a smile crossed Taylor's face. "You were so mad, but Daddy thought it was funny."

Jess could practically feel the emotional weight tugging at the corners of that smile. They hadn't talked nearly enough about him, and she was at fault for that. For not initiating a conversation out of fear that it was "too soon." For not confronting that fear. Instead, leaving it up to a little girl to decide when she was ready. But there was no manual for handling such circumstances.

"If I remember correctly, we all ended up laughing at *me* by the end of it. Especially after he pointed out how I was encouraging you to get on top of a thousand-pound animal and making it gallop as fast as it could. Yet, I was so afraid you'd get burned by the popping grease. But he loved you too much to let that happen," Jess said.

Taylor's eyes were now glossing over. Jess wasn't holding it together much better, but she was determined to.

"Hey. I could use some help with browning the sausage," she said, then whispered the last part. "That's too big of a job for Lizzy and Kat."

That earned her the biggest smile of the morning.

Even though this wasn't their home, something felt so right about being here and cooking breakfast with the girls while Nash fed Mischief. Jess even began putting together a mental list of pots and pans and utensils needed to make this a more functional kitchen. Her imagination sewed colorful new cushion covers for the breakfast table chairs to replace the timeworn beige ones. It added flowers to a vase that otherwise seemed to serve no purpose on the counter other than to collect dust. She'd also get that bronc buster's hands back to work telling time.

The cast-iron skillet, however, would stay. As if any of this was her business. She'd bet it was the same one that she and Nash had used to cook Juicy Lucys dozens of times after practice.

Even though Nash had offered, Jess went ahead and diced the andouille and heated the skillet. He could cut the onion or jalapeno or avocado. In the meantime, her request must have resonated, because Taylor was all of a sudden at her side.

Since Lizzy was through with the eggs and had abandoned her post, Jess moved the step stool in front of the stove for Taylor, even though she was almost tall enough to cook without one. Better to be up too high. Couldn't take a chance on Taylor pulling a hot skillet on top of her.

"Can I stir?" Taylor asked.

Jess looked to the twins, who had moved on to drawing flowers and horses around the edges of the writing on Nash's chore board, so they were safely occupied and she could focus on Taylor's safety.

"I would love that." Jess handed her the spatula but remained poised to dive in at a second's notice. "I'll fry the tortilla strips."

Taylor had just started with the browning process when Nash walked back inside.

"Ladies, I'm home!" he said with what sounded to be exaggerated enthusiasm.

He studied the girls' artwork and looked down his nose at the twins, which made them both giggle.

"That is one funny lookin' horse," he said, pointing to one of the stick figures.

"That's 'cause it's a dog!" Lizzy practically shouted.

For some reason, he didn't look happy about that clarification. Instead, he stuffed his hands in his pockets and wandered Jess's way, stopping to peer over Taylor's shoulder. Behind the little girl's back, he cast Jess the same kind of down-the-nose look as he had done with the twins.

Jess didn't need an explanation for the nonverbal reprimand. She'd gone on and on about the dangers of cooking, and there she was, letting Taylor help with one of the riskiest tasks.

"I'll explain later," she said.

"No need." He proceeded to retrieve a folding chair that had been leaning against a wall and positioned it between two of the others. Tight fit, for sure. The whole process appeared painfully awkward, as if this home had never hosted more than four people at one time.

Once everything was cooked and combined, Jess helped Lizzy do the honors of giving everyone an equal serving of *migas*. Nash got up briefly to help serve the orange juice and milk and coffee, then squeezed back into their tight circle.

"Everything looks and smells amazing," he said. "A man could get used to this."

Jess suddenly craved some fresh air. Instead, she took a bite of *migas*. Then another comforting bite.

"Even better than Pop-Tarts," Lizzy said, right before piling a large bite on her fork and putting the whole thing in her mouth.

"I doubt our breakfast is gonna run off and leave us, but we can always make more. Smaller bites, and a little slower, okay?" Nash admonished.

Lizzy forced a visible gulp, then nodded. Kat and Taylor took a more measured approach.

"Pop-Tarts are good but not as good as pancakes with blueberries and strawberries and raspberries and chocolate-maple syrup and whipped cream," Taylor said.

Although the comment seemed to be directed to Lizzy, Jess felt the not-so-subtle jab. She hadn't made Taylor's favorite breakfast this morning. She'd helped make Lizzy's.

Then again, maybe it was a compliment.

"We'll make pancakes together tomorrow," Lizzy said.

Very diplomatic of the little girl. And quite presumptuous. Nash must have had the same thought as Jess, because they both remained deathly quiet. *Should we do this again?*

"Since y'all were able to join us after all, I take it the *gentleman* wasn't able to fix your sewing machine," Nash said to Jess.

Thankfully, one of them changed the subject, although his emphasis on a certain word was curious. Almost sounded as though he was jealous.

"Not yet. But he's working on it. He'll be back over in a few days with a new part. He really knows his stuff," Jess said, taking another bite of *migas* while searching Nash's expression for some sort of confirmation of her suspicions.

He focused on the feast in front of him, giving nothing away.

"Excellent. You're lucky to find someone. Mostly cowboys in these parts. Not too many gentlemen who can fix things like that." He looked up and took a big bite.

Jess swallowed the one she'd taken and dabbed her napkin at the corners of her mouth.

"Turns out, he's a cowboy, as well." She added a smile.

Nash didn't even blink. "A jack-of-all-trades, huh?"

"More like a knight in shining armor. And he's quite dashing and polite, as knights are rumored to be."

"Dashing, huh?" He grinned and looked down, then picked a pan-fried tortilla strip off his plate and bit it in half. Judging by his expression, that one had sugar.

"What does 'dashing' mean?" Kat asked.

"It means he runs away from things," Lizzy said.

"I think, in this case, it means the cowboy mechanic was cute," Nash said.

"He wasn't cute," Taylor chimed in.

An amused look crossed Nash's face. She felt an urgent need to defend her knight in faded overalls.

"Young lady, that isn't true," Jess said. In her opinion, Vern was adorable.

"He's old, Mommy," Taylor countered.

"Anyone over thirty is considered *old* to her," Jess said to Nash, which seemed to humble him a little since he had also surpassed that milestone. By a few years, if her memory served.

The conversation quickly returned to small talk until there wasn't a morsel left on anyone's plate. Jess rose to clear the dishes, starting with hers, but Nash eased the plate out of her hands.

"You ladies did all the work. Let me take care of these."

"That's a nice offer, but I insist on helping. The girls can go do their own thing and have some fun. I'm afraid I don't have any exciting plans for them today. Not yet, at least." Might as well fess up in advance. Nash would hear about their day, anyway, how Jess kept them trapped inside the B and B while she sewed.

Without waiting to receive the go-ahead, the girls ran back down the hall. Taylor followed.

Together, she and Nash cleared the plates and placed them beside the sink. He let the water run until it turned hot, then plugged one side while Jess added the dishwashing liquid.

"Alone at last," Nash said as he began washing and rinsing the plates, one at a time.

This was a good thing. She wanted to get a read on his thoughts about Taylor. He hadn't offered anything so far.

After the dinner plates were clean and placed in the drainer, he soaped the chipped bowl. He did a thorough job with the task, as if he'd done the same thing every morning for years.

Then again, he'd had to do all the day-to-day tasks by himself, as she'd also been having to do. Exactly how long had Roxanne been gone?

Jess picked up a dry cloth, eased the bowl from his hands and proceeded to dry it. No room left in the drainer, but she'd take care of those next.

"I'm sure you want an update on Taylor's progress," he said.

"Mind reader," she said.

Nash collected the forks and rinsed each as thoroughly as he had the dishes.

"You were right about her talent. But I'm questioning mine. I need a little more time to figure out what's holding her back, because I agree with what you said—she's The One to Watch, for sure." He handed her the utensils to dry, then started on the skillet.

"I have no doubt you'll solve the mystery. You're raising two amazing daughters, by the way. For twins, they couldn't be any more different,"

Nash nodded. "We've been through a lot together. Some rough times but mostly good. Kind of like this old thing." He held up the skillet and pivoted it around as if it were a feather.

Her entire body ached at the nostalgic feelings that piece of cast iron evoked.

"Those Juicy Lucys we used to cook would make any skillet happy. Not to mention, any hungry cowboy or cowgirl," she said.

"Yep."

Even though that one word was all he offered, his smile confirmed he remembered their good times, as well. As with the serving bowl, that wall he'd built had some chips in it after all.

The wall she'd tried to create wasn't faring much better.

FEELINGS WERE NOT part of Nash's plan. But there they were. Right on the surface.

Furthermore, he liked it. He missed all this about Jess. Their long talks. The friendship. Their teamwork in washing the dishes after someone lost the joke swap and had to cook Juicy Lucys.

How I feel when she looks at me.

Most of all, he missed her laughter, although he'd yet to hear it this morning. Roxanne not only didn't have a domestic bone in her body, she didn't have a funny bone, either.

Jess's laugh was contagious. It started out as a giggle, then exploded into a full-throated, open-mouthed, face-to-the-ceiling howl after the punch line settled in.

He came close to telling a joke, wanting to hear that laugh again. But he was already treading on dangerous ground.

Having finished with the dishes, they both turned around and leaned against the counter like they used to do.

"No plans for the day, huh?" he asked. Mostly to make small talk. He didn't expect her to have something unique and exciting for the twins to do at all times. Keeping them entertained was practically impossible.

"To be honest, I was hoping to come up with an idea that would keep them within my field of vision while I got some work done."

Of course she had work to do. Unless she'd received some big life insurance policy, she had to support herself and her daughter. It reminded him of how little he really knew about her. The familiar moments tricked him into thinking that no time had passed between them.

"What kind of work do you do, aside from raising a daughter? Being a single parent is the hardest job in the world," he said, angling himself toward her.

She pivoted to face him, as well. "That's the truth. Parenthood is a full-time gig, but it doesn't pay the bills. I sew. My clients, at least right now, are other rodeo mommies."

He resisted the urge to wince. The more he thought about it, the more he realized her rodeo-circuit clientele might include Roxanne. He hadn't heard whether she'd gone on to have other children. Then again, he'd stopped following all barrel racing news. He didn't want to know.

"Seems we both play two roles. Or, at least I assume you don't have a wife out there somewhere who you haven't told me about," she said.

"Just an ex," he responded without naming names. That seemed pointless at this juncture. Jess was much better at math than he'd ever be. She could add two plus two just fine.

"Does she ever…?" Jess began to say.

"See the girls?"

Jess nodded.

Nash shook his head and hoped that was enough of an answer.

"All I can say is that Taylor's lucky to have a mom like you. And one that sews. I hope she knows that."

"That's about the only thing she likes about me these days."

"I doubt that."

"We share a passion for barrel racing. And all the excitement of traveling from city to city. So there is that. It's more than enough for me to live vicariously through her and her successes."

His breath caught in his throat. He remembered those days.

"I can't imagine doing that now. This ranch is our forever home. Until the twins up and marry and move out. In that order, if I have any say."

Jess laughed softly. "Takes time to really know what you want. Trial and error. Get married too early, and..."

"You end up settling down and planting roots when you don't want to," he said.

"And giving up on what you did," she added.

There. That's what he needed to hear, even though he hadn't wanted to. As much as he could get used to all this—waking up in the same home every morning, and sharing breakfast and feelings with family—it didn't appeal to Jess.

Nash had hesitated asking a question that had been on his mind since she left. However, she'd opened the door, and he was walking through.

"Why did you stop, Jess?"

She gulped hard and stared at him for what felt like the longest minute.

"I've asked myself that question," she said. "I needed a sabbatical. Needed to step away from it all for a while, and that's when Lance stepped in. We got married, I got pregnant, then Taylor was born. All I wanted to do was be there to take care of them. And especially her. Still do."

"From what I can see, you're doing a beautiful job. Besides, you could get back into it." His comment wasn't an idle one. Even though he was entertaining the thought of her having breakfast with them every morning, he was under no illusion that she wanted such a life.

She looked down and scratched at a spot on the counter.

"Right now, I'm focusing on making ends meet. I thought Lance had a good life insurance policy, but he'd cashed it out. Needed the money to pay bills for things I didn't even know he'd bought."

"Ouch."

"Never occurred to me to question why he really needed a new tractor, super-duper tires on his truck, or that the cloth upholstery inside had been replaced with leather. He handled all the finances for us. But he was such a loving dad to Taylor, and a terrific husband to me in many ways."

Nash wanted to say the guy had good taste, too, as evidenced by the fact that he married Jess. But now wasn't the time for such things.

"I'm sorry to hear that." Despite the way their relationship had ended, and all the question marks it left in its wake, he'd never stopped wanting the best for her.

Jess offered a soft smile of appreciation. "Thank you. But, hey, what doesn't kill us makes us stronger, right?"

"How has Taylor handled losing her dad?"

Jess folded her arms and looked to the floor. "I guess as well as any child would. Of course, she doesn't know about the money situation. And I would never tell her. I'd rather she remember only good things about her father. She thinks I sew because I love it. Thank goodness she likes what I make for her, because I couldn't begin to afford…"

Nash inched closer and tugged at her arms until they unfolded. He intertwined his fingers with hers and gave them a squeeze.

He almost admitted he'd had similar issues with Roxanne with the spending but stopped short. He'd felt like a failure for barely meeting her lifestyle expectations. He'd been forced to lower those even further and start saying no after he found out they were having twins. That didn't go over well.

But this moment wasn't about him.

She slipped her hands from his loose grip and gave him a big hug instead, which made any residual inadequacies he'd felt dissolve away. Especially when he hugged her even harder in return, and her form seemed to mold to his.

A trio of giggles erupted from the doorway.

Although he was pretty sure the girls hadn't heard any of their conversation, the long, intimate hug could be interpreted in many ways. And the way they seemed to be interpreting it made them all happy, which only confirmed what he already knew.

His wasn't the only heart in peril.

CHAPTER EIGHT

JESS'S EYES FLEW open when the grandfather clock announced it was 5:00 a.m.

She bolted upright and tried to orient herself to her surroundings, because none of it looked familiar.

It was coming back to her now. She'd gotten up at 3:00 a.m. and come down to the parlor to sew. Must have laid her head down around four and fallen asleep, because she remembered those chimes.

She examined the dot paper where her cheek had been. No drool, thankfully. Just a little smudge from the mascara she'd neglected to remove last night. It was in the shape of a perfect heart, no less. What were the odds? Although she'd lost an hour of productive time, it was unlikely that anyone would wander into the parlor so early.

Judging by the clinking bowls, Georgina was in the kitchen, starting preparations for breakfast. Jess could grab a cup of coffee now from the pot she'd made an hour ago and put on a fresh one for her hostess.

She wasn't quick enough. As soon as she stood, a woman emerged from the kitchen, holding the carafe. Except it wasn't Georgina. Furthermore, the woman wasn't alone. An adorable, sleepy-looking young boy stayed close to her side.

"I thought you could use a refill," she said, adding a warm smile that rivaled her even warmer voice.

Her timing couldn't have been more perfect. This woman was an angel. Sans the wings.

When Jess didn't answer, the woman picked up the cup that Jess had placed on a side table and filled it to the brim, then looked down at the little boy.

"PJ, would you like to offer Jess some cream or sweetener?"

He held up a small carton of milk and some packets of sugar. It had to be the cutest thing Jess had ever seen. She couldn't say no to that face even if she wanted to.

"I'll take some milk. Thank you, PJ."

The little boy took a step forward and offered her both milk and sugar anyway.

"He helped me carry the eggs in this morning, too. Don't think I could manage without him," the woman said, while brushing the almost black hair out of the little boy's eyes.

"I can understand why," Jess said as she tried to piece this pattern into something recognizable. Vern's ranch provided the eggs, but he was usually the one to bring them over. This must be family.

"I'm Vern's granddaughter, Vanessa," the woman offered before Jess had a chance to confirm her theory. "He wasn't up to the task this morning but told me you were here and what happened with your machine. And that you'd probably be awake and working this morning."

A pang of guilt cut through Jess's conscience at the memory of Vern hauling that heavy toolbox up the stairs. Then struggling with that big crate of eggs. And she'd let him.

"Is he okay?" she asked.

"He'll be fine. He gets down in his back sometimes. Tends to overdo it. I offered to make this delivery run for him. I'll be back this afternoon to lead a workshop. At least, I think it's this afternoon."

Vanessa had that mind-spinning look that Jess recognized all too well in herself. That "I have so many responsibilities to juggle, I don't know where to start" kind of expression. Jess knew from experience that that was when it was best to take a step back and regroup. She was standing at that same precipice.

"Care to join me for a cup of coffee?" Jess asked.

Vanessa looked at the carafe and bit her lip. "I don't want to take you away from what you're working on."

"Oh, please, take me away for a minute." Truth was, she could use some hot coffee to sharpen her focus, and she didn't want to have any kind of beverage near the fabric. Not even water.

A smile broke through Vanessa's visible stress. "An offer I can't refuse. Okay. I'll grab a mug from the kitchen. PJ, let's get you something to drink while we're in there."

By the time Vanessa and PJ came back, Jess had organized her next steps to finish one of the Western shirts. For now, she settled into an armchair.

PJ was carrying a glass of milk with both hands. Vanessa eased it from his grip and patted the overstuffed sofa as a directive for him to sit, then eased in beside him.

"Is PJ a nickname or your full name?" Jess asked.

"My real name is Perry Jackson Fraser, but there's a girl in my class named Perry, too, so I got this nickname. I like it."

"If you stay in Destiny Springs long enough, you'll get a nickname, too," Vanessa said. "Except in my case, apparently. Not sure whether I should be insulted or relieved. I don't stand still long enough for them to pin one on me."

Jess couldn't resist. "Really? I got one my second day here. Georgina called me Nash's gal."

Vanessa's brows raised, and her mouth formed an O but nothing came out.

"I had the same reaction. Georgina said she didn't mean it *that* way. And why would she? But you can imagine how I felt."

"There are worse things to be called. Nash is a good man. Gave my cousin Parker a job as a ranch hand, even though he didn't even know what a hoof-pick was used for. Thought it was for cleaning the stalls. Parker denies it, of course. That's another thing about Destiny Springs. You'll hear the most outlandish stories, but they *all* end up being true."

"All?" Jess asked. Vanessa's emphasis on the word was interesting. Vern had already warned her about them, but he said only *some* were true.

Even though hiring a ranch hand with zero experience seemed outlandish, it sounded like something Nash would do. Might be a good topic of discussion between the two of them, instead of dredging up their distant past. Or even worse, the recent past. Yesterday had turned way too personal with that extended hug. She could still feel the softness of his flannel shirt and the strength of his heartbeat.

"I'd like a man like that in my life, but I barely have time for this one." Vanessa reached over and wiped away a drop of milk that had settled on PJ's chin.

The relationship between Vanessa and PJ was at a sweet stage. Hopefully, it would stay that way for her sake. Another single mom, up at the crack of dawn to take care of others, which included Jess this morning with the coffee.

"Cody mentioned a work-life balance workshop. Is that the one you're leading?" Jess asked.

"Yes. Sounds appealing, huh? Specifically, caring for young children and older parents. Some folks call us the 'sandwich generation.' But my workshop adds an extra ingredient—pursuing a new career without the support of a spouse. Some sandwiches have to thrive with only one ingredient and one breadwinner. Themselves."

"I couldn't have said it any better. Are you starting a new career?"

"Sort of. I'm a caregiver. It's the only thing I know. Been doing it since before I was old enough to legally work. But I'm opening my own business in Cheyenne in a few months and will have professionals do the legwork, which will hopefully free up more time to spend with this little man."

"Won't that be fun, having your mommy around more often?" Jess asked PJ.

"Yaaas!" He nodded enthusiastically, then looked up to his mom with the biggest smile.

"Sounds like a good plan, Vanessa," Jess said, stopping short of promising to attend the workshop. She had Lizzy and Kat to think about. Not to mention, her work projects.

"If you ever get tired of sewing everything yourself, you could do something similar. You could design, and someone else could execute it. Might give you more time with your daughter."

"I'd love that, but I'm not so sure how she'd feel," Jess said. "She's at the age where she's testing boundaries and asserting her independence. She retreats into her headphones, but she still seems to like having me near."

"Maybe you could use the quiet time to focus on yourself. Try some meditation or pampering. It sounds like you've earned it."

Now, there was a concept. Hadn't even occurred to her.

"Well, I think you've earned a nickname, Vanessa. I hereby proclaim you Earth Angel. If there's anything I can do to help *you* while I'm here, please let me know."

Except for sewing clothes for PJ, so please don't ask.

Vanessa's phone buzzed. The woman read the message and unleashed a heavy sigh. Another ball must have been thrown into her work-life balancing act.

"Everything okay?" Jess asked.

"Grandpa's girlfriend, Sylvie, can't look after him this afternoon. She's leading a trail ride. I may have to see if the DEBBs can fill my workshop time with something or someone else. Unless Nash can step in and help. He's over there now, checking on Vern." Vanessa maintained eye contact as if making sure Jess was convinced of Nash's selflessness.

No need. She already knew.

"Sounds like something Nash would do." The last thing he needed was to step in and help take care of Vern again this afternoon.

"Like I said, he's a good man. He could use a good woman in his life after what he went through. But you didn't hear it from me."

It seemed Vanessa knew Nash better than she'd led Jess to believe, with the way she'd been hyping him up. But Jess needed more information.

"I'm thinking out loud here, but I can't believe Roxanne could walk away from him. Much less her own daughters," she said.

Of course, Jess didn't know who walked away from whom. But Roxanne was alive and thriving on the rodeo circuit. If it were her being away from her child or children, she'd be too distraught to ever compete again.

"Me, neither. But I think it's a good thing that he has full custody of the twins. He loves those girls so much, and they're crazy about him. He's a good dad."

And a good man, in general. Jess came so close to volunteering to help Vern this afternoon herself, but she didn't know anything about nursing an octogenarian with a bad back. Plus, she'd have the twins, and that might be more than she could manage. However, that gave her an idea.

"I don't know anything about balancing, but I'm pretty good at tying up loose threads. If the DEBBs would be interested in an impromptu sewing workshop in place of yours, I'd be willing to make a fool of myself."

The tension in Vanessa's face softened. "That sounds like a wonderful idea to me, but that's a lot to ask."

Jess wouldn't define it as that, but if it helped her Earth Angel and spared Nash from having to step in and help Vern, she would do it. Besides, a sewing workshop might be fun for the girls. She could give them some felt and glue and rhinestones to play with while she constructed a garment for the belles and beaus.

"I do have something I'd like to ask," Jess said. It was a bold question, but since Vanessa seemed to be playing matchmaker... "Do you think Nash would ever get back with Roxanne?"

Vanessa tilted her head. "I doubt he feels anything for her. I'm not convinced he ever really did."

"Because she wasn't the one who broke his heart?" That was the rumor Vern had mentioned, although Jess had a difficult time believing it.

"Exactly," Vanessa said with a confidence that sent a chill racing down Jess's spine. Whether it was the good kind or bad, she wasn't sure.

Vanessa continued. "Problem is, the only person who knows who did is Nash. And he isn't talking."

"HEALTH IS BETTER than wealth," Vern said. He visibly winced when Nash tugged the heating pad out from under him once he'd shifted to his side.

"Sorry. I'm not the best nurse around," Nash said, although he wished he were setting a better example.

The twins looked on with muted curiosity. Even though he'd wanted to spare them from witnessing the inconveniences of aging and the inevitable aches and pains for as long as he could, they needed to learn how to help. And know that people would be there for them, too, if they ever needed it. That's what family and friends were all about.

Ordinarily, Vern would swing by Nash's and drop off some eggs for his "favorite Destiny Springs bachelor" en route to the B and B. However, Vanessa had called late last night and asked Nash if he wouldn't mind picking up his portion of eggs while she made Fraser Ranch's usual delivery to the B and B. That way, her grandpa wouldn't be left alone for too long, in case he needed help with something.

Nash didn't even have to think twice. It was worth having to rouse the girls out of bed a little early.

He adjusted the heating pad cord, which could present a trip hazard if Vern got a wild hair and decided to get up and walk around. The picture of health, he was not.

"You don't need to baby me," Vern said. "You and the girls go on home."

"We'll leave after you finish what you started to say about health and wealth."

Nash meant it. Although lack of wealth was his main concern these days, that pesky palpitation from a few days ago still haunted him. He'd gotten his heart checked six months ago. The cardiologist ran the requisite tests and informed Nash that he was as healthy as a bull. And Nash believed it.

Then Jess showed up. Ten years had passed, and much more had happened to her than he'd ever imagined.

"Not sure there's much to add," Vern said. "Except that if we can't have both, we should all have at least one or the other."

"If that were the case, you would deserve to be a millionaire today," Nash replied.

"How do you know I'm not?" Vern cackled. "I'm in better shape than I look. It's just that these parts of ours come with limited warranties. All of mine have long expired."

"How'd you strain it this time?" Nash asked. These back issues were becoming a semiregular occurrence with the guy.

"I was trying to impress a lovely young lady by carrying that heavy toolbox upstairs." Vern pointed toward the culprit by the door in the entry. "Her sewing machine broke down, so of course Cody called on me to help. I think you know her. Jess McCoy?"

Nash did a terrible job hiding his huge grin. It came on so fast. She'd led him to believe it was some young cowboy who'd been the gentleman to come to her rescue. *Dashing*, did she say?

"Uh-huh. That's what I thought. You have a crush on that gal," Vern said.

Nash glanced at the twins, who were busy rearranging the knickknacks on one of the side tables and knocking a few to the ground in the process. Thankfully, Vern seemed amused rather than annoyed.

"You *do* know how old I am," Nash said, even though he himself couldn't find a better word to describe how he felt.

"You're never too old to have a crush. I had one on Sylvie for all of one minute before I fell head over heels for her. Couldn't have hidden it if I'd wanted to. But don't worry, your secret is safe with me," Vern said as he gave him the thumbs-up.

"Care to shake on it?" Nash held up his pinkie.

Vern latched on. "Ha! I haven't made a pinkie promise in years."

With his secret safe, Nash covered Vern loosely with a fuzzy blanket, leaving the heating pad exposed. He put another log on the fire and stoked it. Lizzy tried to ease the poker from his hand, but he tightened his grip. This was definitely not a toy.

"Do me a favor, sweetie. Can you and Kat bring Mr. Vern a tall glass of ice water?" He didn't want their input on this topic.

Not after they'd witnessed the hug. And later, when he'd tucked them into bed, they'd asked if Jess was his girlfriend. He had to explain that friends sometimes hugged, too, and that it was perfectly fine as long as both people were okay with it.

Yet, there was something much more special about his and Jess's hug. Even the girls picked up on it.

The front door flew open, and PJ ran inside, followed by Vanessa. She helped her son remove his jacket, then took off her own scarf and draped the items over the existing coats and sweaters and hats.

"Were your ears burning?" she asked Nash as she wandered over.

Not that he should have been surprised. People in Destiny Springs enjoyed a little gossip as much as anyone. Single folks and their personal business seemed to be the preferred topic.

"Girls, come over here and feel my ears. Tell me if they're burning."

He leaned over, and they eagerly complied.

"Yes!" they said in unison.

"I guess the question is, why would they be doing that?" He directed the question at Vanessa.

"I had coffee with someone you know who's staying at the B and B."

Why was Jess up this early?

Nash couldn't say he knew Vanessa well, yet she felt like family because Vern was like family. They'd crossed paths as youngsters. A few months ago, she'd come to Destiny Springs to help with Vern alongside Parker. But, unlike her cousin, Vanessa had bigger plans than to settle down here.

For now, whatever this ear-burning nonsense was, it needed to cool down real fast.

"The lady said she's Nash's gal. That's you!" PJ added.

Nash looked to Vanessa. "What?"

"Georgina inadvertently referred to her as 'Nash's gal' before realizing how it sounded. How funny is that?"

"Jess is a sweet *gal*, that's for sure, but she's not mine." In another week and some change, she'd be on her way to Montana with her daughter.

"Mommy has a nickname, too," PJ said.

"How about you and the girls go play upstairs." Vanessa pivoted him toward the stairway and gave him a kiss on the top of his head before he ran away with the girls hot on his heels.

"And what might that nickname be?" Nash asked.

"Earth Angel."

"Like the song?" he asked.

"No. Like, I brought her a cup of coffee while she was working, and she gave me way too much credit."

Vanessa walked over to Vern and readjusted the heating pad that Nash had just positioned. "Can I get you anything, Grandpa?"

"Not a thing, angel. You don't have to fuss over me."

"Speaking of angels, you saved Jess's life, you know," Vanessa said to Vern, who promptly tried to swat the compliment away.

"She gets up two hours early so she can finish all her sewing commitments before she has to leave for Montana," Vanessa continued.

"She mentioned getting up before the crack of dawn," Vern said. "I hope she can find a better solution. Lack of sleep is hard on the body and the mind."

Nash understood that all too well. He hadn't slept through the night since Roxanne left them the first time. The twins were two handfuls as infants, and it wasn't getting easier with age. Now he realized that he'd handed off that responsibility to Jess every day since she got here. Maybe the trade he'd insisted upon wasn't so equal after all.

Sure, he couldn't fix a sewing machine. But there was something he *could* do to help, starting with offering to feed Mischief in the mornings. The extra time it took her to come back and forth to his house for that could be better spent on her own projects before having to juggle twins.

Besides, it was just breakfast for one additional horse, right?

Right. Kind of like *migas* with the girls had been just breakfast—one that led to an extended hug, which had led to thoughts of something else. Something he'd dared to imagine ten years ago but didn't dare act upon.

Kissing her.

CHAPTER NINE

"DO I LOOK as brokenhearted as I feel?" Nash asked in a low tone.

Jess gulped. The conversation she'd had with Vanessa about Nash and the mystery woman was still fresh on her mind.

"Who broke your heart?" she asked.

His eyes shifted toward Kat, who had followed Lizzy to the parlor entry to look at the crowd that had assembled there.

"Someone isn't happy, although I'm not sure why. I suspect it has to do with me coaching Taylor. Anything you could do to cheer her up would be greatly appreciated."

Not the pressure Jess needed today, with this workshop now on her plate and a parlor full of DEBBs waiting for her to start.

The good news was, what had felt like the worst idea to volunteer ended up being nothing short of brilliant. She was going to use this time to make progress on one of the garments she owed.

"Girls, go ahead and find a spot inside," Jess called out. "I'll be there in a sec, and then we'll get started on some fun stuff."

Jess then turned to Nash. "I was planning to start one of the barrel racing shirts I owe to a rodeo mom as the workshop topic, but I'll distract the girls with felt and rhinestones. Just wanted to let you know, since rodeo stuff is a tender subject."

"I appreciate it. Those shirts look like some she and Lizzy already own, so no concerns. Besides, you're not putting her on a horse or anything."

"No danger of me doing that," she said. He'd been open about his problems, and she wasn't going to add to them.

He softly smiled and nodded for Taylor to follow him.

Once the two were out the door, Jess got situated at the front of the room and looked out at the eager faces of the DEBBs. All she saw was irony.

Those sweet, trusting folks were looking to a self-taught seamstress—one who'd never taken a formal lesson herself, much less presented one—to teach them something.

Lizzy had claimed the big, overstuffed chair nearest the sewing machine. She was a little wiggly but otherwise attentive and ready to help. Jess had a new idea for how to involve her in the process, in a fun way. Even more fun than felt and rhinestones. She'd have Lizzy trace around the sample shirt to make a pattern on the dot paper.

Kat had retreated to a chair in the far back of the parlor. It was almost as if she were stating the obvious: she felt left out. It broke Jess's heart. After all, Lizzy and Jess had bonded over cooking, and Kat's own daddy was bonding with Taylor over barrel racing. Not only that, but the lessons were continuing.

Then a possible solution occurred to her. Jess straightened and served up her most confident smile to the group.

"Does anyone here have a favorite top or skirt or pair of pants that they'd love to duplicate?" she asked.

Nearly all the hands raised.

"I used to have a top like the one I'm wearing. It was my favorite. I paid a little over one hundred dollars, but I made this duplicate I'm wearing for under five. The only difference between the two is that this one doesn't have a fancy label. I'm not sure what material that label was made from, but it couldn't have been worth the extra ninety-five bucks. Especially since no one ever saw it."

That got everyone's attention. Except Kat's. But Jess was just getting started.

"For today's workshop, we'll be duplicating a girl's Western barrel racing shirt from a clone. Lizzy, I'll need your help with drawing the pattern. Dorothy, would you mind helping

Lizzy lay it out nice and flat while I make sure my model fits the prototype?"

"I'd love to," Dorothy said.

It wasn't lost on Jess that she'd now owe the lady a favor.

"I need a model," Jess said, although she already knew who she'd pick. "Let's see, it needs to be someone who fits the sample."

Kat sat up a little straighter but didn't volunteer. At least she'd been listening. Jess walked to the back of the room.

"Do you want to model for me?"

Kat nodded so hard Jess was afraid she'd throw out her neck. Talk about a transformation. Now there was no doubt in Jess's mind that the little girl was interested in the sport.

"Good! Let's run upstairs to my room. I want you to try something on."

Kat hopped out of the chair.

Jess took her hand, and they approached Dorothy. "Would you mind talking to the group about sewing while we're gone?"

It was a big ask, but Dorothy seemed more than willing. At this point, Jess was out of viable options.

Together, Jess and Kat went to the Spandex Room, where Jess fished out the folded top from her work stack and handed it to her little model.

Jess turned around to give her some privacy. "Let me know if you need any help."

After a few long minutes, Kat said, "I'm ready."

Other than the sleeves being nearly an inch too long, it looked like the shirt was made for her.

"I *loooove* it." Kat practically ran over to a full-length mirror and twirled around to see all the angles. "Where is the number?"

"That's something they assign the barrel racer before the competition."

Jess's answer deflated Kat's smile. Not completely, but enough. So much for this bright idea.

"How do you feel about pink?" That may be her only saving grace. She remembered Kat had been wearing a pink puffer jacket when they first met.

The little girl confirmed with a nod.

"Good. Change back into your other clothes and we'll get started making this." Even though this shirt design had a scalloped yoke and Jess didn't have enough contrasting fabric to help it stand out, she could use the same pink fabric and add black piping to fancy it up. She was pretty sure she had rhinestone snaps somewhere, as well. The client was going to love it.

Hand in hand, she and Kat returned to the group. Dorothy had taken full command of the workshop, explaining the different patterning paper.

"Then there's my favorite. Dot paper, also known as alphabet paper, which is what Jess is using here. See how it has these blue marks, evenly spaced in a grid? It's a little more expensive but worth it, in my opinion."

"Thank you for helping, Dorothy. If I get any more speaking engagements, can I hire you?" Jess asked.

"I'd be hurt if you didn't." Dorothy smiled and exited the proverbial spotlight.

Now, for the other smile Jess wanted to see.

She explained the first steps to the group. Specifically, how to fold the material and position different parts of the garment to create the pattern pieces. Lizzy had the important task of drawing around all the edges while Kat looked on with a highly contagious enthusiasm.

Jess added a dotted line around all the drawn pieces and then proceeded to cut them out. For time's sake, she talked through the rest of the process of cutting out the material and assembling the garment. While necessary, it ended up being a bad idea. In the background, she picked up on chattering.

"John had a favorite linen shirt that he wore out. Maybe I'll surprise him and make one like it for our twelfth anniversary," one of the ladies said.

The thought of wedding anniversaries poked at Jess's pincushion of a heart. She'd sewn matching cotton shirts for her and Lance to celebrate their second.

"That is a wonderful idea!" another lady said. "I think I'll pattern some new drapes for our bedroom. We both love plaid. Wesley absolutely hates the red, white and blue ones that came with the house."

Jess closed her eyes and tried to refocus on the task at hand. But the warm memories of decorating her own primary suite as a newlywed sprang to mind. Her bedroom these days was whichever hotel room she shared with her daughter on their way to the next rodeo.

Although traveling so much hadn't been the easiest life for either of them, it was still better than being tied to a so-called home built on a chiffon-thin foundation. But that was a lifetime ago. She had an important task right in front of her now.

She resorted to an old trick she used when barrel racing: focusing on what she wanted most, and pretending as if it were waiting for her at the finish line. In this case, she wanted this workshop to be over with.

After adding the final snap, Jess turned around and stood. The chattering stopped.

She raised the shirt high enough for everyone to see. "Ladies and gents, here is the almost completed project. I wanted to touch on all the steps, but I need to go back and do some finishing."

That was an understatement. At least she hadn't lost any of the attendees, even though she'd gone over the allotted hour.

Jess had finished the top in a decent time frame.

After the DEBBs thanked her and dispersed, she finished the shirt while the girls pulled everything out of her notions toolbox as if they'd discovered some cool new toys. She nudged the pincushion and needles out of their reach. Lizzy zeroed in on the tailor's chalk and was trying to draw on a scrap of dot paper. Kat, on the other hand, seemed to have reverted to her gloomy self.

"You're a natural at modeling, Kat. Maybe you could be one when you grow up," Jess said, realizing a little too late that she shouldn't encourage that traveling-required profession, either, for Nash's sake.

Kat toyed with some of the bright-colored thimbles. "Do models get to keep the shirts they model?"

Jess knew what Kat was asking. She also knew that this shirt wasn't her best work. Definitely not well-made enough for her client. Yet, it had served the purpose for the workshop, if not making Kat completely happy. But one thing might.

"Today, they do," she said. The words were like a vitamin B infusion for the little girl, who pepped right up.

The good ideas kept coming.

Jess rummaged through a couple of travel cases and found a good-sized square of muslin. She then pulled the velvet square that she'd proposed to use for the Dudley project and held it against her heart, hoping it would give her the right answer, because, as Georgina had said in the cooking workshop, there wasn't a fabric store within a hundred miles of Destiny Springs.

"Lizzy, would you mind handing me some black thread, please?" She then turned to Kat. "What's your favorite number?"

Kat didn't even have think about it. "Eight."

"Any special reason?"

"Taylor is eight, and I want to be eight."

"Well, you're about to get your wish. Lizzy, I'll need your help. Can you draw a big number eight on this pattern paper?" Jess marked some parameters so that the little girl would get the proportions right.

"While you're at it, draw a daisy. A big one, about the size of my hand." Jess could make a pink daisy from the scraps and add something in the center. That way Lizzy wouldn't go home empty-handed.

Jess sewed the flower first, adding some backing between the pink layers and a giant black button in the center.

"For you, my lady," she said as she handed it to Lizzy.

"That's pretty!" Lizzy said, brushing her tiny fingers over the petals.

One down, one to go. Jess cut out a square of the muslin and used a zigzag stitch on the edges so they wouldn't fray. She then cut out the number that Lizzy had drawn and trimmed it out of the black velvet scrap she'd brought down. Her scissors rounded the curves like a barrel racer would.

"Did y'all know that the original barrel racing configuration was a figure eight and not a cloverleaf? And that the women received scores on their horsemanship and outfits?"

They both shook their heads. Kat seemed especially intrigued. Lizzy, not so much.

With some careful positioning, Jess sewed the number onto the muslin, tacked all four corners onto the back of the shirt so that it would be easy to remove, and held it up for Kat to see.

"What do you think?" she asked.

Kat didn't have to answer. Her beautiful smile was everything in the moment. If this turnaround didn't impress Nash, she wasn't sure what could.

"Can I wear it now?" Kat asked.

"Sure! We need to try it on anyway. Make sure I don't need to alter anything else."

When they all went back upstairs, Kat couldn't change into the shirt fast enough. But when the little girl turned around, Jess not only saw the competitor's number she'd tacked onto the back, she recognized a whole other layer of irony.

In trying to tread softly around a certain subject, she may have intentionally barreled through it.

NASH ASSUMED HIS old teaching spot on the fence railing. Knowingly this time. But this was as far as it was going to go.

He watched Taylor go through the pattern. Positioning was good coming in. Mischief was supple in his rib cage. They powered out of the turns beautifully. One new thing did stand out today: her start was a little shy, and she still wasn't running home as fast as he thought she could.

The question was, why? The trickiest part was rounding the barrels, and she slayed those.

If he thought taking her through what Jess used to call the lazy daisy drill would help, he would gladly add three more barrels and rearrange them in a loose daisy pattern. But that was a lot of trouble and wouldn't be necessary if his intuition was right. In fact, they could wrap this up today, and he could move on with his life. More importantly, Jess could get back to doing what she needed to do with her work, because the inequality of their trade was now weighing *him* down.

Nash motioned Taylor over. "What do you think about when you're out there?"

She looked away as if searching for an answer. "Um, I don't know. I just try to block out the noise, and I focus on the first barrel."

"Good. Do you give a pep talk to Mischief?"

"Yeah. Sometimes."

"Does he ever give you one back?"

Her brows scrunched. "No. Of course not. Horses can't talk."

Okay, maybe she was a little too mature to fall for that.

"True. But he listens to you, doesn't he? You teach him to focus on what you both want to accomplish through actions. And he answers in his own way."

"I s'pose."

"I want you to try something. Think about how much fun you and Mischief have out there."

That hint of a smile faded, which was exactly the response he'd hoped for.

"Humor me," he said.

"Okay. I'll try," she said.

Once she started, his stopwatch confirmed what was clear to his eyes. Sure enough, this time she was over by an extra five seconds or so. His timing method wasn't too precise, but with that much of a lag, it didn't need to be. That time difference equaled centuries in barrel racing.

Her chin practically touched her chest as she approached him again.

"Sorry," she said.

"No need to apologize. Ever. Let's go inside and get some hot chocolate. With lots of marshmallows."

Taylor gave Mischief a side kick and steered him toward the stables.

"Let him stay out here," Nash called out. "We aren't finished."

No doubt in his mind that her issues had nothing to do with her skill level and everything to do with her emotions. Was Jess pushing, and was this Taylor's way of pushing back? Or was it not fun for her anymore? He was determined to find out.

Taylor sat quietly at the breakfast table while Nash warmed up the milk in a saucepan, added the chocolate mix and poured it into mugs. He topped them both off with an overflowing handful of marshmallows.

From his place across the table, he could easily gauge her reactions. He took a sip and intentionally dipped his upper lip a little too deep before setting the cup down.

"Okay, Miss Simms. Time for a serious talk."

She finished taking her sip, looked up, then started giggling.

"What?"

"You have a mustache!"

"No, ma'am. Not possible. I shaved this morning."

"You do! It's a marshmallow mustache."

He wiped it away. "Better?"

She confirmed with a nod.

His mustache might be gone, but her smile remained.

"We really haven't had a chance to talk," he said. "I'd love to know about your barrel racing journey. When did you discover that you loved it?"

Taylor shrugged. "I don't know. Ever since I was a little girl. Mommy showed me how to do it once, and I liked it and was good at it."

Nash had to blink. Strange, but something about the way she said it reminded him of the first time he put Kat on a horse. She not only liked it, she loved it. Furthermore, she was a natural, too. Little girls and their horses. Such a treasure.

"You're *extremely* good at it. I know it's hard work, but do you also have fun out there?"

Taylor looked away. "Sometimes."

Now he was getting somewhere. Exactly where, he didn't know.

"What happens the other times?"

She shrugged.

"I'm a good listener, if there's anything you want to talk about," he said.

No admissions were forthcoming.

"I have something I'd like to talk about, and I feel like I can trust you with my feelings," he said.

She looked at him. "Okay."

"I'll need a pinkie promise. Do you know what that is?"

"Um, no."

Nash extended his hand across the table, pinkie curled. "It means we're friends and we can talk about whatever is bothering us, without judgment. Hook yours onto mine and we shake."

He suspected that whatever weight she was carrying, he could lift it right off and all would be fine. Jess was a good mom, and Taylor was an otherwise happy and well-adjusted young girl.

She did as instructed. They released and Nash leaned back in his chair.

"Whew! Thank you. I've been wanting to tell someone about this." He wasn't much of an actor, but she seemed to buy it.

Taylor sat up straighter.

"My daddy wanted me to be a bull rider. Started entering me into contests when I was seven. But I hated it so much, I pretended to be sick to get out of doin' it. I was scared of falling to the ground. I have a thing about that, I guess you could say. Have you ever done anything like that to get out of competing?" he asked.

Taylor seemed to think about it. And think…

"No. I was sick once, but it was for real. I threw up and everything. I always want to ride and have fun, but sometimes it makes me sad 'cause Daddy can't have fun anymore because he died."

It was Nash's turn to sit up straighter, propelled upright by the depth of her confession. It didn't have anything to do with Jess pushing her too hard, or the possibility that Taylor didn't enjoy the sport. She self-sabotaged.

He was right about her carrying a weight on her shoulders after all. Yet very wrong about the type and the extent of it. She shouldn't feel such guilt.

"Does your mom know how you feel?"

Taylor looked down and shook her head. "I don't think so. She's so busy, and I don't want to bother her 'cause she has to make lots of clothes."

"Would you like for me to talk with her?"

The little girl shook her head.

He took a few deep breaths while collecting his thoughts. He hadn't prepared for this scenario, so he'd have to speak from the heart.

"Taylor. Look at me and listen very carefully. I'm a father, so I can tell you this with complete authority. No daddy would *ever* want his child to stop having fun just because he wasn't there. In fact, I hope that if something ever happens to me, my girls will have even more fun. I'll be looking down and smiling so big when that happens."

Taylor's eyes started to water. Had he said the wrong thing?

"Really?"

"Yes. I'm totally serious. Your mom would feel the exact same way. Promise you'll talk to her about it whenever you're comfortable. No parent is ever too busy." He took a huge gulp of his now-lukewarm hot chocolate, making sure to get plenty of the marshmallow on his upper lip, then set the cup down.

She nodded in agreement and took a big gulp from her own mug and made sure she got a mustache, as well. Now they both were giggling.

He stood. "I have an idea. Let's go see if Mischief recognizes us."

Together they practically sprinted back to the arena, where the horse greeted them at the fence. Of course, he already knew Mischief wouldn't be fooled, but that wasn't why he'd suggested it. Time for this little girl to have some fun again, and what was more fun than marshmallow mustaches?

Problem was, he was having a little too much fun himself. His intuition was back and ready to compete. Maybe he'd been doing a little self-sabotaging himself the past several years.

The more he thought about it, the more he remembered when he'd stopped having fun. Didn't occur to him to define it that way until now. It was the day he realized Jess had left without so much as saying goodbye. Just when she was reaching her peak as a barrel racer. He'd never felt like more of a failure as an instructor. Took him a while to stop teaching completely. Figured it was nothing more than a temporary slump.

It wasn't.

Not that he couldn't have a comeback, like Jess was having vicariously with Taylor. Unfortunately, if he got back into teaching again, it would take him away from everything else he needed to do. He'd already started the process of rebuilding Buck Stops into a cattle ranch, which had been his father's and grandfather's legacy. Until he inherited the place and decided to focus on horses instead.

Besides, it wouldn't be fair to Kat. How could he justify teaching others but not her?

He couldn't.

With that impulsive thought put to rest, he focused on Taylor. Her helmet was on, and she looked genuinely excited.

"Okay, here's the plan. Visualize something you really want, but don't tell me what it is. Keep that for yourself only. Imagine the thing you want most is waiting at the finish line. The faster you get there, the sooner it's yours."

She nodded and assumed her starting point outside the arena gate. Her first start was fast, and her finish was even more impressive, confirming that she really did have a breakthrough today. The second try was even better.

When Taylor headed back over, he jumped from his perch and applauded. Her enthusiasm was apparent not only at the start and finish. The middle also improved.

Now for the hard part: telling Jess how the breakthrough happened. Taylor promised to share it with her mom. On her own terms and in her own way. That didn't mean he couldn't assist in making that happen, if possible.

For now, he needed a plan to hand the training reins over to Jess and get back to spending time with his own girls.

"I'm so proud of you, Taylor. The officials in Montana should go ahead and give you the trophy, because no one else stands a chance." It wasn't an exaggeration.

At that, she beamed.

Our little girl is back in the game.

Nash's breath hitched. Taylor wasn't his. Not even close. But he felt like a father to her in this moment. All the more reason to wrap up this arrangement. Except he still owed Jess a favor for pulling double duty with the twins. She needed a day off to work on her sewing. And to spend time with her daughter and give Taylor an opening to confess what she'd confessed to him about her dad. The little girl had earned a day off, too.

"Guess what? No practice tomorrow unless you want to. You and your mom are welcome to do so anytime."

"Okay," she said.

"But y'all can't leave Destiny Springs without doing at least one fun thing, if your mom catches up on her work. I can make some suggestions."

"Can you and the twins come with us?"

Not the plan he had in mind. His thoughts immediately went to Jess. The proximity did them no favors last time. At least they'd be with the girls, thus reducing the possibility of another extended hug. Or one of those kisses he'd been trying, and failing, not to imagine. Except, how could kissing Jess ever be considered a bad thing?

The excitement on Taylor's face, combined with the tickle he felt in his heart, made it impossible to say no. So he didn't. It was either the greatest decision he'd ever made…

Or the worst.

CHAPTER TEN

"LADIES, STAY WHERE we can see you," Nash called out, even though he didn't want to see what he was seeing. Specifically, the number tacked on the back of the pink Western shirt that Jess had sewn and let Kat keep.

He hadn't noticed the number when she'd come home yesterday. The girls raced off to their room after collecting a hug, and Nash couldn't take his eyes off Jess.

All three girls looked back. Taylor waved. Lizzy grabbed Taylor's and Kat's hands and tugged them toward the children's corral.

How was it that he could manage such a breakthrough with Taylor but not get his daughter to change the shirt that she admitted Jess sewed for her? Considering how wrinkled the thing looked, she must have changed out of her pajama top and back into it after he'd tucked them in for the night.

His whole purpose for suggesting they spend their "together" portion of the day at the local farmers market was to have some fun and avoid certain discussions. With all the goings-on and music, there was less chance they'd have to tread into deep waters. But now, he didn't have a choice.

Today, the music at the farmers market was not only familiar, it offered a neutral subject.

"Recognize this song?" he asked.

Jess squinted as she seemed to mull it over. "Can't think of the title, but didn't Montgomery Legend sing it better?"

Nash had to laugh. The band wasn't the best he'd heard in town. But that was part of the charm of these weekly events, along with the booths of fresh fruits and vegetables, baked goods and handmade crafts.

"I'll tell Monty you said that the next time I see him," Nash said.

"Monty? Are you serious? You actually know him and are on a nickname basis?"

"Is that a big deal?" he asked, remaining intentionally stoic and leaving out the part that Becca's mom was dating the legend himself.

"Only if it's true," Jess said while rolling her eyes. "Sounds like one of those Destiny Springs rumors I've heard about."

"This town has a few of those, that's for sure. One or two of 'em have turned out to be true."

"One or two?" Jess flashed him a look he couldn't quite define.

"What?" he asked.

She looked down to her boots as they walked. "Nothing."

They stopped within several feet of the tent where the girls had gravitated, directly inside the gate of the children's area. Taylor was seated in a high director's chair while one of the local artists painted a big smiley face on her forehead.

Next was Lizzy, who asked the young man to cover her face in daisies.

Good thing he and Jess wanted to watch and not talk. It was uncomfortable being around her after that hug, to say the least, but in a good way. Not as uncomfortable as seeing Kat take the director's chair and get a number eight painted on her cheek. Now he'd be forced to look at the number coming and going until he could talk her into washing it off.

Even though the face painting was free, Nash pulled a five-dollar bill from his pocket and handed it to the artist as a tip.

"Thank you, sir. What a beautiful family y'all have," the man offered in return.

Nash and Jess looked at each other, but neither corrected him. Jess simply said, "Thank you. We think so."

"We'll keep an eye on your girls if you two want to wander around for a bit." The man pointed to a couple of ladies, who both waved while running herd on a manageable group of kids within the fenced-off area.

Nash knew the women. They'd babysat the twins here a couple of times while he did some produce shopping. Plenty of fun stuff to keep them busy.

"What do you think?" he asked Jess.

"Works for me."

Nash motioned the girls over. He hooked two out of three. "Jess and I will swing back around in a while. Y'all stay here. Let Lizzy know, please."

Kat and Taylor nodded, then ran back inside the corral.

"Good idea. We need to talk privately anyway," Jess said.

His thoughts exactly. As long as the discussion didn't involve Taylor's breakthrough, although that would be much more pleasant than the topic of Kat's shirt.

They wandered past the vegetable tents first. Somewhere between the carrots and the cabbage, Jess asked the dreaded question.

"Any progress with Taylor?"

"As a matter of fact, yes. We had quite a breakthrough yesterday," he said.

"What did the trick?"

Nash inhaled deeply through his nose, then exhaled. Not only for effect, but to relieve the tightness in his chest.

"Breathing the Wyoming air. It can cure whatever ails you," he said.

"There you go again. Another wild Destiny Springs story," Jess said. "Seriously, what happened?"

"It came down to her starts and finishes. Neither were fast enough. She had some hesitation."

"Wow. I never even picked up on that watching her. Very astute of you. How did you help her overcome it?"

"I promised I'd let her tell you."

Jess shook her head. "Then I may never find out."

Nash was tempted to say more, but at least he'd planted the seed that there was something she would care to know.

"Does that mean our training arrangement is over with?" she asked.

Nash paused in his steps. Even though getting back to his own life was important, he'd like to make sure Taylor didn't revert back to her old habits. He was emotionally invested now.

"One more session before y'all leave in a week or so to be certain her improvement wasn't a fluke. In the meantime, the two of you can come over and practice whenever the mood strikes. I'll leave the barrels in place."

Considering Jess's response—or lack thereof—he wasn't sure whether that was a good answer, or a bad one.

"Whatever you think is best. I didn't come all this way to ignore your advice."

It was a subtle reminder that this was, and should stay, a professional arrangement. Since Jess was going to have at least one more afternoon with the twins, there was something he had to get off his chest.

"Follow me. We need to have a chat." Nash led her to the other side of the tents, where some bistro tables were set up and a vendor was making hot beverages.

They took a seat without ordering. She looked nervous, which was nothing compared to how he felt having to bring this up.

"About the barrel racing shirt," he began to say, although he had trouble formulating the rest of the words without sounding ungrateful.

Jess dropped her chin. "I apologize. You'd mentioned she was down. It was the only thing I could think of to cheer her up. I know you're in a difficult spot with the subject, but I figured that once we're gone, she'll move on to something else."

"I did ask for you to cheer her up. You get an A-plus for that. And I'm afraid I'm getting a failing grade on letting her try." He hadn't planned to wade too deep into more reasons than he'd already provided. But there he was, up to his knees in explanation.

"I understand. Barrel racing is a huge time commitment. You're raising two young girls and manage a ranch. You even quit teaching, after all. And you once loved it."

Boy, that was the truth. Another truth was, he was starting to love it again. But he'd learned the hard way that certain loves weren't destined to last, no matter how much you wanted them to.

"I wish things were different, Jess. I've gone to great lengths to discourage anything involving travel. I can't accommodate that right now. But I'll just come right out and say it. The sport is also cost prohibitive."

It was the truth, if not the whole truth. Difficult to admit, but not as difficult as bringing up the part about Roxanne.

Jess cocked her head, then looked down. "And then I came along and messed it up. I'm so sorry."

"Not your fault in any way. I certainly don't regret helping Taylor."

Jess looked up. "You mean that?"

"Of course."

"Good. Then no more secrets. Okay?"

That was a tall order in some ways, but not in a very specific one.

"I'd expect nothing less from my *gal*," he said, adding a wink for good measure. He'd been holding on to this secret and waiting for the right moment.

If a tomato booth had been Jess's backdrop, she would have blended right in with the way her face turned red.

"Vanessa told you?" she asked.

"No. PJ let it slip."

Jess shook her head and laughed. "I could never be upset with that adorable little boy. Her, either, for that matter. Besides, I'm the one who told them about Georgina's gaffe. I think we both know how it's so *not* true."

"Not at all," he said.

"Not in the least. I mean, can you imagine?"

Actually, I have been.

"Right. Grizzled cattle rancher, willingly tied to his property, and the glamorous traveling mother of a rising rodeo star."

Jess looked at him with some level of sympathy, then shook her head.

"Nothing glamorous about me. And at least the property

you're tied to—as you describe it—is providing a warm, wonderful home for you and the girls."

Except for denying the glamorous part about her, everything she said was true. Furthermore, he detected something in her voice that sounded as though she wouldn't mind a warm, wonderful home for herself and Taylor.

"Destiny Springs is a small town, and not very glamorous, but I highly recommend it. There's always room for two more," he said.

Jess sighed, then looked at him, cocked her head and smiled. "When I finally decide to give up the glamour, this would definitely be my first choice."

When. That sure sounded a lot more promising than *if.*

"You'd bring the glamour with you. But you're here now, so we should capture this moment." He pointed to a photo booth across the way. Another couple had exited and were waiting on their photos to print.

"Gosh, I haven't seen one of these in years," she said.

"The girls always have a great time with it. Mostly making silly faces. Wanna try?"

He stood and extended a hand.

Jess gave him the side-eye, then stood. "Okay to the 'trying it' part. But I do NOT want to look silly."

"Me, neither. Let's not even smile." He put on his best serious look.

At that, she not only smiled, she also let out one of those beautiful laughs. After the other couple retrieved their photo, they stepped inside.

"These booths are a lot smaller than I remember." She was forced to half sit on his lap.

"Ready?" He pressed the button anyway.

"No!" she said, right as the first flash went off.

Nash burst out laughing.

"How long between shots?" she asked.

"A decent pause."

"Does it give you a warning? Like a red light or something? I can't remember..." Jess moved her face closer to the glass. Sure enough, the flash went off again.

"You lied! That was more of an *in*decent pause!I'm gonna look hideous!"

"That's not possible," he said.

She looked directly at him now as if deciding whether to take his observation seriously.

Oh, he was serious. Vern was right: you were never too old to have a crush.

Another flash went off, capturing that thought. That moment. It was no longer a question of *if* he'd kiss her, but *when*. This was the perfect moment to do what he should have done ten years ago but didn't dare.

The crease between her brows softened. As they closed the few inches between their lips and kissed, the camera issued its last flash.

Jess's eyes flew open. He'd never closed his. Yet, she wasn't the one to pull away first.

"See what happens when you let down that wall a little?" she asked.

Felt like more than a little. He'd take a wrecking ball to the whole thing right now if he could talk her into staying.

By the time they exited the booth, a few other couples were waiting their turn.

Nash and Jess guarded the photo output bin as if it were Fort Knox. When it finally spit out the print, he grabbed it and they huddled together and fast-walked toward a vacant spot. Both giggling like teenagers the entire way.

Once safe from wandering eyes, they examined the result together. Jess expressed horror at the first two, and fondness for the third. But he barely noticed those.

Maybe he'd avoided talking about his feelings today, but he was doing a pretty good job of showing them. In fact, he was about to steal another kiss. Right here. Out in the open. His phone pulled him away. When he saw that the message was from Parker, another kind of feeling swept over him.

"What's wrong? You turned pale," Jess said.

He reread the text and willed his heart to settle down. He'd taken it around some serious emotional barrels already today.

"There's an emergency at the ranch."

"Did Parker give any specifics?"

Nash shook his head. He tried to return the call, but his ranch hand didn't answer.

"Let's get you back," she said, easing the photo strip from his hand and tucking it into her purse.

Together, they sprinted to the children's area, where they wrangled the girls.

On the drive back, Nash tried to appear normal. No sense making the twins worry when he didn't even know what was going on himself.

"I'll take the girls for a while, just in case it's something the twins shouldn't be exposed to," Jess whispered.

Even though that made sense, Nash shook his head. "That's too much to ask. It's tough enough to entertain two, never mind three."

"I'll come up with something. And it won't include any type of barrels. I promise. I've been wanting to check out Kavanaugh's ever since Cody mentioned it. They might enjoy a girls' shopping trip, as well."

"That's certainly an option, if you enjoy herding kittens. But if you need to get some sewing done, take their whiteboard with you. That's how I keep 'em busy when I have work to do in the house."

Jess nodded. "I like that idea."

"Anything to help. I'll return the favor, I promise." He didn't tell her what a relief it was to not have to worry about the girls in this moment. As a single mom, she clearly understood such things.

"We'll talk about that later, if at all. Right now, I want you to take care of your home and ranch. Let me worry about everything else," she said.

That's my gal.

JESS MAY HAVE been trying to digest a mixed bag of feelings, but one thing was for certain: she wasn't going to take Nash up on his kind suggestion that she get some sewing done.

There was another situation that needed mending first.

The moment Jess entered Kavanaugh's Clothing and Whatnot, she knew she'd leave with the sound of a cowbell ringing in her head like a serious earworm. The thing was tied to the door, which she held open for the girls.

It would be worth it as long as she left with a new top for Kat to replace the barrel racing shirt. She wished he would have admitted the money problem sooner. She, of all people, understood budget constraints.

An earworm might also be helpful in coaxing her thoughts out of that photo booth. Away from the tender kiss she kept playing over in her mind.

A young man looked up from straightening some clothing racks in time to secure his stance before the twins nearly plowed him down. Taylor followed but stopped short of giving him a hug, too.

After he extricated himself from the twins' grip, he came over to Jess, who was taking visual inventory of the place.

"I'm Ethan, the owner," he said. "You must be Nash's gal."

A coincidence? Jess wasn't prepared for *that.* She would have otherwise formulated a comeback.

Ethan broke out in a laugh that Jess could only describe as donkey-like. "Georgina and Vanessa were in here yesterday with PJ. Told me you were taking care of Nash's twins. Overheard 'em talking about the whole *Nash's gal* snafu but how the nickname suits you."

Jess forced a smile. "That's embarrassing. It's not true, you know. I'm not his gal."

Although, after that kiss, maybe she was. But that was staying strictly between the two of them.

"Oh, I know that. Don't be too hard on 'em. When people give you a nickname around here, that means they like you."

"What's yours?" she asked.

Ethan looked to the ceiling and shook his head. "Well, I'll be. I guess I don't have one. And I grew up here."

Ouch. Yet again, Jess seemed to have stepped in it.

"What's Nash's nickname?" she asked.

This time, Ethan really looked stumped. "Seems like he used to have one, but for the life of me I can't remember. If I think of it, I'll let you know. Anyhoo, what can I help you with today? Or are you just browsin'?"

"I'd like to find a blouse for Kat, anything with daisies for Lizzy and a bracelet for my daughter, Taylor."

She could practically feel her wallet getting lighter. Then again, she'd saved money to pay Nash, and he wouldn't accept it. This would be a worthy use of that stockpile.

"The girls are looking at the jewelry right now. We have some writing pens with pretty flowers pasted on the end. One of 'em may even be a daisy, but I'm no expert. They're at the far counter. Unfortunately, we don't carry clothes for little ones."

That confirmed what Jess had deduced at a quick glance.

"In that case, I'll look at your women's tops." If she could find one that Kat liked, fabric-wise, she could either alter it or completely remake a top out of that material.

"Feel free to try on as many as you like. Dressing rooms are over yonder, and there's a full-length communal mirror by the chairs."

"While I'm doing that, would you mind showing Lizzy the flower pens? I'll buy whichever one she wants." No doubt Taylor would find a bracelet she liked, even though the ones she practically lived in were her favorites.

The purchase for Kat would be a little trickier. Jess located a couple of tops that she could work with by the time the girls finished their shopping and joined her. Lizzy flashed a pen with a huge fabric daisy attached to the end. Couldn't have been more perfect. Taylor sported a bracelet with silver intertwined horseshoes.

Then there was Kat, who was wearing the twin to Taylor's bracelet. Although the jewelry looked junior in design, the items were sized for a grown woman's wrist. The girls must have helped each other figure out a way to clasp them so that they wouldn't fall off.

Now Jess had not only sewn Kat a barrel racer shirt, it looked as though she might be buying her a horseshoe bracelet. At least it wasn't specific to barrel racing, and the little girl was an equestrian anyway.

Besides, the fabric of the items Jess picked out couldn't begin to compete with that. Maybe she should give up and they should all go to the drugstore with the old-fashioned soda fountain instead. See if they were expecting Nash's gal there, too. That would make her day complete.

As Jess was in the process of surrendering the tops and skirts and dresses to their racks, Lizzy tugged at one of the garments.

"Don't put this one back. Daddy would like it." The little matchmaker gave Jess the most mischievous grin.

A floral maxi skirt. Jersey, cut on the bias. She'd grabbed it because it had enough fabric to transform into a short dress with long sleeves. The background was black, and the flowers were faded. Subtle. Sophisticated but girly. Paired with some boots and leggings, it would look beyond adorable on Kat.

Jess held up the skirt. "Your daddy would like this, huh? Then we should definitely buy it for him. Do you think this one will fit, or would he need a larger size?"

"Not for him. For you!" Lizzy insisted.

"Daddy would like this one, too. You should try it on." Kat tugged at one of the blouses in Jess's other hand. Meanwhile, Taylor had collected several more tops and sweaters.

This was getting way out of control, in more ways than one.

"I'm limited to three items. Oh, well." Jess shrugged, made a frowny face and pointed at a sign that was clearly posted.

"Just ignore that. I know the owner personally," Ethan called out, then unleashed the donkey again.

Now all three little girls were wearing matching grins.

"Okay. I'll try them on." But that's all she would do. At least it would keep them entertained for a while.

Jess handed her purse to Taylor for safekeeping since there wasn't so much as a chair in the dressing room.

"I'll come out and model the things that I can fit into." For once, she was glad she'd gone up a size. The things they picked out looked quite small.

Jess first tried on the blouse that Lizzy had picked out. Even though there wasn't a mirror in the room, she already knew it wasn't working. Too frilly for her taste, but she drew the curtain back and showed the girls anyway. They all looked at her as if they didn't recognize her.

One down, a dozen to go.

Next, she tried on the floral maxi skirt that Lizzy had picked out. If Kat wasn't interested in the fabric, she would be. It couldn't have been a better fit, that was for sure. She could pair it with her tall black boots. This time, when she opened the curtain, they all smiled and nodded.

"Buy that one, Mommy," Taylor said.

Jess's first thought was, *I could make this for a fraction of the cost.* But since Taylor liked it so much, it was worth whatever the price tag read.

"That skirt is thirty percent off, but I'll give you another ten," Ethan called out.

Sold.

Once she pulled the curtain closed, she realized they may be there for a while if she actually tried everything else on. She had to admit, this was fun, but she, for one, was getting hungry. They had to be starving, as well, even though they were too excited about this little experiment to have noticed.

Then there was Nash, and whatever was happening. She and the girls could get some food to go and eat together at the ranch. Assuming the coast was clear. In the meantime…

"I have some candies in my purse, if you'd each like one," she said. At least, she hoped she still had enough. Butterscotch was her mindless pleasure. She could polish off half a bag before stopping to breathe. She'd get them something healthy after this, like a good mom would do.

Her own summation threw her a little. She really did think of the twins as hers for a split second, which was crazy. More than that, it was a reminder that the twins didn't have a mother.

Jess shook off that sad thought as quickly as she did the sweater and maxi skirt and contemplated which outfit to try on next. In fact, it was actually quiet enough to think for a change. The girls, who had been chattering nonstop, were now dead silent. Which meant they must have found the candies.

Crisis averted, for now.

A wave of discomfort washed over her as she reached for one of the sweaters that Taylor had picked out.

The photos…

Time felt as though it were standing still, until the giggles from the other side of the curtain turned into shrieks and laughter. Lizzy first, followed by Taylor. Even Kat joined in.

Jess shifted into overdrive, paying zero attention to what she put on, then drew back the curtain.

One look at their faces, and there was no doubt in her mind that they'd seen it.

The kiss.

Judging from their impish smiles, they liked what they saw.

"What else did you find in my purse besides the candies?"

Lizzy let out a giggle. "You kissed Daddy."

It had been easy enough to explain away the hug they'd witnessed. But this required a response from both parents. Bottom line: she needed his help with this one.

Jess extended her hand. "And he kissed me. Grown-ups do that sometimes when they really like each other. May I have my purse back, please."

Taylor relinquished it. Jess reached for her cell phone inside and tried to dial Nash. He hadn't left a message, nor was he answering.

That left her with only one conclusion. As badly as she needed his help right now, he might need hers even more.

CHAPTER ELEVEN

IT TOOK SOME GUESSWORK, since Parker hadn't provided any logistics, but Nash finally spotted his ranch hand outside in the far distance with one of the heifers.

He sprinted past the calving barn and caught up with them.

"I was putting down some fresh hay and got the swinging gates all mixed up. She made a run for it," Parker explained. "What do I do?"

Nash willed his heartbeat to normalize. Unless it was a breach, this wasn't an emergency. His first inclination was to call Jess and let her know everything was okay. But in the blur of panic, he'd left his cell phone inside the house.

"First, we stay calm and get her back into the calving barn," Nash explained while evaluating the heifer. "She's still in stage one. Going on twelve hours now at my best estimate."

"How long does it take?"

"In my experience, anywhere from four to twenty-four."

"What if we can't get her back in the barn?" Parker asked.

Nash was sure that was doable, but Parker obviously needed reassurance. And an education in case something like this happened again when Nash couldn't get back as quickly.

"She'll give birth out here, and we'll get both of 'em back inside."

Better for something like this to happen today rather than

in the next couple of days when a rainstorm was predicted to move through the area.

"Should I saddle up Tiger and Sassy?"

"Nah. Not for only one. Helps to have the visibility, but you need to know how to herd on foot."

Nash took the lead, explaining the steps to Parker along the way.

"You gotta be aware of their flight zone. That's the distance that'll cause her to flee. Also, be aware of the balance point, which is where you place yourself. Figure out which side you need to be on to get her to move in the direction you want."

"I'd understand if you fired me," Parker said as they successfully herded the heifer back to the calving barn.

His ranch hand seemed serious. Unfortunately, Nash couldn't muster the energy to tease him at the moment. But he could tuck this incident away in his proverbial pocket to torture the guy with later.

"Let's give her a little privacy. We'll check on her about every thirty minutes," Nash said, once the mommy-to-be was situated inside.

Now that Nash had time to breathe and look around, he was pleasantly surprised. Parker really had spread out fresh hay, and the other heifers were partitioned off in their own bays.

"Perfect," Nash said, until he noticed something about the way sunlight was hitting the ground around the mommy-to-be. As if she were on stage, in a spotlight. "Looks like we have another problem, though."

"Uh-oh. What did I do this time?"

"Nothing. Unless you've been shouting from the rooftops about how much you love Hailey." He pointed skyward.

A few of the shingles had come off. Nothing a ladder and a little time couldn't fix. He'd bet the ranch that he wouldn't be able to get a roofer out before the rain started.

"I'll let you take your pick. You can either go into town and get some roofing materials, or you can stay here and check on our new mama and her baby in thirty. If it ends up being a breach, don't panic. Call me immediately."

"I'm not even going to ask what that is. I'll grab the keys."

"Grab my cell phone when you get back, too. I need to let Jess know what's going on."

"Will do, boss. But before I go, I have something else to tell you," Parker said.

Nash anchored his boots into the dirt. "Go on."

"I met a fella the other day. A retired cattle herder who needs to burn off some energy. He'll work for you for free, and I could use the help."

Now, there was some possible good news. Too good to be true, in fact. At the same time, it would mean breaking in yet another ranch hand.

"What's his name? Is he from around here?" Nash asked. Maybe he knew the guy.

"Gus something or another. Lived near Jackson Hole for several years but has been staying with some relatives in Destiny Springs until he finds out where he's going to land."

Not so helpful. And not good if this guy had no ambition beyond burning some time. Not to mention, he might not even decide to stick around. Sounded as though he went whichever way the wind blew. At least with a paid employee, he knew that person needed the work and was serious. Then again, once a cowboy, always a cowboy.

Nash's defenses crumbled at the thought.

"All right," Nash said. "I'll talk to him. But no promises."

Parker's huge smile was a bit overenthusiastic. No doubt he would be relieved to have some help on the ranch. Nash would, too. Plus, an experienced cowboy would be able to distinguish between a true emergency and something they simply needed to keep an eye on.

"I bet you won't be able to say no," Parker said.

Funny, that seemed to be Nash's dilemma with Jess. But this Gus fella wouldn't have the same kind of charms, so it should be a breeze to make a good decision.

After Parker made a swift exit, Nash went through the calving barn with a fine-tooth comb, searching for anything else that needed mending. Other than getting his ranch hand comfortable with the gate configuration, he hadn't come across anything that couldn't wait a week or two.

He wandered back to his heifer, who was quickly entering the next stage. Looked like she was ready to get this part of the process over with.

Still, the gal didn't know how good she had it. His grandfather had built this calving barn, and his dad had updated it with superior ventilation. With the gate configuration Nash had put in place, it sported six bays that could hold about twelve calves each. With only four heifers expecting, each had her own private suite, so to speak. At least, for now.

His dad would be none too pleased that the barn had been used to store hay, among other things, for the past fifteen years since Nash inherited the ranch, sold off most of the cattle and focused on horses instead. But he'd certainly be proud that Nash was taking it seriously now.

Before hardly any time had passed, he heard the frantic tires of a truck in the distance. Nash had to laugh. The guy couldn't hightail it out of there fast enough.

If Parker was going to be squeamish at all, he left just in time. The heifer was now full-on stage two, which forced Nash's anxiety into another stage, as well. He braced himself.

One thing Nash didn't have to worry about was keeping the girls entertained or safe at this moment, many thanks to Jess. That was always tricky. They would wander off in an instant. Wasn't easy being responsible for so many lives in a given moment.

Perhaps his hopes were a bit premature regarding Parker because the sound of footsteps quickly approaching set off a new alarm. Except it wasn't Parker who was running into the barn. It was arguably worse.

Jess stopped several feet away, completely out of breath. The girls were nowhere in sight.

After a confusing, terrifying moment, where his mind started wandering down some dark alleys, she broke the silence.

"I'm here to help."

JESS WISHED SHE could take a picture of Nash's expression. His mouth was open but absolutely nothing was coming out. She could only imagine what he must be thinking.

"Don't panic. I handed off the girls to Parker. He's taking them with him to town. Said you needed this." She handed him the cell phone, which he promptly checked, then typed something in.

What she didn't say was that she'd promised Parker she'd make an appearance in his upcoming DEBBs workshop in exchange for babysitting. His idea. The poor guy was afraid no one would show up for *Your Home Is Your Business*, his portion of the dual workshop. She could always bow out of the other portion of the workshop, whatever that was, and get back to sewing.

Jess rolled up her shirtsleeves and walked over to the heifer.

Nash grabbed an extra pair of gloves from a workbench and handed them to her.

"Do we know when the water bag appeared?" she asked.

"About an hour ago. Presentation is normal, thankfully. Last thing we need is a breach."

She exhaled some pent-up tension and took a step back. "Hopefully, we can just monitor her from here. Is that what you're thinking?"

Nash simply stared, but then a smile slowly emerged.

"What?"

"Where did you learn about all this?" he asked.

"It was one of the skills I honed during my marriage."

"Lance was one lucky rancher," he said. "Brains, beauty and calving skills."

Her breath hitched a little, although she tried not to let it show. *You could have been the lucky one.*

They held their gaze for the longest time, until the mommy-to-be let out a serious moan.

"Oh, look! It's happening," Jess said.

They both stood ground to assist, if necessary, but otherwise gave the heifer a bit of room as the miracle unfolded. The birth of…

"A son," Nash said after a quick examination of the calf. "Except the little guy needs help breathing."

Together, they proceeded to clean the fluid from the calf's nose and mouth, then tickled the inside of his nostril with a piece of straw until the calf coughed.

"Finally, a baby boy in the Buchanan family," she said, which made him smile, as if a son was on his wish list.

They finished and took several steps back to observe one of the scariest parts, in her opinion.

"I hope mom doesn't reject her baby," Jess said.

Nash's warm smile cooled instantly. "Some tend to do that."

"You've been through that before, I take it," she said.

"Yeah. On a personal level. Roxanne rejected her babies."

Jess's heart could have stopped in that moment. She hadn't made such a connection when she'd spoken those words, even though she pretty much knew Roxanne had been the one to leave. Just not so heartlessly.

She closed the space between them and gave him a big hug. "I didn't mean to remind you."

Nash returned her embrace for a long moment, then pulled away enough to look at her.

"No reminders necessary. I live with that fact every day."

Her heart ached for him and the girls during what should have been a very special moment. The cow was rejoicing in her newborn.

She wasn't quite sure how, or even if, she could make things better.

But then he straightened and pointed to the roof. "I'm guessing Parker told you that was the reason he needed to go into town."

She looked up. As if he needed one more emergency to deal with.

"He mentioned a roof problem but not the extent of it. I'll reclaim all the girls as soon as he returns. Give you and him time to fix it without the distractions."

Nash's cell phone dinged. He checked the message and texted something back. Then he smiled a tortured smile.

"I'd texted Hailey to see if she could look after the girls for a while, but she can't. She can babysit tomorrow afternoon and evening, though."

"Good. That will give you a chance to keep an eye on these two," she said, pointing to the cow and her calf.

"Actually, I asked her about babysitting all three of the girls. If you're comfortable with that."

"I don't understand."

"I owe you a Juicy Lucy for helping with this. I'm cooking."

No, she wasn't entirely comfortable, but it had nothing to do with Hailey babysitting Taylor. It had to do with her being alone with Nash because that kiss had temporarily blurred her common sense. She'd meant it about settling down in Destiny Springs if she ever settled down. But that couldn't happen any-time soon. Not with Taylor's career taking off.

She'd wrestle with those feelings tomorrow. The issue at hand was still unresolved.

"I'll take you up on that. But I still insist on taking the girls today when Parker returns."

"Only if you promise to go back to the B and B and work. They can keep themselves entertained with the whiteboard."

"Is that your final offer?" she asked. Sounded like she was getting the better end of the deal.

"My final offer for today," he said.

That clarified nothing except what she dared to hope.

If all of this was negotiable, so was a continued relationship with him.

CHAPTER TWELVE

SIXTEEN FEET MIGHT as well have been a thousand.

Nash stared at the ground below. He had no intention of falling, but no one ever did. Maybe that's why he was already feeling the pain of falling for Jess, even though he'd yet to hit the ground.

He didn't have the luxury of imagining the possibility of injury right now. Getting the shingles battened down before the sky fell in on the mama and her newborn below was the priority.

"You still awake up there, Dad?" Parker called out.

Nash snapped out of it and looked down at his ranch hand, who was holding the bottom of the ladder steady. Parker had started climbing up himself to patch the roof, but Nash wouldn't let him. Hence Nash's new nickname: *Dad.*

Sure beat the one Vern called him every once in a while: Mr. Grumpy Pants. Well deserved, if he were being honest. But those pants only fit when he was hungry. Now that he thought about it, his stomach was starting to growl a bit.

Once he got his footing, Nash used screws instead of nails to secure the shingles to the horizontal joints. He needed to replace all the nails with screws at some point, but he'd have to save that for another day. This patch was good enough to get them through the rainstorm.

Parker tightened his grip on the ladder as Nash descended.

"I don't know about you, *son*, but I've worked up an appetite. Let's rustle up something to eat."

They made the trek back to the kitchen, where a sparsely stocked refrigerator and freezer stared back at them. Nash realized there was something perhaps even more important he needed to take care of before the rain set in: groceries.

"How do shrimp tacos sound?" Nash asked. They could head out to eat, then swing by the store on their way back.

Parker looked over Nash's shoulder and into the same abyss. "Will they magically appear?"

"In a way, they will. You just gotta know where to look. Let's go out."

"Shrimp Lake, here we come! I'll grab the nets. You carry the ice chest," Parker said.

Nash closed the refrigerator door. "I was thinking something a little closer and easier."

"Who's going to hold down the fort?"

That was the million-dollar question. Back in the day, he had a handful of people to rely on. The number had dwindled over the years. That was about to change. By focusing on cattle again, and eventually hiring more hands, he could turn everything around. Maybe even find time to go to a local rodeo or two, just to watch.

Feelings of selfishness, or perhaps stubbornness, about denying his horse-obsessed daughter the joys of the rodeo had begun to creep in. He'd just have to make sure Roxanne wasn't on the ticket. He'd still have to put his foot down about competing. Couldn't have the twins' names appearing anywhere. But perhaps Kat could do the drills at the ranch, just for fun.

Then again, where was the fun in that?

In any event, he needed Parker's help. And even this Gus person's, he reluctantly admitted.

"We won't be gone that long," he said. They'd taken care of most chores and checked on all the animals. The new mommy and her baby were safe and settled in.

Nash put on a fresh flannel shirt, and the two cowboys donned their respective Stetsons. This was one of the few times they'd done anything together that wasn't ranch related.

The ride to Ribeye Roy's was quiet, even though they had plenty to talk about. Once inside, the waitress seated them at a table for two in a dark corner. Would have been the perfect setting to stare into Jess's warm hazel eyes. Instead, Parker's cool blue ones were looking back.

"I'm glad we have a chance to sit down and talk," his ranch hand said.

"Me, too."

"We need to get some things out in the open. And I'm not talking about any more heifers. I was giving some thought as to how we can make the ranch more efficient and profitable, aside from adding more cattle. You have, what, thirty-five?"

Nash was impressed that Parker was thinking of their future. They'd never really discussed it. Back in his father's and grandfather's days, they had about two hundred head. But something was holding him back.

Must be the weight of responsibility.

"Thirty-six. You forgot about our newest addition."

Parker smiled. "Not a chance I could forget about that little guy. How lucrative was your barrel racing business?"

Nash felt his stomach seize at the mere mention of it.

"Not as lucrative as my dad and grandad's cattle ranch. Why would you ask?"

"Hailey tells me you used to be one of the most sought-after teachers in the world."

"She's prone to exaggeration. You should know that by now," Nash said.

"She teases. Like someone else I know, whom I happen to be looking at right now. But she doesn't exaggerate."

Nash had to think about it, but he made a valid point.

"How much land do you have? About a thousand acres?" Parker asked.

"Eleven hundred, counting the house."

Parker looked to the ceiling as if contemplating the possibilities. This should be interesting.

"So, you could possibly have five hundred head of cattle with the anticipated forage supply."

"I'd pare it down to about three hundred fifty, max. Allot

fifty percent for future forage, and about fifteen percent for wildlife," Nash explained.

"You thinking dairy or beef?"

To be honest, he had trouble thinking about his cattle in those terms. "Can't I do both?"

Parker looked at him. "I don't know. You tell me. What do you envision?"

"I'd like to be able to provide milk to some folks around here, like Vern does with the eggs."

"Whoa! Let's not be too ambitious," Parker said, feeling around his pocket and retrieving a pen, then stealing Nash's napkin.

It took a moment for Nash to realize his ranch hand was being sarcastic.

"So, for that scenario, your profit would be…" He jotted something down and held up the napkin. "Less than zero."

All of a sudden, Nash felt quite silly. Not that he ever needed the type of fancy math skills that Parker had developed as a former business consultant in Chicago. But if that big-city boy could learn ranching, then there was hope for Nash.

"Look. I'm not saying this to make you feel any sort of way," Parker said. "I'm just playing devil's advocate. Let me see your family's ledgers from as far back as you have. And any financial statements that you can line up with the activities at the time, whether it be cattle ranching or teaching. I'll put together some numbers."

"I'll leave out the ledgers from my teaching years. If I ever get the itch, I'll let you know and you can work your magic."

Nash didn't want to admit that the itch had grown and was now just beneath his skin. But there was no use going down a dead-end road. He didn't have a head for numbers, but he knew he wouldn't turn a big enough profit anytime soon. The girls would be grown up with families of their own by the time that happened. Not to mention the way it would make Kat feel in the meantime, having to watch him teach others.

"An itch can be a good thing, you know," Parker said. "You could focus on the horses and barrel racing. I could focus on the cattle. I have to admit, coming back and seeing that newborn calf was a rush I hadn't expected. Kind of wish I hadn't missed it."

"Most doctors advise against scratching itches. If you don't, they'll usually go away on their own. Cattle ranching only," he said. He looked Parker straight in the eye to let him know that the barrel racing training was off-limits.

Not that he hadn't been entertaining the idea. But the more he and Jess discussed their lifestyles, and the reminders of the past and how expensive and time-consuming the sport could be, the clearer the obstacles came into view. Too many barrels to circle, too little time.

Judging from Parker's expression, he got the message. Where were those fish tacos anyway? He was starving.

"Understood," Parker finally said. "I still need to see all the ledgers. Trust that I know what I'm doing."

Not that he didn't appreciate what his ranch hand was trying to do. But Nash had been at this a lot longer than Parker, and focusing on more than one goal wasn't as easy as it might look on paper.

"You got a rush about the calf because you're gonna be a daddy yourself someday soon," Nash said in an attempt to steer this conversation into another direction.

He'd never seen Parker smile that big. "I bet you're right."

"It's been known to happen."

Parker's expression turned serious. "There's one other thing I noticed that I wanted to point out. Jess."

"She's hard not to notice."

"I can tell you feel that way. Question is, what are you gonna do about it?"

So it began. The *feelings* discussion. And to think he almost got away with dodging it. The man gave up riches to win over the love of his life. Nash wasn't going to get out of this dark corner without giving the guy something to chew on.

He didn't need a professional forecaster to tell him that there was at least a 50 percent chance she was going to leave and never return, and a 100 percent chance that he had to stay. Wanted to stay. This time, he was emotionally prepared.

Or was he?

Parker raised his brows as if seriously expecting an answer. The guy was relentless. That's what had made him so successful in business, and why Nash could rest assured he'd succeed in ranching. He also had a way of making people think anything was possible. It was a gift. And it was working on Nash.

"We need to pick up some cheese and hamburger meat, among other things, at the market on the way back to the ranch."

"That's a bit off topic," Parker said.

"I promised Jess a Juicy Lucy. I'm cooking dinner for her tomorrow night. Hailey offered to babysit. Maybe even have a slumber party. Just waiting on confirmation. That is, if you're okay with that."

Parker nodded slowly. "If it makes my wife happy, then I'm all for it. But this isn't about her happiness. I think I see where you're going with this plan."

Unfortunately, the place Nash was likely going was the hard ground below. Definitely more of a *when* than an *if.* Too late to stop the fall, and no way to assure a soft landing. Hopefully, that was enough of a *feelings* share for his ranch hand. Which reminded him…

"Do we have any metal sheet scraps left from the roof repair?"

"I think so. Why?" Parker asked.

"Just making sure we had some left in case of any emergency."

Like patching the inevitable hole in my heart.

AS IF THE day couldn't get any stranger, Vern was exiting the B and B just as Jess and the girls were making their way up the steps. Cody trailed behind him, familiar toolbox in hand.

"Did someone need a knight in shining armor?" Jess asked.

What she really wanted to ask was, shouldn't Vern be resting his back?

Cody shook his head. "Vern here is as stubborn as any bull I've ever been on. He located a working motor for your sewing machine and wanted to surprise you, even though he should be on the sofa with a heating pad instead."

"Surprise!" Vern said. "It's working again. Your machine,

that is. My back is a work in progress. I'll get the motor I ordered in another day or two and then you'll have a spare to take with ya."

She set the whiteboard down and gave him a gentle hug. "You're the best."

Jess watched as they walked to the truck and played tug-of-war with the toolbox until Vern finally relinquished and allowed Cody to place it in the truck bed. Then something else caught her eye. Dorothy, standing alone in the parlor. Admiring Becca's sewing machine.

Jess barely recognized her outside of the group. Come to think of it, though, she often saw other DEBBs together without Dorothy.

"Girls, wait at the bottom of the stairs for a minute please. Kat, you take this." Jess handed the board to the twin.

As the girls started heading toward the stairs, Jess held Taylor back.

"Will you do me a huge favor, my dear? Let's not talk about barrel racing around Kat," she said, softly enough that the twins couldn't overhear.

"How come?"

"Because it might make her feel bad since her daddy can't let her compete in rodeos right now."

"Why not?"

"Because he has a big ranch to run. You can still talk about horses," Jess offered. Telling young equestrians not to talk about horses wasn't remotely doable, after all. It would be like Jess getting together with Dorothy and not talking about sewing.

Taylor looked at her feet. "I'll try."

"That's all I ask."

Almost. Jess did have one more question. "Nash tells me you had a big breakthrough in the training. I'd love to hear all about it, and your thoughts on him as a coach."

The little girl's expression brightened. "Nash is great. I like him a lot."

Not as much information as she was hoping to hear, but it definitely cheered her up to know that Taylor was happy and thriving in the arena. That was what this whole trip was about, after all.

Jess smiled and nodded. "Wait for me over there with the twins. This will only take a sec."

Once she made sure the girls were waiting, as requested, Jess approached her sewing soulmate.

"I'm sure Becca wouldn't mind you using that if you need to mend anything. The one in my room is fixed," Jess said.

Dorothy tore her gaze away from the machine and smiled. "I haven't stopped thinking about your workshop. You really inspired me to get back into it. Pull out my old Singer."

A certain sadness passed over the woman's face. Jess couldn't pinpoint it.

"Is anything wrong?" she asked.

"Everything's fine. I'd like it to be *more* than fine, for a change. That's all."

Now, *that* Jess could relate to.

"What would make it more than fine for you?" Jess asked.

"To be at home more, yet stay productive."

Jess's first thought was that it must be nice to have such choices. She didn't have any. She *had* to work to make ends meet. Yet, she understood the fear of being idle, as well. The fear of feeling as though she wasn't needed in any measurable way. She'd experienced that a bit as a domestic engineer and stay-at-home mom herself.

"You could always do what I do. It's surprising how many people don't even know the basics, and you're well beyond that."

Dorothy nodded. "I was thinking of doing it more as a hobby, but I like that idea."

"I'm happy to go into more detail with you, if you want to talk later."

Again, the woman nodded. Only this time, she didn't add anything to the conversation.

Jess hated leaving her like this. Alone and seemingly sad. But Jess was destined to plunge into those same feelings if she lost her clients because she didn't deliver.

Once Jess and her crew got to the room, the girls claimed their spots and started entertaining themselves. Kat and Taylor hovered over the whiteboard, whispering and taking turns drawing and erasing. Lizzy kept busy grooming her new flower pen, lovingly straightening out the petals.

It didn't take long for Jess to accept that this suggestion of Nash's to bring back the whiteboard was brilliant. She was able to pattern and trim out the pieces for a Western shirt, leaving only one of its kind to go. Plus the crop top. The girls' chatter couldn't even break her focus. But something else sure did: the cry of tortured dot paper.

Lizzy had located the roll and was poised to take that pretty little pen to it.

No! Jess had barely enough left to pattern the rest of the items for Montana. She sprang up from the chair and gently reclaimed her property. "Let's get you something else to draw on, okay? This is for my job, and it's all I have left."

Lizzy looked a little sad and confused. No doubt Nash had difficulty telling either of the twins no.

Jess could go downstairs and scavenge for some loose paper. Then she remembered the box of retired pattern pieces she always kept with her. Sometimes, she'd rob body parts from the stash while putting together another garment. But that rarely happened, so she wouldn't miss a piece.

She took the lid off the box and offered up the bounty, which made Lizzy smile. "Take your pick of shapes. You could draw some flowers on one and give it to your daddy."

At that, Lizzy lit up again.

Taylor and Kat weren't paying any attention, but she had a suggestion for them, as well. "Kat, how about you and Taylor draw some horses on the board for Nash? He's working really hard today, and I know that would make him smile."

Her cell phone dinged, so she stepped away. A message from Mrs. Dudley.

Sorry it took so long for me to get back with you. I love what you've suggested so far. Especially the chiffon and velvet trims. If it turns out as pretty as it sounds, I'll mention it in my Dudley's Delightful Duds section.

Jess's breath hitched. This was huge. But that wasn't all. A second message from Mrs. Dudley followed on that one's heels.

Your design is also in the running to be featured on my blog. I select three per month. If you're interested, I'll need the completed suit when I see you in Montana.

Interested? Are you kidding?

Except, where would she find the velvet to replace the fabric she'd used for Kat's shirt? *Don't panic.* There had to be a store in or around Billings. At least those details could be added after most of the construction was done. But still, that would be cutting it close. She was leaving for Montana in a little over a week. Once there, she'd intended to focus on Taylor exclusively for a change.

Yet, the news couldn't have been better. Even the pending rainstorm had its perks. She'd have Taylor in the morning, then drop her off at Hailey's at high noon, per the woman's request. Jess would have every reason to stay inside the B and B that afternoon, where she could sew up a storm of her own.

It was an entirely different storm she was currently grappling with: the one brewing within her. Nash's voice, combined with the memory of their kiss, made her thoughts zigzag. Add to that the fact that they'd be making Juicy Lucys tonight. Without the girls around. How she'd managed to focus at all since that kiss had been nothing short of miraculous.

The phone rang this time. *Nash.* It was as if he'd read her thoughts.

"How are all my girls doing over there?" he asked.

Funny, but she'd made a similar slip within her own thinking.

"Everyone is having a good time. I was able to make some progress on my own work, so thanks for insisting."

"Glad to hear it. Parker and I are grabbing something to eat, and we'll be back at the house soon. We can swing by and pick up the girls."

That would be easiest for her. But she wanted to spend at least a few minutes with Hailey and make sure Taylor was comfortable with the idea of being left there with the twins tomorrow night. Besides, her hands were beginning to cramp. She needed to give them a brief break from sewing.

"That's a nice offer, but I'll drop the twins off in a while. I'm taking the girls to Sunrise Stables. I wanted to meet Hailey in person. Text me when you're home."

"You'll love her," Nash said.

From everything Jess had heard, she had little doubt about it. With the plan in place, she set down the phone.

"Lizzy and Kat. Let's finish the artwork for your daddy, then we'll all head over to Miss Hailey's."

She walked over to Kat and Taylor first, but they quickly wiped away whatever they'd been drawing.

"Why did you do that?" Jess asked.

At first, they both shrugged. Then Taylor said, "We didn't like it."

"Yeah. We didn't like it," Kat concurred.

She wasn't sure what to make of the alliance those two were forming. Hopefully, they weren't talking about barrel racing. Not after Jess had asked Taylor not to. She had overheard Kat mention her horse, Sugar Pie, so that was probably it.

Nash was in a difficult position. She understood that now. Yet, it put her in a difficult, if not impossible, one with Taylor.

Then there was Lizzy, who must be feeling more and more excluded. Having only one child, and being an only child herself, Jess felt inadequate as far as navigating sibling bonds.

So much for those parenting skills she'd been convinced she had moments ago.

"We can't give your daddy a blank board, Kat. How about we think up a joke, and he'll have to figure out the punch line?"

"I don't know any jokes," Kat said.

Jess gave it some thought. "How about this one. Why can't your head be twelve inches long?"

The girls looked at each other and shrugged.

"Because then it would be a foot." Jess retrieved a measuring tape from her sewing box and laid it out. "See. These are the inch marks, and twelve of these equal a foot."

That earned a modest giggle.

"I like it," Taylor said.

"Do you think your daddy will guess the answer, Kat?"

"Prob'ly not. He's not very good with math. Sometimes he asks me to help him count things."

At that, Jess had to snort. *From the mouths of babes...*

"Then I think it's the perfect joke. I'll write it down." Jess sat cross-legged on the ground. Taylor handed her the board, and Kat passed her the marker.

"I'm three feet tall and five and a half inches, and Kat is only five inches," Lizzy called out.

"I'm more than five inches," Kat responded.

It was all Jess could do to not break out laughing as she finished writing the setup on the board.

"There. I can't wait to see what he says." Jess popped the cap back on the marker and scooted on her behind to where Lizzy had resumed drawing. It was nothing short of amazing that the flower pen had any ink left in it. She had created so many daisies.

"That's gorgeous! Your daddy is gonna love it."

Upon closer inspection, she recognized the pattern paper that Lizzy had selected. The little girl must have dug to the bottom of the box to find the largest piece: a wedding gown skirt with train. More specifically, Jess's "dream" gown. Much more opulent than anything else she'd created or sewn. It was designed with a long church aisle in mind. But her once-in-a-lifetime event had happened at the justice of the peace to save money. The dress would have been way too much for the courthouse.

Now the pattern piece was covered with flowers, with all the important markings buried beneath the landscaping. Jess saw it as a not-so-subtle sign that it was time to stop entertaining the possibility of a future built on a solid foundation that couldn't tear beneath her.

Unless it was a sign that somehow it could.

CHAPTER THIRTEEN

NASH HAD TOLD Jess that she'd love Hailey. Now she understood why.

The cowgirl ran outside to greet them as they drove up. She gave all the girls a hug first but saved the longest one for Jess without introducing herself. Not that an introduction was necessary. Jess felt as though she already knew her.

"I appreciate you letting us come over," Jess said as Hailey led them to the barn, without saying why.

When Hailey slid open the barn door, no explanation was needed. The place was a wonderland. The girls ran over to a goat pen. The three little seasoned equestrians avoided the ponies altogether.

"Anything for Nash's gal," Hailey said, adding a sly smile.

Jess blinked. "He told you about that?"

"Nash? Are you kidding? I heard it from Parker, who heard it from Vanessa's little boy, PJ. Not that Nash isn't an open book in many ways. He just has a few footnotes that he keeps to himself."

Her brain felt as scrambled as those eggs in the *migas* recipe. "You may have to repeat all that more slowly."

Hailey's cell phone rang. She looked at the screen, held up one finger and answered it.

While Hailey was steeped in conversation, Jess surveyed the girls. So far, so good. Taylor and Kat weren't joined at the hip.

Jess tried to piece together what Hailey was implying about Nash and the footnotes, as well as the chain of gossip. Seemed like everyone's lives here were intertwined, either by family or marriage or friendship. Perhaps she should assume that everyone knew her nickname by now. That way, she wouldn't get caught off guard again.

Hailey ended the call and slipped her phone into the back pocket of her jeans. "That was Parker. He and Nash finished eating and are waiting on the check. You should take one of my goat yoga classes while you're here. Or, better yet, I could show you some moves now since you have a little time."

"That sounds…interesting."

"It's catching on slowly. People come here to play with the silly critters more than exercise with them, though," Hailey said.

Taylor walked over with the twins on her heels. "Mom, can we ride Hailey's horses?"

Jess hadn't intended to make this a long afternoon, but that sounded a little better than goat yoga. Plus, having the girls occupied would give her an opportunity to get to know Hailey a little better.

"It's up to our hostess," Jess said.

"Horses are what we're about here. Everyone, follow me," Hailey said.

As if they didn't hear the "follow me" part, the girls ran toward the stables, leaving the grown-ups in their dust.

"The horses need some exercise anyway since I don't have any trail rides booked for tomorrow, even though the rain isn't supposed to move through until the evening. Unless you'd like to go on one."

"I've heard your rides have an interesting story behind them," Jess said, without committing. She was interested, but she needed to keep sewing.

"They sure do. My tour guides are much better at it than I am. You would totally fall in love with the young man I hired."

Hailey managed to reroute the girls toward the tack room,

where she contemplated which equipment they'd need. "Lizzy, you're familiar with Blaze, so you ride him."

Lizzy nodded her approval.

"And Kat likes Whiskey, don't you?" Hailey asked.

The little girl nodded enthusiastically, giving Hailey permission to pull the appropriate tack for that horse and rider, as well.

"Of course, I don't mean she likes *that* kind of whiskey," Hailey whispered to Jess, who got the joke.

Hailey looked at Taylor. "Let's put you on Charmed. I'd say No Regrets, but he still has issues with boulders. Hence the giant fake rocks spaced out in the arena."

Jess had noticed them but assumed it was some sort of weird landscaping design. Now it made sense.

Hailey and Jess put the tack on the horses, then took a seat on a nearby bench and watched as the girls went through some random warm-up drills, stopping and chatting every once in a while. It was fun watching the three of them. Part of her wanted to saddle up and join in. But having this opportunity to talk with Hailey alone had its perks.

"Tell me about this tour guide gentleman you think I'd fall in love with," Jess said.

Hailey grinned. "Well, he claims to be six feet tall, but he's definitely shorter. When it comes to personality, though, he's got tons of it. Lots of energy."

At least the description ruled out Nash. Not that he'd have time to assist with trail rides. He was a good six foot two, and his energy level seemed fairly moderate to her.

"Interesting way to sell it, if that's what you're doing," Jess said.

"Not at all. Besides, you're Nash's gal. I just wanted to add a little mystery and tempt you to take me up on my offer if you ever have some free time. No pressure, and no charge," Hailey said.

Although she couldn't accept the offer, there was something *Nash's gal* wanted from Hailey. Footnotes.

"Speaking of mysteries, I heard a rumor that it wasn't Roxanne who actually broke Nash's heart." A bold question, but Hailey had opened the door.

"Same here. I asked him outright one day if it was true. All he said was, 'I don't have any confessions to make at this time.' Kinda sounded like a confession to me, but I can't be sure of it."

"He used to confess a lot to me, but it was always things like, 'I have a confession… I like American cheese for my Juicy Lucy and not that sharp cheddar stuff,'" Jess said.

Hailey laughed, but all of a sudden, it wasn't funny. Jess put her elbows on her knees and cradled her face. Maybe she didn't want to know if there was another woman besides Roxanne.

"Hey, you okay?" Hailey asked, snapping Jess back to the present.

Jess looked up and nodded. "Yeah. Just thinking about what you said about Nash."

"The man is definitely sporting some deep wounds, which is why I don't poke around too much. All I know is that he pours all his love and attention into those girls. He deserves to have a good woman in his life."

"If you say so." Jess stared at Hailey, hoping for some deeper insight. Instead, Hailey looked straight ahead at the girls.

Jess was about to cradle her face in her palms again, when Hailey shouted, "Way to go, Kat!"

Jess snapped her attention to the scene playing out in front of them. Taylor must have shown Kat some moves and explained them in detail considering Kat's mock performance around three of the boulders. Not the perfect cloverleaf proportions and distance, but unmistakable.

A knot formed in her gut. Make that a boulder. Her cell phone dinged, forcing her to look away from the nightmare playing out before her and read the text from Nash.

We're home. Missing my girls, but y'all take your time at Hailey's.

Jess only wished they could. But she'd stayed way too long.

As she approached the fence, the girls stopped. Taylor looked guilty, as she should. Wouldn't even look Jess in the eye. Yet, she gave her mom a side hug as they were walking to the truck, which rendered Jess helpless against confronting the barrel racing topic.

Then there was the fact that Kat looked so...*happy.* Genuinely, and for the first time since they had met. Jess's heart was torn between respecting Nash's situation and trying to help a little girl's newfound dream come true.

Even though she needed to start wrapping up their trip, this was now a loose thread. Jess hated those. Yet, this was one she knew better than to yank.

This one she would have to cut.

"WHO IS THAT, and what have you done with my daughter?" Nash asked, pointing to Kat.

He wasn't sure how Jess managed it, but his normally quiet, reserved twin was all smiles and energy. He couldn't help but feel uplifted.

Jess froze. "What do you mean?"

"I've never seen her so happy, that's all."

Did Jess not notice the transformation? Or had his joking-around skills atrophied? Not that he needed to resurrect their joke-swap shtick. Not with the clock winding down to her departure from Destiny Springs. Eight more days, if his math was correct.

Jess started to say something, but Taylor jumped between them and offered him a pinkie handshake, which tickled his heart.

The three girls huddled and whispered something, then looked at the adults and giggled before running down the hall to the twins' room.

"I'm glad they've been getting along so well. I hope they weren't too much of a handful," he said.

"Not at all." Jess eased onto the love seat and patted the cushion next to her. He took a seat next to her and tried to keep as much distance as possible. Didn't need a repeat of the photo booth incident with the girls nearby. Which reminded him...

"Whatever happened to those photos we took? Wouldn't want those falling into the wrong hands." He nodded in the direction of the hallway.

Jess looked down at her own hands and laughed. "I'm afraid they already did."

Nash squinted. "So that's what the whispering and giggling was all about."

"I'm afraid so. The good news is, little girls generally move on pretty quickly from one thing to the next. I know. I used to be one," Jess said.

Nash only wished that were true about his daughters.

"The bad news is, the twins inherited my difficulty in letting things go. At least they got their mom's looks."

Jess looked away.

Oops. Maybe not the best thing he could have said to a woman who had become more than a friend.

"About Roxanne..." Jess said.

Nash held his breath and waited for the inevitable questions about the relationship.

"I was always a bit jealous of her," she continued.

"Why?" He was genuinely perplexed. Roxanne had to work for every trophy she got, whereas barrel racing had come naturally for Jess.

Same went for their appearance, if that's what she meant. Sure, Roxanne turned plenty of heads, but she put a lot of effort into it, what with all the fancy clothes and hair and makeup. Whereas Jess was the most natural beauty he'd ever seen. She'd turned heads back then, too—and his had been no exception. In fact, he had trouble taking his eyes off her now.

He couldn't say he understood any of this. When Jess didn't offer up an explanation, he had to ask, even if it meant opening an old wound. Then again, he was all but convinced that it never fully healed. Just like the heart that was practically beating out of his chest right now.

"Is that why you stopped coming to lessons?" he asked.

She pulled in her elbows tight against her rib cage, as if she were trying to disappear.

"You could have at least said goodbye. Or returned my call. I was devastated when you didn't." That was putting it mildly, but she needed to know.

"I figured you'd barely notice my not being there. Roxanne was able to corral you personally, but also professionally. Even on my time. Honestly, I felt shut out."

By me.

That was an unexpected gut punch. Not that there was any other kind, but this one was delivered with a twist. It wasn't jealousy that had ultimately driven her away. It was how he'd treated her, as if she wasn't as important as Roxanne, which couldn't have been further from the truth.

"Was I putting up one of those walls you've mentioned?"

Jess shook her head. "Not at all. That actually would have made leaving easier."

"I'm so sorry, Jess. Roxanne was very assertive about what she wanted, and I obviously didn't handle it the right way." Another understatement. He'd had the bad judgment to marry her, after dating for two years. It wasn't that she was a bad person. She simply wasn't a "for better or for worse" one.

"It wasn't that. I quit because… I had a crush on you." Jess shrank back into the cushion and looked down again.

Once the words set it, it felt as though a million tiny zaps of electricity flooded his body. As if he could feel every blood cell coursing through his veins.

"You must be good at keeping secrets. I had no idea." Because, if he had, his whole life would look a lot different today. He'd had a serious crush on her. Of course, he'd kept his own feelings a secret, as well, so who was he to judge?

"Really? I thought it was fairly obvious," she said.

Perhaps it had been, and it had been his mistake for not realizing it.

"I figured you thought of me as a teacher and friend and Juicy Lucy buddy."

"I did. I thought of you as all those things, too."

Yet, instead of treating him like a teacher and a friend, she did what all the women who claimed to love him ended up doing: left without saying goodbye.

His mom had been the first, but he had long since forgiven her. She was so sick. She'd promised him she would never leave him, and by the following morning, she had.

Nash gulped back the painful memory and tried to focus on this new revelation. Only one thing could cut the tension between them now, and it wasn't a confession. Rather, it was something she'd least expect.

He took a deep breath. "Wanna hear a roof joke?"

The look on her face could have only been described as incredulous. Couldn't blame her after she'd just bared her soul.

"O-kay," she said hesitantly.

Nash smiled and bit his lip. "Good. The first one's on the house."

JESS WAITED FOR the punch line. And waited. It wasn't until he started laughing that she realized he'd already delivered it.

The first one's on the house? Even though the joke was awful, in her opinion, there was nothing better than seeing him laugh again. He didn't return the sentiment about the crush, which she wasn't expecting him to. But that wall he'd constructed had crumbled even more, allowing her to see the friend she once knew so well. Besides, he deserved to know the truth about why she couldn't face him.

"Nice try, my friend, but you still owe me that Juicy Lucy," she said.

"What? That was a joke."

"Barely. Regardless, I'm still ahead."

"I'm not so sure about that. But I *am* sure you dropped the ball just now. Did you forget how the game worked? We have to come back within a certain amount of time," Nash said.

"I remember. I thought you'd decided not to play along anymore, so I didn't come prepared. But since you're game, here's one. What do you call a sleeping bull?"

Nash thought about it. "I give up."

"A bulldozer."

He let out a painful-sounding howl.

"Oh, no! I wish I could unhear that." He dropped his head back against a cushion and just as quickly sat up and rubbed his hands together as if summoning a genie from an invisible bottle.

"What did one boat say to the other?" he asked.

Jess was determined to get this one. As she thought about it, Nash hummed the theme to *Jeopardy!*

"Stop it! I'm trying to concentrate," she said, swatting at his arm. But she couldn't come up with the answer.

After a few moments, he leaned in and whispered, "How about a little *row*-mance."

Jess gulped. Hard. She recognized the punch line now. She also recognized the seriousness of the moment. And how close they were sitting.

And how Nash had yet to lean back.

Shrieks and giggles from down the hall were enough to make their spines stiffen. They pooled to their separate sides of the love seat, which still left them quite close.

They seemed to be on the same page about the risk of crossing the friendship line again anywhere near the girls. At least until they could figure out a few more things, such as…

"What did the boats say when one was anchored to a single port, and the other was destined for many?" she asked.

He turned serious, as if he understood exactly what she was saying, then reached over and squeezed her arm. But he didn't have an answer, either.

The girls reappeared. Lizzy first, followed by Taylor and Kat, who were practically joined at the hip.

Jess stood, then Nash.

"Girls, say your goodbyes to Taylor and Jess."

The twins gave Jess a hug, and her heart felt as though it might melt right down to the soles of her feet and spill across the floor.

The girls released their grip. Taylor hooked pinkie fingers with Nash, then let go and headed out the door.

Nash walked Jess to the door, but paused. Neither seemed to know quite what to say.

"Thanks again for the jokes. And for offering to make Juicy Lucys tomorrow. It'll be a nice thing for us to share before I have to leave Destiny Springs."

The last words hung in the air between them, as more of a "definitely" rather than a "maybe."

"It's worth it to see you laugh again," he said.

A bittersweetness stuck in her throat as she attempted to swallow. *So this is how closure tastes.* She'd never really had it before. It was always too easy to abandon an uncomfortable situation and avoid confrontation altogether.

Taylor was already in the truck, and Jess was halfway down the stairs when Nash called out.

"Hey, Jess, one more thing."

She was almost afraid to ask. The pause felt like an eternity before he finally spoke.

"I had a crush on you, too."

CHAPTER FOURTEEN

I HAD A crush on you, too?

What was she supposed to do with that information?

Jess had been expecting a joke. Not a confession that would change the whole way she looked at their past. It was like how Lizzy had drawn daisies all over Jess's dream wedding dress pattern, altering those memories forever.

Not to mention, how it opened the door to the possibility of a future with Nash, even though all the other obstacles still blocked a viable path.

Jess was somehow able to focus enough to use the morning as originally planned and get the second Western shirt done for the rodeo moms, along with patterning the crop top.

She'd hoped to have some free time to talk with Taylor, especially since she wouldn't see her tonight or in the morning. Maybe even find out more about that mystery insight that helped with her breakthrough. But the morning had already come and gone.

So many mysteries, so little time.

Maybe tonight, on their dinner date, she could extract at least a hint from him.

Date. She hadn't really thought of it in the traditional sense of the word. Until now. It was supposed to be two friends, making Juicy Lucys for old times' sake.

For now, she needed to get the two of them moving. Dropping off Taylor at noon would give Jess plenty of time to come back and put a dent in the Dudley job. That one required the most focus, so the free afternoon would be invaluable.

Jess stood and stretched, then walked over to Taylor and motioned for her to remove her headphones for a second.

"Ready for your slumber party?" Jess asked.

Taylor nodded enthusiastically, which was a good thing. Taylor was completely on board with it.

The two of them got ready and landed at Sunrise Stables right on time, where an older woman with a long silver braid was tacking up the horse Jess recognized as Charmed.

"You must be Jess and Taylor. I'm Sylvie," the woman said as they approached. Sylvie was old enough to be a grandma but looked to be much more fit than Jess felt.

Hailey wasn't anywhere in sight. However, the short-but-energetic young man that she'd teased Jess about was there. It all made sense now.

Max ran over to greet her, but instead of a proper hello he launched into a story.

"A zillion years ago, Hailey's grandma and her boyfriend rode the trails we're gonna ride on. He gave her a bracelet, and they ended up loping."

Jess raised a brow and looked to the woman.

"Taylor and Jess aren't going on the ride, Max," Sylvie said as sweetly as possible.

The little boy looked crestfallen.

"The noon couple canceled at the last minute," Sylvie said, which explained why four horses were tacked and no one else was around.

Max perked up and pointed at a truck coming down the long drive. "Maybe that's them!"

Jess shielded her eyes from the sun. But the closer the truck got, the more familiar the vehicle and driver were to her. And the passengers. Nash was dropping off his girls for the slumber party. At high noon, as well.

What a coincidence.

Jess redirected her attention to the immediate issue at land.

Sylvie had cast a sympathetic look toward Jess, which matched what she felt in her own heart. The little boy obviously loved his job and was looking forward to the ride.

"I would have guessed the horses would walk or trot instead of loping, but y'all are the experts," Jess said, encouraging Max to finish his story. It was the least she could do.

"They eloped," the woman clarified.

"Yep. Loped," Max confirmed.

"Ah! Okay, that makes more sense," Jess said.

Hailey emerged from the barn and headed their way as Nash and the twins were getting out of the truck. She came over and gave Jess and Taylor a big hug first, then Nash and the twins had their turn.

"I'm glad everyone is on time. I need all the girls' help with perfecting the new moves I'll be offering in my goat yoga class," Hailey said. "Jess, you're free to join. You, too, Nash. Or maybe you two could fill in for the couple that canceled. My horses need the exercise now because that rainstorm is supposed to last twenty-four hours."

Nash moved to Jess's side and whispered, "What do you think?"

She whispered back. "I think I need to get back to a big sewing project. Then, I have some very important plans for the evening."

"A woman who has her priorities straight. Gotta love that," Nash said, then cleared his throat and answered Hailey and Sylvie. "I'll go on the ride, then I'll help work your other horses when we get back."

The thought of the calf birth, and Nash's reliance on Parker, immediately sprang to mind. If Parker called with another emergency, Nash wouldn't be available.

"How long is the ride?" Jess asked.

Sylvie and Hailey looked at each other, with Hailey nodding to the older woman for decision approval.

"This can be a short one. How about one hour? Fifteen minutes on the trail, thirty minutes lunch, then back home. Can't let Hailey's amazing grilled cheese sandwiches go to waste."

Jess wanted to say that perhaps the girls could eat the sandwiches, since they were staying behind to help with goat yoga. But she knew exactly what was going on here. Furthermore, she didn't mind it. One more hour wouldn't make a huge difference in her sewing progress.

"Okay. I'll go, too," Jess said.

"You sure?" Nash asked.

Jess nodded.

"Max, come inside with me and get the snacks for Sylvie," Hailey said.

The precious little boy did as he was told and followed Hailey's lead. Jess found herself admiring his adorable cowboy outfit. She would love to embellish the jean pockets for him. Silver studs in the shape of bulls. Or, perhaps purple to match his sparkly riding helmet.

Yeah. In my spare time.

"Which horse do I have the honor of riding today?" Jess asked.

"How about Gabby? She's a sweetheart," Sylvie said, pointing to the nearest horse. "Nash, you take Blaze."

Max reappeared, carrying a couple of thermal bags. Sylvie tucked the bags in Charmed's gear and helped Max mount Star, then she and Jess and Nash followed suit. With Sylvie in the lead, Max in the middle, followed by Jess and Nash, respectively, they headed out the back gate and across the grassy field.

Jess soaked in the warmth of the sun as the bluegrass turned to meadows dressed in colorful wildflowers.

"Has Lizzy ever drawn a landscape like this?" Jess asked Nash.

"She's been all about daisies. I'm trying to get her to expand her horizons. Try something new."

Right away, Jess's mind went to Kat and how badly *she* wanted to "try something new." In fact, she'd been thinking about the financial aspect of barrel racing being one of the issues Nash had brought up. Jess had been looking for sponsorships for Taylor. There could be one out there for Kat, too, in case that possibility hadn't occurred to him.

Of course, there was still the time issue, but maybe by the time Kat was ready to compete, he'd have more help with the ranch. Until then, there were the area rodeos. Or, just barrel racing on the ranch for fun and exercise.

But such a conversation should be done in private.

They meandered along to the sound of hooves and an occasional elk bugling somewhere in the distance, until Max broke the silence to continue his story.

"I forgot to tell you the parents wouldn't let Miss Hailey's grandma get married, so her boyfriend couldn't get her a ring, and so he made a bracelet out of their horses' hair instead," Max said in one galloping sentence, which clearly winded him.

"That's a fascinating story, Max," Jess managed to say.

"The kicker is, it's true. And there's more. Hailey inherited the engagement bracelet, which she gave to my boyfriend, Vern, so that he could propose to me. Let's stop and have our snack, and I'll tell you more," Sylvie said.

Nash helped Max spread a blanket on the ground while Sylvie and Jess secured the horses. That's when Jess noticed the bracelet that Sylvie was wearing.

"Is that the one?" Jess asked, pointing to Sylvie's wrist.

The woman twisted the bracelet around delicately, as if it might easily come undone.

"Yes, it is. Funny thing about it, I used to make these out of hair from my horse's tails when I was a little girl. Gave one to all my friends."

"Friendship bracelets? Taylor and her buddies love to make those, too, but theirs are from a kit. She would absolutely adore these."

"I'll write down the steps when we get back to Hailey's. Then perhaps you can show her how to do it. Same concept as the kits, I imagine."

They all got situated on the blanket. Max took the liberty of handing out sandwiches and chips and drinks.

"Vern tells me you're a professional seamstress," Sylvie said.

Professional? Jess had taken a huge bite of her grilled cheese sandwich and swallowed it in one gulp. "I'm trying to be."

In fact, she should be deep into the Dudley project at the moment, rather than being on this trail ride. She could work a couple of hours when she got back from the ride, though.

"I sewed all my kids' clothes and my husband's. I miss it," Sylvie said.

"It's like riding a bike. You can jump back in at any time," Jess said.

Sylvie looked out over the landscape. "I may do that someday."

"I can ride a bike, but I like riding horses better," Max said.

"You can do both," Nash offered.

Max seemed to think about it, then scrunched his brow. "How?"

He was so cute, Jess nearly choked on a chip she'd just popped into her mouth. It took a moment for her to realize that he thought Nash was proposing the impossible.

"Not at the same time, of course," Nash clarified. "You'd probably fall off one or the other. Or both."

"That would hurt," Max said.

"Falling usually does," Nash said, only this time he was looking directly at Jess.

"You'd only have to try it once to end up not wanting to do either ever again. If you survived to tell about it. So whatever you do, don't try it," Jess added, in case Nash had inadvertently put a bad idea in the little boy's head.

Seemingly satisfied with the explanation, Max took another big bite of his sandwich.

Meanwhile, Nash seemed to have an idea of his own. He leaned in and whispered quietly enough that only Jess could hear, "What if the potential gain outweighs the possible pain? Wouldn't it be worth a try?"

"Love is that way, too," Sylvie said, as if knowingly picking up the thread. "Your heart gets all skinned up, and you swear you'll never try again. For widows, it's even worse. Our lives come completely apart at the seams, don't they? Feels impossible to mend."

Sylvie was right about that. Such a thing created a hole in the fabric of one's life unlike anything else.

"You should put a Band-Aid on it," Max said.

If only it were that easy.

"You could do that, until a charming fella comes along and heals it altogether. No better feeling than that," Sylvie said.

"I'm never gonna fall in love," Max said. "Yuck!"

All three adults exchanged knowing glances.

"I think you'll find that you don't have a lot of control over certain things, Max. I didn't plan to fall in love again. Then I met Vern. Can happen to you, too." Sylvie took a long moment to look at Jess, then looked to Nash, who was clearly suppressing a smile. She wasn't doing much better.

Max shook his head vigorously. Could he be any more precious? Jess could relate to the defiance. His face looked the way she felt inside most days. Trying so hard not to fall for Nash again but feeling completely helpless against it.

I had a crush on you, too...

"No, it won't," Max insisted.

Sylvie laughed. "I didn't mean you, sweetie."

"Are you and Miss Jess getting married?" Max asked, causing Nash to nearly choke on his sandwich.

"What makes you think we might?"

"'Cause I heard Mommy say that Miss Jess is Nash's gal."

"It's just a cute nickname," Jess assured him. "Apparently everyone has one. Except for Nash."

"Not true," Sylvie said. "According to Vern, Nash can be a little unpleasant when he gets hungry. In fact, Vern calls him 'Mr. Grumpy Pants' when that happens. Isn't that right, Nash?"

The poor guy turned a diluted shade of crimson.

Max dropped backward on the blanket and started giggling. Jess had to laugh, as well. She'd experienced that side of Nash before and always thought it was rather cute and harmless. Nothing a Juicy Lucy couldn't fix. Or, hopefully, grilled cheese.

Nash took his time chewing and swallowing a bite, then slowly wiped his mouth with a napkin.

"I can confirm," was all he said, and he did so with a smile.

The trail ride back to Sunrise Stables was quiet, but the noise in Jess's mind was louder than ever.

Hailey and the girls were waiting when they returned. While

Hailey had Nash's attention, the girls took Jess by the hand and pulled her several feet away from the others.

"What's this about?" she asked.

"We think you should wear your new skirt tonight for your date," Lizzy said.

"But we're making Juicy Lucys. They're pretty messy."

"Daddy has an apron," Kat offered.

She looked over to Nash to see if he'd noticed she'd been kidnapped. How was she going to explain this conversation?

Then again, maybe she could negotiate a conversation trade. He'll tell her what Taylor had revealed, and she'll tell him about how his twins were future matchmakers. As if they both hadn't already figured that out.

"I'll think about it," Jess said, which was enough for the girls to release her arms and run over to Nash.

Jess followed behind as quickly as she could. If they were bold enough to give her wardrobe suggestions, no telling what advice they'd give him. But the only thing they seemed to be exchanging were hugs.

"I've gotta get back to the ranch," he said as Jess approached. "I'll see you tonight. Pick you up at seven?"

"I'll come to you," she said, if only to disabuse all the curious onlookers of what their evening was sounding like more and more: a date.

Surprisingly, Nash didn't argue. He tipped his hat to all, and Jess watched as he drove away.

Hailey handed the thermal bags to Max and filled the void that Nash had left behind.

The little boy ran to the house as if he'd finished rounding the third barrel at the world championships.

"Smart kid," Jess said.

"He's a sweetheart. Just like his parents. He's lucky to have the two of them. Becca was doing a wonderful job of raising him alone, but little boys need a daddy. So do little girls."

"What? I didn't realize she had been a single parent."

"Oh, yes. Secret baby. Cody found out less than a year ago that Max was his son. Now, he's making up for lost time by being the best daddy ever."

"That would be quite a secret for a guy to learn about. And for a woman to keep."

"Just goes to show that love really can overcome huge obstacles."

Sylvie reappeared before Jess could make a counterargument.

"Here are the instructions for the bracelet. Let me know how it goes. I'm going to finish untacking these lovely horses." Sylvie walked away, leaving Jess and Hailey where they left off.

"Thank you for hosting the slumber party," Jess said instead.

"Thank *you* for letting us. Parker and I can't wait to have a home full of children," Hailey countered.

"Wrangling those three might make you change your mind."

But as soon as Jess said it, she realized she'd lied. Wrangling those three was nothing but rewarding. In fact, she hadn't even left Hailey's and she already missed the girls. All of them. How was it going to feel when she had to leave for Montana and say goodbye to the twins?

Seemed Nash wasn't the only one in an increasingly difficult situation.

THAT CHORE BOARD of Nash's had turned into an Etch A Sketch in his absence. This time, it read:

• Pull ledgers.
• *Workin' on it. Got sidetracked.*
• Pick out something clean to wear for your date.

No brainer.

Nash grabbed a towel and wiped the board, once again.

Clean clothes, yes, but there was no point getting too spiffed up. Juicy Lucys could be quite messy to make, and even messier to eat. The girls had been whispering and giggling and hinting around that they could tell he and Jess liked each other. Yet, the writing was on the wall, where it couldn't be erased. Jess and Taylor were leaving soon. He could put a big fat period at the end of that line item.

If anything good could come from them leaving, it would

be that the matchmakers in this town would shift their focus to someone else.

Parker busted through the back door just as Nash was wiping away the last remnants of his handwriting.

"Why did you do that?" he asked.

"I could ask you the same thing. I can't let my girls see this."

"I didn't mention a dog this time."

"But you did mention a date. They're already a little too giggly about seeing us hugging. And kissing. Don't ask."

"Don't really have to. But could your girls even read that word?"

"Taylor's eight, so she probably could."

As soon as the response slipped from his lips, he realized his gaffe. He already thought of Taylor as a daughter. Couldn't deny it.

Parker squinted. "I think I see."

"Think again. This is not a *date* date. It's—" Nash stopped short. He wasn't quite sure what it was.

"Dinner?" Parker asked.

"Exactly."

"If you're done with me here, I have a date with my lovely wife. And *your* girls."

"You're sounding like an old married couple. Y'all are still in the honeymoon phase."

"And we're going to stay there forever, which is why we're ready to move forward with adopting a little boy we met."

"Are you serious?"

"As a heifer giving birth to her calf. We talked about an infant, and we will someday. But this little fella captured our heart, and he's up for immediate adoption. Just need to make some arrangements."

Nash felt as though his chin needed to be forklifted off the floor. Things were happening so fast.

"That's terrific!" Nash said. And he meant it. Still, he had a million questions. Such as, how could an adoption happen so fast? No doubt, Parker and Hailey would make wonderful parents, but wasn't an enormous amount of vetting and paperwork and legal mumbo jumbo involved?

Then again, there wasn't any vetting for regular couples to have little ones of their own. If there had been, Roxanne's lack of maternal instinct might have been flagged.

"I know what you're thinking. That I won't be available to help around the ranch as much. But I assure you that isn't the case. Remember that ranch hand I mentioned? I'll bring him by after the rainstorm moves through."

No use arguing. Parker had clearly made up his mind. Nash honestly hadn't thought about how Parker and Hailey's eventual adoption would impact his own situation. Still, he wouldn't change anything.

"Bring him by whenever you wish," Nash said.

With that, Parker tipped his Stetson and exited out the back door.

Dinner. *Right.* He didn't fool Parker, or himself.

Nash remembered his parting words from yesterday. *I had a crush on you, too.* Not that he could forget. That big, fat period he'd mentally put at the end of the writing on the wall was looking like a question mark. There was only one way to figure out which it was, and that was to be alone with her. Only then could he begin the process of letting her go.

Or convincing her to stay.

CHAPTER FIFTEEN

"YOU MUST BE at the wrong house," Nash said.

If Jess wasn't already standing on his porch, wearing a knockout long skirt and boots and holding a brown bag, he would have told her not to come.

Not because it looked like an anvil was about to be dropped on the entirety of the town and he didn't want her to be out in this kind of weather, although that was true. Rather, once again, he was having visions of her being a permanent fixture in his life. Only thing missing tonight was the girls to make the vision complete.

Seeing her all dressed up, he wished he'd put on something nicer than an old-but-clean pair of jeans and a well-worn flannel shirt.

"Since I'm already here, perhaps you could invite me in," she said.

"Please." He ushered her inside with a wave of his hand and closed the door behind her. Thankfully, he'd had the wherewithal to throw some wood on the fire at the last minute.

Jess set the brown bag by the door. "These are some drawings for you from the girls."

"Really? How sweet. I'll look at 'em when they get back," he said, as tempted as he was to look at them now.

Jess removed her coat and put it on a hook.

He could have stood there all night and admired her. Instead, he turned on his heels and motioned her to follow him to the kitchen.

"I thought we'd jump right into dinner while the den warms up. I'm starved. How about you?" he asked.

"Same."

Nash grabbed an apron that had been freshly washed and folded.

"Here. Even though I'm doing the cooking, you might need this. Wouldn't want to get hamburger grease on that pretty skirt of yours."

He hadn't meant to be so forward, but it practically begged to be complimented. She always looked pretty, but this skirt took it to a whole other level.

She paused for a moment as she held the apron, then smiled as if he'd given her a gift as she tied it around her waist.

"*We're* doing the cooking, so I'll take you up on it. Lizzy picked out the skirt for me at Kavanaugh's. She wanted me to buy it because she thought you'd like it. How cute is that?"

It did look like something Lizzy would gravitate toward.

"I should've had her pick out my outfit, too. I'm afraid I'm not very fancy."

Jess bit her lip and smiled.

"What?" he asked.

Her smile spread. "I'm just glad you decided not to wear your grumpy pants tonight."

"Mr. Grumpy Pants promises not to crash our party if we feed him soon, so let's get started. You fix the patties, I'll add the cheese."

"Because I can't be trusted to use American instead of cheddar?"

He neither confirmed nor denied. Truth be told, her Juicy Lucys had always tasted better than his, in spite of her cheese choice. Although it took some time for him to pinpoint why, it seemed to have to do with how thick she made the patties, the amount of salt and pepper she used and how she forced a bit of a well in the center, which made them cook evenly.

He retrieved the cheeses from the refrigerator. Both American and cheddar.

"I thought we'd try combining them. Once slice of each, per burger. Who knows? Maybe they'll be even better this way."

Jess raised her brows and nodded. "Interesting concept. That said, you're the chef de cuisine. I'm a mere sous-chef tonight. It's your reputation on the line."

Nash smiled. "I'll take my chances."

Together, they went through the steps. Jess added a big pinch of salt to the ground beef, separated and rolled it into four equal balls and shaped them into flat patties.

"I hope the girls are okay," she said.

Nash added one slice of each cheese and closed them in between two patties each, sealing the edges.

"They're in excellent hands. With both Parker and Hailey there, they'll be one big happy family."

She added the perfect well in the center of each set, then salted and peppered the tops while he sprinkled the bottom of the heated skillet with a pinch more of salt.

"Bigger than you think. Hailey told me Parker was venturing out to pick up some guy named Gus and bring him back to Sunrise Stables."

That was odd. How well did Parker even know the guy? Then again, his ranch hand's plan was probably to coach Gus on the answers he should give Nash for the informal interview. For some reason, Parker was obsessed with having this particular person help with the herding.

Nash couldn't say he blamed Parker. He'd probably teased the guy a little too much on his lack of skills.

With the burgers officially prepped, it was time to start cooking.

"You time. I'll flip. They're pretty thick, so five minutes a side," he said.

"Three. Respectfully," she countered.

"You sure? The cheese might not melt enough. Especially with two slices, one being cheddar."

"Excellent point. We should account for that. Let's check

'em at four. We don't want a repeat of the hash browns incident. *Ahem*."

Nash squeezed his eyes closed and half laughed. "Good to know my angels can't keep a secret."

"Maybe you should have made them pinkie shake on it."

He gulped. He knew she'd witnessed it between him and Taylor, but since she hadn't asked, he hadn't offered. Unless Taylor had decided to tell her mom everything, which would take him off the hook because Jess really needed to know.

They cooked the burgers in silence for their agreed upon four minutes per side. Once done, Nash cut into one of the patty combos. It couldn't have turned out more perfect.

"Now, this is an example of good teamwork," he said.

She pulled two plates from the cabinet and set up the buns and condiments. Then they put together what he would consider the best Juicy Lucys he'd ever tasted. They didn't even bother to sit down at the table before digging in. Instead, they leaned against the counter.

"So you noticed my pinkie shake with Taylor," he said as Jess bit into the cheesy center of her burger.

She finished chewing and wiped her mouth and chin.

"Did it have to do with the whole breakthrough thing?" she asked.

He nodded and took a bite of burger, as well, if only to give himself a few moments to come up with a response.

"I'll tell you anything you want to know, as long as she tells you first," he said.

"It has to do with her dad," Jess said.

"Then she did tell you."

"Nope. But I got you to reveal something."

Nash shook his head, wagged his finger at her and smiled.

"I can't say I'm surprised," Jess said. "She and I have a hard time talking about him."

Nash's heart ached for both of them. He wanted to say it would get easier, but his situation seemed to have only gotten worse with time. Pretty soon, the twins would want to know more about their mother, and he didn't have a clue what he was going to say. In the meantime, he was determined to put off the inevitable for as long as possible.

"I have a question for you," he said.

"Go ahead," she said, taking another bite. It was almost as if neither of them had eaten in days.

"Has Kat brought up the subject of barrel racing?" he asked, hoping it didn't sound too accusatory.

Jess washed down the bite with some ice water. Then some more, before taking a deep breath. "She had some general questions on that first day. At the time, I suggested she talk with you and that maybe you could show her some moves. Then you asked me not to encourage her, and she and I haven't talked about it since."

Her soft stare and slow blink convinced him she was telling the truth.

"Thanks. I appreciate that."

"Maybe someday you'll be in a position to let her learn," Jess said.

He'd dared to entertain that possibility lately because of the similarities Kat had with Taylor as far as riding, which Hailey had pointed out. As a teacher—former teacher—he also had an eye for talent.

"You may be right. But *someday* is a little too far away right now."

Jess nodded. Another period of silence followed as they finished eating, but it was nice. He remembered them well, those long stretches of quiet where they were together but didn't have to say a word.

Nash moved to the next step of their ritual and put on a pot of coffee. Once the coffee maker stopped burping, they each grabbed a cup and retreated to the den.

The rain had slowed to a sleepy pulse, which made him wonder if they'd dodged the worst of it. In any event, he would insist on driving her back to the B and B. He could deliver her truck in the morning and ask Becca or Cody to give him a lift back to Buck Stops. With a little luck, Jess would offer to drive him back instead.

Nash privately smiled at how he'd inadvertently come up with a possible way to spend a little more time with her.

The den had warmed to a perfect temperature. They settled in on the love seat once again. Except this time, it felt different. Maybe because everything was different. Even though they'd sat in this proximity dozens of times before, he'd never felt so close to anyone. He would have been fine to spend the rest of the evening simply enjoying being with her.

"My turn to ask you a question," she said. "Are there any other secrets I should know about?"

Just one. The fact that Roxanne had not only left him once, which Jess already knew, but that she had done it twice.

"If I share it with you, then it won't be a secret anymore, will it?"

She shrugged. "I can't make you tell me anything. Obviously. But be warned—I already know something about you that no one else in this town knows."

"No one else? I highly doubt that." He liked her confidence, though.

Jess put her finger on his chest, directly over his heart and paused.

"There's a tiny hole, right there," she finally said.

Nash gulped. That was a whole other subject. A whole other story that he wouldn't begin to know how to explain. He'd been born with a small hole in his heart. Atrial septal defect, the doctors had called it, although it wasn't diagnosed until after his mother died.

Shortness of breath. Heart palpitations. Easily written off as stress. Any five-year-old might display such symptoms under the circumstances of losing a parent. But when his legs swelled up, his father took him to the doctor.

Nash was convinced that losing his mom had created the hole, even though the doctors insisted it was there at birth. Supposedly, it closed on its own. That much he believed. The tests all proved that was the case. But Nash would never be convinced that it hadn't been ripped back open.

Maybe it had never shown up on a transesophageal echocardiography, but he'd felt it. Until this very moment, he'd blamed

Roxanne for that. Blamed her for leaving him and the girls. The whole thing even launched a rumor in Destiny Springs about there being another woman who'd broken his heart. Which he denied. But they'd known something that even he didn't know. It was so clear now.

Jess had been the one to put it there.

"HOW DID YOU KNOW?" Nash asked.

Jess couldn't even begin to describe his expression. So serious. It was almost as if she'd hurt his feelings by pointing it out. A tiny hole in a shirt wasn't anything to be ashamed of. It was going to eventually happen with a cotton flannel work shirt.

"Don't worry. I won't tell anyone. Besides, I can barely see it. I wouldn't worry that anyone else has noticed. Nothing I couldn't mend in a few minutes. Do you have a needle and some blue thread?" she asked.

He blinked hard, then looked down and examined the place she'd pointed out. He tugged at a frayed edge of the hole, then let out a nervous laugh.

"I have a hole in my shirt. Right here." He pointed at it and laughed as if someone was tickling him.

Weird.

"I'm glad you can accept it," she said.

Nash leaned back on the pillows, looked to the ceiling and laughed a little more.

"You already know that Roxanne abandoned us. Walked out on me and the girls when they were less than two weeks old."

Jess's breath caught in her throat. Less than two weeks? She, quite literally, did abandon her babies. Nash was stating it so matter-of-factly. Then again, some people laughed out of nervousness or fear or even grief. Perhaps that's what was happening.

In one way, she was relieved that he'd decided not to reveal what Taylor had confided in him. If he had, she might have been forced to mention the whole barrel racing event at Hailey's. After everything Nash had done to help her daughter, that wasn't the way for the little girl to repay him, even though Taylor was too young to fully grasp the depth of Nash's predicament.

"I'm so sorry," she said.

"It gets better. She came back around again when they were barely past toddlerhood, wanting another chance. The engine hadn't even had time to cool on her Jeep before she up and left again."

Wow.

"Is that why you don't go to events anymore? Kat said she'd only seen part of one."

He nodded. "Some years ago, I heard through the grapevine that Roxanne was talking about *her* girls and wanting to see them. As far as I'm concerned, she forfeited her place in their lives."

"Totally understandable."

"No matter. I lost my love for the sport before that," he said.

So it *was* Roxanne who broke his heart. Not someone else. That Destiny Springs rumor wasn't true. But the worst part was, he hadn't moved past it. She'd had to compete with Roxanne ten years ago. Maybe she still was.

"Thank you for confiding in me." She extended the pinkie of her right hand. "I won't tell anyone."

He hooked his pinkie with hers. "I appreciate that. While we're at it, promise you won't leave Destiny Springs without saying goodbye."

"If you'll promise not to put up any more walls," she said.

"Then promise the twins and I will see you and Taylor again at some point in the future, after y'all leave for Montana," he said.

"It's a deal."

At that, they squeezed each other's pinkies so hard she thought they might break. Furthermore, she felt the power of it.

Nash finally softened his grip and released. He picked up his coffee and took a sip. Even though the confession about Roxanne must have been difficult, there was a lightness about him now. Getting something that heavy off his chest must have felt good. Kind of like her confession about her crush.

They sipped their coffee in silence. The fireplace could have used another log, but she had to get going anyway.

"The rain stopped. I'd better get back and get some sleep." Then get up early and sew.

"I'll drive you," he said.

"That's not necessary. I'm a big girl. I've driven in worse weather than this."

"I know. But it's a convenient excuse to see you again tomorrow."

It was true; she didn't need to be taken care of in that way. She'd been taking care of herself for years. But the chivalry was beyond sweet. And, if she were being honest, she was looking forward to more time with him after he'd let her in a little more.

"Then I insist on mending that hole, as payment," she said, pointing once again to the tear in his flannel shirt.

He glanced down at the thing again and then back up. "You're the only one who could."

Jess rolled her eyes. She could think of at least two other people who were good with a needle and thread: Dorothy and Sylvie.

"You're giving me way too much credit, but I appreciate the vote of confidence."

They looked at each other for the longest time before leaning in for a gentle, extended kiss that felt perfectly natural and expected. This time, she kept her eyes open, and he did, too, softening any suspicion she'd just had about him not being over Roxanne.

She searched for any holes in that wall that he'd constructed. Only to realize that he was no longer hiding behind one.

CHAPTER SIXTEEN

NASH FELT LIKE a nervous groom, waiting for his bride to walk down the aisle.

Except the "bride" in this scenario was supposedly a seasoned ranch hand, the venue was his greenhouse and the aisle was lined with yet-to-bloom potted gerbera daisies.

They were coming along. Probably needed about two more months, if Nash didn't mess things up. This was his first attempt at raising florals.

Otherwise, he would have taken a daisy with him and presented it to Jess when he dropped off her truck at the B and B, which didn't go entirely as planned. Vern had made a late run with the eggs and insisted on giving Nash a lift back to his place.

Just as well. Nash used the extra time to locate all the ledgers. Parker had texted that he and Gus were heading his way. Since Vern managed to get him back to Buck Stops first, Nash decided to check on the progress of this future surprise for Lizzy, since she and Kat were still at Hailey's and probably eating Pop-Tarts about now.

He looked around at the other aisles. Plenty of open space, but until he got some more help around here, he wasn't inclined to develop it. Maybe Gus had a green thumb and could take on extra duties.

In fact, Nash was getting a little excited about the possibilities.

The door to the greenhouse opened, and Parker strutted in. Alone. As he watched his "best man" walk down the aisle, a certain fear struck him.

"Did Gus get cold feet?" Nash asked, trying to mask his disappointment.

"Not at all. But I didn't want him to get 'em wet, so I left him in the house."

"Gus isn't one of your city buddies in wing tips, is he?" Nash asked, although at this point he couldn't imagine what else it could be. A seasoned ranch hand wouldn't mind getting his boots a little muddy.

All of a sudden, this felt like a huge waste of time. No matter how highly Parker thought of this stranger, Nash would have to stand firm if he wasn't a good fit. No help was better than bad help.

Same went for relationships, for that matter. Being alone was better than being with the wrong person. He may have a bad relationship track record, but at least his intuition and judgment were usually spot-on when it came to the ranch.

"No comment on the shoes. I'll let you make your own judgment about that," Parker said.

Not helpful.

"Okay. Let's see what you've gotten me into."

Once they reached the house, Parker went straight inside after wiping his boots. Nash took a little extra time while contemplating how to put an end to all this nonsense without hurting Gus's pride.

Even that might have to wait, because once he stepped inside, he was staring down a different kind of problem. Looking up at him was the most adorable Australian shepherd he'd ever seen.

"What's going on? Where's Gus?" Nash asked.

Parker looked down to the dog. "Gus, beg for the job."

The dog took the cue and sat on its hind legs.

Nash tried to make sense of it. Was this some kind of joke?

"You said Gus was an experienced ranch hand."

"I said he was an experienced cattle herder. Worked at the Tanner ranch for ten years. Old man Tanner said you're welcome to call him for a reference."

Nash knew of the place. Buck Stops was a dot on the map compared to them.

"They replaced him with a younger dog since they've added more cattle. And they put Gus up for adoption. They let me bring him home and introduce him to the family to make sure it was a good fit for everyone involved."

So much for Nash's grand plan of giving Gus even more responsibilities. He rubbed his eyes and blinked a few times.

"What's with not getting his paws dirty?" he asked.

"Oh, he'll have no problem with that. I just didn't want him to track mud back through your clean house."

That begged the question…

"Do Lizzy and Kat know about *you know who*?" Nash asked, nodding sideways toward the dog.

Parker shook his head. "Gus spent the night in the stables with the horses. We want to introduce him to Hailey's cat, Sergeant, when there aren't three other little terrors running around. The poor kitty went into hiding last night and hasn't come out."

The dog seemed to study Nash's every expression, as if Nash was the one being interviewed instead of the other way around.

"What do you think? Does he get the job? We can round up any cattle and move 'em to higher ground. Hailey wants to keep the girls a little longer. She'll bring 'em back this evening."

Nash wanted his little ones back more than anything. It was always tough being away from them for even one night. The more he thought about it, the more he realized that Gus was the perfect solution to the dog problem. The girls could have one around to play with sometimes, but Nash wouldn't have to take care of him.

"Okay. Don't say anything to the girls or let them see this adorable little guy until I have a chance to talk to them."

"The not-saying part I can do. The not-seeing part might be a little tricky. I'll need to take him back to the house for an hour because I'm leading half of a workshop over at the B and B. I'll be back here to finish up any chores after. I have a feeling my topic isn't going to draw a big crowd, so I might be talking to an empty room. Unless Jess makes an appearance like she promised when I took the girls off her hands, which she's certainly not obligated to do."

"If Jess said she'll do something, she will. She's amazing that way," Nash said.

Judging from Parker's stoic expression and the absence of a clever comeback, the guy was taking the statement too seriously.

Nash looked at the pup, who cocked his head as if still waiting on an official offer. Hopefully, Nash wouldn't regret what he was about to say next.

"Gus can stay here with me."

"Said like a man in love."

Nash squinted. "Gus is good lookin', but he isn't my type. And don't leave without taking that box."

"I wasn't talking about Gus." Parker tipped his hat and headed toward the front door this time, collecting the ledgers on his way out.

That's when Nash noticed the brown bag Jess had brought over. Drawings that the girls had done, did she say? How could he have forgotten about those?

He took the sack to the twins' bedroom, set it on the edge of Kat's bed and looked around. Even with all the stuffed animals and dolls and Breyer horses, the room should have felt larger without them in it. Instead, it felt smaller. Emptier. Colder. Is this how it would feel in twelve or so years, when they left the nest? If so, how did parents stand it?

Although he wanted to wait until they got home, his curiosity got the best of him. A quick peek wouldn't hurt.

He pulled out and unfolded the enormous piece of paper first. Oddly shaped and filled with daisies in all different sizes.

Next, he turned over their whiteboard, except there wasn't a drawing on it. Only a question.

Why can't your head be twelve inches long?

Nash had to laugh. "Because then it would be a foot."

Of course he'd pretend not to know the answer for Kat's sake. Except, this probably wasn't her joke. Definitely wasn't her handwriting. But something else caught his eye. Faint, layered loops in the background. As if whatever had been drawn didn't get fully erased.

He turned on the overhead light and tilted the board for a closer look. They'd started to draw one thing, then something over it. The darker marks could have been the leaves of one of Lizzy's giant flowers. Or...*a lazy daisy.* Those also had six petals.

He compared Lizzy's artwork that she'd drawn for him. Many of those had six petals, but not all. He retrieved his cell phone and pulled up the photo he'd snapped of her drawing the other day on his board. Those daisies had too many petals to count.

The slightly darker, semi-erased marker on the girls' board appeared to only have three loops, which wouldn't qualify as any kind of flower he'd ever seen. Now he wished he had forgotten about the brown sack, because this was enough to raise some serious doubts he thought he'd never have to raise with Jess.

The handwriting was hers. And one of the drawings beneath it was a cloverleaf.

Dear Ms. McCoy—I can't stop thinking about all those fun details you're including on the suit. I would love for Meghan to wear it to a celebration dinner in Montana. I want to feature it this month instead of next. Meghan's in the morning slack. I can collect the garment then and there. Yours truly, Mrs. Carol Anne Dudley.

Jess literally gasped. She looked up and around, wanting to share the good news with Taylor. In fact, throughout the morning, she'd kept looking around for her. She'd even saved her a seat at breakfast in the barn.

But Taylor hadn't been there, since Hailey had kidnapped all the girls yesterday and was still holding them hostage. Taylor was such an integral thread in her life, it felt as though she would fall completely apart without her.

Then another kind of reality sank in. She hadn't made any actual progress on Mrs. Dudley's outfit, aside from patterning and daydreaming. And she'd used her last scrap of black velvet for the number on Kat's shirt.

Jess glanced at the clock, which reminded her of the workshop that Parker was leading. The one she'd promised to drop in on, only she was late. She slipped her boots on, combed through her hair and brushed her teeth.

By the time she got downstairs, the parlor was packed with DEBBs. She considered slowly turning around and going back upstairs. Except she'd caught Dorothy's eye. The woman patted the empty seat next to her on one of the sofas.

Another surprise: Vanessa was standing next to Parker. Jess was hoping she'd get to see her again.

"I'll fill you in on what you missed later," Dorothy whispered as Jess squeezed into the small space.

Jess turned her attention to Parker. The cowboy looked as comfortable in front of a crowd as Nash did in jeans.

"Now for the part you've all been waiting for," he said. "Accounting software for your home."

That earned a few chuckles from the audience.

"Does anyone currently use any software, either for home budgeting or business? Or both?" he asked.

Jess was the only one to raise a hand.

"Good! Then I'll let you take over from here, Ms. McCoy," Parker said, then pretended to walk away.

Unfortunately, she wasn't prepared to speak on such an important topic. As with her sewing, her budgeting and software skills had been self-taught out of pure necessity. But if he was okay with that—

"He's teasing, Jess," Vanessa said, grabbing Parker's arm and pulling him back to his post.

Jess exhaled. Yep. That woman was an angel, for sure.

"Vanessa is right, as usual. But since my cousin didn't let me get away with it, I'm going to hand the workshop over to her instead. After a quick wrap-up."

At that, Jess perked up. She'd been thinking about what Vanessa had suggested about her hiring someone to help with the garments. Hopefully, she'd delve into that concept more. If so, all the anxiety of taking the time to come down here would be worth it.

"Instead of putting the room to sleep, I'll post a link on my website where you can download a free trial to a couple of my preferred accounting software programs," Parker said. "With that, I'll let my cousin Vanessa take over from here and share her part of the workshop on work-life balance for the 'sandwich' generation. We'll both hang around for a little while afterward to answer any questions that you're too embarrassed to ask in front of your friends."

Again, that earned him a few chuckles and plenty of smiles.

"My cousin is a tough act to follow, but I'll try." Vanessa looked down at some notes, then looked back up. "I met someone here in Destiny Springs the other day. I won't name names, but I saw myself in her."

Vanessa had been scanning the room, but her gaze settled on Jess long enough to suggest the woman was talking about her.

"I also know that at least one of you is caring for a spouse because of major health issues while holding the whole sandwich together on your own," Vanessa continued. "We don't have much time left, but I want to give you a few pointers and resources on not only balancing our responsibilities to others, but also our responsibilities to ourselves and our own future goals and dreams."

Dorothy shifted and wiggled as if Jess was sitting too close. They were all sandwiched in, which seem to be the food reference of the day. Jess glanced at her sewing soulmate just as the woman dabbed away a tear, and she realized she was sitting next to the main ingredient in Vanessa's last scenario.

Her sewing soulmate had mentioned being interested in getting back into the craft and doing that from home. At the time, Jess assumed it was because she wanted a productive hobby. Now she realized it went much deeper.

In fact, Jess looked around at all the women and men in the room. She'd assumed they all had spousal support—emotional or financial, or both—and that this was nothing more than a fun retreat they gathered for each year. She'd been wrong.

"This isn't a phenomenon that only affects women. Many men are juggling home life and work on their own, too—like at least one local cowboy I know. He could use a partner in his life. Preferably someone who can do accounting spreadsheets, because I'm afraid he's a lost cause in that area," Parker added.

Again, that earned a laugh from some of the DEBBs. Parker

didn't even have to say Nash's name, although his identity wouldn't be obvious to the others. Except Jess. And she'd bet the cowboy knew it.

Was the whole town in cahoots?

That was the least of her concerns at that moment. Jess squeezed her eyes closed. Whatever Vanessa had started explaining turned into white noise, although she recognized much of it from their private talk. There was no way she could finish the Dudley project without some help. And there were two working sewing machines in the house.

What if...?

Jess began to see the possibilities. Her mind suddenly felt as though she'd been sleeping like a champ, when in reality, she'd been lucky to get in four hours a night.

The sound of Parker and Vanessa's voices wrapping up the meeting, and the rustling of DEBBs starting to leave, reeled Jess back into the moment. And back to Dorothy, who thankfully looked somewhat uplifted.

"What did you think of all that? I found it helpful but a bit overwhelming. Vanessa and Parker made it sound so easy to have a home business, but I wouldn't know where to start." Dorothy's eyes were now dry but tinged in red. She slipped something into the pocket of her sweater. Looked like a tissue.

"I know Vanessa talked about having to go it alone, but what if you didn't have to?" Jess asked.

Dorothy seemed confused. No surprise. Jess wasn't too clear herself on what she was about to propose, but it seemed like a possible solution for both of them.

It also might be a good way to test the waters for what she was contemplating. A work from home situation…in an actual home instead of an apartment. Maybe with a sewing studio, or just an empty corner she could call her own.

"You mentioned wanting to sew again. I'm desperately behind on a project with a tight deadline. I could pay you a standard hourly rate, if Becca is okay with us continuing to use her sewing machine."

Dorothy sat up straighter, and her expression lightened.

"Honestly, I'd do it for free. It would take my mind off certain things. I have a sewing machine at home, as well, if it still runs."

Jess wanted to say that this couldn't wait until they returned home from their workshops, but this deadline was her fault and her problem. Not Dorothy's.

"There is no way I'd let you work for free. Your time is precious, and it might take away from your experience here."

Dorothy fidgeted with her nails. "Well, I've missed out on a lot already. The DEBBs were so sweet to have the retreat here this year so that I could go back and forth to my house."

"You live in Destiny Springs?"

"About fifteen minutes outside of the town, in an even smaller one."

That explained why Jess didn't always see her. It also confirmed what she suspected about Dorothy's situation. In fact, maybe being around these men and women, who appeared to be happier and less burdened by life's senseless tragedies, reminded Dorothy of easier times. Just like it was doing with Jess.

Still, the choice was Dorothy's.

"Give it some thought. I stand to gain a lot from the completion of this project, so free labor is off the table."

"Okay. If you insist. Can't say I couldn't use the extra money," Dorothy said.

The woman didn't ask for further details, and Jess was happy to omit that the outfit would be featured on a prominent blog. Yet, even though it was Jess's design, she wouldn't be the one to assemble it. This could backfire. The woman could do a less-than-stellar job, in which Jess would take the fall.

All Jess knew for certain was that she couldn't finish the garment without spending every available waking moment on it. She wasn't about to shortchange the twins or further alienate her own daughter.

Or see less of Nash. Not if she absolutely didn't have to.

"Terrific! I have it all patterned out, and I'll provide you with the fabric and notions. All I'm missing is the black velvet for some trim, but I'll come up with something," Jess said.

Even though Jess was taking a huge chance, she felt lighter already. But there was something else. She hadn't heard much of the workshop, but she did hear Parker's and Vanessa's indirect message to her about a certain local cowboy they knew needing a partner in his life.

For the first time, Jess believed that so many people couldn't be wrong. That maybe she had been wrong about certain things, like feeling confined by planting roots. And about Taylor not needing a stable father figure because Jess should be able to handle both roles.

Most of all, maybe she'd been wrong to think that this relationship wasn't meant to be. She felt safe with Nash in a way that she hadn't for years.

It was time to trust that feeling again.

CHAPTER SEVENTEEN

FOR THE FIRST time ever, the twins burst through the front door and halted without giving their daddy a hug.

Nash didn't want it any other way.

Even though he hadn't seen his girls since yesterday afternoon and had been suffering serious hug withdrawals, the look on both of their faces was priceless.

Kat stood, slack-jawed. Lizzy started crying happy tears.

Gus knew exactly what to do to comfort her. He ran over with his backside wagging furiously, giving her slobbery doggy kisses.

"Before you get too excited, he doesn't belong to us. He's Parker and Hailey's. But he's going to be a Buck Stops employee, so we'll get to play with him every day."

Parker followed behind and leaned on the door frame. "And I'm open to letting him spend the night every once in a while, if it's okay with your daddy."

The twins obviously didn't hear a word that either had to say. They were too busy hugging the happy little fella.

Nash nodded for Parker to join him. His ranch hand came inside and closed the door behind him.

"Hope I didn't overstep my bounds by suggesting a slumber party," Parker said.

"No worries, as long as it gets me out of having to adopt one myself," Nash said.

"My evil plan has been exposed. Plus, it might be good for the girls to have a distraction while you make some important life decisions." Parker flashed a large envelope. "These are the preliminary suggestions I promised, based on annual summaries for each year. I wanted you to mull everything over before I spend many hours in the weeds, pulling together specifics and a working budget. You had quite a business going back in the day. I'm impressed."

"I'm not as bad with numbers as people think," Nash said.

"I've found that most people are better than they think. Numbers are like relationships," Parker said.

Nash looked at him sideways.

"You have to work at them sometimes. But when everything adds up, it's a beautiful thing," Parker said.

"And when it doesn't?" Nash didn't mean to sound so cynical. In fact, he'd almost forgotten how some things in his life—and, admittedly, his relationship with Jess—didn't add up as easily as he wanted them to.

"That often means you didn't try hard enough," Parker said, relinquishing the envelope.

Nash pulled out the binder-clipped stack of paper and glanced at the summation.

- Primary source of income: teaching (barrel racing).
- Secondary source of income: cattle (dairy and/or beef production).
- Optional income stream: growing crops (farmers markets, or branching out).

Nash looked Parker square in the eye. "Pretty sure I asked you to leave barrel racing out of the equation. Or did I dream that?"

"No. I concur that happened."

"And you agreed, as I recall."

"I said I understood."

"Same difference. I know you're doing this as a favor, and

I appreciate it. But please try again." At that, Nash placed the envelope on the hall table between them, folded his arms and prepared for a witty comeback.

His ranch hand obviously sensed Nash wasn't in the mood.

"I'm going to check on our momma and her baby," Parker said in a calm but cooler tone than before. The cowboy then turned on his heels and left.

Nash closed his eyes and rubbed his temples. His mind returned to another situation where his request had been ignored. His thoughts kept going round and round those faint loops he'd noticed on the whiteboard. Running in circle eights and cloverleafs and daisy petals until he couldn't tell which was which. Maybe there was a way to get some clarification.

When he opened his eyes, his girls were standing there with Gus. Watching. Time to pull himself up by his bootstraps and paste a smile on his face. Maybe even get some clarification.

"Girls, I brought the drawings home that you did with Jess. Remember? They're in your room, and I can't wait to see them."

They looked at him for a long minute before they remembered, which eased his guilt over forgetting.

"Can Gus come with us?" Lizzy asked.

"Absolutely!"

The twins each took a hand and practically dragged him down the hall. Gus followed, his entire back end wagging so hard he could have knocked a hole in the wall.

Lizzy unfolded hers first. "They're daisies. Miss Jess let me draw on some of her special paper."

"Those are the most beautiful flowers I've ever seen," Nash said.

Lizzy produced a pen with a flower on the end. "She bought me this to draw with."

"That was awfully nice of her."

"And I picked out a skirt for her. It's really pretty," Lizzy added.

Now *that* he hadn't forgotten.

"Did you get a pen, too, Kat?"

"She got a bracelet like Taylor's," Lizzy said.

"Let me see," Nash said. Kat held it up. Horseshoes, intertwined.

"That's beautiful. And did you draw something for me, too?"

"Miss Jess drew a joke for you instead 'cause I can't draw," Kat said. She reached into the sack, pulled out the board and handed it to him.

"I wouldn't say that. Your stick ponies are amazing. Can you help me read this?" he asked.

As Kat pointed to each word, Nash took the lead in sounding them out for her. "Why can't your head be twelve inches long?"

He then pretended to think about it. "Gosh. I don't know."

"'Cause twelve inches is a foot!" Lizzy called out.

"That was my joke. You ruined it!" Kat yelled.

The earth could have stopped rotating. Kat had never pushed back that hard against Lizzy. Unless it had to do with cupcakes versus sugar pies. And even then…

Nash's hope of getting any insight into the faint markings on the board was superseded by the need to put a stop to this argument and calm the waters.

He stood and offered one hand to Kat and one to Lizzy. "C'mon ladies. Cupcake and Sugar Pie miss you. We need to stretch their legs, but we're gonna walk. Not ride."

Hand in hand, they went to the stables, Gus trotting happily beside them. The arena was reasonably dry, but he didn't want to risk any injuries to the horses or the girls. He'd exercise them himself later. Or have Parker do it, if the guy was even speaking to him. He hadn't meant to come across as ungrateful, but what Parker had proposed would create more problems than it would solve.

Together, they put the halters and lead ropes on their horses. Once done, Nash claimed his teaching spot on the fence and observed.

"Be careful. It's muddy in places," he called out.

It had become only a minor point that the barrels were out there. One more session with Taylor, and they'd go back into storage, even though he'd considered getting rid of them completely. But he'd gotten reattached to them over the past few days, at least enough to hold on to them for a while.

Lizzy went through her usual walking drill around the perimeter of the arena. Gus followed her and Cupcake instead of Kat. Lizzy seemed to relish every moment of it.

Kat, on the other hand, deviated from her usual drill and took Sugar Pie around the barrels. Right turn around the first, left turn around the second. Another left turn around the third.

His stomach seized. No way that was accidental. He jumped off his perch and joined them in the arena.

"Where did you learn to do that?" he asked Kat.

She stopped and looked down. "I don't know. I saw Taylor do it."

That was believable. She had caught a glimpse of Taylor going through the drills. Once. Maybe he didn't know a lot about six-year-old girls. And he was pretty sure he wasn't biased in believing that Kat was smarter than the average kid. But he was certain it took more exposure and practice than that to pick up that much detail.

"Miss Jess let us all barrel race at Miss Hailey's around rocks at her house while they watched," Lizzy said.

What?

"Is that true?" he asked Kat.

The little girl nodded. Poor thing looked terrified, which wasn't his goal.

"Did you have fun?" he asked, to let her know he wasn't upset. Not at her.

She lit up a bit and nodded harder.

He pulled out his phone and dialed Hailey, but she didn't answer. Then again, he hadn't talked to her about not encouraging Kat. This one was on Jess. She'd said she wanted to stop by tonight. Had a surprise for all of them.

Hopefully, she'd also have an explanation. Trying to make a relationship like theirs add up, even in the best-case scenario, might not be easy. He would have been willing to try. But if honesty and transparency weren't there…

Maybe he wasn't good at math, as Lizzy and Kat always

joked about. But he could add a cloverleaf drawing and bracelet and competition shirt together just fine.

And it equaled a breach of trust.

CUPCAKES AND SUGAR PIES Didn't get much sweeter than that.

Jess balanced the grocery sacks, filled with all the necessary ingredients for the girls' favorite desserts, on her hip and knocked on the front door of Nash's house.

She wasn't sure how a relationship between them was going to work, but she wanted to try. What he'd said on the trail ride, about the potential gain outweighing the possible pain, convinced her that he felt the same way.

That wasn't all. She had Becca's permission to fix pancakes with fresh strawberries and blueberries and raspberries and chocolate-maple syrup and whipped cream for Taylor tomorrow morning in the B and B kitchen. Just the two of them.

It was a small thing that she should have done for her daughter a long time ago, and more often.

At first, she'd felt guilty about not bringing her daughter, but Jess wanted tonight to be one-on-two time with the twins, making cupcakes and sugar pies in the kitchen. The main course being some one-on-one discussion with Nash in the den while the girls decorated the treats. Becca had stepped in to help by inviting Taylor to "movie night," with her own little family.

The sun had already begun to set, and smoke was rising from the chimney. It was the only movement against a backdrop that otherwise looked like an Albert Bierstadt painting, except for a few cattle stirring in the distance.

When Nash opened the door, she felt a certain chill, even though she could see and hear the fireplace crackling from where she stood.

"C'mon in," he said, barely looking at her before walking away and leaving the door open behind him.

Someone's a little grumpy. Looked like she'd arrived in the nick of time with sustenance.

Jess took a deep breath, crossed the threshold and struggled to push the door closed with her knee.

"Miss Jess!" The girls ran over to greet her, along with an unfamiliar face: an Australian shepherd.

"And who's this?" Jess asked as she struggled not to topple over.

"Gus, and he's our new dog! But he really belongs to Miss Hailey and Mr. Parker," Lizzy said.

Jess looked to Nash for clarification while still struggling with the groceries. He had to realize her immediate predicament.

"Sorry. Let me take those off your hands," he said, rushing over to relieve her of the two paper bags but without making any further eye contact.

"Thanks." *I think.*

"Gus is the ranch's newest employee. Cattle herder. I offered to keep him tonight for Parker and Hailey. He doesn't get along with the cat." He paused to look at the girls. "But he's not technically ours. Okay?"

Lizzy's chin dropped, but she quickly recovered once the pup went over and snuggled with her. Animals were so perceptive that way. People, not so much. Jess could use a snuggle from Nash right now. Didn't have to be a full-on hug or kiss.

"Those go in the kitchen," she said. "I come bearing food."

"Actually, we just ate," he said. Nothing else. No curiosity. No *thanks anyway.*

She clearly wasn't welcome here. And she didn't have a clue as to why. She halfway expected him to hand the sacks back to her.

Instead, he carried them to the kitchen. Jess stayed behind and tried to make some sense of his cold reaction. If they hadn't already eaten, she would have assumed he was wearing his grumpy pants. Except they didn't look the least bit cute on him tonight. Instead, he was decked out from head to toe in attitude.

She got the same knot in her stomach as she did less than two weeks ago, when she knocked on his door after so many years. When she'd hugged him and he barely hugged her back.

Not that she had blamed him. The difference now was that he knew she was stopping by tonight. They shared more than a history of training sessions and bad jokes and Juicy Lucys.

They shared hugs, secrets, a pinkie promise. Kisses. And, most important, hope for a future together.

Jess summoned her courage and joined them in the kitchen.

"I bet Gus could use a walk. Take him around the house a couple of times. No farther," Nash said to the girls.

Lizzy collected the leash, and together the twins managed to attach it to his collar. Nash checked to make sure it was secure, then opened the door and watched them exit, leaving it cracked open for their return.

"I wanted a chance to talk with you, alone," he said.

What could have been that moment of privacy she'd hoped for tonight was something she now dreaded. The person looking back at her wasn't Nash. It wasn't even Mr. Grumpy Pants. She didn't know who it was.

"I guess my coming over to bake cupcakes and sugar pies with the girls wasn't the best idea," she said, even though the thought of that being the reason for his sour mood was ridiculous.

Nash exhaled and looked down at his feet. "This doesn't have anything to do with desserts. It was nice of you to think of the girls."

"Then what does it have to do with?"

"Lazy daisies and a cloverleaf," he said.

"I'm confused."

"You don't remember?"

"Of course. The lazy daisy was our version of the six-barrel drill," she said. The cloverleaf was self-explanatory.

"Did you show Kat either one of those?"

Jess's mind was a blur. No one knew about their lazy daisy drill except her and Nash. And Taylor. But there was one possible explanation.

"A lazy daisy is also an embroidery technique. Hence the name. I showed Lizzy how to draw one."

"On their board?"

No. Taylor and Kat were drawing on that.

"On a piece of pattern paper," she said. Her stomach tightened.

Nash nodded and didn't blink.

"I'll come right out and say it. She's been coached by someone, Jess. It's unmistakable. Was it you? All I'm asking is for you to be honest with me."

She knew exactly what he was asking now, and nothing about that question was simple. Jess replayed the past week in her mind. How Nash had helped Taylor in the arena. How the two had formed a bond. How her little girl was happy again.

The simple answer to Nash's question would be *yes*. The honest answer would be that Taylor had been instructing Kat beyond what she'd witnessed at Hailey's, as Jess suspected. Yet she hadn't done enough to prevent it. And maybe part of her—that little girl she used to be who fell in love with barrel racing and was encouraged to pursue it—didn't want to.

She wanted to ask him if he'd cared that it had made *his* little girl happy. But that issue wasn't simple, either.

"Sounds to me like you have the only answer you need." That was as much of a confession as she would offer. At least, until he made one of his own. "Now I need an honest answer from you."

Nash blinked. She took a deep breath and asked a form of the question she should have asked ten years ago when she should have confronted a fear but ran away from it. "Are you still in love with Roxanne?"

"What? Of course not! How could you even think that, after what I told you?"

"Because I don't think this is about whether Kat was coached by me or anyone else. I know you'd let her pursue this in a heartbeat. You'd find a way around the time and money constraints. Because, guess what, I did. Except Roxanne is still in your life. And she's calling the shots."

Nash shook his head in denial. "You're wrong. I've gone to great lengths to make sure she isn't. And doesn't."

"I know you have. You've created a safe home for the girls. You protect them from the big bad world, like any good father would and should do. Your daughter wants to try barrel racing, but she's afraid to talk to you about it. Just like Taylor seems to be afraid to tell me what you two discussed."

Nash nodded in concession. "You deserve to know. She wanted to be the one to tell you, but maybe she's not quite ready. I'd tell you now, but she trusted me with her secret. I hope you can understand."

"I sure do," she said. *And I trusted you with my heart. Difference is, you're breaking it.*

She understood other things in that moment. She still wanted to explore the world, and the rodeo was a big part of that. He still wanted to hide from it. She believed in doing whatever a parent had to do to help make their child's dreams come true, even if it meant facing demons. He did not.

That was what she'd tried to do by coming here in the first place and by asking for his help. And that's what she ended up getting.

In a way, he'd been right on that trail ride, because all the pain she was feeling right now was ultimately worth the gains she'd made for Taylor. But there was one thing she did want to take responsibility for.

"I take the blame for letting this get personal between us," she said. After all, she was the one who had admitted to having a crush in the first place. If she could take all of it back, she would.

Nash unfolded his arms and straightened. "I share the blame for that."

A softer look crossed his eyes. For a moment, she thought he was going to take it back. Say he didn't regret it for a minute and then embrace her so hard she couldn't run away. Tell her that they would find a way through this. Instead, he stuffed his hands in his pockets and looked away.

Just as well. There was nothing remotely appealing about hugging a wall.

"All that said, I want to make sure Taylor is good for Montana. If you're still okay with one more session, first thing in the morning tomorrow," he said.

There they were. Back to being friends. Not even that, really. A former teacher and his student. That was what it should have been all along.

"I'll pay you for your time."

"That's not—"

The girls busted through the door, all smiles. Jess willed herself not to cry.

"Gus is fun, Daddy! Can we adopt him?" Lizzy asked.

Nash's entire demeanor transformed. The wall came crashing down for his girls. That smile of his busted through it.

"I have an idea. Since Gus is older, let's see if he will adopt both of you. He can take y'all on walks instead. Who wants to try on the leash first?" he asked.

When Nash reached for them, they let go of Gus and tried to run. But they didn't get far. He scooped them up, one in each arm. Gus started barking as if trying to protect the twins, which made them giggle even more.

Jess rubbed her arms. It was too cold in here for those who didn't belong. Too cramped. She stepped out of the kitchen, most likely unnoticed. She pulled a pen and slip of paper from her purse, along with two butterscotch candies, and jotted down a note.

Lizzy and Kat—I had to leave, but I'll take a rain check on baking. In the meantime, here are a couple of sweets for two of the sweetest gals on this earth.

Jess slipped the pen back inside her purse, exited through the front door and locked it behind her.

Sure, they didn't have the skills yet to read the letter, but Nash did. She hoped he would convey the sentiment.

She needed to focus on her own world now. The one that embraced her. She and Taylor were all each other had when they came to Destiny Springs. And all they'd have when they left, even though it hadn't felt that way for a while. Nash broke his promise not to put up a wall, but in a way she was grateful.

She was about to break one, too.

CHAPTER EIGHTEEN

NASH NEARLY CHOKED on a sip of coffee as he looked out the back window. A woman was sitting on the fence, facing the arena.

Jess?

She'd slipped out last night while he was playing with the girls and Gus, which was a bit unsettling. Sure, they'd had a confrontation, but nothing was resolved to his satisfaction. They had nearly a week to see if it could be.

At least Jess had left a note and candy for the girls, saying she had to leave. But he figured she'd be back this morning with Taylor since she hadn't proposed a later day. He simply hadn't expected them so early.

He set down the cup and called out to Parker. He'd only caught glimpses of his ranch hand this morning. "Watch the girls for a few, please?"

"Yes, sir," Parker called back.

The formality was annoying. Nash shouldn't have acted so ungrateful about the proposal, but his ranch hand had driven him to it. They'd have to hash it out and talk about their *feelings* another time, however.

Nash put on his Stetson and headed outside. As he approached, he realized it wasn't Jess after all.

Relief swept over him, because he wasn't sure what he would

have said to her. She'd broken his trust. Yet, his own daughter had been secretive, too. After a couple of talks, he'd thought—hoped—Kat understood his situation, even though a child that age shouldn't have to.

Turned out, he was the one who hadn't understood how important this was to her, and his role in denying her. In a twisted-logic way, Jess was right about Roxanne calling the shots. And Kat was paying the price.

Then again, so was he. He'd given up something he loved. Make that two things: teaching and Jess.

"What are you doing here?" he asked.

Hailey half smiled. "I thought you could use a friend this morning, since you're running all the others off."

Nash didn't have to ask. No doubt his ranch hand had told his wife what had happened.

"Parker's a professional. He'll get over it. He's inside playing with Gus, in case you didn't know," Nash said.

"I know. I don't have the heart to watch, so I thought I'd come check on you."

"Why is it hard to watch Gus?" Nash asked.

"Because Parker is convinced that he isn't cut out to be a daddy. Can't get Gus and Sergeant to coexist peacefully. I told him to give it some time. We'll figure out something, together. At least, that's the way it *should* work."

Nash needed to figure out something, as well. How to run off the person who might be the only friend he had left. Not permanently, however. He simply didn't want Hailey to be there when Jess and Taylor arrived.

He turned on his heels and headed to the stalls to check on the horses, except something was different. Mischief's stall was empty.

The air escaped his lungs. He ran over to make sure he wasn't imagining it. The gate wasn't opened. The horse couldn't have gotten out.

Hailey came up behind him. "Becca called me this morning. Said Jess and Taylor checked out before dawn."

The blade of abandonment was swift. Nash froze. Everything

around him seemed to do the same. He felt beyond sick. Pressing his hand into his stomach didn't begin to tame it.

In Jess's note to the girls, she'd mentioned she had to leave. But it didn't sound like goodbye. She'd even mentioned a rain check for baking, albeit without a proposed time or day.

"I'm sorry," Hailey said.

Nash straightened his back but couldn't look at her. He proceeded to feed the other horses through the pain while Hailey maintained a respectful distance.

"Sorry for what? Jess got what she came here for," he said when it was clear that Hailey wasn't taking a hint and leaving.

"And what was that?" Hailey asked.

"To get my help with Taylor. I thought we had one last session. I must have misunderstood. No big deal."

"I really thought you two had something good going on," Hailey said.

"So did I." He didn't mean to say it out loud, but he was hurting too much to hold it in.

"Let's go sit on the fence. Watch the sunrise." She took his hand and led him to his old teaching spot.

As they sat there in silence, Nash stared at the way the sun started glinting off the barrels, and thought about how he should have said no to Jess in the first place and avoided reopening that hole in his heart. He could feel it now, as sure as he felt the wooden railing beneath his seat and the frigid air in his lungs. No doctor or fancy tests would ever be able to convince him otherwise.

"You were saying," Hailey said.

Nash breathed in and exhaled slowly. "Jess was training Kat to barrel race against my explicit directions. I confronted her about it. I know you saw it happening, so don't deny it."

"I saw Kat rounding the boulders like she would the barrels. Taylor was doing it, too. Jess put a stop to it."

"She admitted she'd trained her, Hailey."

"Jess said that?"

Not in so many words, and he'd memorized all of them from last night.

"She didn't deny it," he said.

For once, Hailey didn't have a response, which always struck fear in him. That meant her brain had shifted into overdrive. This time was no exception. Except, there wasn't much she could say. Not if she wanted to remain his friend, of which the numbers had dwindled. If she was a good one, she wouldn't take Jess's side in this.

"I..." She took a deep breath and started to say something, then paused.

He gripped the railing beneath him.

"I admitted to Parker the other day that I knocked his favorite coffee mug off the kitchen counter and broke it. But it was Sergeant."

Nash looked at her sideways. "Okay. I won't tell your hubby. He isn't speaking to me anyway. Cats tend to do that sort of thing. He'll get used to it."

"That's true. But I didn't want Parker to be mad at Sergeant. I'd rather he be mad at me."

"You're strange."

"Says the man who ran off the love of his life. Have you talked to Kat about what happened?"

"I'm gonna get whiplash if you keep changing the subject," he said.

"I'm staying on point. You'll see if you answer the question."

"No. I haven't spoken with her."

"I'll tell you what I bet happened. Taylor has been the one teaching Kat."

The thought had briefly crossed his mind, but then Jess took the blame. Kind of.

"If you're right, and I'm not saying you are, why wouldn't Jess say so?" Nash asked.

"Gosh, I don't know. Maybe because she didn't want you to be mad at Kat. Or Taylor. Like I didn't want Parker to be mad at Sergeant, so I took the fall for the kitty. And I'd do it a million times over 'cause he's my baby."

If Hailey was right, and she usually was, that would mean that he and Jess were both protecting Taylor. Furthermore, they both wanted what they thought was best for Kat. Except he was the only one who *wasn't* trying to make that happen.

Nash blew out a long breath. "You really believe that's what happened?"

"Like you said yourself, I was there. I saw what Jess saw. Talent and drive. The pure excitement on Kat's face as she raced around the boulders. I never realized she even had dimples when she smiles that big."

Kat has dimples?

"I put up walls," he confessed. "Is that something you can see, too?"

"Are you kidding? You could quit your day job and start a construction company. You'd make a fortune. Should I ask my hubby to put together some numbers for that?"

"Absolutely. Anything to get Kat involved in barrel racing. Or whatever sport she wants."

Hailey simply stared.

"What?" he asked.

"Oh, just wondering why you didn't think about that sooner."

Nash blew out a long breath. "I haven't stopped thinking about it lately. I wanted to avoid crossing paths with Roxanne, at all costs. Turned out, that decision has cost a lot more than I bargained for. Jess thinks that's why I'm against Kat getting involved in the rodeo. She even asked me if I was still in love with Roxanne."

"You're not in love with that woman. Jess is smart enough to know that."

"I know. I'm not in love with Roxanne. I'm in love with Jess. Is she smart enough to know that, as well?"

Instead of waiting for an answer, Nash jumped from the fence and hightailed it to the house. He turned around long enough to shout, "Tack up Sugar Pie, if you don't mind."

"Yes, your highness."

Nash shook his head, grateful he hadn't run her off. Then again, that woman would never let something like a wall get in her way.

Once inside the house, he followed Lizzy's and Kat's shrieks and Gus's bark and Parker's laughter to the den.

Nash gave Lizzy a wink but didn't make eye contact with

his ranch hand quite yet. First, he had a very important bridge to build.

He knelt to Kat's level and searched for those dimples she supposedly had. Not even a trace. One thing was for sure: he wasn't letting this little girl out of his sight until she revealed them to him.

"I want to watch you and Sugar Pie run around the barrels," he said.

"Really?" she asked.

"Only if you want to."

Kat nodded so hard, he was afraid her pretty little head would come right off.

He looked to Parker. "You and Lizzy stay here and play with Gus. It's important that the pup get used to hanging around here more often."

Thankfully, the comment went right over Lizzy's head, because he didn't want to get her too excited until he had a chance to talk to Parker and Hailey about a possible solution to all their problems. Perhaps they could share custody if the dog and cat couldn't stop fighting. Or Nash could adopt him outright, and the Donnellys could have unlimited visitation.

"What did Hailey tell you?" Parker called out.

Nash paused in his steps without turning around. "Everything I needed to hear."

By the time he and Kat reached the arena, Hailey had tacked up Sugar Pie. She handed Kat a pink riding helmet, and together, she and Nash gave the little girl a leg up. Nash led her to the starting point.

"I want you to trot through this first. Start with whichever barrel you want. I'll call out instructions if you get turned around."

He and Hailey took their respective places, once again, on the fence. He intentionally didn't call out for her first round. Wanted to see how much she'd learned. Turned out, she didn't need any direction to get through the basic pattern.

"Are you seeing what I'm seeing?" Hailey asked.

"Everything except those dimples of hers that you'd mentioned."

Hailey smiled. "I have a feeling you'll be seeing a lot of those from now on."

Now, *that* made him smile. So did the idea of teaching again, now that he'd stopped resisting the urge to scratch that itch. He also realized what a friend he had in Parker, even though the guy didn't listen. Then again, Nash wasn't finished talking.

There was another itch begging to be scratched. To have a life with Jess. She was…*everything*. Friend, joke swapper, Juicy Lucy buddy. In other words, the perfect woman for him. Always had been. The icing on the cupcake and the sugar on the sugar pie was that Jess was exactly the kind of mom the girls needed. Yes, she'd broken their promise not to leave without saying goodbye. But he'd broken his first by putting up a wall.

There was only one way to possibly fix everything: a road trip. Him, the girls and a horse named Sugar Pie.

AVOIDING CONFRONTATION MAY have worked for Jess in the past, but it was backfiring royally now.

Taylor was sad again, and any chance Jess might have had with Nash was in the rearview mirror. Another horrible consequence: she'd abandoned the twins.

Just like their mom had done.

Hopefully, Nash would read them the note and they'd know that she cared, as small of a gesture as it had been.

Jess had also abandoned her responsibilities when it came to her sewing. Dorothy had handed over what she said was the completed Dudley project, which would have been next to impossible to execute in such a short amount of time. Jess hadn't summoned the courage to open the box that her sewing soulmate had placed it in. Might as well have been a casket for Jess's career. But by getting to Montana earlier than planned, she would have time to fix any problems once they got settled into their hotel.

A diner's lights were on, up ahead. Might be a good time and place to stop and get something to eat, since Taylor was wide awake.

They were still a couple hundred miles from Billings, having stopped halfway at a friend's dude ranch outside of Wyoming to exercise Mischief. The family was even kind enough to put out barrels and let Taylor practice, which only underscored how horribly Jess had messed up by leaving. Her daughter seemed to have slipped back into slow beginnings and slower finishes.

Jess wouldn't have stopped at all, but their room in Billings wasn't going to be ready until later anyway. And the morning had arrived, even though the sun had yet to make its announcement.

They had their choice of booths. Taylor led them to the one with the best view of their trailer through the glass. Her little eyes didn't veer from it.

The waitress was promptly at their side.

"What can I get for you ladies?"

"Coffee for me, please. What would you like, Taylor?"

"I'm not hungry."

"I'm starved." Jess scanned the menu and found what she was looking for. "I'll have pancakes. Tall stack. Do you have strawberries and blueberries and raspberries and chocolate-maple syrup and whipped cream?"

That got Taylor's attention. She cast a hopeful look to the waitress, who was mouthing the list to herself and processing it.

"Ohh-kay. I can do strawberries, blackberries, blueberries, and I can bring you some chocolate syrup and maple syrup, but you'll have to mix 'em yourself."

"I think we can manage. How about whipped cream? And milk and orange juice for her," Jess said.

It took a minute, but the waitress caught up with jotting the order down on a pad. She promptly returned with the beverages, along with the silverware and an extra plate.

At least Taylor hadn't returned to gazing out the window. She wasn't looking at her mom, either. The diner was quiet, their food was being prepared and Jess had a captive audience. It was now or never. She took a deep breath.

"I messed up, Taylor. I owe you a huge apology."

That earned some eye contact.

"We shouldn't have left without telling Lizzy and Kat and Nash goodbye," Jess continued.

Taylor looked down again, this time at her friendship bracelets. It tore at Jess's heart that, once again, she'd so brutally yanked her away from her newest friends, as swiftly and impulsively as one of those threads. Although this time felt like the cruelest of all.

It also gave Jess a brilliant idea.

They sat in silence until the waitress brought the pancakes, with the fixings on the side. "Let me know if you need anything else. I'll swing back around in a little while and check on you."

"Wait! Do you mind keeping an eye on our food for a few minutes? We need to run out to the trailer."

"Happy to," the woman said.

"C'mon," Jess said as Taylor reluctantly eased out of the booth. She took her daughter's hand and led the way to the trailer.

Jess opened the truck cab and retrieved her notions box. She pulled out her scissors, a square of suede she'd been hauling around for a while and a needle and thread. With those in hand, she walked around to the side of the trailer and consulted Mischief.

"Forgive me for what I'm about to do, but I need your help," Jess whispered to Mischief. She walked farther down, reached through a slat, and snipped some of the hair from his tail. Once she felt she had enough, they went back inside.

Jess served up the biggest smile as they both eased back into the booth.

"Can you help me assemble these pancakes? You always do such a good job," Jess said, tucking the notions and horse hair away for now.

Taylor took the lead, and Jess followed. Together, they put quite a dent in the feast, which gave Jess time to summon her thoughts, and courage.

"I want to tell you something, but I need for it to be just between us. For now, at least. Can we pinkie promise on it?" Jess asked.

Taylor took a good long time contemplating it, but finally nodded.

"I miss Nash. A lot. In fact, I love him. I'd like to drive back to Destiny Springs after the rodeo. But that would mean missing the one in Nevada. I'll make it up to you," Jess said.

Taylor sat up straighter. "Can I see Lizzy and Kat again?"

"Absolutely! Y'all became good friends?"

Taylor deflated a little. "The best. But..."

"You can tell me anything, sweetie."

"Kat was asking a million questions about barrel racing, and you said I wasn't supposed to talk about it, but she said her daddy wouldn't talk to her about it, so..."

You coached her.

"You wanted to be a good friend, which you were. You still are. Since y'all are such good friends, we can't go back to Destiny Springs empty-handed. But I'll need your help, because you're a lot better at this than I am."

Jess pushed their plates to the side and cleared a spot on the table. She wasn't sure how the management would feel about her placing unwashed horse tail hair on the dining table, but she'd offer to clean it up. And leave the waitress a very good tip.

She spread out several napkins and placed the notions between them, along with Sylvie's written instructions. Together, they started making friendship bracelets while taking periodic breaks to check on Mischief.

The first couple Jess made were a mess. Taylor's were much prettier. They could always make more in Montana. What they were accomplishing now was perfect.

Once they'd finished five, Taylor spread them out on the table. The early sunrise coming through the window illuminated the beauty of what they'd created together.

"Which one do you like best?" Taylor asked.

Jess had a favorite, all right. She pointed to the last one Taylor had made. It was going to look perfect next to those friendship bracelets that her daughter loved so much.

Taylor picked it up and double-checked the ties to make sure they were stitched on tight, then reached over and draped it across her mom's wrist.

Jess's breath hitched. This couldn't be happening.

"A friendship bracelet? For me?" she asked.

Taylor secured the tie. "Of course. You're my friend."

It was all Jess could do to hold back her tears. Meanwhile, Taylor inspected the others they'd created together.

"Which one do you think your daddy would have liked?" Jess dared to ask. "We'll take it when we visit him at the cemetery."

Whether it was the right thing to say in the moment, or completely wrong, Jess knew that Lance had been Taylor's friend, too. Maybe even her best friend.

Taylor sat up straighter and selected the bracelet with the thickest weave, then picked it up.

"This one," she said.

Jess nodded. "I agree. I think we've earned a hot chocolate for the road. What do you think?" Not that either of them needed more sugar, but the diner was beginning to fill up and they'd best head out anyway.

Taylor nodded, looked directly at her and smiled.

Jess waved at the waitress.

"More pancakes?" the woman asked.

It was a reasonable question. Between the two of them, they'd cleaned the plate.

"Can we get two hot chocolates to go? And the check, whenever you're ready."

"Extra marshmallows please," Taylor added.

"That's the only way to drink it." The waitress finished tallying the damage, tore it from the pad, and placed it on the table.

Jess took possession of the scissors while her daughter collected the thread and remaining strands of horsehair. Taylor picked out one of the bracelets that Jess had made and wrapped it around her own wrist while struggling with the tie.

Jess reached over to help.

"Thanks, Mommy. I really like this one."

The waitress returned with their hot chocolate in the biggest insulated to-go cups Jess had ever seen.

"Hope these fit in your drink holder. Needed plenty of room for those marshmallows."

Taylor pulled the top off hers, peered inside and took a long sip. When she came up for air, she had the biggest grin. Along with a white marshmallow mustache.

"Hmm, looks like my friend is being silly," Jess said.

"Nash taught me this after he showed me how to pinkie shake," Taylor said.

That. She'd all but forgotten.

"Do you think Daddy would be proud of me?" Taylor asked.

The question took Jess aback.

"Of course. He was your biggest fan." She wanted to add *next to me*, but this wasn't about her. Maybe it never had been.

"Mr. Nash told me that Daddy would want me to have fun, even though he isn't here to have fun with me."

Jess took several moments to process the fact that this was what Taylor had revealed to Nash. The thing that he'd left her daughter to reveal. Furthermore, he was right to do so. This moment was so special. Furthermore, she and Taylor didn't even need a pinkie promise for it to be revealed. They had something even stronger: a mother-daughter friendship.

"Mr. Nash was exactly right. So let's go have lots of fun in Billings. Then we'll go back through Destiny Springs so you can see your friends and have even more."

With that, all of Jess's grand plans unraveled, along with her confidence. What if the fact that they'd both broken their promises to each other didn't level the playing field, much less raze that wall of his?

All she knew was that she had to try. If nothing else, she wanted to repair any damage she'd done to the twins, even if it required a full-on confrontation with their daddy.

She realized that sometimes the most logical plans and patterns benefitted from alterations and could even end up with a more perfect fit. With any luck, he would realize that, too. She'd found her perfect fit in Destiny Springs. With Nash.

If it wasn't too late.

CHAPTER NINETEEN

"THERE YOU ARE, Parker. We need to talk," Nash said.

Parker had hightailed it out of the house and to the calving barn the moment Nash walked back into the house with Kat. Even Gus had trouble keep up with the guy.

His ranch hand stopped petting the calf, rose from his squatting position and brushed off his hands. "I'm all ears."

"First, I owe you an apology," Nash said.

"For what?"

"For being so hard on you for not listening. And for putting up a wall. At least, that's what I do, according to Hailey. And Jess. I put one up with you. I know your heart is in the right spot. By contrast, my heart's been all over the place lately."

Parker straightened his cowboy hat, widened his stance and folded his arms.

"That's one lousy apology, Nash. I can't accept it."

Huh? It felt as though he'd spilled his deepest thoughts and feelings and they were both neck-deep in it.

"And why's that?" Nash asked.

"Because I *did* listen to you in putting together the proposal."

"Um. No, you didn't. With all due respect, you're as stubborn as your grandfather."

"That's quite a compliment. Hopefully, I'm as wise. Although Vern is more eloquent."

Why did Nash feel as though he were losing this argument, even though he was the only one making sense?

Parker continued. "I stand by my proposal. I listened, but more to what you *didn't* say. Your lack of enthusiasm for cattle ranching. The smile that you failed miserably to suppress when you talked about coaching Taylor. The footnotes in your ledgers."

"I wrote footnotes?"

"Yeah. Read more like a diary. Most of the comments were about Jess."

Nash closed his eyes. It started coming back to him. He had written notes about the progress of the students. Thankfully, nothing personal. Or had he?

"I even know how you sneak out to the greenhouse," Parker continued. "Which is why I suggested adding some crops. We could start small. Cucumbers, tomatoes, eggplant. Maybe even participate in the farmers market. Expand from there. You have a lot of land that could be put to use if you don't go the full-on cattle ranch route."

"You've been spying on me?" Nash tried to joke.

The fact that Parker had nailed it so precisely based on what Nash *hadn't* said was a little unsettling. Nash had read the proposal, in its entirety, last night when he couldn't sleep. It managed to keep his mind from wondering why Jess had snuck out of the house. And, ultimately, out of his life once again.

Now he knew why. He'd never let her in. Not completely. Only for certain moments, and he shut her out as quickly.

"You're hard to miss, so I suppose I spied on you accidentally. As far as walls go, those don't deter me. I can see right through them. It's my superpower. You just need to have a little trust," Parker said.

Nash shifted his stance. "I disagree with one thing."

"Oh, yeah?"

"You're as eloquent as Vern, if not more so. I'm glad you didn't listen to my words, because I accept your business proposal. Perhaps with a few modifications. And I trust you to look after the ranch while the girls and I go to Montana for a few days. Gus can even sleep at my house. Just move anything he might be tempted to destroy."

Ambitious and impulsive, perhaps. Yet, the other three heifers weren't due for another week or two, and the new momma and baby were doing fine. No storms were on the horizon. Except for one, and that was only if he didn't try to fix this situation with Jess right away.

Parker was all smiles, which was somewhat comforting. Except confidence wouldn't be enough to get him through some of the issues he might encounter.

"Before you get too excited, I want reinforcements in place," Nash said.

"Since I knew you'd eventually come to your senses and go with my proposal, I've already put out some feelers. Grandpa's ranch hand Trent offered to be on call in case I need help, and Cody made a standing offer to pitch in. Then there's Gus. Free labor all around."

"Which brings me around to my proposal. Since Gus and Sergeant seem to have irreconcilable differences, how about he stays here with me and the girls at night, or whenever he needs to? That way, he'll have two families who care for him. Two homes. And you'll get to see him all day because, yes, I want to hire him," Nash said.

Parker dropped his head. Was the guy about to cry?

"You win. Your proposal is better than mine," his ranch hand said.

"I don't know about that. I didn't type it up and put it on fancy paper like you did. But I appreciate the vote of confidence."

Parker extended his hand, but Nash pulled him in for a solid cowboy hug instead.

"I'll let Gus take over from here. I have something to add to the chore board. Do you mind watching the girls outside for about ten minutes, if I send 'em your way?" Nash asked.

"It would be my pleasure."

Once alone in the house, Nash grabbed the marker, jotted a clear directive on the board, then snapped the cap back on and admired his artwork. Only one word.

YES.

Yes to letting Kat learn about barrel racing and seeing where that leads. *Yes* to getting a dog that they could share with the Donnellys. *Yes* to teaching again, although this time he'd focus on the students who were most important…and not get distracted.

Nash hopped online and submitted a late entry for Kat in Billings. If they kicked back for any reason, he still had connections over there. He'd pull some strings. Kat was a rookie, but it was an open rodeo. She wouldn't even advance beyond slack, but that was fine. Kat wasn't ready to compete. Not by a long shot. Neither was Sugar Pie. Although the horse was sound, she needed instruction. Plenty of time to perfect that.

However, time felt as though it was running out when it came to winning Jess back, and that meant convincing her that his wall-constructing days were over. He never wanted to give her any reason to run away, ever again.

He did have one more idea that might help win her over.

The girls busted through the door right at the ten-minute mark. He pulled out all the ingredients that Jess had left behind.

"Ladies, I need your help. We're gonna make cupcakes and sugar pies to take on the road tomorrow. We'll need enough to leave some for Parker, and to share with Jess and Taylor when we get to Montana."

It took the girls a few minutes to realize the magnitude of what he was saying. Lizzy was especially excited.

"We're going to Montana *and* we get to make cupcakes?" Lizzy asked.

"And decorate them with daisies if you want to," he added.

"Yesss!" Lizzy practically jumped out of her skin.

"We get to watch Taylor in the rodeo?" Kat asked.

It wasn't lost on him that she didn't care anything about the desserts in this moment.

"We sure do. We'll also get to watch you, if you want to go around the barrels. Nothing faster than a trot. That's my only rule."

Kat looked at him in disbelief. Then her smile grew so big that he caught a glimpse of those dimples before she wrapped her arms around his neck.

"I guess that's a yes," he managed to say. That made two *yeses* he'd collected so far.

He had one more very important, life-changing one to go.

JESS ALWAYS LOVED the morning slack times. So much fun to watch the talent within the overflow of contestants, but without the noisy crowds that the performances drew.

Today, however, she had a different reason for being there.

The bleachers were quite stark, so she had her pick of the seats. She went to the top for the best view. Taylor was in the warm-up pen, as were the other contestants, so Jess was on her own.

All of her rodeo mom projects had been completed and delivered to their respective hotel rooms except for the one she was holding. The box containing the Dudley project.

She'd finally mustered the courage to peek inside in case she needed to make any last-minute modifications. What she found was a beautifully executed two-piece yellow-and-black tweed suit, with pale yellow satin lining, black chiffon cuffs and black velvet trim. No wonky stitching. No uneven hems. No loose threads. Dorothy had exceeded Jess's expectations. Hopefully, she'd exceed Mrs. Dudley's, as well.

The wait, it seemed, was over. Although they'd never met in person, Jess recognized the woman from her blog. Jess set the box down, then stood and waved.

The woman waved back and navigated the myriad steps to join her.

After they introduced themselves and were situated, Jess got down to business and handed her the box.

"Feels like Christmas," Mrs. Dudley said with a huge smile as she ran her palms over the lid.

Jess bit her lip, grateful that there wasn't a lump of coal inside the box. If the garment hadn't been up to par, Jess would have taken full ownership of it anyway. She also proudly refused to learn her lesson about not being honest about everything. Her unwillingness to throw Taylor under the bus had backfired, but she'd do it all over again to protect her daughter from any blame Jess should ultimately shoulder. Same applied to her sewing soulmate.

The competition started in the arena, and they both watched the first barrel racer. Wasn't either of their girls.

"The time of 24.184 seconds going to Angie Cartwright, Dallas, Texas," the announcer said over the loudspeaker.

Second competitor, same story. It was neither of their girls.

Being seasoned at this, they both knew they had about thirty seconds to chat before the next one's turn.

Mrs. Dudley opened the box. When she pulled out the jacket, she audibly gasped. Same with the skirt.

She pulled out a folded piece of paper and flipped it over, where someone had written Jess's name on the front. Jess hadn't even noticed it inside the box. Must have been buried at the bottom.

"Looks like this is for you, dear," Mrs. Dudley said.

Jess opened the note.

Thanks for letting me help. I hope I did your heart justice. Thankfully, I was able to rob some black velvet from my room-themed gift bathrobe to add the accents you wanted. Hope that's okay!

It was way more than okay. If Dorothy were there, Jess would assure her that she'd gone above and beyond what was expected. As soon as she and Taylor got back to Destiny Springs, Jess would request the Velvet Room, if available, and she'd send that complimentary robe to Dorothy.

"That will be a time of 20.132 seconds for Sophie Pendleton, Flagstaff, Arizona," the speaker announced.

The next rider took her position at the gate.

"Oh! That's Meghan!" Mrs. Dudley said. Jess squeezed her arm, hoping for the best while secretly rooting for her own daughter.

"Time of 19.520 seconds to Meghan Dudley, Albuquerque, New Mexico," the announcer said.

The best time so far. This was the first run, though. Still a chance for Taylor to beat it.

Mrs. Dudley returned her attention to the suit, examining the yellow satin lining. "I love this! Makes it so expensive-looking. And these chiffon cuffs are precious! I'm not a seamstress, but it must have been tricky to get these so perfect."

Jess nodded. *Yes, it must have been.*

They glanced up in time to see the next rider, who looked to be one of the youngest ones, based on her size. She didn't appear completely confident in her seat.

"Isn't that the cutest thing you've ever seen?" Mrs. Dudley asked.

"Adorable." Especially the way the little girl trotted around the barrels instead of running. Upon a closer look, the pink shirt with the black piping looked awfully familiar. As did the horse. And the girl herself.

When Jess finally figured out why, her breath caught in her throat. *It can't be.* The crowd, which had grown in size, went wild as the little cowgirl took it home with a determined trot.

"We have a time of 49.538 seconds going to Katherine Buchanan, Destiny Springs, Wyoming," said the announcer.

That did it. Jess couldn't have stopped the waterworks if she'd wanted. She searched the stands for Nash and Lizzy through the blur of tears but didn't see them. They were probably with Kat behind the scenes, smothering her with hugs and kisses.

"Well, what have we here?" Mrs. Dudley asked as she turned the jacket inside out.

Jess wiped away the moisture from her eyes and cheeks with the back of her hand. She'd all but forgotten the woman was there, looking at the garment that could possibly launch the next phase of Jess's career.

"Looks like a tiny yellow heart," the woman said.

Or a mistake. Jess leaned in closer. Definitely a little heart, embroidered into the inside front panel in dark yellow thread that complimented the lighter yellow lining. A hidden treasure. That wasn't in her design specifications to Dorothy. The woman must have added it as her special touch.

Yet, didn't Dorothy write that she hoped she'd done Jess's heart justice?

Jess remembered clearly now. She'd fallen asleep on the pattern paper, and her mascara had left a mark in the shape of a heart. Dorothy must have thought it was intentional and added her interpretation of what the mark meant.

"That's exactly what it is," Jess said. "Western wear with heart."

Mrs. Dudley looked at her square in the eye. "That would make a wonderful company name. Not that your name alone isn't lovely, but a proper one would look good on a garment label, too. Just thinking out loud."

"Mrs. Dudley—"

"Please, call me Carol Anne."

Jess smiled. "That is a brilliant suggestion, Carol Anne. I'll have to clear it with my associate, Dorothy Lawrence, but I'd love to use it. For now, for this project, I want Dorothy to get full credit for executing this garment so beautifully. I'll give her your contact information for the blog, if that's okay."

"Are you sure, dear? Isn't it your design?"

"Very sure. My design was nothing more than a vision in my head, and lines and curves and notches on pieces of dot paper. Dorothy breathed life into it."

"Well, either way I'm thrilled. I can't wait for Meghan to try this on. Better go check on her now, if you'll excuse me."

"Of course!" Jess had some checking on to do herself. She'd yet to see Nash or Lizzy, but her peripheral vision had been working overtime.

Taylor hadn't had her turn yet, either, and Jess wasn't about to miss it.

She stood and did a visual sweep of the bleachers as another racer took her turn. That's when she noticed three familiar people standing at the bottom. One big one. Two little ones. Looking up.

At me.

Her heart was beating out of her chest, but it was tamed by Nash's smile. One odd thing, however. His arms were crossed. The twins, by contrast, were wiggling and giggling and waving. She headed down the steps as fast as her feet would take her.

They had the same idea and headed up the stairs. At the

halfway point, she found herself eye level with the crush of her dreams.

"I'm not going to let you run away again, Ms. McCoy. Not until you know how sorry I am for shutting you out. And not until you mend this. You're the only one who can." Nash placed his hand over his heart. Over that tiny hole in his threadbare flannel shirt.

"You said it wasn't necessary."

"I was wrong."

The breeze blew his hair ever so slightly over his eyes, but he didn't blink. Neither could she.

"Daddy! It's Taylor!" Lizzy screamed, breaking the trance.

Jess peeked around Nash in time to see Taylor glance up at the stands and wave.

"Everyone sit," Nash demanded.

They all clamored for the closest seats, and just in time. They seemed to hold a collective breath as Taylor made a strong start, then circled the barrels and took it home in record time.

"That was 17.316 seconds! Let's hear it for Taylor Simms, Rock Springs, Wyoming," the announcer said.

Jess jumped up from her seat. They all did. It was Taylor's personal best, and she was in the lead so far. Barring any mistakes on the second run, the little girl could win the top prize tonight.

And barring any mistakes on her own part, Jess could, too.

CHAPTER TWENTY

WHAT ARE YOU thinking about out there, Taylor? Jess was dying to know.

Whatever it was had put a fire beneath the little girl as she rounded the first barrel, then the second, then…

Jess held her breath and didn't dare blink. She did take a quick glance at the man sitting beside her, along with his two adorable daughters, if only to assure herself that this wasn't a dream.

Jess's guy. That would be a good nickname for Nash, because she was going to insist that he retire his grumpy pants. The new nickname would complement the long list of keepers: friend, teacher, Juicy Lucy maker, joke swapper…

Back in the day when he was all of those, Nash had asked her what thoughts went through her head during a competition. She remembered that answer so clearly, because it always resulted in a win.

I imagine the thing I want most is waiting at the finish line. The faster I get there, the sooner it's mine.

She didn't even have to hear the time to know that Taylor had won. Didn't need to hear the roar of the crowd, or the loud-and-proud "Bravo!" from *her guy.* Jess knew.

The whole crowd knew.

"C'mon, ladies. Let's go back there to see her," Nash said.

They shimmied past a family and rushed down the steps. Lizzy and Kat launched into a run.

"Slow down, girls! Stay where we can see you," Nash called out, but they kept going.

He turned to Jess. "Nobody listens to me."

"Did you say something?"

Nash pulled her in and gave her a huge lip smack on the side of her head.

The twins turned around, ran back and circled around her and Nash.

"Looks like you spoke too soon," Jess said.

Lizzy took the lead. "I should be a barrel racer, too."

Nash dropped his chin in a gesture that looked like defeat.

Jess put her arm around his waist and rested her head on his shoulder. "You've got this."

The girls spotted Taylor, who was having her and Mischief's picture taken by people on their cell phones. Lizzy unapologetically photobombed the whole thing, while Kat had the discipline to stay out of the frame.

Nash and Jess stopped even farther away, but close enough to breathe it all in.

But there was something that needed to be said, in the spirit of total transparency.

"You probably already know. But in case you don't, Roxanne is here tonight. Somewhere."

Nash didn't even miss a beat when he looked at Jess and said, "Roxanne who?"

"It's okay. She's part of your past."

Nash kissed the tip of her nose, then moved down to claim a quick kiss on the lips.

"You're right. My past. *Not* my future. Or even my present. I didn't even think to consider whether she'd be here tonight."

Jess knew he was telling the truth. He hadn't looked around even once.

Nash continued. "I can't protect the girls from everything for the rest of their lives. We'll face other obstacles. Plenty of 'em."

"But we can face them together," she added. *And never run away.*

"Don't tell Taylor this, but she wasn't the main reason we came all the way to Billings," Nash said.

"Oh, I know. You realized that barrel racing is what Kat is destined to do and what will make her happy. You get bonus points for making it happen," Jess said.

"There's that, too. But my trip here is more about what you and I are destined to do."

A thrill raced up Jess's spine. "And what's that?"

Nash looked at her with those soft brown eyes. "Make cupcakes and sugar pies. What else? You told the girls you'd take a rain check. I'm holding you to it."

"I know. I also left without saying goodbye." Jess knew she was stating the obvious, but if they were destined to move forward, they needed to put everything out in the open.

Nash took a deep breath and blew it out. "I don't blame you, Jess."

He looked at her now, the softness of his eyes warming her back up.

"I have trouble embracing confrontation, but if you're willing to embrace what I'm about to tell you, that's all that matters." He pulled her in. "I'm going to start teaching again, but I need a partner. In love and in life, and in everything that entails."

Was that a marriage proposal? Kind of sounded like one. It could also be a business proposal. Or maybe both.

"I'll let you know if I think of anyone," she said, adding a smile. Not quite a joke, but she needed to be sure.

"I have someone in mind, but I'm afraid that if I say her name out loud, one of Destiny Springs's most popular rumors will be put to rest. That won't leave folks much to talk about," he said.

"Which rumor? There are so many," she said.

"The one about Roxanne not being the one to break my heart and drive me away from teaching. That there was another woman."

Jess's breath hitched. "I heard that rumor. If you'll tell me her name, I promise to never repeat it."

"I'm pretty sure people will figure it out. For now, let's call her Nash's gal."

He winked.

She melted.

"Be honest. You have more than one gal, don't you?" Jess asked.

As expected, Nash pulled back and pinched his eyebrows together. She nodded toward the twins.

"Ahh, yes. You're right about that. And my little barrel racer might soon become The One to Watch," he said.

Jess's competitive spirit nudged her to respond.

"I'm afraid you may be right. But she'd have Taylor to thank for that." Realizing what she'd just done, Jess clapped her hands over her mouth.

Nash pulled her even closer. "It's okay. I know she coached Kat."

"How did you find out?" Jess asked.

"Hailey sold me on the theory. You just confirmed it."

Jess shook her head. Although Nash and Hailey weren't siblings, they could pass as fraternal twins much of the time.

"I hope you won't be mad at Taylor," she said.

"That isn't possible. As long as she hasn't revealed our secret weapon without clearing it with me first."

"She told me about how you convinced her that her daddy wanted her to have fun."

"There is that."

"You mean there's something else she hasn't told me?"

"Apparently," he said.

Jess squinted. "I do wonder what she was thinking about today, and what she envisioned was waiting at the finish line."

At that, Nash cocked his head. "So she *did* tell you what we discussed."

There it was. Another accusation. Jess matched his gesture for effect. "No. Why would you think that?"

"Because that's what I told her to think about to get her over the hump. To imagine that what she wanted most was waiting for her at the finish line and—"

"The faster she gets there, the sooner it would be hers. You're really gonna take credit for my secret formula?" Jess asked.

Nash pulled away, put his hands on his hips and huffed. She matched his body language. They had a stare-off for a good fifteen seconds, until he caved. He dropped his chin, then covered his face with both hands and shook his head.

"You did tell me that, didn't you?" he said.

"Um, yeah. I'm afraid so," she said.

"I guess that means you ultimately get credit for helping her."

Jess looked to Taylor, who was waving at them. Make that, waving at Nash. Maybe Jess deserved credit in a roundabout way, but she had no intention of taking any of it.

Once the little girl finally looked away, Jess presented her pinkie finger to Nash. "I won't tell her about it if you don't."

Instead of hooking his pinkie onto hers, he straightened out her hands and kissed the top of her ring finger instead.

"I'd rather we make a promise to each other in a more permanent way."

Jess gulped. Was this really about to happen? She didn't get a romantic proposal the first time, from Lance. Nor did they get a proper wedding, complete with bridesmaids and organ music and lots of flowers. Not that she needed any of those things to be happy with someone. But she had given up her career to build a home—one that ended up being built on shifting sand.

This time, it would be on solid ground, and in a town that she'd fallen in love with as deeply as she had with Nash. Now, the thought of having a home was...*freeing.*

But she was getting ahead of herself. They weren't at the finish line quite yet.

"Is there something you want to ask?" She offered up her most dreamy look. Might as well give him an encouraging nudge because the suspense was killing her.

He shifted his stance and looked to the ground. Instead of kneeling, he crossed his arms and said, "As a matter of fact, I do."

"I'm listening," she said.

The poor guy looked terrified.

"What did the cowgirl say to the rancher when he asked her to marry him?"

So much for the romantic proposal, although it was super adorable. As was his nervousness. She knew the answer to this one, but she simply smiled instead. She wasn't going to make it that easy for him, although she was determined to get everything she wanted.

Hopefully, Lizzy would be willing to give the bottom half of her wedding dress pattern back—the piece that the little girl had drawn all over—if only temporarily. Even though Jess hadn't officially accepted, she already had the perfect spot for their nuptials in mind. She also intended to have the original wedding dress of her dreams, because it would fit in beautifully there.

With one very important modification.

OKAY, SO HIS setup for the proposal didn't get the punch line response he'd hoped for. She hadn't said no, either. Nash still had one thing left in his bag of tricks.

"While you're thinking about that, do you mind corralling the girls? Looks like they're wrapping things up in the ring. I need to run to the truck," he said, then sprinted away before she asked any questions.

He reached to the floorboard of the back seat of the cab. Fortunately, neither twin had stomped on the box. Taking it slow and easy, he carried it back to the pen area where he'd left all his gals, dodging enthusiastic little barrel racers and their friends and family along the way.

No doubt Jess would be expecting a much smaller box with something less fragile inside, but that was next on his list. For now, this should be a sweet surprise.

As he approached, he noticed how the girls seemed to be hanging on Jess's every word. He didn't know what they were talking about, but they turned silent as soon as he approached. They also smiled in unison, so whatever it was had to be good.

He pivoted the box so that the flap was facing them, then opened it.

"Our cupcakes and sugar pies!" Lizzy called out.

"Yes. But these are special. I decorated these after you ladies went to bed." Nash reached into the box and retrieved the one he'd decorated with Taylor in mind. It had a lopsided icing barrel drawn on top. For Kat, he'd executed a squiggly number eight. For Lizzy, he retrieved the one with her favorite flower. Or, at least a reasonable facsimile.

"It's a lazy daisy, like you taught me to draw with six petals," Lizzy said to Jess.

"It's also a barrel racing drill," Nash said. "Maybe Taylor and Jess can show Kat how to do it."

The little girls looked at each other, then back at Nash with huge smiles.

"Are we splitting that one?" Jess asked about one that had nothing more than a smear of vanilla icing.

"Nope. That's mine. This one is yours." He pushed aside a piece of tissue paper that had separated one of the cupcakes from the others. He'd piled this one with flowers of all shapes and sizes and colors, taking inspiration from all of Lizzy's drawings. What it lacked in floral beauty, it made up for in height.

Jess lifted it out of the box and cradled it as if it was topped with a cluster of diamonds.

"Hopefully it will taste better than it looks," he said.

She smiled. "What do you mean? It's beautiful! But I'll let you know," she said, taking a huge bite out of the thing. Nash took a bite of his cupcake, as well. And another. Before he was halfway through, the girls had already demolished theirs and had started on the sugar pies.

While the twins were distracted, he turned his full attention to Jess. There was something he needed from her.

"I'm still waiting for an answer," Nash said, launching into the *Jeopardy!* tune. Not that a marriage proposal was a joking matter, but he'd never been so nervous in his life. The longer she took to answer, the worse it got.

Jess finished her last bite of cupcake, wiped her hands on a napkin and motioned for him to follow. They stopped far enough away from the girls that they wouldn't be able to hear. All of a sudden, a sharp pain shot through his heart at the possibility that she intended to let him down easy.

She faced him and took both of his hands in hers. "What was that question again?"

Nash cocked his head. Even though he'd concluded that his original proposal wasn't the least bit romantic, it wasn't forgettable.

Yet, he recognized this as a second chance to get it exactly right. And he was going to take it. After all, he got another chance with their relationship. From now on, he vowed not to make the same mistakes. He'd probably make some new ones, but hopefully she'd be just as forgiving of those.

Nash gave her hands a gentle squeeze and looked into her eyes. *Those eyes.* He took a cue from Parker and listened to what she wasn't saying. Sure enough, he got the answer he wanted. The only thing left to do was take it home. He cleared his throat.

"Will you be my gal, forever?" he asked.

She opened her mouth to answer, but he was faster.

"No…wait. Let me start over. Will you marry me, Jessica McCoy? Because I love you. I always have and always will."

"I love you, too. My answer is yes. There never would have been any other."

Nash didn't care who saw what he was about to do next. He leaned in and kissed her. After a moment that probably lasted only a few seconds but would stay with him forever, she pulled away and licked her lips. "Wow. That was really sweet."

"In more ways than one." It wasn't merely a cliché. The moment was sweet, as was the residual taste of the cupcakes between them. Then he noticed something else. How could he have missed it?

Easy. He'd been lost in her eyes.

Should I tell her? He couldn't hide his grin.

"What?" she asked.

"Oh, nothing. I've just never kissed a woman with a mustache before."

Her eyes widened. She wiped at her upper lip. "Why didn't you tell me?"

"Because I'd rather you see me smiling instead of crying if you'd said no." It wasn't a complete lie. He'd been too caught up in and nervous about the proposal to notice the icing.

"You thought that was a possibility?" she asked.

"The fact that you're standing here at all makes me believe that anything is possible." With his thumb, he wiped the last remnants of icing from above her upper lip.

"You still have one, too," she said, doing the same for him. "When should we tell the girls?

Nash looked at them and exhaled. As perfect as this all seemed, they had a lot of things to figure out. Jess needed to know what she was getting into. Full transparency.

"How do you feel about semi-adopting a boy?"

Jess's eyes widened. "Um, I haven't given it any thought, although I love the thought of having a boy. I'm not familiar with semi-adoption. Is that like fostering? Can we wait until after the honeymoon to decide?"

Nash put on his most serious expression and shook his head. "I'm afraid not. In fact, I've already committed to letting Gus live at our house as long as necessary. Maybe forever."

Jess squinted and looked at him sideways. "Parker's dog?"

Nash nodded.

"As long as you don't let him sleep between us," she said.

Nash pulled her closer. "Not a chance. What I really wanted to ask was, are you willing to embrace being the wife of a cattle-ranching, barrel-racing teacher who grows crops in his greenhouse and sells them at the local farmers market?"

"Only if you're willing to embrace a rodeo mom who is the CEO of her own company."

Her own company? Nash closed his eyes and tried to remember if she'd told him about that, even though such information would be hard to forget. His mind drew a blank.

"Don't look so nervous," she continued. "I have a sewing soulmate who wants, and needs, the work. You can thank Parker and Vanessa for putting that idea in her head, and the idea of thinking about having a home business with employees in mine. It would free me up to do more of the actual designing and pattern making, which are my favorite parts of the process anyway. Oh, and marketing, starting with Kavanaugh's. I'll have more flexibility to take our girls to compete in rodeos if you can't get away."

"I'm good with anything you and the girls want to pursue, as long as you promise to come back every time."

"If the door is open to me, I'll always come home."

Nash made a mental note to thank Parker and Vanessa. Oh, and Hailey and Vern and the rest of Destiny Springs for helping him realize that the walls he constructed at times didn't protect him. Rather, they kept out the love he wanted.

That much was clear. Otherwise, his brain felt scrambled even thinking about how to juggle their combined responsibilities, and shuffle two—maybe three—little girls to and from rodeos around the country. Also, he and Jess might be apart from each other at stretches.

For now, she was in his arms, and there was only one thing to do about it.

This time, their kiss lasted more than a few seconds. He was hoping to exceed Kat's barrel racing time of 49.538. Maybe set a new national record. And he would have, except it was interrupted by something even better than winning. And infinitely sweeter than icing. A trio of giggles only a few yards away. From the girls.

Our girls.

EPILOGUE

Two months later

"NICE FRIENDSHIP BRACELET," Parker said, pointing to Nash's wrist.

Nash pulled up his black tuxedo jacket sleeve, bent his elbow, held the horsehair jewelry eye level and rotated his hand like he was some sort of royal in a parade, waving at the crowd.

In reality, he was standing in his own arena, smack-dab in the middle of the three barrels that now had flowers painted all over them. His and Jess's closest friends and relatives were sitting patiently in uncomfortable-looking wooden foldout chairs that framed the imaginary dirt aisle.

"Thanks. My daughter Taylor made it for me."

Technically, his soon-to-be legally adopted daughter. Nash couldn't wait to get that process started, along with Jess adopting the twins.

Parker lifted his jacket sleeve, as well. "She made one for me, too."

His ranch hand raised his wrist so they could both get a closer look, twisting the bracelet around to the opposite side to show off the suede tie details.

"Good. Saves me from having to make you one since you're my best friend and all," Nash said. He had to bite his lip to keep from laughing. From the corner of his eye, he could tell that his ranch hand was about to burst.

Today, Parker was more than a ranch hand, or even a best friend. He was the best man.

"That hurts. I was going to make one for you, but now..." Parker said.

At that, Nash snorted. Couldn't hold it in any longer. That's all it took to make Parker start shaking as he attempted to contain the laughter. The guy's eyes were even watering. After all, this was a serious occasion. And they had an audience.

Truth be told, that bracelet was one of the sweetest gifts Nash had ever received, and he was certain Parker felt the same way. The laughter was more out of nervousness. The wedding was supposed to start twenty minutes ago, and all sorts of awful scenarios were stampeding across his imagination.

He corralled such thoughts with a more reasonable one: Jess had been one busy gal lately.

Even though she was staying at the B and B, Nash had given her a key to *their* house. She'd already transformed the kitchen. The curtains and chair cushions were new, the cabinet was stocked with all sorts of cookware, and the scent of fresh-cut flowers greeted him every time he walked through the door.

Then, when Taylor picked up a sponsorship from a national boot company, Jess helped secure Kavanaugh's Clothing and Whatnot as a sponsor for Kat. All while selling Ethan on the idea of carrying children's clothing from her and Dorothy's new company—Western Wear with Heart.

And, of course, there were the rodeos: Taylor had been in two more competitions since Billings—and placed first both times.

It wore him out just thinking about all that Jess had been up to.

Nash had been busy, too, building a student roster that wouldn't pose a conflict of interest with his most important student of all...his own daughter. Thank goodness Lizzy got over the itch to compete. Instead, she'd been mastering the art of cupcake baking and decorating. She even made the wedding cupcakes for all their guests, with Georgina's help at the B and B.

Speaking of his go-getter, she entered the arena, running at full speed. The little bridesmaid was out of breath by the time she reached him.

"Is everything okay?" he asked.

"Yeah. We're almost ready. Miss Dorothy had to sew her in her dress." Lizzy bolted back toward the house before Nash could ask what that even meant. Wasn't going to attempt to explain anything to all the folks staring at him with questioning looks.

Instead, Nash crossed his hands in front of him and tried to resist the urge to rock back and forth on his heels.

Parker leaned in and whispered, "I feel like we should sing or tap dance or something."

Nash was about to say, "Maybe you could entertain 'em with one of your workshops," but the officiant finally appeared, saving him and his best friend from a bad joke.

"She's getting sewn into her dress, so..." Nash explained to the lady once she got situated.

The officiant nodded and smiled as if it were perfectly normal.

Maybe it was. He had no recollection of his wedding to Roxanne. For the life of him, he couldn't remember anything about the dress she wore, either.

Finally, the twins appeared on horseback. Both in matching pink satin pantsuits with faux fur cropped jackets and white cowgirl boots. They walked their horses around the cloverleaf, single file, with Kat in the lead and Lizzy following behind. Once done, Kat and Sugar Pie stood on Nash's side. Lizzy and Cupcake stood on Jess's, leaving room for the maid of honor, Nash assumed.

Next came Taylor, on foot, looking so grown-up in a long fitted pink satin dress and cropped faux fur jacket that matched the twins'. She was carrying a small bouquet of daisies, held together with a satin tie, her hands slightly shaking.

Is she cold? With the sun about to set, the temperature had started to drop. The twins looked comfortable.

Nash couldn't stand it any longer. He removed his tuxedo jacket, then stepped over and draped it across Taylor's shoulders before assuming his groom position again. That earned him some smiles and *awws* from the group.

Next down the makeshift aisle was PJ, keeper of the rings. Vanessa had been walking behind him but took a seat with the others. The little boy didn't seem to remember where he was told to stand but ultimately settled in the right place. Next to the best man.

"Earth Angel," Nash said, a little too loud.

"Pardon?" Parker asked.

"Your cousin. That's her nickname."

His best man snickered.

"Is that funny?" Nash asked.

"No. She is an angel. I was thinking about how that's going to throw all the good people of Destiny Springs off. Someone started a rumor that she's more of a *fallen* angel. Not in a bad way. She hasn't had an easy life is all. Maybe this nickname will shut that one down."

Speaking of rumors, Jess hadn't believed Nash that day at the farmers market when he'd claimed to be on a nickname basis with country music star Montgomery "Monty" Legend. But she would believe him as soon as she walked down the aisle and saw him, or at the reception later on.

They stood there for another good five minutes. Nash began softly humming the theme song to *Jeopardy!* as a stress reliever.

"Shhh," the officiant gently admonished.

Not that it was necessary. The whole world seemed to turn quiet when Jess walked into the arena on her father's arm, while her mom looked on through teary eyes. No music, no talking. Not even any nickering from the horses. Only the sound of her dress *swooshing* with every step she took.

He didn't know a lot about wedding gowns, but weren't they usually white or ivory? Her skirt looked to be covered in some sort of pattern.

As soon as she joined Nash, he recognized the pattern as the drawing that Lizzy had done on that big piece of paper. Right down to the size and number of petals on each of the daisies, best he could tell. Except, the flowers were softer and more muted. The fabric they were printed on was a sheer layer that appeared to float over the white part underneath. How did she do that?

He was about to ask, but the officiant cleared her throat and began. The ceremony itself was a bit of a blur as he got lost in Jess's eyes and didn't come up for air until the "I do's." No telling what he agreed to, but that didn't matter. He was totally present for the most important part: the kiss.

A few camera flashes went off in his periphery, and all of a sudden, they were back in that photo booth. Only this time, he'd have the pictures framed. He was pretty sure that little Max hadn't taken a flattering one, but he held out hopes that Georgina had, since she was a wedding planner in addition to making herself indispensable at the B and B.

As they struck a few more poses for the cell cameras, Jess said, "Sorry I took so long. The special fabric I ordered didn't get delivered until this morning. I wanted this to be perfect."

He kissed the top of her hand. "It was already perfect the moment you said yes."

She wrapped her arms around his neck while smiling for the camera, then turned back to him.

"I respectfully disagree. It was perfect ten years ago. We simply didn't know it."

He couldn't argue with that.

"I almost ran down that aisle tonight," she said.

That gave him an idea.

"We could run down that aisle right now. Toward the finish line so we can start our lives together as fast as possible. I'll help carry the train. It'll be a good workout for my arms," he teased. That really was some dress. Abundantly beautiful, like the flowers that graced the fabric. Most of all, beautiful like her.

"No need to strain yourself. I have what I've always wanted most, even though it took ten years instead of sixteen seconds."

The camera flashes reduced to distant stars in his periphery.

Imagine the thing you want most is waiting at the finish line. The faster you get there, the sooner it's yours.

"Is that a confession?" he asked. Back when she first told him about her formula for winning, he hadn't asked what it was that she'd wanted most.

"I suppose it is."

He looked at each of their girls, who were becoming the focus of the wedding paparazzi. If Jess had revealed it a decade ago, they all wouldn't be standing here today. Like this.

Maybe it was his perfect mistake not to ask.

He still wasn't a math whiz. Probably never would be. But he could safely subtract "mistake" from that self-assessment, because what was right in front of him now was nothing short of…

Perfect.

* * * * *